I0668759

Redemption

Phil M. Williams

© 2021 by Phil M. Williams

All rights reserved. This book or any portion thereof may not be reproduced or used in any manner whatsoever without the express written permission of the publisher, except for the use of brief quotations in a book review.

Printed in the United States of America.

First Printing, 2021.

Phil W Books.

www.PhilWBooks.com

ISBN: 978-1-943894-74-1

A Note from Phil

Dear Reader,

If you're interested in receiving my novel *Against the Grain* for free and/or reading many of my other titles for free or discounted, go to the following link: http://www.PhilWBooks.com.

You're probably thinking, *What's the catch?* There is no catch.

Sincerely,

Phil M. Williams

PART I: MICHELLE

We convince ourselves that we know the other person well, but do we really know anything important about anyone?
—Haruki Murakami

Not until we are lost do we begin to understand ourselves.
—Henry David Thoreau

Chapter 1: Y2K

Michelle fast-walked down the hallway, nearly breaking the no-running rule. The hallway was decorated with holiday paraphernalia. Excited little voices and holiday music filtered into the hallway from the classrooms. Michelle typically taught a class for gifted and talented students at that time, but her principal had let her leave a few hours early.

Mrs. Levitt walked toward Michelle, coming from the teacher's bathroom. The old teacher gave Michelle the evil eye and glanced at her watch as their paths crossed, but Michelle didn't acknowledge her existence. The rumor was that Mrs. Levitt was jealous of Michelle's beauty, wealth, and connection with the kids.

Michelle never thought of herself as beautiful. Her brown hair was too straight, and her breasts were too small. She did have large blue eyes, a symmetrical heart-shaped face, and an athletic build. It was more than enough to win a hypothetical beauty pageant among the Radnor Elementary School staff.

Mrs. Levitt made Michelle pay for her good fortune by scheduling recess during gifted support time, forcing Michelle to explain to the kids why they couldn't go to recess. And Mrs. Levitt wasn't the only one. A gaggle of the old guard secretly wished for Michelle's demise.

Michelle stepped outside, the cold air nipping her nose. The wind whipped her dress around her legs, as she hurried to her car. She pressed her key fob, her 1999 BMW flashing in response. Her new car did nothing to quell the jealousy.

One teacher had been bold enough to say, "Must be nice to have a rich husband."

Another had asked, "Why do you even work?"

She drove from Radnor Elementary School to her neighborhood in Villanova, Pennsylvania, less than three miles away. It was a dream commute, one that saved her from being late each morning. She drove into her exclusive neighborhood of mansions on two-acre lots. The trees were barren, yet not a leaf covered the dormant lawns. The landscapers had removed every last leaf in the neighborhood in preparation for Christmas.

Her house was faced with stone and stucco, with multiple peaks, multiple chimneys, and a four-car garage. Michelle parked her BMW inside. She sighed and thought, *I should've known.* Her husband's M3 wasn't in the garage. Michelle went inside, tapping the beeping keypad, disarming the alarm. She walked past the laundry room, into the open-plan kitchen, with a center island, commercial grade appliances, and hardwood floors. She set her keys and her purse on the granite countertop, grabbing the cordless phone from the receiver. She called Jason at work. His administrative assistant, Tori, put her through to his desk.

"I'm sorry," Jason said in lieu of a greeting.

"Does that mean you won't be home soon?" Michelle asked.

"I'm swamped. I have clients freaking out about Y2K. They should be freaking out about the tech crash that's coming."

"*I'll* be freaking out if you're not home soon. We'll be stuck in holiday traffic."

"Would it be okay if we left tomorrow morning?"

Michelle slumped her shoulders. "Don't do this. You *promised.* I left work early."

"I know. I'm sorry. But I'd rather finish so I'm not stressed over the holiday break. Besides, there'll be less traffic on Christmas Eve."

"I told my mom that I'd help her with dinner."

"We'll be there in plenty of time to help with dinner."

"She'll have everything done by two. Then she'll complain that I didn't help."

"We'll leave early tomorrow morning. I promise."

Chapter 2: Girl Meets Boy

Jason drove Michelle's BMW on 322 West through the Allegheny Mountains. Michelle sat shotgun, content to be a passenger. Normally they'd take Jason's M3, but her four-door sedan was more suitable to haul the mountain of presents in the back seat.

Jason turned down the music: Christmas-flavored R&B, Michelle's choice. "We're not going out to any bars, are we?"

"We might. A bunch of us are planning to get together at Maguire's on Christmas night."

Jason shook his head. "I'd rather not."

Michelle pursed her lips. "You never want to go out."

"All they do is talk about high school. If you're not from Loganville, it's like you don't exist."

"You just need to open up a little. Let everyone see what I see."

"I don't think that'll work. I think the whole town wanted you to marry Danny."

Michelle turned in her seat toward her husband. "It's not like that. If you go into every social situation with a negative attitude, what do you think will happen?"

Jason frowned. "Fine. I'll do my best."

"Thank you."

"Who'll be at dinner tonight?"

"The usual suspects. My parents. Obviously. Then probably just

Susie and Cody and Becky."

"Why does everyone in Loganville have a name or a nickname that ends with the *E* sound? Danny, Susie, Cody." His eyes flicked to Michelle. "*Shelly.*"

She mock-frowned. "People think it's cute. Sus*ie* thinks Co*dy* might propose over Christmas." Michelle emphasized the *E* sound at the end of their names.

Jason nodded. "Good for her."

"You like Cody, don't you?"

"I don't know him very well, but he seems fine."

"My parents are over the moon. Susie hasn't had the best of luck with men."

Jason changed lanes, passing a pickup truck pulling a camper. "How much of that is her fault?"

Michelle shrugged. "I know she's had her struggles, but I think she finally has her life together."

"I hope so, for Becky's sake."

"Speaking of Becky, she was disappointed that we didn't make it to my parents' house last night. My mom told me that she wanted to play with you. She said to my mom, 'I like Jason but don't tell Aunt Shelly.'" Michelle giggled.

Jason laughed.

"You two have a special connection."

Jason nodded, thinking for a moment. "I'd like to think I understand what she's going through. It's not easy growing up without a father."

"I love that you spend time with her, when we visit my parents."

Jason flashed a small grin toward Michelle.

They drove in silence for a minute. Michelle peered out over the gray mountaintops.

Jason interrupted the silence. "Who else will be there on Christmas Eve?"

Michelle turned from the window, back to Jason. "I think that's it."

Jason glanced at Michelle, with raised eyebrows, and said, "You *think* that's it?"

"You know my mom. She opens up the house on Christmas Eve, so we might have some friends and relatives stop by."

Jason glared at the road. "Friends, like Danny?"

"Probably not, but maybe."

"That's bullshit, and you know it. He'll be there, like always. Do your parents not understand how disrespectful it is to me to have your ex-boyfriend over when we're visiting?"

Michelle let out a breath. "It's not like that. They don't even think about it."

"Because they like him better than me."

"That's not true. He's just more open. More outgoing. And he has that police connection with my dad."

"You're making my argument for me."

She reached over and placed her hand on his thigh. "You're missing one very important thing." She squeezed his leg. "I love you, so my parents love you."

He grinned, showing his dimples.

Michelle leaned over, stretching her seat belt, and kissed him on the cheek. She sat back in her seat, admiring her husband. He was thirty-six, eight years older than Michelle. Danny and some of her childhood friends had made fun of the age difference, playfully chiding Michelle for marrying for money. But Jason wasn't rich when they met five years ago.

It was the summer after her first year teaching at Radnor Elementary. Michelle was at home, when she had heard a woman yelling outside her window on a Saturday afternoon. Michelle had parted her curtains. The middle-aged woman had pointed and yelled at a tall, dark, and handsome man. They were standing in front of an old Honda Accord, parked with the hood raised.

The woman had said, "You can't work on your car in the parking lot. I'm calling the homeowner's association." She'd stomped back to her condo, slamming the door in her wake.

The man had been dumbfounded, but he hadn't lashed out at the woman. He was thin, but his arms had muscle definition. He was clean-shaven, his brown hair cut short. His nose was a little off-kilter, but he had a handsome face and dark eyes. It had been over a year since Michelle and Danny had broken up. She'd only been with one man in the interim, and he had been a distant second to her vibrator.

So, she had gone to the mailbox, checking the empty box, and checking him out on the way. He had been installing a battery, not noticing her. Michelle had stopped behind him and cleared her throat. He had turned from the engine bay, his eyes narrowed.

Michelle had smiled and asked, "You need any help?"

"No, thank you," he had replied.

"That's good because I don't know anything about cars."

He had laughed, and that was it. They'd spent nearly every second together since then.

As she stared at her husband, she thought he was still that handsome man who she'd fallen in love with.

He glanced from the road and asked, "What are you looking at?"

"You."

Chapter 3: *El Diablo*

Her parents' house was a brick rambler that her father, Frank, had built himself. Jason pulled into the driveway, parking next to Frank's F-150, and in front of the two-car garage. The garage housed Frank's tools and fishing boat, along with Ruth's Ford Taurus.

Michelle glanced at the clock on the dashboard. "We're late. My mom's probably already cooked dinner."

"It's barely two o'clock," Jason replied.

"Pop the trunk."

They carried their luggage inside, along with whatever presents they could manage. Michelle led them into the living room, without ringing the doorbell. They walked into the kitchen and dining room, the smell of cooking meatballs and sausage in the air.

Frank stood from the dining room table, a cup of coffee and the local paper nearby. He was a tall burly man with a full face, short feathered hair, and a goatee. He grinned at Michelle. "Shelly."

Ruth aka Ruthie turned from the stovetop, where she tended several simmering pots, and frowned. "Nice of you to join us, honey." Michelle's mother was tall with a paunch and fleshy hips. Her hair was still blonde but mixed with white.

"Merry Christmas, Mom. Merry Christmas, Dad," Michelle said.

"Merry Christmas," Frank said.

"We should put our stuff in my room."

Frank smirked. "It looks like you're moving in."

Michelle rolled her eyes. "Ha, ha." Frank told the same joke every time Michelle visited with her entourage of luggage.

Jason said hello to her parents, and they carried their luggage to Michelle's childhood bedroom. A queen-size bed dominated the small room. Framed photos hung from the walls of Michelle with her family or with friends from high school and college. There'd been multiple photos of her and Danny the first time Jason had visited, but Michelle had since put them in the closet. Her Penn State diploma hung on the wall as well. Bachelors of Science in Elementary Education.

Jason left the room, headed for the kitchen. At least that's what she thought. She went to the bathroom, then walked toward the kitchen. She stopped along the way. Jason was in Frank's office, gawking at the team pictures of various girls' basketball teams.

Michelle knitted her brow. "What are you doing?"

Jason turned from the photos of the six- to eight-year-old girls in shorts and basketball jerseys. "Just looking. It's nice that your dad coaches."

"He loves it."

When they returned to the kitchen, Michelle hugged her father, then her mother. Ruth also planted a lipstick-laden kiss on her cheek. Jason received a strong-gripped handshake from Frank and the same lipstick kiss from Ruth. Jason discreetly wiped off the lipstick.

"What can I do to help?" Michelle asked, her gaze sweeping over the pots on the stovetop and the already set dining room table for eight.

"It's all done," Ruth said, wiping her brow.

"I told you that I would help."

Ruth held out her hands. "Well, I wasn't sure. You were supposed to be here yesterday."

Michelle's voice went up an octave. "Jason had to work."

"Well, I didn't know if he had to work today too."

Michelle gave Jason an I-told-you-so look.

The doorbell chimed.

Ruth said to Michelle, "You can get the door for me."

Michelle went to the front door as everyone sat at the dining room table to visit. She opened the door to find Officer Danny Gibbs, standing in his Loganville Township Police unform, holding a plate of cookies. He was tall, like Jason, but more muscular and athletic. He was more rugged too, with a strong jawline and a scar under his left eye from a fight with a heroin dealer.

Danny smiled. "Merry Christmas, Shelly."

She smiled back. "Merry Christmas, Danny."

"My mom asked me to drop off these cookies for your parents, and I need to talk to your dad."

"Of course." She stepped aside and waved him in. "They're in the dining room."

He stepped inside, shutting the door behind him. He stood perilously close to Michelle and whispered, "You look beautiful."

She blushed and stood frozen, catching her breath.

"New car?"

Michelle opened her mouth to speak, but nothing came out.

"Must be nice." Danny walked into the dining room. "Merry Christmas, Frank. Ruthie."

"Merry Christmas, Danny," her parents replied in unison.

"My mom wanted me to drop off these cookies."

"Oh, that's so nice of her. Please thank her for me," Ruth said.

Michelle walked into the dining room, watching her parents dote on Danny.

Ruth moved her centerpiece to feature the plate of cookies.

"What's up, sport?" Danny said, lifting his chin to Jason.

"Not much," Jason replied, barely above a whisper.

Michelle sat next to Jason, her gaze on Danny.

Danny turned his attention to Frank. "I wanted to talk to you about the girl who disappeared."

"Isn't it awful?" Ruth said, sitting down after displaying the cookies.

Danny addressed Ruth. "It's the worst case I've seen since Heather Sample disappeared."

"Have a seat," Frank said, gesturing to the table.

Danny sat across from Frank, removing his hat and setting it on the table.

Frank leaned forward, his elbows on the tabletop. "Any leads?"

"We have nothing." Danny scanned the group. "I would appreciate it if you would keep this between us. A lot of people know this, but still."

"Of course," Ruth said.

Michelle nodded.

"The parents don't even know if she made it home from school or not," Danny said. "They both work two jobs, so they're not home when she gets home from school."

"That's terrible," Ruth interjected. "She's only six."

Danny acknowledged Ruth, then turned his attention back to Frank. "Nobody saw her enter their apartment, and the place was locked. No sign of a struggle. We canvassed the neighbors, but they didn't see or hear anything."

"What about her friends?" Frank asked. "The kids who ride the bus with her and walk home from school with her?"

"She doesn't ride the bus. She's a walker at Loganville Elementary, but she doesn't have very many friends. She's only been at Loganville for a few weeks. Nobody remembered seeing her walk home from school."

Frank leaned back, rubbing his goatee. "Are there any cameras on the route from school?"

"There's a convenience store, but they record over their tapes every night." Danny blew out a heavy breath. "This girl disappeared without a trace."

"*Hmm.*" Frank thrummed his fingers on the table. "Anyone mention a work truck or a van with a ladder rack?"

"No. Why?"

"When I was working the Heather Sample case, one of the witnesses talked about a suspicious van with a ladder rack." Frank had retired from the Loganville Township Police two years ago.

Danny drew his eyebrows together. "Why was it suspicious?"

"The witness said it was parked on the street for hours, but she never saw any workmen. It was a block from where we thought Heather disappeared."

"Did you ever find the van?"

"No."

"What's her name?" Michelle asked.

Danny turned to Michelle. "Nina Diaz. I think her parents are illegals. They didn't report her disappearance for almost three days."

Frank shook his head. "She might've been taken by a coyote. These illegals come here with help from a coyote. Then they owe. If they don't pay, maybe the coyote snatches their kid. It might be worth asking the parents."

Danny nodded. "Good idea. I'll let Detective Gaines know."

"Is the FBI involved?"

"Two guys from the regional office. Not much help so far, although one of them can speak Spanish."

Frank grunted. "They were no help with Heather Sample."

Danny hesitated for a second, then said, "There's another thing that's strange with this case. The mother. She seems a little off. She's claiming it was *El Diablo.*"

"The devil," Jason said softly to himself.

Chapter 4: Christmas Eve

"I know guys like Danny. He's an asshole," Jason said, sitting on Michelle's bed.

"He didn't do anything," Michelle replied, brushing her brown hair in front of the mirror in her childhood bedroom.

"He called me *sport*, and he was practically drooling over you."

Michelle turned from the mirror and frowned. "He was not."

"Believe what you want to believe."

The front door opened, followed by footsteps and excited voices.

"I think my sister's here," Michelle said, setting her hairbrush on the dresser. "You coming?"

"I'll be there in a minute," Jason replied, not making eye contact.

Michelle left the room, headed for the kitchen. Everyone stood in the kitchen near the counter. Susie chatted with Ruth, and Cody talked to Frank. Becky stood next to Ruth, tugging on her pants.

"What, honey?" Ruth asked, bending down toward Becky.

Becky whispered to Ruth.

"There you are," Susie said, smiling at her older sister. Susie was a slightly younger and slightly more beautiful version of Michelle. Her straight brown hair hung to her chest. Like Michelle, Susie had striking blue eyes and an athletic build, but she was a few inches taller. She wore heavy makeup, but, like her clothes, both were expensive and well worn.

Michelle hugged her sister. "Merry Christmas, Susie."

When they separated, Susie said, "I have big news. Huge actually." The spotlight was on Susie. She held up her left hand, showing her large diamond ring. "We're engaged!"

"Oh, my Lord," Ruth said, beaming. "How could I have missed that rock?"

"Congratulations," Michelle said.

Frank shook Cody's hand. "You do know about her debts, don't you?"

"*Dad.* I pay all my bills, thank you very much," Susie said, glaring at Frank. "When Becky and I move in with Cody, I'll be able to save even more." Susie grabbed Cody's hand. "Right, baby?"

"That's true." Cody grinned at his fiancé, his dimples obscured by his manicured beard.

Becky tugged on Ruth's pants again. "Ask him."

"In a minute, honey," Ruth replied.

"When are you two shacking up?" Michelle asked.

"It's not shacking up if we're gonna get married," Susie replied.

"Susie's lease is up in a few months, so probably then," Cody said, glancing at Susie, as if corroborating their story.

"We would do it now, but Cody wants to fix up a room for Becky, and he wants to clean out his house to make room for us." Susie turned to Cody. "Hopefully, now that you're not working two jobs, that'll happen sooner."

"I'm working on it." Then Cody addressed the group. "My dad's getting ready to retire, so I've been more involved with the properties. I was burning the candle at both ends, trying to work as an EMT at the same time. I'm a full-time property manager now."

"Do you like that better than working as an EMT?" Ruth asked.

"I love being an EMT, but seeing people in pain has really worn on me over the years, and I knew I would eventually take over for my father."

Frank clapped Cody on the back. "I'm sure they'll miss you at the hospital."

Cody had met Susie at the hospital, where she worked as a nurse. Cody was the most eligible bachelor in Loganville. He was two years ahead of Michelle in high school, and her friends had described him as drop-dead gorgeous then. He had aged like a fine wine, filling out his tall frame with athletic, but not bulky muscles, to go with his family's reputation as the wealthiest in town. Wealth that would soon be his alone. Rumors swirled that his father wasn't long for this world. Susie had reeled in a whopper.

Jason walked into the kitchen. Becky goggled at Jason, smiling, and showing her missing front teeth.

"Hey, Susie. Cody," Jason said, as he approached the group.

"They're engaged," Michelle said, bringing him up-to-date.

"Congratulations." Jason made eye contact with the happy couple. "When's the big date?"

Susie's expression darkened. "We haven't discussed that yet."

Michelle thought maybe they had, and Cody hadn't committed to a date yet.

Jason seemed oblivious. He bent over and said, "Hey, Becky. Are you looking forward to Christmas?"

Becky grinned and nodded. Then she tugged on Ruth's pants again and said, "Ask him."

Jason stood upright.

Ruth said to Jason, "She wants you to take her downstairs to see the presents. She's afraid to go down to the basement alone."

"I can take her down there." Jason agreed to this quickly, as if he wanted an excuse to get away from the adults.

"You can look but don't touch," Ruth said to Becky. "We'll open gifts after dinner."

Since Michelle and Susie had left the nest, it had been a tradition

17

with their parents to open gifts on Christmas Eve. Frank and Ruthie preferred to sleep in on Christmas Day.

Becky nodded again. Then she held out her hand to Jason. He took it and walked the six-year-old towhead to the basement to see the pile of presents.

***

Christmas music played through the CD player. Michelle and Ruth cleaned up the trash from the gift exchange. Jason put together Becky's plastic dollhouse, with her acting as his assistant, asking what piece he needed next, then handing it to him. It would've been easier for Jason to grab the pieces himself, but Becky beamed every time he thanked her for being such a good helper.

Cody and Susie sat on the couch, drinking beers. Frank sat in his recliner, doing the same. A dozen empties were on the coffee table.

"Did you want to keep her toys here?" Ruth asked Susie. "Otherwise, you'll have to move them twice."

"Just leave them here," Susie replied. Her speech was slightly slurred.

"Can I stay here tonight?" Becky asked Ruth.

"If you want Santa to come, you have to sleep in your own bed," Susie interjected.

"But I wanna stay here." Becky's voice was whiney.

"Not tonight, Becky. Maybe tomorrow."

Becky crossed her arms over her chest, her face red. "No. I wanna stay *here*."

"I said, *not tonight*." Susie stood from the couch, her legs a little wobbly. She addressed her mother. "We should go. Becky's getting tired. If we stay too much longer, she'll have a meltdown."

"I wanna stay!"

Michelle turned to Becky, a garbage bag full of wrapping paper in hand. Jason sat on the floor, still assembling the dollhouse, seemingly oblivious to Becky's distress.

"Come on, sweet pea. It's time to go," Susie said, holding out her hand to Becky.

"No."

"Do you want Santa to come?"

"No."

Susie let out a long breath. "Don't do this tonight. Come on, sweet pea."

"No."

"We'll come back tomorrow."

Cody stood from the couch and said, "I'll go warm up the car."

"Good idea," Susie replied.

Cody thanked Ruth and Frank and left.

Jason stood from the completed dollhouse. "We can play tomorrow."

"Wanna play *now.*" Becky went to the dollhouse and started to play, as if she didn't have to leave.

Susie kissed her mother on the cheek. "Thank you for everything."

"You're welcome, honey. Are you okay to drive?" Ruth asked.

"Cody's driving."

Susie gave Frank a hug, while he was still sitting in his recliner, and another hug for Michelle. Susie smelled like alcohol. Then she went back to Becky, who was playing with her dollhouse. Susie held out her hand again. "Let's go, Becky."

Becky ignored her.

Susie addressed Frank. "Dad, can you carry her to the car? She's getting too heavy for me."

Frank stood from the recliner with a groan and approached Becky. "Come on, munchkin. Time to go home." Frank scooped her up. Becky screamed and flailed her arms and legs, trying to free herself from his grasp. Becky's screams echoed through the house, as Frank carried her upstairs and outside to the warming car.

Chapter 5: Bad Boys and Bad Girls

Moonlight filtered into her bedroom through the curtains. Michelle lay on her side in her childhood bed, listening to the rhythmic breaths of her husband. He lay on his side too, facing away from her. She thought about how kind he'd been to Becky. She tapped his shoulder. "Are you awake?"

He groaned.

She tapped him again. "Are you awake?"

"I am now," Jason replied, rolling to his back.

"I can't sleep."

He rubbed the sleep from his eyes. "What's wrong?"

Michelle snuggled tightly to Jason, her leg and arm draped over his body. She spoke quietly, so her parents across the hall couldn't hear. "I was just thinking that I love how you are with Becky. My family's getting wasted, and you're playing with Becky totally sober. It's sweet." She pecked him on the lips.

Jason spoke barely above a whisper, following Michelle's cue. "I hope Cody can be a good father to her. It's no fun to have a steady stream of boyfriends coming by to have sex with your mom."

"Susie's not like that."

Jason gave her a look.

"Not anymore. I think Cody's the one."

"He seems more like the player type than the marrying type."

Michelle glowered at Jason. "That's not true. He might be good-looking, but he's never been a big partier. His family has more money than God. He certainly didn't have to work as an EMT for like eight years. He did it because he cares about people."

"So you think he's good-looking?"

Michelle sat up, grabbed her pillow, and smacked Jason across the face. "That's what you got out of that?"

Jason flashed his palms in surrender. "Fine. He's a great guy, and your sister and Becky will live happily ever after."

Michelle snuggled against Jason again. "I sure hope so."

"What about Luke? Does he ever come to visit Becky?"

Luke Miles impregnated Susie when she was nineteen. He was a senior from Texas and the backup quarterback for Penn State at the time. After he graduated, with Susie six months' pregnant, he left her and went back to Texas to work for his father's business on an offshore oil rig. Before he left, he signed away his rights to Becky but vowed to send money when he could. Susie received the odd child support check, but that was the only contact they had. Rumor has it that he battled substance abuse.

"He's never visited her once," Michelle said.

Jason winced. "That's awful."

"I'm so lucky to have you."

Jason cocked his head. "Really?"

"*Yes*. Really. My sister's prettier than me, and she's had a tough time."

"I don't know about that."

"You don't think she's prettier than me?"

"No. I don't like all the makeup. It's too much."

Michelle raised her eyebrows. "You can tell me the truth."

Jason frowned. "You don't think I'm telling the truth?"

She winked. "Just checking." Michelle slid atop Jason and straddled him, her nightgown riding up and showing her cotton underwear. She kissed him openmouthed, their tongues swirling together.

When their lips parted, Jason asked, "What are you doing?"

She sat up, still straddling him, a wry smile on her lips. She rubbed her crotch against his, her hands on his thin chest. The old bed squeaked.

He hardened beneath her. "Your parents will hear," he whispered.

She leaned forward and whispered in his ear, "We'll be quiet." She kissed his ear and tugged on his earlobe with her teeth. Michelle kissed her way down his bare chest, kissing the outline of his penis. She removed his boxer briefs and kissed his exposed erection. Then she took him in her mouth.

He gasped.

A creaking came from the hallway. Michelle sat upright, and Jason's eyes were wide open.

He looked at the bedroom door and mouthed, "Lock the door."

Michelle shook her head, chewing on her bottom lip. The forbidden concoction of having sex in her childhood bed and the possibility of getting caught was too much to resist.

One of Michelle's parents opened and shut the bathroom door. The bathroom was separated from Michelle's room by one thin wall. Grunting noises and sounds of raising the toilet lid came from the bathroom. Then a steady stream of urine. It was Frank.

Michelle straddled Jason again, rubbing the crotch of her cotton underwear against his shiny erection, the movement causing little bed squeaks.

Jason mouthed, "Stop."

But she didn't. She reached between her legs and moved her underwear to the side. She grabbed his erection, lifted up, and placed the head of his penis in position. When she sat back down and straddled him again, he pushed deep inside her. Michelle let out a long sigh, her head tilted upward, and her eyes half open.

The sound of running water came from the sink in the bathroom.

They moved together in rhythm, like rolling waves. They adjusted their movements each time the bed squeaked, trying to keep quiet, but they were moving stronger, their breathing heavier. Jason gripped her hips. She leaned back, her mouth parted, grinding her clitoris against him, his penis deep inside. She was close.

A knock came on her door.

Michelle sucked in a sharp breath, her eyes like saucers. Jason was paralyzed, like a deer in headlights.

"You okay?" Frank asked through the door.

"We're trying to sleep," Michelle said in an annoyed tone.

"Sorry. Good night."

"Good night, Dad."

Her parents' bedroom door opened and shut.

Michelle smiled in the moonlight and mimed wiping sweat from her forehead. She started to grind again. Jason moved his hands up her nightgown, cupping her breasts. They rolled like waves again. Steady yet growing. Her eyes were closed.

Then he went still. She opened her eyes. He whispered, "I should get a condom. We shouldn't."

Through heavy breaths, she replied, "Just a little longer. I'm close."

He moved his hips in rhythm again. She kept grinding back and forth. Harder, stronger. So close. He was in the perfect spot. The perfect angle to take her over the edge. Her face was flushed, her lips swollen. She shuddered. Heat radiated through her body, from the tips of her toes to her fingertips. He must've felt it too. He pushed faster, his penis spasming inside her.

The bed squeaked unmistakably, but neither of them thought about it in that moment.

Chapter 6: Frenemy

Maguire's Irish Pub was packed with childless twentysomethings, searching for a place to party and to escape their families on Christmas night. A bar ran along the east wall. Three bartenders, all wearing Santa hats, tended the throng of drunks. Neon beer signs popped in the dim lighting. A fake Christmas tree stood in the corner, decorated with beer cans, hung by the tabs.

Tables and chairs filled half the room. The other half was the dance floor and the stage. A Def Leppard cover band was onstage, singing a familiar hit. Headbangers did exactly that, banging their heads to the beat, dressed in faded Def Leppard shirts and black leather pants. Many of the women and even a few men had big hair for the occasion, teased and set in place with Aqua Net.

Michelle stood far from the stage, nursing her rum and Diet Coke. Danny and Susie flanked her. Michelle had convinced Jason to go to the bar with Susie and Cody. Jason had been having a good time, until Danny walked through the door.

"These guys are pretty good," Danny said, leaning in, so she could hear over the noise.

"They sound just like them," Michelle replied, leaning in, close enough to smell the beer on his breath and the cologne on his neck.

Danny nodded and surveyed the crowd. He leaned back in. "What happened to your boy?"

"Jason?"

He grinned. "You got another boy I don't know about?"

Michelle shrugged. "I don't know where he went."

Susie butted into their conversation, also reeking of alcohol. "He's too good for us."

Michelle glared at her sister. "What the hell is that supposed to mean?"

Susie rolled her eyes. "Nothing."

Cody came from the crowd with a beer and a Long Island iced tea in hand. He handed the mixed drink to Susie.

The lead singer said into the mike, "This is for all you lovers and sexpots out there."

The guitarist strummed the cords to the beginning of a slow song.

"I love this song!" Susie said something in Cody's ear, and then they were off to the dance floor.

Danny took a swig from his beer and leaned in again. "You wanna dance?"

Michelle shook her head. "No thanks."

"I'm surprised …"

"I don't like this song." That was a lie. She didn't want Jason to see them dancing, but, if she said that, Danny would make fun of Jason as insecure.

"No. I'm surprised you married him."

Michelle frowned.

He smirked. "You usually go for athletes."

"He's athletic."

Danny snickered. "For an accountant."

Michelle's face felt hot, embarrassed that Danny was making fun of her husband. "He's not an accountant."

"He's in finance, right?"

"Yes."

"Same difference."

"Who should I have married then?"

Danny popped his collar and grinned again.

A fake blonde with a fake tan and pink lipstick strutted toward them in a tight dress, her perfect gym body on display.

Michelle chugged the last of her rum and Diet Coke and said, "She's why I didn't."

Danny turned to the blonde and winced.

The blonde smiled at the two of them as she approached, a cranberry mixed drink in hand. Michelle gritted her teeth.

"Hey, Carrie," Danny said, lifting his beer to the woman. "Merry Christmas."

Carrie arched her eyebrows, a smirk on her face. "What are you two doin'?"

Michelle narrowed her eyes. "I was just leaving."

"Looking for your husband?"

Michelle cocked her head, confused.

Carrie simpered. "He was just hittin' on me. I thought about it, but I turned him down."

Michelle clenched her fists. "My husband wouldn't touch a skank like you with a ten-foot pole."

Carrie threw her drink at Michelle, soaking her light-blue fleece with cranberry and vodka. Carrie admired her handiwork with one hand on her hip and one side of her mouth raised in contempt.

Michelle rushed her with her fist reared back. Danny grabbed Michelle around the waist, holding her back.

Michelle shrieked at Carrie, "You *fucking* bitch!"

The surrounding patrons laughed and pointed at the scene. A bouncer approached and pointed at Michelle. "She has to go."

"*Me?*" Michelle pointed at Carrie. "She was the one."

The bouncer gestured with his chin for the exit. "Let's go."

"I got her," Danny said, taking Michelle by the arm.

Michelle snatched her arm from Danny's hand. "Leave me alone."

Danny showed his palms. "Fine."

Chapter 7: The Stain

The burly bouncer escorted Michelle outside. The parking lot was dimly lit by the nearby streetlights. She was freezing in her jeans and fleece pullover, especially with the cold cranberry juice seeping through her fleece. She had left her coat in the car. She opened her purse and fished for her keys. "*Shit.*" Jason had the keys.

She walked to her BMW on the off chance it was unlocked. It was running, exhaust coming from the tailpipe. She peered into the car. Jason lay in the back seat. She opened the front passenger door and climbed inside, slamming the door behind her. Jason sat up, rubbing the sleep from his eyes.

She turned to him, annoyed. "What are you *doing?*"

He scowled back. "I got sick of being ignored in favor of your ex-boyfriend."

"I wasn't ignoring you. I was being social."

He squinted at the dark stain on her fleece. "What happened?"

"Carrie Fuller happened."

He knitted his brow. "*The* Carrie Fuller?"

"Yes. That one." Michelle crossed her arms over her chest. "Did you hit on her?"

"*What?* No. I've never even met her."

"She's a fake blonde with a fake tan. Nice body. Wearing a skintight black dress. Did you hit on her?"

"I didn't hit on *anybody*. Nobody even talked to me. That's why I'm out here."

"She said you hit on her, and she turned you down. I told her that you wouldn't touch a skank like her with a ten-foot pole."

Jason laughed. "You said that?"

Michelle uncrossed her arms and dropped her hands to her lap. "Yes."

"Let me guess. Then she threw her drink on you."

"Exactly. Then I tried to punch her fucking face, but Danny held me back, and the bouncer kicked me out."

Jason's mouth turned down. "I'm sure Danny loved putting his hands on you."

"I yelled at him. Told him to let me go. Carrie was my best friend, and Danny cheated on me with that bitch. That's why we didn't get married. You know that. You're the one I want. Not him."

"Then why did you ignore me? This happens every time we go out in Loganville."

"I'm sorry for neglecting you. I get around the Loganville party scene, and it's like I'm twenty-one again. I know that's not an excuse, but I'm sorry. Can we just drop it?"

Jason let out a heavy breath. "Okay." He exited the back seat, reentering the car from the front driver's door.

Jason drove them across town, back to Michelle's parents' house. Once inside, they walked toward Michelle's room. Ruth was in the hallway in her pajamas, arguing with Becky.

"I don't wanna go to bed," Becky whined. "I want you to play with me."

"It's late, honey," Ruth replied. It was after ten.

"Hi, Mom," Michelle said, as they approached.

"Hi, dear," Ruth replied, then stared at her fleece. "What happened to your shirt?"

"Someone spilled a drink on me." Her parents didn't know about Carrie and Danny. The whole thing had been humiliating, so Michelle had never told her parents the specifics about their breakup, only that it had been Danny's fault.

"Well, that stinks. Did you two have fun?"

Jason looked down.

Michelle lifted one shoulder. "It was okay."

"I take it Susie and Cody are still out?" Ruth asked.

"Yes. They'll probably be out until last call. Are they supposed to pick up Becky?"

"No. She's sleeping over with Grandma tonight." Ruth bent down closer to Becky. "Aren't you, honey?"

Becky tugged on Ruth's pajama pants. "He can play with me."

"Your sister's a night owl, just like this one." Ruth stood, facing Michelle and Jason again.

"Ask him."

"I can play with her for a few minutes," Jason said.

"You're a dear." Ruth bent down to Becky again. "Thirty minutes and then it's time for bed."

"Let's play Ice Cream Shop downstairs," Becky said, holding out her hand to Jason.

Jason took Becky's hand and smiled at Michelle.

Michelle smiled back.

As Jason and Becky walked away, hand in hand, headed for the basement, Michelle thought, *He'll be a great father.*

Chapter 8: Baby Fever

Michelle lay on her childhood bed, reading *Speak* by Laurie Halse Anderson. It was a recently published YA novel that some of her sixth-grade girls had been reading on their own. The themes were a bit too mature for eleven-year-olds, but her gifted kids read well above their age level.

Jason stepped into the room, shutting and locking the door behind him. He wore his pajamas, his hair still wet from the shower. Jason hung his towel on the closet doorknob, and placed his toiletry bag into his open suitcase.

Michelle set her book on the bedside table facedown, next to the lamp. "All clean?"

Jason nodded and removed his pajamas, revealing his boxer briefs. "I hate smelling like smoke."

Michelle had showered, while Jason was playing with Becky. "Did Becky go to bed?"

He climbed into bed. Jason and Michelle lay on their sides, facing each other, the blanket covering their lower halves. He replied in a low voice, "She's sleeping with your parents. She wouldn't sleep in the guest bedroom."

"She could've slept with us."

Jason frowned. "That wouldn't be appropriate. I'm not her father."

"It would've been fine, but it doesn't matter. As long as she's sleeping."

"She's crashing now. Probably coming down from her sugar high. I think your mom let her eat too many Christmas cookies."

Michelle sighed. "My mom always has too much junk around. Especially at Christmas."

"I got her to brush her teeth before she went to bed. I thought with all that sugar …"

Michelle kissed Jason on the lips, sucking his lower lip for a beat.

He grinned. "What was that for?"

"For being you. I think you'd make a great father."

"I don't know."

"No, that's wrong. I *know* you'd make a great father." Michelle leaned in and kissed him again. When they separated, she said, "I want a baby."

He pulled back, his brow furrowed. "Now?"

"Not necessarily tonight, but I think we should start trying."

Jason rubbed the back of his neck. "I wanted to talk to you about that. I'm a little worried about last night. We didn't use anything."

Michelle frowned. "I doubt I'm pregnant, if that's what you're asking. I just had my period."

Jason nodded again, a wave of relief passing over his face. "I thought we were going to wait, so we can have some time with each other."

"We've been together for five years. How much longer?"

"We've only been married for three."

"I may not get pregnant right away. We should start trying."

He rolled away from her, now on his back. "I don't know if I'm ready. I don't want things to change yet."

Michelle reached out and took his hand. "Our children won't have the same childhood that you had."

"I know."

"Then what are you afraid of?"

"I just need a little more time."

Michelle let go of his hand and rolled to her back. "Is it me? Do you not want children with *me?*"

He rolled to his side, closing the gap between them. "Of course I do."

"We're financially secure. It's time."

"Soon. I promise." He pecked her on the lips.

Michelle kissed him back, openmouthed, her tongue in his mouth. He responded in kind. She slid her hand down his boxer briefs, his penis hardening in her hand. He slipped his hand between her legs, rubbing her clitoris. She moaned, moving her pelvis against his hand. She tugged on the waistband of his boxer briefs, signaling what she wanted.

Jason got the hint. They removed their underwear, like they were on fire, the bed squeaking under their sudden movements. Michelle lay on her back and spread her legs. He was inside her immediately afterward. They were in perfect sync, moving as one for several minutes. Michelle edged close to her climax, but Jason pulled out, grabbed a condom from his bag, and rolled it over his erection.

"No. I want to feel you," Michelle whispered.

"I know what you want," Jason replied.

When they resumed, the synchronicity was gone. He came, but she didn't get what she wanted. They didn't say anything to each other when he rolled off her, slipped on his pajama pants, and went to the bathroom.

Chapter 9: The Nightmare Begins

"God damn it!" Frank shouted.

Becky cried.

Michelle woke in the darkness, her parents arguing across the hall. She glanced at the clock on the bedside table—*1:03 a.m.*

"She peed the bed," Frank said.

"It's fine. I'll clean it," Ruth replied.

"It's seeping into the mattress."

Michelle turned on the lamp in her bedroom.

Jason groaned and rolled toward Michelle. "What's happening?"

"I think Becky peed the bed. I should help."

"Can you turn out the lamp before you go?" Jason rolled away from the light and covered his head with his pillow.

Michelle exited the bed and dressed in pajama pants and a PSU sweatshirt. She turned off the lamp and went into the hallway. Ruth came from her room, leading Becky by the hand.

Becky sniffled, her face tear streaked.

"Do you need any help?" Michelle asked.

"Can you help your father strip the bed and wash the sheets?" Ruth replied.

"Sure."

"Thank you, dear."

Ruth took Becky into the bathroom to get cleaned up. Michelle went into her parents' bedroom. Frank pulled the comforter from the bed, dumping it in a heap on the floor.

"The mattress is ruined," Frank said, one side of his mouth raised in disgust.

Michelle walked to the side of the bed, opposite Frank, and stripped the top sheet from the bed. "Maybe. You can always flip it over."

Frank undid the corners of the fitted sheet on his side of the bed. "Or I can burn it."

"Come on, Dad. It's only pee." Michelle removed the pee-soaked fitted sheet from mattress, placing the sheet on the floor.

Frank scowled at the dark pee stain in the middle of his mattress. "This is why I never let you kids sleep with your mother and me. Looks like a map of Russia."

Michelle laughed and shook her head. "You're ridiculous." She scooped up the sheets from the floor. "I'll take these down to the wash."

Michelle went down to the laundry room in the basement. Wet clothes were in the washer, and dry clothes were in the dryer, so she had to put the dry clothes in a laundry basket and then move the wet clothes to the dryer to make room for the sheets. Ruth had the bad habit of forgetting about clothes in the wash, giving them a mildew smell.

Once Michelle had the sheets in the wash and the machine running, she went back upstairs to help Frank clean the mattress and to make the bed. Frank paced in the hallway with clenched fists and a clenched jaw, holding a Ziploc bag with what appeared to be underwear inside.

"What's wrong?" Michelle asked.

Franks stopped pacing and pivoted to Michelle. "Your mother found dried blood in Becky's underwear."

Michelle glanced at the Ziploc bag, holding the bloody underwear, her face etched with concern. "What happened? Did she hurt herself?"

Frank spoke through gritted teeth, his lower jaw jutting forward. "Becky said that a man hurt her privates."

Michelle was stunned and slack-jawed. "What man?"

Frank gestured to his shut bedroom door. "That's what your mother's trying to find out."

"*Jesus.* Is that what she said exactly? A man hurt her privates?"

Frank shook his head. "She said, 'A man hurt my pee-pee part.'"

"What are we going to do?"

Ruth exited the bedroom, her eyes puffy from crying. "She won't tell me. She keeps saying she doesn't know."

"We need to call the police." Frank addressed Michelle, "Call your sister. Tell her to come over immediately."

Chapter 10: Doth Protest Too Much

Susie and Cody made it to the house before the police. They smelled like smoke and alcohol from the bar and still wore the same clothes Michelle had seen them in earlier that night. Becky was asleep in Frank and Ruth's freshly made bed. Jason rose and dressed, after hearing about the alleged sexual assault. Everyone sat at the dining room table, waiting for the police. The Ziploc bag containing Becky's bloody underwear was now the centerpiece.

Ruth had placed a dish towel over the bag. "I can't look at that anymore," she had said.

"Who has she been around?" Frank asked Susie.

"Nobody really," Susie replied, her eyes puffy.

"That's not good enough. We need to know every male who she's been in contact with over the last week."

Susie looked at Jason. "She was with him."

Everyone at the table turned their attention to Jason.

Jason showed his palms and spoke rapidly. "I never touched her. I would never do that. *Never.*"

Susie's lips curled into a sneer. "I didn't say you did. I said you were with her, which you were. Several times. *Alone.*"

"Don't do that," Michelle said to her sister. "Dad and Mom were alone with her. I bet you and Cody too. Do we start suspecting you guys?"

Susie glared at Michelle. "We didn't immediately start professing our innocence."

"Who *else* has she been alone with?" Frank asked.

"I don't know. Teachers. Counselors at the after-school program." Susie tapped her lips, thinking. "Danny gave her a ride home from school twice last week, but she seemed perfectly happy when she came home, excited about riding in a police car."

Susie and Becky lived in a condo within walking distance of Loganville Elementary School.

"Do you think you would've noticed the blood on her underwear?" Frank asked Susie.

"What difference does it make?" Susie replied.

Frank leaned forward, resting his elbows on the table. "If you didn't notice it, then who knows when this happened? The blood's dry."

"I think I would've noticed it, but I don't know. Becky dresses herself."

Frank raised his eyebrows. "Does she change her underwear every day?"

"Probably."

"*Probably?*"

"I told you. She dresses herself." Susie huffed. "*Jesus*, you're acting like this is my fault."

A hard knock came from the front door. Everyone knew it was the police. Normal people didn't knock like that. Frank went to the front door. He spoke to the officers for a few minutes, their words inaudible from the dining room. Frank led the officers into the dining room. Two muscled Loganville Township Police Officers flanked a petite blonde detective, wearing a pantsuit and flats. The detective wore latex gloves and held a plastic evidence bag, information already scrawled on the label. One of the officers was Danny Gibbs.

Frank gestured to the female detective. "This is Detective Wells."

"Hello," Wells said.

Everyone at the table nodded or said hello.

"Where is the underwear?"

"It's right here," Frank said, reaching for the dish towel.

"Don't touch it," Wells replied, holding up her hand.

Frank retracted his hand, a scowl on his face. "I know what I'm doing."

"Please let me handle this, Mr. Murphy."

Frank flashed his palms.

Wells removed the dish towel, then placed the Ziploc bag and underwear inside the plastic evidence bag, sealing it tight. She handed it to the officer standing next to Danny, and he took it outside, presumably to the detective's car.

"Where's Becky?" Wells asked.

"She's sleeping in my bed," Ruth replied.

"Okay. We'll have to wake her up and take her to the hospital for an exam." Wells surveyed the people seated around the kitchen table. "Which one of you is Becky's mother?"

Susie raised her hand. "I am."

"What's your full name?"

"Susan Murphy."

Wells nodded to Susie. "Ms. Murphy, you'll come to the hospital with me and Becky." She glanced around the table. "I would like the rest of you to go to the police station with Officer Gibbs to be interviewed. This is not mandatory, but, since all of you obviously care about Becky, I would be surprised and dismayed if anyone refused."

"Nobody has anything to hide," Frank said, interjecting, still standing near Danny.

"Great." Wells stared at Jason for a split second, then said, "Within the next few hours, we'll have crime scene investigators here."

The officer who had gone outside, reentered the house, and marched back to the dining room.

"I don't want anyone going into the basement until they've finished their work." Wells gestured to the officer. "Officer Harris will guard the scene until it's been processed."

Michelle wondered why they were so concerned about the basement. *Do they think she was abused there?* Then it hit her like a bolt of lightning. *Jason was in the basement, with Becky, ... alone.*

Chapter 11: Suspicious

Michelle sat in the waiting room of the Loganville Township Police Station alongside her parents. Detectives were separately interviewing Jason and Cody. Frank stood from his plastic chair and walked to the nearby vending machines.

Michelle turned to her mother and whispered, "Why are they checking the basement? What did Dad tell the detective?"

Ruth turned to her daughter, not whispering. "I assume your father told them the truth."

Frank returned with a cup of coffee. He must've heard their conversation because he said, "Jason was alone with Becky in the basement several times over the past two days."

"Twice," Michelle replied, glaring. "Not several times. Two times. I don't appreciate you and Susie throwing Jason under the bus. He didn't do anything."

Frank stirred his coffee. "If he didn't do anything, he has nothing to worry about."

***

"What did they ask you?" Michelle asked, sitting in the front passenger seat of her BMW in the parking lot of the Loganville Township Police Station.

Jason rested his head on the steering wheel. "They think I did it."

Michelle arched her eyebrows. "The police said that?"

Jason sat up and took a deep breath. He turned toward Michelle. "Not exactly. They were very suspicious. They asked me about what Becky and I did in the basement, which is fine, but then they started asking me if I touched her. When I said no, they kept asking." He mimicked the male detective. *"Are you sure you didn't brush against her? Was it an accident? You can tell us. I bet you'd like to get it off your chest. If you talk now, things will be much easier for you."* Jason shook his head. "It was an hour of that bullshit. They were trying to get me to confess. It was stupid of me to talk to them without an attorney."

Chapter 12: From Bad to Worse

"I don't think I should go in." Jason parked the BMW in the hospital parking garage.

Michelle reached over and grabbed his hand. "If you don't go in, it'll look bad."

"It already looks bad. You saw the way Susie was looking at me at your parents' house. The cops are looking at the basement, where I was alone with Becky." He swallowed hard. "I have a really bad feeling about this. Your dad already doesn't like me—"

"That's not true."

"Really? Come on, Michelle. He tolerates me. He actually likes Danny. That's another thing. I really don't like it that your ex-boyfriend is part of the investigation. He's already biased against me."

"You're jumping to conclusions."

Jason broke eye contact and removed his hand from hers. He peered through the windshield at the concrete wall of the parking garage. "I'm going home. If you want to stay, that's fine, but I'm leaving."

They had planned on staying for a few more days.

"You can't leave. That'll look *really* bad," Michelle said.

"I *know* how it looks." Jason turned back to Michelle, scowling, his fists clenched. "It doesn't matter. They are *already* looking at me. I can't be around people who think I could do such a thing. I *can't*. They can all fuck off."

Michelle hung her head and rubbed her eyes. She raised her gaze to Jason again. "I can't believe this is happening. This is crazy."

Jason closed his eyes. When he opened them, a tear slipped down his cheek. "Can we go home? Please."

Michelle nodded. "Okay. Let me check on Becky, and then we'll go. You can wait in the car, if you don't feel comfortable, but I don't think my family really thinks it was you—"

"I'm not going in."

"That's fine. You know what? Maybe it was nobody. Maybe Becky saw something in a movie. Susie lets her watch R-rated movies."

Jason shrugged. "I hope so."

"I'll be back." Michelle leaned over and kissed him on the cheek, then exited the BMW.

Michelle left the parking garage and entered the hospital. She found her family in the pediatrics waiting room. Ruth and Cody sat in chairs, one chair between them. Cody leafed through an automotive magazine. Ruth stared into space, like a zombie. Frank paced, like a man possessed.

Michelle approached her father. "What's going on?"

"Susie and Becky are still with the doctor," Frank said, his face twisted into a scowl.

"I was thinking that it's possible that nothing happened. Maybe Becky was just repeating something she saw on TV."

Frank shook his head, his lower jaw jutting forward. "Susie said the exam showed vaginal trauma." He took a deep breath, his hands on his hips. "There was penetration, ... probably from a finger."

Michelle winced. "Oh my God. Did she say who it was?"

Frank shook his head again, his face red with rage. "No, but that's not all. Based on what Becky said, she was probably forced to perform oral sex."

Tears welled in Michelle's eyes. She wiped the corners of her eyes and said, "I ... I don't know what to say."

"Where's Jason?"

"He's in the car."

"Why didn't he come in?" Frank narrowed his eyes, searching Michelle's face.

Michelle sniffled. "He's feeling a little persecuted at the moment. The police were tough on him."

"That's their job. They're not concerned about his feelings. They're concerned about the truth."

Michelle pursed her lips. "It's not just the police. Susie was quick to point the finger at him. So were you."

"That's bullshit. Let me tell you something." Frank pointed at Michelle. "If Jason did have something to do with this, he better hope the cops get to him before I do."

Chapter 13: DNA

After the hospital, Jason and Michelle had packed up their belongings and drove home to Villanova, Pennsylvania.

Over the next nine days, Michelle had talked to Ruth three times on the phone. She had said Becky was physically healthy, and she was seeing a child psychologist who specialized in sexual abuse. Michelle had wondered if Becky would ever emotionally recover from the trauma. The police hadn't made any progress in the case. At least, that's what Ruth had said. Michelle hadn't talked to Frank or Susie since Jason and Michelle left Loganville on December 26. She was still pissed that they were pointing the finger at Jason.

Michelle placed the marinated steaks on the indoor gas grill. She washed her hands. Humming came from the garage door opener. Then the throaty exhaust from Jason's M3. Michelle went to the side-by-side refrigerator, fishing out lettuce and vegetables for the salad. As she was cutting the tomato, Jason walked into the kitchen, his mouth turned down and his shoulders slumped.

"Hey, honey. Dinner should be ready in about ten minutes."

"I'm not hungry." He set his briefcase on the counter, along with his keys.

Michelle set down the serrated knife and approached her husband. "What's wrong?"

"Detective Wells showed up at my office today."

Michelle inhaled sharply. "What did she want?"

He grunted. "My DNA."

"Your DNA? For what?"

"I think they want to compare my DNA to a sample from Becky's exam."

Michelle hesitated for a second. "Did you give them a sample?"

Jason exhaled a tired breath. "I did. She swabbed the inside of my cheek."

Michelle smiled. "This is actually really good. They'll compare your DNA to their sample, and this'll clear your name."

"That's what Detective Wells said."

"Exactly. This is a good thing."

"Then why do I feel sick to my stomach?"

Chapter 14: Objects in Motion

Eleven fourth-grade gifted students crowded around the ski slope, which was a six-foot long piece of plywood covered in wax paper and propped on Michelle's desk. Two students held stopwatches at the ready. Michelle leaned over her desk, holding two six-inch-tall aluminum foil skiers at the top of the slope. Popsicle sticks were taped to their feet as skis. A fan was set up at the finish line, blowing air up the slope, causing resistance. The skiers were low and bent forward to reduce wind resistance. The race was the culmination of their lesson on Newton's laws of motion.

Michelle said, "Ready. Set. Go." She let go of the skiers at the same time.

The aluminum foil skiers raced down the slope, the students cheering. The skier on the right won by a nose. The students with the stopwatches recorded their times for the leaderboard.

"Great job, you two. Notice that Allison and Jake added foil to the bottom of their skis to reduce friction." Michelle held up two more skiers. "This is Samantha on the right and Kevin on the left."

The classroom telephone rang. Michelle handed the skiers to an adorable little brunette. "Emily will be the starter, while I answer the phone."

While the students continued the downhill skiing championship, Michelle answered the phone on the wall. "Hello. This is Michelle Lewis speaking."

The students cheered the aluminum foil skiers.

"This is Tori. I'm so sorry to bother you at work. Jason asked me to call you." Tori was Jason's administrative assistant.

Michelle's heart pounded. It had been a week since Jason's DNA had been collected. "What's wrong?"

"He was arrested by the Loganville police. Jason told me to tell you to hire an attorney and to meet him in Loganville at the police department."

Michelle dropped the receiver on the linoleum.

Chapter 15: The Defense Attorney

After notifying her principal of the family emergency—she didn't go into specifics—Michelle sent her gifted students back to their regular teachers and left school. She drove home in a trance, her mind overloaded with apocalyptic thoughts. As she pulled into her driveway, she slowed the car, her stomach doing cartwheels. Three police cruisers and a van crowded her driveway. One was unmarked. Most of the vehicles were from the Loganville Township Police, but one cruiser was from her local department—the Radnor Township Police. She parked behind a cruiser.

Are they going to arrest me?

Michelle exited her car and fast-walked toward the front door, the winter wind biting at her ears and cutting through her slacks. Detective Wells stood with two uniformed police officers, everyone watching Michelle.

At the bottom of the stoop, Michelle asked, "What is this?"

Detective Wells stepped toward Michelle and handed her a piece of paper. "We have a search warrant. Open the door, please."

Michelle glanced at the search warrant, her heart pounding. She skimmed something about confiscating computers and searching the premises. Michelle stepped up to the stoop, her legs wobbly. At the front door, she fished through her purse for her keys. She dropped her keys on the stoop. One of the officers picked up her keys and handed them to Michelle.

"Thank you," Michelle replied, barely above a whisper. With shaky hands, she unlocked the door.

Before Michelle opened the door, Detective Wells placed her hand on the door and said, "I'm sorry. You have to stay outside while we conduct our search."

"How long will that be?"

"I'm not sure. It's a pretty big house. At least six hours."

"I need the phone, and I need to go on the internet to find an attorney."

Detective Wells shook her head. "You'll have to go somewhere else for that."

Michelle clenched her jaw. "I need to disarm the alarm."

"Okay."

Michelle went inside and disarmed the alarm, with Detective Wells breathing on the back of her neck. Michelle left, driving away from her neighborhood, leaving the officers to search her home. She cried as she drove, scanning a strip mall for a pay phone. She spotted a phone booth on the corner and parked nearby.

Michelle called the one person who could help her but worried that he wouldn't.

"Hello," Frank said.

Michelle sniffled and choked out one word. "Dad."

"They picked him up, didn't they?"

Michelle wondered if her father knew the arrest was coming. "He didn't do it." Her voice was whiny.

"If he didn't do it, it'll all work out. I promise."

Michelle sniffled again. "I have to find an attorney, but the police won't let me in my house. I'm at a pay phone. Do you know a local defense attorney I could call?"

Frank was silent.

"Please, Dad."

Frank let out a heavy breath. "Yeah. I know somebody."

After a phone call and some begging to an administrative assistant, Michelle was on the line with the best defense attorney in Loganville. Her voice was shaky. "My name is Michelle Lewis. I'm Frank Murphy's daughter. My husband was arrested this morning."

"What was the charge?" Norman Tuttle asked.

"I don't know specifically, but I think it was sexual assault." Michelle couldn't bring herself to say rape.

"Do you know if the alleged victim is an adult or a minor?"

Michelle cleared her throat and said barely above a whisper, "A minor."

Norman exhaled.

She stood with slumped shoulders. "He's innocent. My husband would never …"

"Defending alleged child molesters in a small town isn't very good for business."

"Please, Mr. Tuttle." Tears blurred her vision. Her voice quivered. "I'm assuming you know my dad?"

"I do. He was a tough and honest cop."

"If I thought my husband was guilty, I wouldn't want anything to do with him."

Norman was quiet for a long moment. "What's your husband's name and date of birth?"

"Jason Lewis. August 20, 1963."

"Let me make a few calls, and I'll call you right back."

"Thank you."

"I'm not committing yet. I'll call you back."

Michelle gave Norman the pay-phone number and hung up the receiver. She zipped up her coat and stood in the phone booth, alone with her thoughts. She hoped nobody would come to use the phone. *I'll give them $20 to go somewhere else.*

***

Sixteen minutes later, Norman called back.

Michelle answered on the first ring. "Mr. Tuttle?"

"Jason was arrested and charged with two counts of involuntary deviate sexual intercourse with a child and two counts of aggravated indecent assault of a child. Each of these charges are first-degree felonies. Involuntary deviate sexual intercourse with a child carries a forty-year maximum sentence. The other charge carries a twenty-year maximum sentence. If Jason's convicted, and the judge chooses to run the charges and counts consecutively, he's facing 120 years in prison."

Michelle gasped. "One hundred and twenty years?"

"That's worst-case scenario, but twenty to forty years in prison is very realistic for those charges."

She leaned against the phone booth, her legs weak. "Don't they need evidence to do this?"

"They have evidence. They don't make arrests without evidence."

"What evidence do they have?"

"I don't know yet."

"We need your help, Mr. Tuttle. Please."

"My fees are $300 an hour, and I'll need a $50,000 retainer."

"Whatever you need."

"Jason's initial court appearance and arraignment is tomorrow morning at 8:30. At the arraignment, the judge will set the bail amount. Given the charges, I think bail could be as high as $500,000. Based on the felony bail schedule, it won't be less than $200,000."

Michelle hung her head. "My God. That's so much money."

"It's a standard amount, based on the charges and Jason's likelihood to flee. If you can't come up with the bail money, I can help you with a bail bondsman. They can loan you the money, but they'll charge you 10 percent. Do you understand how bail works?"

"Not exactly."

"Let's say the bail is $300,000. You would either pay the court yourself or hire a bail bondsman to do it for you. If you pay it yourself, when Jason appears at trial, the court will refund your money. If he disappears, that money is forfeited. If you use a bail bondsman, they take 10 percent as a fee."

A burly man stood outside the phone booth, his arms crossed, and his feet tapping the asphalt.

Michelle raised her head and stood up straight. "We have the money. Jason wouldn't want me to pay the fee."

"Okay. Great. Where do you bank?" Norman asked.

"PNC."

"Perfect. There's a PNC around the corner from the courthouse. I don't know if you have half-a-million dollars in your checking account ..."

The burly man knocked on the phone booth.

Michelle flinched, then turned her back to him. "We don't have that much. Most of our savings are in a money market account with PNC, but I can move money into our checking pretty easily." Jason had recently sold their stocks in anticipation of a stock market crash.

The man banged on the phone booth.

"Please hold on, Mr. Tuttle," Michelle said.

The man tapped his watch.

Michelle opened up the phone booth door and shouted at the man, "Would you *please* give me a fucking minute of privacy?" She slammed the door shut.

The man glared, his arms again crossed over his chest.

"I'm sorry, Mr. Tuttle," Michelle said.

"It's all right," Tuttle replied. "I suggest you go to PNC immediately and move $500,000 into your checking account, so you can write a certified check for the bail, once we know the amount. It might be smart to call the PNC in Loganville and let them know that you'll be coming in for a large certified check tomorrow. Just in case I forget to tell you tomorrow, you'll make the check out to the clerk of the court."

Michelle took a deep breath. "Thank you, Mr. Tuttle."

"Don't thank me yet. This is just the beginning. I'll stop by the jail today and introduce myself to Jason. I want you to meet me tomorrow morning at the courthouse at 8:15."

Chapter 16: Arraignment

Yesterday, Michelle went to PNC and moved half-a-million dollars from their money market account to their checking account. She took off another day at work and drove 110 miles to Loganville in the early morning hours on Wednesday, January 12.

Michelle was so worried about being late that she made it to the Loganville courthouse forty-five minutes early. She parked in the paid lot across the street from the gothic courthouse that resembled a cross between a haunted mansion and a church. It was barely light outside as she walked from the lot to the courthouse. She dipped her head into the wind as she walked, the cold air piercing her skirt suit and tights.

She went through the metal detectors, her legs wobbly and her hands shaky. A deputy eyed her with suspicion but said nothing. She had been too nervous to eat, and now she was even more jittery because she hadn't eaten. Even though her dad was a retired police officer, she'd never been to court.

Once through the metal detectors, she followed the well-dressed crowd. Most of the people ended up at a glass-protected bulletin board, with the day's dockets printed and hung inside. She found Jason's arraignment, which would take place in courtroom 2F.

Michelle took the stairs to the second floor and found 2F. She tried to open the door, but it was locked. She checked her watch. It was only 7:44 a.m. The arraignment didn't start until 8:30, and she was supposed to meet Tuttle at 8:15. Michelle sat on the bench in the hall, her legs crossed.

Various people meandered to the courtroom. Many checked the locked door, as Michelle had. She glanced at each person, hoping not to recognize anyone. Thankfully, they were all strangers. At eight o'clock, a bailiff opened the courtroom, and the small crowd filed in. Michelle remained on the bench, waiting for Jason's attorney.

At 8:15 on the nose, a tall white-haired man walked toward the courtroom, holding a briefcase. He looked exactly as he had described himself. Michelle stood from the bench, as the man approached.

"Mrs. Lewis?" he asked.

"Yes," she replied.

"I'm Norman Tuttle."

They shook hands.

Norman wore a tailored suit. He was fit for an older man. His eyes were gray and squinty. His lips were thin. His face was taut and surprisingly wrinkle free, the beneficiary of a recent facelift.

Michelle patted her purse. "I have your retainer check. I don't know if you need that before you ..."

He gestured to the bench. "Why don't we sit down?"

They sat on the bench.

"Were you able to move the bail money to your checking account?"

"Yes." Michelle fished the personal check for the retainer from her purse, and handed it to the attorney. He placed the check into his wallet.

"How was Jason?" Michelle asked.

"A little rattled but I've seen worse," Norman replied. "He told me that your niece is the alleged victim."

Michelle bowed her head. "Yes."

Norman nodded. "That's tough. I imagine you'll be under extreme pressure from your family to abandon Jason. If you truly believe he's innocent, it's important that you don't abandon him. You and I are all he has, but I'm the only one who doesn't have to believe he's innocent." He leaned toward Michelle and raised his eyebrows. "Do you understand?"

"I think so."

***

The courtroom was half filled, the audience sitting on rows of wooden pews. Michelle and Norman sat in the second row, the old attorney next to the aisle. The pews were separated by a short wooden divider from everything else—the tables for the prosecution and the defense, the tall desk for the judge and witnesses, and a jury box with twelve empty chairs.

They had watched three different men in black-and-white striped pajamas—like prisoners from an old cartoon—make their pleas, receive their bail amounts, and being led back the way they came. These men were all represented by the same public defender, who didn't know their names without checking his files.

Jason was the fourth man to be led into the courtroom by a bailiff. Like the others, his hands were cuffed, and his feet were shackled, with a chain and leg cuffs that made him shuffle. Unlike the others, he was dressed in the suit he wore when he was arrested. Norman had made the request with the jail. He had said to Michelle, "We don't want him looking like a criminal."

Norman stood and pushed through the swinging door of the divider, meeting his client at the defense table, then sitting next to each other.

A name placard in front of the judge read Honorable Cynthia Ames. She was middle-aged with strawberry-blond hair. Her black robe nearly swallowed her petite frame. She said, "This is case number zero-seven-dash-three-eight-eight-two, the Commonwealth of Pennsylvania versus

Jason Lewis. The defendant has been charged with two counts of involuntary deviate sexual intercourse, a violation of Title 18 of the Pennsylvania Code, Section 3123, subsection B, which is a first-degree felony and carries a maximum sentence of forty years in prison and a $25,000 fine for each count."

A few people in the audience gasped. Michelle's face felt hot with shame.

Jason looked down. Norman sat ramrod straight next to him, looking up to the judge. Cynthia Ames had a reddish tint to her skin that exuded mild irritation, even though it was a constant feature.

Judge Ames continued, seemingly unfazed by the outburst. "The defendant has also been charged with two counts of aggravated indecent assault of a child, a violation of Title 18 of the Pennsylvania Code, Section 3125, subsection B, which is a first-degree felony and carries a maximum sentence of twenty years in prison and a $25,000 fine for each count."

Judge Ames raised her gaze from the file, showing her lazy eye and thin lips. "In the matter of the Commonwealth of Pennsylvania versus Jason Lewis, how do you plead?"

Norman nodded to Jason.

Jason looked up and said, "Not guilty."

Judge Ames nodded, then leafed through her planner. "I'd like to set the preliminary hearing for next week, Wednesday, January 19 at 8:30 a.m. Mr. Tuttle?"

"That'll be fine, Your Honor."

Judge Ames addressed the heavyset man, sitting behind the prosecutor's table. "Mr. Elliot?"

"That works for the commonwealth, Your Honor."

Judge Ames made a note in her planner, then addressed the prosecuting attorney again. "I'll hear from the commonwealth regarding bail."

Mr. Elliot rose from his seat. He was short, with a Santa-like gut, double chin, and thick neck. The top button of his shirt was undone, despite the tie. "Mr. Lewis lives in Villanova and has considerable means. Given the heinous nature of the crimes and the age of the victim, we believe Mr. Lewis is a serious flight risk and a danger to the community."

Judge Ames flipped through the file, her face twisted in disgust. She eyed the prosecuting attorney. "Mr. Elliot, does the commonwealth have a recommended bail amount?"

"We're recommending bail be set at one million dollars."

Michelle winced, knowing that she had only moved half that amount to her checking account.

Judge Ames looked at Norman. "Mr. Tuttle?"

Norman rose from his seat. "This is egregious. One million dollars is five times the recommended amount of the bail schedule for these charges. Mr. Lewis is not a flight risk. He does not have a criminal record. Not even so much as an unpaid parking ticket. He may have the money to flee, but, by that logic, nearly everyone who comes to this courtroom has enough for a bus ticket to Canada."

Judge Ames frowned. "I'll set bail at $400,000, but Mr. Lewis is not to come into any contact with anyone under the age of eighteen years old, and he is to stay at least one hundred yards away from schools and events where children are present." She banged her gavel.

Chapter 17: Loyalty

After the arraignment, Norman led Michelle downstairs and showed her where to pay Jason's bail. They stood in the hall, just outside the office of the clerk of the court. Norman gave Michelle directions to the nearby jail, where Jason would be released in a few hours.

Norman said, "I'd go with you, but I doubt you want to pay me $300 an hour to sit on my butt."

Michelle nodded. "What happens now?"

"I expect a plea offer before the preliminary hearing next Wednesday, but Jason already told me that he won't plead guilty or even no contest. He's adamant that he's innocent, so unless the commonwealth drops the case, we're going to trial."

Michelle swallowed, her throat dry. "Do you think they'll drop the case?"

Norman frowned. "Not a chance. The DA wants blood on this one."

Michelle winced. "What happens at the preliminary hearing?"

"This is where the commonwealth will have to prove probable cause exists to prosecute, meaning they'll present their evidence, and the judge will determine if there's enough to proceed to trial."

Michelle stood up straight, hanging on to a thread of hope. "If they don't have enough evidence, then you can make it go away."

Norman shook his head. "Theoretically, but that's highly unlikely.

Jason's arrest had a warrant. Chances are they have sufficient evidence to go to trial. Otherwise, they wouldn't have made the arrest. I'll have a better idea of what we're facing once I've gone through the evidence."

Michelle slumped her shoulders, deflated.

"I'd like to meet with you two on Monday in my office to go over the case. How about 10:00 a.m.?"

Michelle thought about taking off from work. "That's fine. This is so much to process."

Norman searched her face for a beat. "One thing at a time, Michelle. Don't worry. You're not alone. Go get your check and bail out your husband. A trial is a marathon, not a sprint."

Michelle went to the Loganville PNC Bank, then back to the courthouse to pay Jason's bail, then to the Loganville Sheriff's office and jail. She checked in with a deputy, who was a poor excuse for a receptionist, and sat in the waiting room, her butt hurting from the wooden pews in the courtroom.

Deputies came and went from the restricted area. Each time Michelle watched the doorway, hopeful to see Jason. She sat there for over two hours. Jason had barely been gone twenty-four hours, but it felt like an eternity. The door opened again, a deputy opening the door for Jason to walk through. His suit was rumpled, and he had dark circles under his eyes.

Michelle stood and rushed toward him. They embraced in the waiting room. The receptionist looked at them side-eyed. Jason buried his face in her hair.

He spoke into her ear. "Thank you. I was worried you wouldn't come."

When they separated, she said, "I wouldn't leave you here."

"Can we go home?"

She took his hand. "Let's go."

Michelle and Jason walked outside to the salt-stained parking lot of the Loganville Jail. Michelle zipped up her long coat, condensation coming from her breath. Piles of dirty snow were on the edge of the lot. The sun was obscured by gray clouds. At the car, Michelle handed her keys to Jason.

He didn't take the keys, like usual. "Would you mind driving? I'm still a little shaky."

She tilted her head. "Have you eaten anything today?"

"I had breakfast. I'm not hungry. I'm just … a little off."

Michelle climbed into the driver's seat and started the car, cranking the heater. Jason sat next to her in the passenger seat.

"How did you find Tuttle?" Jason asked.

"My dad," Michelle replied, putting on her seat belt. "I have a good feeling about Norman."

Jason creased his forehead. "Your dad helped you find me an attorney?"

Michelle nodded. "I know it seems like he's against you, but I think it's just because he was a cop. He's always really suspicious."

"I can't imagine he's on my side."

"I think he cares about what's true. I also think he knows things about your case, things that Norman doesn't even know yet."

Jason turned in his seat to face Michelle. "What makes you think that?"

Michelle started the engine. "When I called him for help, the first thing he said was, 'They picked him up, didn't they?'"

"He knew I was going to be arrested?"

"I think so."

"What else does he know?"

Michelle's eyes widened, and she turned in her seat to face Jason. "We should go over there and find out."

Jason showed his palm like a stop sign. "I'd rather not see anyone right now, especially your father."

"I understand. You can wait in the car."

"Let's just go home."

Michelle shook her head. "This is your life. This is *our* life. If he knows something that can help you, he's going to fucking tell me."

He leaned over and hugged her. "Thank you for believing in me."

She kissed him on the cheek. When they separated, she said, "We'll get through this. I love you."

He cracked a small smile. "I love you too."

They drove across town to her parents' neighborhood of ramblers and colonials on quarter-acre lots. Michelle parked next to Frank's F-150, in front of the garage. "I'll be right back."

She exited her BMW and peered into the garage window. Her mom's car wasn't there, which wasn't uncommon on a school day. Ruth taught English at Loganville Middle School. Michelle walked along the front walk to the front door. She rang the doorbell and tried to open the door, but it was locked, which was odd for her parents.

After several doorbell chimes, Frank finally answered the door. "Michelle? What are you doing here?"

"I need to talk to you," Michelle said, her hands on her hips.

Frank glanced at the driveway, probably wondering if Jason was there, but Michelle's car was obscured by Frank's truck. "I need to talk to you too." Frank let Michelle inside.

They sat across from each other at the dining room table. Michelle unzipped her coat but didn't bother taking it off.

"You knew that they were going to arrest Jason, didn't you?"

Frank rubbed his goatee before answering. "I thought they might arrest him, but I didn't know. When you called, you were upset, so I figured ..."

"I feel like you're keeping something from me."

"I didn't know anything until this morning." Frank clenched his jaw. "I gave Jason the benefit of the doubt. That's why I helped you find an attorney. I regret that now."

Michelle glared at her father. "He didn't do it. You and Mom and Susie were so quick to point the finger at him. That's why the cops zeroed in on him."

Frank glared right back. "I know from a very good source that they found semen on Becky's underwear."

Michelle's eyes were like saucers. "What?"

"Yeah. The semen matched Jason's DNA. That piece of shit raped Becky."

Michelle winced, as if she'd been slapped. "That can't be right. There has to be an explanation."

Frank's lower jaw jutted forward. "Yeah, there's an explanation. Your husband's a goddamn pedophile."

Michelle was stunned and slack-jawed for a moment. "This is insane. I know Jason. He wouldn't do this."

Frank leaned forward, spittle coming from his mouth. "How else do you explain his semen on her underwear? He raped my granddaughter!"

Michelle thought for a few seconds, grasping for an explanation. "We had sex on Christmas night."

Frank held up his hand. "I don't wanna hear this."

"Hear me out. He used a condom, and he threw it in the trash in the bathroom. Maybe someone took it and put it on her underwear, or it was some kind of lab mistake."

Frank sneered. "Impossible. Your mother and I were the only ones to touch the underwear. Detective Wells bagged it right in front of us. And labs don't make mistakes."

"Everyone makes mistakes."

"This is no mistake. I'm gonna tell you something, and I suggest you listen real good because you're at a crossroads. If you support Jason, you're on the side of evil. Do you understand that?"

Michelle opened her mouth to speak, but nothing came out.

Frank pointed at Michelle, his finger jabbing the air between them each time he said *you* and *your*. "If *you* support Becky's rapist, what do *you* think that'll do to *your* relationship with Susie or Becky or *your* mother or me? What about *your* career? Everyone will wonder if *you* knew, if *you* condoned it."

Michelle blinked, and tears slipped down her cheeks. "There has to be a mistake."

"It's not a mistake. Even if he finds a way to weasel out of the charges, he's still guilty in my mind."

Michelle shook her head. "I can't believe it. I can't."

Frank's demeanor softened. "Stay here tonight. We can go down and get your stuff tomorrow. Divorce him. Wash your hands of him. You need to show this family that you support Becky and Susie. That's the only way to salvage anything in this fucking nightmare."

Michelle kept shaking her head, her vision blurred by her tears. "I don't believe you. He would never. You don't know him like I do." Michelle stood from the table.

Frank stood from the table. "Women are fooled all the time by these creeps. It's not your fault. Now that you know, you can do the right thing and stand with your sister and Becky."

"This isn't right. This isn't right." Michelle turned and hurried to the front door.

Frank ran after her, catching her near the door, grabbing her by the upper arm, and nearly yanking her off her feet. "He's a *pedophile*."

Michelle caught her balance and shouted, "Let me go!"

He let go, stunned by the volume of her voice.

She turned to her father, her eyes like lasers. "You're wrong about him. I know my husband." Michelle left the house, slamming the door in her wake.

Chapter 18: Theories

Michelle ran to her car, entering, and sliding into the driver's seat. She reversed wildly into the street.

"What are you doing?" Jason asked, his eyes wide open.

Michelle stomped on the accelerator, the rear end fishtailing before righting, and ripping down the street.

"Slow down," Jason said, putting on his seat belt.

As her parents' house faded from her rearview mirror, she eased off the accelerator and took a deep cleansing breath.

"What the hell happened?"

Michelle turned onto Pleasant Valley Boulevard. She didn't look at Jason. "They found your semen on Becky's underwear."

"*What?* That can't be. It has to be a mistake, or someone planted it somehow." Then he came to the same conclusion that Michelle had. "When we had sex on Christmas night, I put the condom in the bathroom trash. The cops could've planted it or Danny or …"

Michelle cast a side-eyed glance toward Jason. "Or who?"

"Frank."

Michelle gripped the steering wheel, showing the whites of her knuckles. "My dad wouldn't. Neither would Danny."

Jason hung his head and rubbed his temples. "Someone did."

They didn't talk for a few minutes. Jason stared out the window in a trance. Michelle drove them away from Loganville on I-99 South through the mountains. The traffic was light. Winter winds pushed against the BMW.

Michelle finally broke the silence. "We have to figure this out."

Jason turned from the window to Michelle.

Michelle continued. "Let's think this through from the beginning. We had sex on Christmas night, and you used a condom. You went into the bathroom and threw it away. I'm assuming you threw it in the trash? You didn't flush it down the toilet, did you?"

"Of course not. You're not supposed to flush condoms. It can cause plumbing issues."

"Okay, so you threw it in the trash. Did you wrap it in tissue, or did you just throw it in the trash?"

Jason frowned. "I wouldn't just throw it on the top of the trash for your parents to see. There wasn't a lot of toilet paper left, but I used the last of the roll to wrap it up as best I could. It was more than enough to cover it."

Michelle glanced from the road to Jason and back again. "Did you put it on the top of the trash or did you put something on top of it?"

"I don't make a habit of digging in the trash. I'm sure I put it on top. Someone would have to open it up to see that a condom was inside."

Michelle nodded, remembering the sequence of events. "Then we went to sleep, and a few hours later my dad was yelling about Becky peeing the bed. My mom took Becky to the bathroom to clean up and noticed blood in her underwear. Becky told her that someone touched her. Then my mom gave the underwear to my dad, who put it in a Ziploc bag. If that's all true, how does your semen end up on the underwear?"

"The only thing that makes sense to me is Danny planted it. He has motive and opportunity."

Michelle pursed her lips, thinking for an instant. "What if my mother put the underwear in the trash, and it touched the condom?"

Jason shook his head. "But the condom was wrapped up, and your mom said she gave the underwear to your father. She didn't say anything about putting the underwear in the trash. Would she put the underwear in the trash or in the laundry?"

"I guess that depends on the condition of the underwear."

"Did you see it?"

"It was hard to tell. It was folded inside the Ziploc bag. It didn't look new though." Michelle exhaled. "There has to be an explanation."

"It's possible that Ruth doesn't remember putting the underwear in the trash. Maybe she threw them away, then asked Becky about it. Ruth was understandably upset. Maybe she grabbed the underwear from the trash, realizing it was evidence—"

"But she was so distraught that she forgot about throwing it away," Michelle replied, finishing Jason's sentence.

"Exactly," Jason replied. "But that doesn't explain how there's transference when the condom is wrapped in toilet paper."

Michelle moved to the right lane to let the truck riding her bumper pass. "Semen can leak through thin toilet paper. You said there wasn't much toilet paper left."

"Maybe. But my semen was *in* the condom. It won't leak through latex. And even if the condom did leak, which is unlikely, gravity would make it leak down. If your mother put the underwear in the trash, she would've had to put it under the wrapped up condom."

"Maybe she didn't want bloody underwear visible, so she moved some trash to cover it."

"If she did all that, do you really think she'd forget putting it in the trash?"

Michelle shrugged. "Maybe."

"I still think it was Danny."

They drove for a long time in silence. Jason peered out the window. Michelle thought about the case. One question occupied her mind.

What if Jason's guilty?

Chapter 19: Choose

The next day both Michelle and Jason went to work. There wasn't much to do about the case, until the meeting with Norman on Monday. Despite their upcoming meeting, Jason said he'd call Norman Tuttle from work to tell him about what Frank had told Michelle, plus their theories on how Jason's DNA had ended up on Becky's underwear. They both felt the information was too important to wait until Monday.

Michelle wasn't at her best, sleepwalking through the school day. Five different students asked her if she was okay. It took all her strength not to dissolve into tears.

After work, Michelle made dinner like usual. Jason barely talked and barely ate. He was a zombie, hunched over his food, swirling his mashed potatoes with his fork. With his plate still half full, he said, "Do you mind if I go to bed? I'm sorry. I'm not very hungry."

"Do you want me to lay down with you?" Michelle asked.

"No. I want to be alone. I haven't slept at all the last two nights."

"Okay. If you need me, just let me know."

He left the table, leaving his plate and wine. Normally, Jason cleaned up afterward, since Michelle cooked, but this wasn't normal.

Michelle picked at her honey-glazed salmon, sitting at the white linen-covered table for eight, with a chandelier overhead. She thought about what was to come. Monday, they'd meet with Norman to strategize. Wednesday was the preliminary hearing. There'd be witnesses. Michelle set down her fork, suddenly sick to her stomach. *Everyone will be there. My family. They must hate me.* She wiped the tears welling in her eyes with her index finger. She thought about Becky. *If Jason didn't molest her, who did? Is she still in danger?*

Michelle stood and cleared the table, making three trips from the dining room to the kitchen sink. She washed the dishes, loaded the dishwasher, and started the machine.

The phone rang. Michelle went to the kitchen phone, picked up the cordless receiver, and said, "Hello."

"It's me."

Michelle sucked in a sharp breath. "Susie. Um, how are you?"

"How do you think I am?" Susie replied.

Michelle stood by the counter. "I'm so sorry this happened."

"What are you sorry for?"

"I … I'm sorry that that happened to Becky. It's … awful."

"It was child rape. You can't even *say* it, but Becky had to *live* it."

Tears welled in Michelle's eyes again. "You're right. I don't even want to think about it. I'm so sorry."

Susie spoke with an undercurrent of rage. "Then why the *fuck* are you standing by her rapist?"

Michelle felt woozy. She leaned against the counter. "I know it looks bad, but I swear to you, he's innocent. I know my husband—"

"*No.* You can't say that to me. There's DNA evidence."

"I know, but Jason and I had sex that same night. His condom was in the bathroom trash. It's possible that Mom put the underwear in the trash and—"

"Don't defend him! If you don't leave that *fucking* pedophile, you're dead to me."

"Please, Susie. There has to be an explanation—"

"Go to hell!" Susie hung up.

Michelle set the cordless phone on the counter. Tears slipped down her face. *I know Jason. He wouldn't do this. I know he wouldn't.* She went to the living room and collapsed on the couch. *But what if he did?* She pulled her knees to her chest and sobbed.

Chapter 20: Concession

On Monday morning Michelle and Jason met Norman Tuttle at his office in Loganville. Tuttle and Associates occupied the top floor of a five-story office building. Norman's corner office was filled with dark wood and black leather. Thick legal texts adorned the floor-to-ceiling bookshelf. The picture window featured a view of downtown Loganville, which consisted of churches, weathered brick office buildings, bars and restaurants, the courthouse, and a ten-story apartment building that used to be a railroad parts factory.

Michelle and Jason sat in plush leather chairs across from Norman at his mahogany desk.

"I just got off the phone with the DA," Norman said. "He's offering to drop the two counts of sexual intercourse with a child in return for a guilty plea on the two counts of aggravated indecent assault of a child—"

"Absolutely not," Jason said, through gritted teeth.

"I figured, but I'm obligated to inform you of any plea offers."

Michelle wrung her hands in her lap. "Would he go to prison if he took the deal?"

Jason shot Michelle a look that could kill. "It doesn't matter. I'm *not* pleading guilty."

Michelle dipped her head and shrank in her seat.

"The deal's ten years in prison, no parole," Norman said.

"I don't care if it's one day in prison," Jason replied.

Norman flashed his palms in surrender. "Okay. Then we better get to work on your defense. Let's start from the beginning. Tell me what happened. Don't leave out any details, no matter how mundane."

Jason took a deep cleansing breath. "I went to the basement with Becky on Christmas Eve because she wanted to look at the presents, but she was afraid to go down there alone."

Norman's fingers were steepled before him. "Why did she choose you?"

Jason shrugged. "I don't know. I guess because I play with her when we go to visit. We have a good relationship. At least I thought we did."

"What happened when you went down to the basement on Christmas Eve?"

"Nothing really. She was proud that she could read her name, and she was showing me which presents were hers. I taught her to read *Santa*. She picked that up really quick. Then we played Ice Cream Shop."

Norman narrowed his eyes. "How exactly do you play Ice Cream Shop?"

"She has plastic ice cream stuff and likes me to be the customer. I pay her with imaginary money. I ask for different toppings. I pretend to eat the plastic ice cream, and I tell her how good it is. There's not much to it."

"Did she ever touch you accidentally or rub up against you?"

Michelle searched Jason's face for signs of guilt.

Jason frowned. "No. Apart from holding her hand sometimes, we never touch. She's not a touchy-feely kid. I don't think we've ever even hugged."

Norman raised his eyebrows. "You don't think you've hugged, or you know you haven't?"

"I'm not sure."

"She hugs *me* sometimes," Michelle said.

74

Jason turned to Michelle. "You're her aunt. I don't think she's ever hugged me."

Jason then went on to detail the second time he was alone with Becky in the basement, the next day. It was forty minutes or so, after he and Michelle had come back from Maguire's Irish Pub on Christmas night. They'd played with her dolls and her new dollhouse, and they'd played Ice Cream Shop again.

"How much did you have to drink at Maguire's?" Norman asked.

"I had one beer," Jason replied, his tone slightly annoyed.

"Any drugs?"

"No." Jason glared at Norman.

Michelle reached over and squeezed Jason's hand. "He's just trying to help."

Jason clenched his jaw but didn't respond.

Norman said, "If I call you to the stand as a witness, Greg Elliot will cross-examine you. He may look like a teddy bear, but he's a shark. He'll ask the hard questions. You have to be ready to respond without getting upset."

"Do you think you'll call Jason as a witness?" Michelle glanced at Jason, so he didn't feel as if she were talking about him, like he wasn't in the room.

Norman thrummed his fingers on his desk. "I don't know yet. That's why we're having this conversation. I don't normally call defendants, but, if I have a likeable, smart, and attractive client, like Jason, I might."

***

Michelle drove them on I-99 South through the mountains toward home. The winter sun made a rare appearance, heating the inside of her BMW like a greenhouse. Jason stared out the window in a trance. Norman Tuttle had the police report but little else. He had said that they'd have a much better sense of the commonwealth's case after the preliminary hearing and pretrial discovery. Michelle worried about what they might say about Jason in open court.

Jason turned from the window and said, "I think we should sell the house and my business."

Michelle flashed Jason a confused look. "*What*? Why?"

"Even if I'm acquitted, my reputation will be ruined. If I wait, my business may be worth nothing, and then we can't afford the house."

"I think you're jumping the gun a little."

He shook his head. "No. The preliminary hearing is in two days. I might be too late."

Michelle gripped the steering wheel, staring at the road. *If he's innocent, why would he give up so easily?*

Chapter 21: The Preliminary Hearing

Judge Ames sat behind her desk on high. The courtroom clerk sat to the judge's left, behind a shorter desk. Three deputies were strategically positioned around the packed courtroom. The audience crowded into eight rows of wooden pews separated by a center aisle.

Michelle sat in the front pew, on the left-hand side, directly behind the defense table, separated from Jason and Norman by a short wooden partition. From her perspective, she saw the back of Jason's head. He hadn't looked back during the hearing. Norman had instructed him to keep his eyes forward and to not show any emotion.

Michelle scanned the audience, recognizing many people, her stomach fluttering with nerves. Frank, Ruth, and Susie sat on right-hand side, a few rows back, along with neighbors, former classmates, and Danny. Susie sneered at Michelle. Michelle turned back around, listening to the prosecuting attorney.

Greg Elliot stood behind the podium, between the prosecution and defense tables, facing the judge. He opened the folder and held up a small stack of stapled papers. A red tab was at the top, identifying the exhibit. Elliot spoke into the mike. "The commonwealth's exhibit number seven is the lab report completed on January 10, 2000, by the Pennsylvania State Police Crime Lab, and authored by Ashley Watson, who performed the DNA testing. Your Honor, this report indicates with mathematical certainty that the semen found on the victim's underwear matches the DNA of the defendant. May I approach the bench?"

A murmur of hushed whispering came from the crowd.

Michelle already knew about this evidence, but she reddened, embarrassed by the revelation in open court.

Judge Ames motioned for Elliot to bring her the DNA report.

Elliot delivered the exhibit, then returned to the podium.

Judge Ames thumbed through the report, then she addressed Elliot. "Please proceed, Mr. Elliot."

"The commonwealth calls Ruth Murphy to the stand," Elliot said, glancing back to the audience.

One of the deputies led Ruth through the small door in the wooden partition to the witness stand, next to the judge. After the court clerk swore her in, Greg Elliot asked her questions about the events leading up to finding the bloody underwear and the events immediately afterward.

Ruth talked about Jason being alone with the victim on Christmas Eve and Christmas night in the basement. Becky's name was never mentioned, always being referred to as the victim or Alice, her pseudonym to protect her privacy. Ruth talked about "Alice" wetting her bed late on Christmas night, and, in the process of cleaning her up, noticed dried blood on her underwear. When she asked why she had blood on her underwear, Alice stated that the man hurt her pee-pee part.

Michelle gazed at her mother on the stand and thought, *We may never speak again.*

Norman cross-examined Ruth, asking her about what happened to the victim's underwear between her removing it and it ending up as police evidence. Norman did his best to try to trip her up and to make her question or contradict her prior testimony, but Ruth was competent, even though she appeared nervous, as she wrung her hands.

After Ruth, Greg Elliot said, "The commonwealth calls Lori Ross-Grasso."

A petite woman with stringy dirty-blond hair and tight jeans emerged from the audience. She appeared to be in her thirties, with hooded eyes that were too wide set. She was led to the witness stand by a bailiff, where she was sworn in by the court clerk. Michelle knew her by name but had never met Jason's half sister or his mother. He had said that he had to cut them out of his life because they were toxic.

Greg Elliot stood from the prosecution table. His belly hung over his belt, putting downward pressure on his pants. He hitched up his pants and took his place behind the podium. "Could you give your full name for the court and your relationship to the defendant?"

Lori spoke into the microphone attached to the witness stand. "I'm Lori Grasso. That's my married name. I used to be Lori Ross. I'm Jason Lewis's half sister."

"For the court, could you please point out Jason Lewis."

Lori pointed at Jason. "He's right there in the gray suit."

Jason stared straight ahead, not looking directly at his half sister.

"Let the record show that Mrs. Grasso pointed out the defendant," Elliot said to the judge. Then he turned his attention back to Lori. "How long did you live in the same house with the defendant?"

"Until I was fifteen, and he went away to college. So, I guess fifteen years," Lori replied.

"How much older than you is the defendant?"

"Three years and a few months."

"Did he ever molest you as a child?"

Jason still stared straight ahead, showing no emotion.

Michelle cringed, her stomach turning.

Norman shot out of his seat. "Objection, Your Honor. This is extremely prejudicial. What Mr. Lewis allegedly did as a minor has no relevancy in this case. This is pure character assassination."

Elliot said, "It's very relevant, Your Honor. It's the exact same crime. It establishes a prior pattern of deviant behavior."

Judge Ames pursed her lips, thinking for a moment. "I agree with Mr. Tuttle. Unless Mrs. Grasso has knowledge pertinent to *this* case, her testimony is inadmissible." Ames addressed Lori. "You may step down, Mrs. Grasso."

A bailiff led her back to the audience.

"Does the commonwealth have any other witnesses?" Judge Ames asked.

"Yes, Your Honor, the commonwealth calls Detective Jessica Wells."

The petite fortysomething detective emerged from the audience, wearing a dark-blue pantsuit and heels. She was sworn in and sat at the witness stand. Detective Wells identified herself and her connection to the case. Elliot asked a few questions about her experience in law enforcement, establishing her competency.

Greg Elliot held up the folder and said, "These are the commonwealth's exhibits, numbered eight and nine. These are the transcripts from Detective Wells' videotaped interview with the victim in the early morning hours of December 26 and again on December 30." Elliot waddled to the judge, handing her the evidence. Then he returned to the podium and turned his attention back to Detective Wells. "*Did* the victim identify the defendant as the perpetrator?"

"Yes, she did," Wells replied.

"What exactly did she say? If you can't remember, I'm sure Judge Ames will let you borrow the transcript."

"I remember." Wells glared across the courtroom at Jason for a beat. "I asked her who hurt her private part. She said, 'Jason,' without hesitation."

Jason dipped his head.

A few whispers came from the audience.

Michelle swallowed the bile creeping up her throat.

Elliot pushed his glasses up his nose. "Did you ask her what he did specifically?"

"Yes, I did," Wells replied.

"What was her response?"

"At the time we were using dolls to identify where she was hurt. She said, 'He poked me with his finger.'"

Murmuring came from the audience. Michelle cringed again. The room swirled around her.

Detective Wells continued. "When she said that, she pointed to the doll's crotch area. She also said, 'He made me put my mouth on it.'"

A collective gasp came from the audience. More than a few angry eyes looked toward Michelle and Jason. Michelle cowered, her face hot with shame.

"The victim demonstrated oral sex by placing the crotch of the boy doll on the girl doll's face."

Michelle stood from the pew. Everyone gawked or sneered at her. She staggered from the courtroom, nauseated, her world spinning. She went to the ladies' room, opened a stall, fell to her knees, and prayed to the God of Porcelain, leaving red bile from her empty stomach as an offering. She dry-heaved, tears streaming down her face. When she finally stopped retching, she sat on the cold tile, catching her breath, her throat raw and burning.

She staggered to her feet, went to the line of sinks, and washed her hands. The bathroom was empty. Then she cupped her hands under the faucet, collecting a small pool, and brought it to her mouth. Michelle rinsed out her mouth and spat several times. She looked in the mirror, leaning on the counter. Her mascara had run down her cheeks. Her eyes were red and puffy. She wiped off her mascara with a damp paper towel. *What the hell am I going to do? How did I not know?*

Michelle left the bathroom, nearly running into Danny Gibbs. She stopped in her tracks, bowed her head, and said, "Excuse me." She expected a lecture that she couldn't stomach.

"You okay?" Danny asked, wearing slacks and a button-down shirt.

Michelle shook her head, and the tears welled in her eyes again.

Danny reached out and embraced her.

Michelle was limp and surprised at first. Then she reciprocated, burying her head in his neck, sobbing.

He rubbed her back, holding her tight. "It's okay. It's okay."

She sniffled and said, "It's my fault. I brought him to Becky."

"No. It's *his* fault."

Michelle let go of Danny and stepped back. "I'm sorry. I should go."

"Where?"

Michelle rubbed her eyes. "I don't know. I don't have anywhere to go. I can't go home. I can't stay with my parents. I can't …"

"You can stay with me for a few days, until you figure out what you wanna do."

Michelle hesitated, searching Danny's face. At that moment, she didn't see the man who had cheated on her with her best friend. She saw the beautiful boy she'd fallen in love with at fifteen. She sniffled and said, "Thank you."

They left the courthouse together.

Chapter 22: It's a New Day

Sunlight slipped between the blinds, warming Michelle's face. Her eyes fluttered and opened. For a few seconds, she thought it was all a nightmare, but then she remembered. She lay on Danny's queen-size bed, under his plaid comforter. His bedroom was small compared to what she was used to. She rose from the bed, placing her bare feet on the carpet. She crept to the attached bathroom. Danny's T-shirt hung to midthigh, covering her underwear.

She peed, washed her hands, and brushed her teeth. Danny had given her a new toothbrush to use. While she brushed her teeth, she replayed the preliminary hearing in her mind. *I still can't believe he did it.* Michelle swallowed the lump in her throat, resisting the urge to cry. *My marriage is a lie. My life is a lie.* She washed her face and combed her hair, using Danny's comb. Then she returned to his bedroom, found some socks and cotton sweats from his dresser.

The clinking of plates and silverware and the crackling of bacon frying came from the kitchen. Michelle left the bedroom, walking down the short hall to the living room. A big-screen TV dominated the living room, along with a black leather couch and a full bar. Danny's blanket and pillow were still on the couch from the night before. He had been kind enough to take the couch.

Michelle stepped into the kitchen.

Danny worked two skillets at the same time, one with scrambled eggs, the other with bacon. He took the bacon skillet off the burner and turned to Michelle. "Good morning, sleepyhead. Hungry?"

She lifted one shoulder. "Not really."

Danny frowned. "You really need to eat something."

Michelle hadn't eaten in twenty-four hours. She nodded and replied, "Need any help?"

The toast popped.

"I got it." He gestured to the nearby kitchen table for two. "Have a seat. Relax. What do you want to drink? I have OJ, water, milk, coffee."

"Water's fine."

Danny served scrambled eggs, toast, and bacon, with water for Michelle and coffee for himself. He sat across from Michelle and said, "Dig in."

They ate in silence for a minute.

"Thank you … for everything," Michelle said, her voice barely above a whisper.

Danny swallowed his bacon and replied, "Anytime." He sipped his coffee. "Have you decided what you wanna do?"

Michelle hesitated.

"I'm not trying to rush you. You can stay here as long as you want."

Michelle let out a breath. "I have to reconcile with my family, and I have to divorce Jason. What other choice do I have?"

Danny shrugged. "I don't know, but it sounds like you gotta good plan."

"I thought about it a lot last night. I let my feelings for Jason cloud my judgment. My dad tried to tell me." She stared at her plate. "I didn't listen."

"Well, you're listening now. That's what matters. I'm sure your parents will forgive you." He sipped his coffee.

Michelle looked up. "What about Susie? She hates me."

He set down his Fraternal Order of Police coffee mug. "That might be more difficult, but none of this was your fault."

She pushed her eggs around with her fork. "Why do I feel so guilty and so *stupid?*"

Danny frowned again. "Don't do that. Don't beat yourself up."

Michelle shook her head. "It's hard not to. I'm a teacher. I'm around kids every day, and I'm married to a fucking pedophile."

"Stop. You're spiraling. You need to keep your head."

"I don't know if I can."

***

After breakfast, Michelle drove to her parents' house, wearing the skirt suit she'd worn to the preliminary hearing the day before. She parked next to Frank's F-150, stepped to the front door, and rang the doorbell. She didn't dare walk in without being invited.

Frank came to the door with a knitted brow, guarding the threshold. "What are you doing here?"

"I came to apologize. I didn't …" She choked up, her eyes glassy. "I didn't know. I'm so sorry."

Frank stepped onto the stoop and hugged his daughter. He kissed the top of her head. "I know you didn't."

When they separated, Michelle sniffled and said, "I'm leaving him."

"Good. Let's get out of the cold." Frank led her inside to the dining room. "Did you have breakfast?"

Michelle nodded. "Danny made eggs and bacon."

Frank turned to Michelle with raised eyebrows.

"Nothing happened, Dad."

"I always thought you two were perfect for each other."

Michelle sighed. "So did I."

Frank sat at the dining room table, his paper and coffee before him. "What's the plan, Shelly?"

Michelle took off her jacket, hung it on the chair, and sat across from him. "Obviously, I need to talk to Susie."

Frank nodded.

"I don't think I can teach. I'm not emotionally healthy right now. It's not fair to my students. I was thinking about taking a leave of absence, so I need to talk to my principal."

"You're welcome to stay here, if you need to."

"Thanks, Dad. Maybe just until the trial's over." Michelle leaned forward, her elbows resting on the table, and her hands clasped like she was praying. "And I need to tell Jason it's over."

Chapter 23: Fifty Percent of Marriages …

Michelle sat on her childhood bed, the door to her room shut. She held her parents' cordless phone, her heart beating a mile a minute. With a shaky finger, she dialed Jason's office, but he wasn't there. Then she tried their home phone. He picked up on the first ring.

"Michelle?"

"Yes," she replied, her tone icy.

"Thank God. You disappeared at the trial. I was so worried about you. Where did you go? I had to rent a car to get home."

Michelle swallowed hard. "I want a divorce."

His tone was desperate. "Please don't do this. I know the hearing was bad, but it was all bullshit. All of it. I swear on my life—"

"Did you molest your sister?"

He hesitated. "It's not what it seems—"

"Yes or no, Jason. Did you molest her or not?"

He blew out a ragged breath. "Yes, but—"

"Stop." Michelle stood from the bed, her body tense. "I don't want to hear your *fucking* bullshit. You *disgust* me. I never want to see you again. *Never.* Do you understand me?"

He didn't respond.

"I'm coming for my clothes tomorrow. *Don't* be home." Michelle hung up.

The phone rang seconds after, causing Michelle to flinch.

On the third ring, Frank picked up, his voice booming from his bedroom. "Hello?"

Michelle pressed Talk on the cordless receiver and put it to her ear.

"May I speak to Michelle?" Jason asked.

"You gotta lot of fucking nerve. Don't *ever* call my house again. And stay away from Michelle. You better hope you end up in prison. If you don't, I'll see that justice is served. *Personally*." Frank hung up.

Jason said, "Michelle, I know you're there. Please listen. I know all this looks awful. I can't explain it, but I swear to you that I'm telling the truth. You know me. You know I'm not a liar—"

Michelle hung up.

Chapter 24: Making Amends

Michelle drove a few miles to Susie's apartment complex, parking in a visitor's spot. The setting sun was low on the horizon. The wind swirled a dusting of snow around the lot. The complex was a collection of three-story brick buildings, housing twelve apartments in each building. Susie's red Ford Mustang was parked along the front of her apartment building.

Michelle exited her BMW. She went to the front door and punched in the code, freeing the lock. Michelle had been to her sister's more than enough times to memorize the never-changing code. She climbed the stairs to the second floor and walked to apartment 2B. She took a deep breath and knocked.

Susie opened the door, guarding the doorway, her face puckered, as if she'd smelled something rotten. "What the *fuck* do you want?"

Michelle dipped her head. "I came to apologize. I'm so sorry for being on the wrong side in court yesterday. I believed him, but I was wrong. I'm so sorry, Susie."

"You brought that sick fuck into our life." Susie pointed at her sister. "*You* did that."

Michelle raised her gaze. "I know. I'm so sorry. I don't expect you to forgive me. I just wanted you to know that I know I was wrong. I told him that I want a divorce. I'm leaving him."

Susie rolled her eyes. "I would hope so. *Jesus*. You don't deserve a medal for leaving your pedophile husband."

"I'm just telling you. I'm not asking for anything."

Susie put one hand on her hip, the other still on the door. "I'm suing the *shit* out of him. I wouldn't expect to get anything in the divorce."

"I'm not expecting anything. I just want him out of my life."

"I already have an attorney. He said, once Jason's convicted, we'll have a strong civil case."

Michelle nodded. "Good for you. How's Becky doing?"

"How do you think? She's either scared, depressed, or acting out."

Michelle winced. "Is she still seeing the child psychologist?"

Susie narrowed her eyes.

"Mom told me."

"She'll probably have to see a fucking shrink for the rest of her life."

Michelle swallowed hard. "I really am sorry. I'll do whatever I can to help. Whatever you and Becky need."

Susie stared for a long moment, then she sighed. "You really want to help?"

"Whatever you need."

"You can help me shuttle Becky to her therapy appointments."

"I'd be happy to."

Becky appeared beside Susie, wearing her pajamas, and carrying a blanket. "Aunt Shelly."

Michelle smiled and bent down to her level. "Hi, sweetheart."

"Will you play Ice Cream Shop with me?"

Michelle stood and eyed her sister. "That's up to your mom."

Susie stepped aside from the doorway. "You want a drink?"

"Sure." Michelle stepped into her sister's apartment and back into her life.

Chapter 25: Leave

The next day, Michelle sat in her principal's office, told him about Jason and the charges, and asked to take a leave of absence for the rest of the school year.

The middle-aged principal rested his forearms on his desk. He frowned and shook his head. "This is a shock. You must be devastated."

Michelle nodded, holding back her tears.

"How's your niece, if you don't mind me asking?"

"She's struggling, but she's seeing a child psychologist, so hopefully in time …"

The principal nodded. "I can understand why you'd want to take a leave of absence. I think it's a good idea, and we should be able to accommodate."

"Thank you, Principal Harrison."

"Of course. I hope to see you back next year. You're one of the good ones. I'd hate to lose you."

***

After her appointment with Principal Harrison, Michelle drove home to pick up her clothes. She pulled into the driveway of their ten-thousand-square-foot stone-and-stucco mansion, hit the garage door opener on her visor, and parked inside. Jason's M3 was parked in the garage.

She let out a tired breath. "God *damn* him." She thought about turning around and getting her things another day, but it was a long drive, and she needed her clothes and toiletries. She was wearing her skirt suit for the third day. Thankfully, she had been able to purchase fresh underwear.

Michelle went inside through the garage door. The alarm was off. She walked through the laundry room and the kitchen. Then she climbed the spiral staircase to the master bedroom. One of the double doors was open. The king-size canopy bed had a Jason-size lump under the comforter. She tiptoed inside, hopeful that she could pack her things and leave without Jason waking. Heavy rhythmic breathing came from the bed. Michelle went to her walk-in closet, grabbed two suitcases, quietly unzipped one, and started packing it with her clothes and shoes. She had too many clothes to take everything, so she was selective. Once it was full, she grabbed her duffel bag, went to the bathroom, and packed her toiletries. She saved her dresser for last, since it was right next to the bed. She carried her luggage to the hallway for a quick getaway.

Michelle reentered the master bedroom, taking the second empty suitcase to her dresser. The dresser was oak with a dark brown stain and an attached mirror. She glanced in the mirror, checking the lump. Jason was still motionless, except for his steady breathing

She opened the suitcase, working the zipper slowly. Then she opened the top drawer, grabbing bras and underwear by the handfuls and setting them in the suitcase. After her underwear, she packed her socks. She shut the drawer a little harder than she had intended. Her gaze immediately went to the mirror. The lump moved, and his breathing quickened.

Jason sat up, rubbing his eyes. "Michelle?"

She stiffened, still looking in the mirror. "Go back to sleep. I'll be gone in a few minutes."

"Don't leave me. Please." His voice sounded like a little boy.

Michelle swallowed hard, opened her T-shirt drawer, grabbed a stack of shirts and tossed them in her suitcase.

"I don't have anyone."

Becky came to mind, the thought vanquishing her empathy. Michelle packed her sweats and shorts.

He stood from the bed and inched closer. She continued to pack, ignoring her husband. He reached out and touched her shoulder.

She wheeled around and slapped him. "Don't *touch* me."

Jason stepped back, his hand on his cheek. His hair was disheveled. His eyes were red-rimmed. He had a five o'clock shadow. He wore sweatpants and a sweat-stained T-shirt. He blinked, and tears slipped down his face.

Michelle went back to her suitcase, zipped it shut, and hurried from the room. In the hallway she grabbed the rest of her luggage and left.

He didn't follow.

Chapter 26: Blast from the Past

Over the next nine days, Michelle settled into a routine with her family. The trial wasn't until the end of March. She lived with her parents in her childhood bedroom. She helped Susie by babysitting Becky and taking her to therapy, so Susie could spend more time alone with Cody. Amid the chaos, they still hadn't set a formal wedding date, but they were shooting for late summer. Cody still needed to do some remodeling to make room in his house for his new bride and stepdaughter. In addition, Michelle did what she could to help her parents. Anything to keep her mind off Jason.

Michelle parked her BMW in front of the apartment building, next to Susie's red Mustang. Michelle peered at Becky in the rearview mirror, sitting in her car seat, playing with her Bratz doll. Becky had been quiet on the ride back from her therapy appointment. Michelle wasn't comfortable with the doll's short cheerleader skirt and impossibly skinny proportions, but it had been a gift from Susie, and Michelle was in no place to criticize.

"You ready?"

Becky nodded.

Michelle exited her car. The afternoon sun was covered with gray clouds, casting everything in a dingy aura. Michelle's fingers, ears, and the tip of her nose felt the bite of winter. She accessed Becky from a rear passenger door. Michelle unbuckled the car seat and kissed Becky on the forehead. Becky wore her puffy jacket and a knit cap with a pink ball on top.

"Will you carry me?" Becky asked.

Michelle smiled. "You're getting too big for me, sweetheart." Michelle held out her hand. "Come on. I'll walk you up."

Becky climbed out of the BMW and grabbed Michelle's hand. Michelle shut the car door and walked her to the apartment building. Michelle punched in the code, releasing the lock.

As they walked up the steps, Becky asked, "When can Jason play?"

Michelle cringed. It had been a week since she'd mentioned Jason. Michelle had hoped she'd simply forget about him. "Jason can't play anymore, sweetheart."

Becky looked up at Michelle, her little nose wiggling back and forth. "How come?"

"Because he's a bad man."

"What if he stops being bad?"

At the top of the stairs, Michelle hugged Becky and said, "He won't."

After dropping off Becky with her mother, Michelle drove to Weis Markets to grocery shop for her parents. Michelle wore her knit hat low over her eyebrows, not wanting to be recognized.

Michelle waited in line for a few minutes. When it was her turn, she loaded the conveyor belt with groceries and pushed her cart to the bagger. Michelle helped the young man bag her groceries.

Once the groceries were scanned, and her cart was full, the cashier asked, "Do you have a Weis card?"

"I think so," Michelle replied, fishing through her wallet.

The middle-aged woman behind her groaned.

Michelle glanced at the stone-faced woman. *She knows.* Michelle had a bad habit of attributing every negative interaction to Jason's crime. Michelle continued to search, with the added pressure of the long line behind her. Finally, Michelle said, "Can I give you my phone number?"

"Of course," the cashier replied, her tone upbeat.

Michelle gave her parents' phone number and received the Weis discounts.

After Michelle paid and pushed her cart away from the line, the woman behind her said, "It's about time."

Michelle ignored the woman and pushed her grocery cart through the automatic doors. She waited at the curb for a few salt-stained cars to pass. Michelle pushed the grocery cart toward her car near the back of the crowded lot.

She parked the cart next to the trunk of her BMW. Michelle popped the trunk and loaded a few grocery bags inside. Someone beeped their horn, causing her to flinch. She turned to the sound to see Danny in his Dodge Ram 4x4. He parked next to Michelle and hopped out of his truck.

"Hey, girl," he said, grinning as he approached.

Michelle forced a smile. "Hi, Danny."

"What are you doing?"

"Getting groceries for my parents."

"Let me help you." Danny grabbed the last few bags and packed them in Michelle's trunk. He shut the trunk lid.

"Thank you."

"Of course. I've been meaning to call and see how you're doing."

Michelle nodded.

"How *are* you doing?"

Michelle shrugged. "I don't know. I think I made a mistake coming here. It's a little cramped at my parents' house. I miss having my own bathroom. To be honest, this whole town is too small. Everyone knows everyone's business. I feel like people are always giving me dirty looks."

"*I'm* glad you're here. I'm sure your family's happy to have you back.

Nobody else matters. You know how people are around here. They see a beautiful, classy woman with a nice car, and they're jealous. I wouldn't pay them any mind."

Someone else beeped at them. They both turned to a purple Dodge Neon, with a temporary spare as the front left tire. A twentysomething blonde stopped her car and rolled down her window. "I thought that was you," she said, beaming at Danny, as if Michelle were invisible.

"Hey, girl," Danny said, giving the same line and grin that Michelle had received minutes earlier.

"I just wanted to thank you for helpin' me the other day. Maybe I can take you out sometime."

"That's really nice of you, but, *uh*, it's against department policy."

She pouted. "Well, I'll think of somethin' *else* I can do for you." She winked. "See you around, officer." She drove away with a wave.

Danny turned his attention back to Michelle.

"Who was *that*?" Michelle asked.

"Nobody. I helped her change her tire the other day."

Michelle smirked. "You're blushing."

Danny mock-frowned. "I am not."

"Against department policy?"

Danny laughed. "That's my go-to. You'd be surprised how often that happens."

Michelle shook her head. "A handsome man in uniform. Not surprised at all."

"You think I'm handsome, huh?"

"One compliment and you're already getting a big head."

Danny laughed again.

"It was good to see you," Michelle said, fiddling with her keys.

"Have you eaten?"

"Not since breakfast."

"Would you like to have lunch with me? My treat."

"Oh, *um* …" Michelle touched her trunk lid. "I need to take these groceries home."

"It's twenty-five degrees. Nothing's going bad."

Michelle hesitated, then said, "Okay."

They drove around the corner to Sal's Pizza and Subs. It was a place they'd been to many times when they were younger. It was a small place that catered mostly to takeout and delivery, but they had a few tables and booths for eating in too. It was late in the afternoon, well past lunch, so the place was deserted. Michelle sat in a booth along the wall. *Their* favorite booth.

Danny smirked at her, as she slid into the familiar booth. "You want your usual?"

"You remember my usual?"

"Grilled chicken salad, balsamic vinaigrette on the side, with a hot tea."

Michelle smiled. "I'm impressed."

Danny went to the counter to order. She watched him joke with Sal, the owner, and put $5 in the tip jar, giving it some much needed green to go with the silver. Danny was tall, built, and rugged. A man's man. Michelle thought about how she'd gone for someone so different after Danny had slept with her best friend. In many ways, Jason was the polar opposite. For the first time since the affair that had destroyed her engagement and her friendship, she thought about what her life would've been like had she forgiven Danny.

He returned to the table, all smiles. "Sal said he was glad to see us back together."

She raised her eyebrows.

He showed his palms. "I told him we were just friends. You know what he said?"

"What?"

He mimicked Sal's Italian accent. "*That's a how it starts.*"

***

After a lunch of reminiscing, Michelle helped Danny clear their table. They both waved goodbye to Sal, and walked to their cars, which were parked side by side.

"Thank you for lunch," Michelle said.

"Anytime," Danny replied.

"I think I really needed to live in the past for a little while. It was nice."

They stopped next to Michelle's BMW. She searched in her purse for her keys.

"It doesn't have to be in the past," Danny said.

Michelle extracted her keys and looked up to Danny. "What do you mean?"

"Exactly what I said. *We* don't have to be in the past."

She furrowed her brow. "Are you saying you want to get back together?"

Danny took a deep breath. "Look. I know we can't just pick up where we left off. I'd like to spend time with you. That's all."

Michelle nodded. "I'm not exactly available emotionally."

"I know things are hard for you right now, but I'm not asking for you to be emotionally available to me. I'm asking to be there for *you*, to be your friend."

"That's really nice of you, Danny, but …"

"Let me be there for you. I care about you."

Michelle pursed her lips. "Okay."

Danny grinned. "I'm off this weekend. We could get out of here. I think you need a break from this town."

"That's probably true."

"We could go to Blue Knob." Blue Knob was a ski resort about forty-five minutes away. "We can get two beds, if you want—or separate rooms even."

Chapter 27: Second Chances

They made it to the ski resort, but they never made it to the ski slope. Danny rolled off Michelle, his breathing elevated. They lay in bed, side by side, naked. She rolled partially on him, her arm across his chest, and her leg across his thighs. They lay silent, catching their breath in the dimly lit loft. Michelle thought about what it all meant. She silently chided herself for jumping into bed with him. *This wasn't supposed to happen. It's too soon. How long has it been since I left Jason? It was at the preliminary hearing. That was what, ten, eleven days ago? This is seriously self-destructive. What the hell am I doing? Danny's a player. I know he sleeps around. This is what he does.*

She rolled off him to her back.

Danny turned to her. "I liked you there."

"You sure?"

He turned on his side and scooted closer, so their bodies were touching again. He kissed her on the lips. When they parted, he said, "This isn't casual for me—if that's what you think."

"It's not?"

He shook his head. "For the last six years, I've thought about what I did to you. I'm so sorry, Shelly. It's, by far, the worst thing I've ever done in my life. And I did it to the person I love the most in this world."

Michelle took a deep breath.

"It was the biggest mistake of my life."

She turned on her side, facing Danny. "I should've forgiven you."

He shook his head again. "No. You were right to walk away. I wasn't ready to treat you the way you deserve to be treated, but I am now. If you give me the chance, I'll prove it."

Chapter 28: Surprise

Michelle kneeled before the toilet in her parents' bathroom and vomited. A mixture of dull red and green chunky liquid splashed into the toilet water. She spat and caught her breath, sitting on the tile. The house was quiet. Her mother was at work, and her father was helping his police buddy, Bryan McCloud, finish his basement. She struggled to her feet, went to the sink, and washed out her mouth. She looked at her reflection in the mirror and had a revelation.

"Oh, my God." She thought, *When was my last period? Think. Today's February 16.* She winced. *I'm late. I should've had my period by the tenth.* "Shit." She thought about the sex she'd been having with Danny. They'd used protection, but condoms weren't 100 percent. *When was the first time? It was in Blue Knob. End of January.* She went to the kitchen and checked the magnetic calendar on the refrigerator. *It was a Saturday. It had to be January 30. What about my January period? Did I have my period then?* She couldn't remember having her period then either. Then she remembered the unprotected sex she had had with Jason on Christmas Eve.

Michelle leaned against the kitchen counter, her legs wobbly, the room spinning. "I can't believe this is happening." She would've been elated two months ago. Now, she was possibly carrying the child of a pedophile. *What will Danny say? Will he want to be with a woman who's pregnant with another man's child?* Michelle took a deep cleansing breath. She went to her room, changed from her pajamas to jeans and a fleece, and left the house.

She drove to the nearby Rite Aid. She browsed the pregnancy tests, picked one with attractive blue and pink packaging, and checked out. She walked out of the automatic doors, and stopped dead in her tracks, her hand over her chest. Jason's M3 was parked next to her BMW, and he stood next to her car. She shoved the pregnancy test into her purse and grabbed her keys for a quick getaway. Then she marched across the parking lot to her car. Jason met her in the middle of the lot, and walked alongside her. His hair was disheveled. He had a scruffy beard. His eyes were bloodshot.

"I really need to talk to you," he said.

Michelle continued to her car, not breaking stride, gripping her keys. "What the hell are you doing here?"

"I know your parents don't want me to come to their house, so I ..."

Michelle stopped at her car and turned to Jason with a look that could kill. "So, you *followed* me?"

He opened his mouth to speak, but nothing came out.

"Don't make me report you for stalking."

He dipped his head. "Please, Michelle. It's all a big mistake. I swear. I never touched Becky."

"You admitted to molesting Lori."

"It's not the same thing. I was—"

"Save it for the judge." Michelle pointed at her husband. "If you come near me again, I'll go to the police so fast it'll make your head spin." She climbed into her BMW and drove away, leaving Jason in her wake.

Chapter 29: The Big Lie

Michelle gaped at the plus sign on the pregnancy test for a long moment. Then she placed it in the bin and covered it with trash. She knew Danny didn't have to work until noon, so she called him.

"Hey, beautiful," he answered, knowing the phone number from his caller ID.

"Hey. *Um*, I have to talk to you. It's important," Michelle said.

"What's up?"

Michelle walked from the bathroom to her bedroom, her parents' cordless phone to her ear. "Do you mind if I come over? I think it's an in-person conversation."

"Yeah. Now you got me worried. Are you okay?"

Michelle grabbed her purse. "I don't know. I'll be there in a few minutes."

She left her parents' house and drove across town to Danny's apartment. It was another gray winter day in Loganville, making the white siding on Danny's four-story apartment building appear dirty. His apartment was on the ground floor. When he had moved in, he had volunteered to take a ground-floor apartment, as they were more susceptible to break-ins.

She knocked, and he opened his door almost immediately. Michelle stepped inside and removed her coat, hanging it on the coat rack near the door. He wore athletic gear from his morning weightlifting at the gym. They walked into the living room.

"You got me seriously worried," Danny said, sitting on the black leather couch.

Michelle sat next to him, her body turned toward him. "I'm sorry."

"Did I do something wrong?"

Michelle shook her head. "Absolutely not. The past couple of weeks with you have been really great."

Danny grimaced. "I feel a *but* coming."

Michelle took a deep breath and said, "I'm pregnant."

Danny was slack-jawed and wide-eyed for a few seconds.

Michelle reached out and put her hand on his knee. "I'm so sorry."

He smiled and said, "Wow. I wasn't expecting that. I mean, I thought we would eventually get married and have kids, but years down the road."

Michelle frowned. "It's not what you think."

"Hold on. Maybe this is a blessing—"

"It's Jason's."

Danny winced, as if he'd been punched in the gut. He ran his hand over his face and said, "Fuck."

"I know. I'm so sorry. This wasn't planned. It happened over Christmas. Obviously, before you and me and before I knew about what he did."

Danny exhaled. "What are you gonna do? If you have this child, he'll have visitation rights. If he has a good lawyer, which he does, you might be forced to visit him in prison so he can see his kid. Jason will be in your life *forever.*"

Michelle hung her head. "I know. I don't know what to do." Tears welled in her eyes. "I can't have Jason's baby, but I can't have an abortion. I won't. My baby's innocent." She sniffled. "What am I supposed to do?"

Danny took Michelle's hand. "I wish the baby was mine."

Michelle raised her gaze and wiped her tears with her index finger. "So do I. More than anything."

Danny hesitated. "What if we said it was?"

Michelle tilted her head. "What are you talking about?"

"Why couldn't we say the baby's mine? The only person who might know will be locked away in prison for life. Think about it. We raise this child as if it's mine. We never tell anyone. *Ever*. You never have to worry about seeing him again. The child never has to go through the trauma of finding out that his or her father is a pedophile."

Michelle was slack-jawed. "Are you serious? Isn't that illegal?"

"Nobody will know."

"We'd be living a lie."

"Would you rather our child know that their father is a pedophile?"

Michelle stared at Danny.

He squeezed her hand. "We can make this work."

Michelle leaned forward and kissed him on the lips. When they parted, she replied, "You said, '*our* child.'"

Chapter 30: The Announcement

A week later, Michelle and Danny had dinner with her parents. They sat at the dining room table in her parents' house, eating spaghetti and meatballs, with side salads.

Frank leaned back in his chair and patted his belly. "I'm stuffed."

Danny swallowed and set down his fork, his plate clean. "This was really great. Thank you, Ruth."

Ruth beamed. "You're welcome, Danny. It's nice to see you two reconnecting as friends."

Michelle took a drink of water. "I have something to tell you two."

Frank sat up straight.

"Let me guess." Ruth pointed across the table at Michelle and Danny. "You two are dating?"

Danny smiled.

"I always thought you two would end up together."

"How did you know?" Michelle asked.

"Because I have eyes," Ruth replied. "I see the way you look at each other. And Danny's been calling the house for you."

"What about your divorce?" Frank said, frowning.

"I'm working on that next week. I already have an appointment with a divorce attorney," Michelle replied.

After dinner, Frank and Danny went to the basement to watch television. While the boys watched TV, Michelle helped Ruth with the dishes.

Ruth turned off the faucet and said, "I need to ask you something, and I want an honest answer."

Michelle set a plate in the dishwasher and stood, facing her mother. "What is it?"

Ruth glanced around to make sure nobody was listening. The men were still downstairs. Ruth spoke in a hushed whisper. "Are you pregnant?"

Michelle was stunned for a second. She whispered back. "No. Why would you think that?"

Ruth frowned. "You're a terrible liar. I found your pregnancy test when I took out the trash."

Michelle's shoulders slumped in submission.

Ruth shook her head. "Oh, Shelly. I'm assuming it's Jason's child."

Michelle hesitated for a beat. "No. It's Danny's. Do you really think Danny would be with me if I were carrying another man's child?"

Ruth raised her eyebrows. "He would if he didn't know."

"*Mom.* I can't believe you think I'd do something like that."

"I'm not judging you. I know it's a difficult situation, but I'm pretty sure you've only been seeing Danny for a few weeks. I doubt you'd already know you're pregnant that quick."

Michelle hesitated again. "It wasn't that quick. Danny and I had an affair over Christmas break. I'm not proud of it, but it happened, and I don't regret it. Jason always wore a condom. He never wanted children." She touched her stomach. "This is Danny's baby. I'm certain of it."

"Okay, honey." Ruth didn't sound convinced.

"I would appreciate it if you didn't tell anyone. Not even Dad. We're worried about what people will say. You know how people are around here. They'll say our baby has a pedophile for a father. We're not telling anyone until after the trial and after my divorce. This is hard enough as it is."

"I won't mention it." Ruth gave her daughter a hard stare. "I understand if you don't want Jason in your baby's life, and I'll go along with whatever you say. That's your decision, but I sure hope Danny knows. You can't build a relationship on a lie."

Michelle dipped her head, chastened. "He knows."

Chapter 31: The Crib

The day after Michelle had told her parents about her rekindled relationship, Danny asked Michelle to move in with him. She accepted. Michelle loved her parents, but she didn't want to live with them anymore, and she wanted more privacy to conceal her pregnancy. Her parents often had friends and family popping over.

Over the next month, Michelle settled into Danny's apartment and his life. She cooked his meals and doted on him. They watched movies on his big screen, cuddled on his couch. They made love often, unconcerned about contraception.

Now, Michelle stood in Danny's kitchen, wrapping the receiver cord around her finger, the phone pressed to her ear.

Her divorce attorney said, "Jason won't sign until after his trial. He seems to think you'll change your mind if he's acquitted. I know that's not what you want to hear, but the trial is less than two weeks away. We might as well wait. It'll take much longer if we take this to court, not to mention the expense."

The trial was scheduled for March 27.

Michelle exhaled. "I just want this to be over."

"It will be soon."

"Okay. I guess I have to wait."

"I'll be in touch."

"Thank you, Les." Michelle hung up the phone. She rubbed her temples. Then she went to the cupboard, grabbed the Utz barbecue potato chips and went to Danny's leather couch. She turned on the television, flipping through the channels. She stopped on MSNBC. Talking heads chattered back and forth, with stock tickers scrolling at the bottom of the screen. A headline just above the stock ticker read, High Flying Tech Stocks Grounded. She thought about Jason's prediction for a stock market crash. She pushed Jason from her mind, flipping through the channels for something mind-numbing. She settled on a trashy reality TV show.

Several minutes later, the lock turned, and Danny pushed open the front door. He carried in a large cardboard box.

"Could you get the door?" Danny asked.

"What's that?" Michelle asked.

"It's a surprise." Danny carried the box toward the office, which had mostly been a place for Danny to play computer games.

Michelle turned off the television, shut the front door, and met Danny in his office. There was a picture on one side of the box. It must've been facing away from Michelle when Danny brought the box inside.

"What do you think?" Danny asked, gesturing to the picture of the white crib on the side of the box.

Michelle held out her hands, a scowl on her face. "What were you thinking? Nobody can know I'm pregnant."

"Nobody saw me."

Michelle dropped her hands and exhaled. "I'm sorry. I'm on edge with the trial coming up, and my attorney just told me that Jason won't sign the divorce papers until after the trial. I guess I'm just feeling stressed."

Danny wrapped her up in an embrace, kissing the top of her head. "It's gonna be okay."

"What if he finds out?"

They separated.

Danny took her hand. "He won't. You're not showing yet. The doctor said it usually takes longer to show with your first pregnancy. Nobody will know. Not until long after the trial and your divorce. Then he'll be out of your life forever."

Michelle and Danny had gone to an OB/GYN two weeks ago. They'd found out that conception was likely on December 25, 1999, and she was eleven weeks pregnant. Thirteen weeks now, as of March 14, 2000. The due date was September 18, 2000. She'd had an ultrasound and told the technician that she didn't want to know the sex, but the technician had said that it was too early anyway. The OB/GYN gave Michelle a clean bill of health for her and her baby.

Michelle chewed on her bottom lip, still nervous. "What if he gets off?"

Chapter 32: The Question

It was unseasonably warm. The leafless canopy overhead allowed the bright sun to reach the forest floor. Michelle followed Danny up the Allegheny Mountain trail. Sweat beaded on her hairline. Her jacket was tied around her waist, covering the tiniest of baby bumps.

Danny turned his head and said over his shoulder, "Have you decided about the interview?"

Danny had spoken to his father, Gerald, earlier that day on the phone. Gerald Gibbs was the principal of Pleasant Valley Elementary, which was an eight-minute drive from Danny's apartment. Principal Gibbs had mentioned that he had some openings to fill for the next school year and inquired about interviewing Michelle.

"I don't know," Michelle replied.

Danny stopped next to a massive oak. Standing on a tree root, he turned and waited for Michelle to catch up. When Michelle stopped in front of him, he asked, "What don't you know? My dad would hire you in a second."

Michelle frowned. "We talked about this. I'm due in September. I doubt your dad would want to hire someone who immediately goes on maternity leave."

"It might be worth talking to him at least, maybe mentioning that you wanna start the following year. You don't have to tell him why."

"I know. I'd like to get through this trial, my divorce, and my pregnancy before looking for a job. I should have more than enough money to take a year off with the baby." Michelle let out a heavy breath. "Unless Susie takes everything."

Michelle still had full access to her joint accounts with Jason, even though they were separated and headed for divorce. Although, Michelle had spent very little since she'd left Jason.

Danny nodded and looked away.

"You think I'm an asshole for worrying about marital assets."

Danny turned his gaze back to Michelle and showed his palms. "I'm not judging, but, if Susie takes everything, like she says she will, we'll be fine. I have savings. I can take care of you and *our* baby, until you're ready to go back to work. We're in this together. I think you forget that sometimes."

Michelle stood on the same tree root as Danny. "It's a lot to take in. A few months ago, you were a bachelor without a care in the world. I just …"

"What?"

Michelle inhaled the mountain air. "I'm worried that you'll meet someone better, someone with less … complications." She dipped her head. "I'm worried that you'll leave me." Michelle almost said, *again*.

Danny reached out and grabbed her hand. "You're not a *complication*. Neither is our baby. I know I screwed it all up before, but I never wanted anyone but you." Danny pulled her into an embrace. They kissed slow and openmouthed, his hands running along the curve of her hips.

When their lips parted, she hugged him tight for a few seconds, before releasing him. "Tell me everything will be okay."

"Everything's gonna be great." Danny smiled. "It already is."

She smiled back.

He motioned to the trail. "You ready?"

They continued up the trail for several minutes, Danny leading. He glanced back and said, "We're almost there."

Danny led Michelle to a collection of large boulders on the side of the mountain. He climbed one of the boulders, the irregular rock filled with easy footholds and handholds. At the top, he offered his hand and heaved Michelle on the boulder. They walked across another boulder, then up another rock the size of a pickup truck. Like the first boulder, the second had many crevices and irregularities to help their ascent. Danny helped her again to the top. Here, they were open to the sky, not even the naked forest canopy to provide a modicum of shade.

Danny walked near the edge, wearing a backpack.

Michelle stood a few paces back, not comfortable on the edge, but the view was no less stunning from her perspective. They had a bird's-eye view of the valley below and the mountains beyond. It was covered in deciduous trees on the verge of waking. The sky was bright blue, with a sprinkle of wispy white clouds. Renewal and rebirth were coming.

Danny turned to Michelle, watching her step tentatively in his direction. "It's beautiful, isn't it?"

"It is," Michelle said.

"Come closer."

Michelle shook her head. "You come here. You're making me nervous."

He walked a few paces back to Michelle. "Better?"

"*Much* better."

He took off his backpack and sat on the boulder. "You hungry?"

Michelle sat next to him. "I'm always hungry. I hope you still like my butt when I'm huge."

"You know what they say. More cushion for the pushin'."

Michelle twisted her face in disgust. "*Gross.* Don't ever say that again."

Danny cackled. Then he handed her a bottled water, a small bag of potato chips, and one of the turkey sandwiches, which Michelle had made for the hike.

They ate identical lunches, sitting on the boulder, enjoying the mountain view.

"I'm worried about Monday," Michelle said, in between bites of her sandwich.

"Don't be. He's the one who should be worried," Danny replied.

Michelle swallowed and said, "I wish I didn't have to go."

"Apart from testifying, you don't."

"I don't want to disappoint my family. I've done that enough."

"None of this is your fault."

Michelle lifted one shoulder. "I should be there to support Becky and Susie. Greg Elliot wants me there too. He says my support for the prosecution is a powerful message to the jury."

"It is." Danny gulped his bottled water.

Michelle chewed on her bottom lip. "I don't want to see him."

Danny reached out and placed his hand on her knee. "Don't worry. I'll be there with you. I took off all week."

Michelle nodded. "What if it goes longer than the week?"

"Then I'll take leave without pay if I have to."

Michelle stared at Danny. "Why are you so good to me?"

"Because I love you."

"I love you too."

Danny grabbed his backpack and unzipped the pocket. He extracted a small felt-covered box and set it on the boulder between them.

Michelle gaped at the box. "What's that?"

"Open it and find out."

With trembling fingers, Michelle grasped the box in both hands. She opened it to find a gold ring with a single diamond that was much smaller than her engagement ring from Jason. She eyed the ring in a trance, thinking about all the reasons it would never work. Lying about the baby. His history of cheating. Her divorce.

"You okay?" He paused for a beat. "I know it's not a very fancy ring."

Michelle looked up to Danny with tears in her eyes. "It's perfect." She slipped the engagement ring on her left ring finger.

Danny beamed. "You're not supposed to put it on until you answer the question."

"Yes. The answer is yes."

Chapter 33: Opening Statements

On Monday morning, the courtroom was packed with friends, neighbors, and family. Danny sat to the right of Michelle in the audience, a few rows back from the prosecution table. Frank, Ruth, Susie, and Cody sat to Michelle's left. The petite redhead, Judge Cynthia Ames, sat on her elevated desk, presiding over the trial. Jason sat next to his attorney, Norman Tuttle, his attention on the trial. District Attorney Greg Elliot had expected Norman Tuttle to invoke the rule, denying witnesses access to the trial until their testimony. This would've barred some of the defense's biggest adversaries from the courtroom, including Frank, Ruth, Susie, and Michelle. After the stalking incident at Rite Aid, Michelle wondered if this was Jason's doing. Maybe he wanted her to be here for some sick reason. Michelle expected Jason to turn around and find her in the audience, but he never did.

Michelle watched the portly prosecutor approach the twelve jurors, who sat behind a short wooden partition in two rows of six chairs.

"Good morning," Greg Elliot said.

A few jurors mumbled, "Good morning." Most simply nodded.

"Thank you for being here this morning to fulfill your civic duty." Elliot surveyed the jury. "This is a particularly heartbreaking case. It will be up to you to serve justice for the victim, the victim's family, and this community." Elliot paused for a moment. "Christmas is the most magical time of the year, especially for children. But, on Christmas Eve and Christmas night, the defendant"—Elliot pointed and glared across the courtroom to Jason at the defense table—"Jason Lewis, committed the most heinous of acts against a six-year-old little girl."

Elliot turned back to the jurors, his mouth turned down. "To protect her anonymity, we've agreed to refer to the victim as Alice." Elliot took a deep breath, his gut rising and falling. "On Christmas Eve and Christmas night, Jason Lewis penetrated Alice with his finger and forced that little girl to perform oral sex on him."

Gasps came from the courtroom audience.

Judge Cynthia Ames glowered at the audience.

Elliot shook his hanging head, letting his statement sink in with the jury.

Michelle glanced at Danny, her eyes glassy. She wanted to take his hand, but they'd agreed that it wasn't smart to show that they were a couple at the trial. She turned her attention back to the district attorney.

Greg Elliot raised his gaze to the jury. "Don't listen to me. Listen to the evidence. The evidence will show that Jason Lewis's semen was found on Alice's underwear, the very same underwear that she was wearing on Christmas night when she was alone with the defendant." Elliot paused again to catch his breath. "You'll see Alice in a videotaped deposition, describing what happened to her and identifying the defendant, Jason Lewis, as the perpetrator."

Elliot nodded, scanning the jurors.

Some of the jurors nodded along with Elliot. They all paid careful attention to the DA.

"You'll hear from several witnesses, who will testify that Jason Lewis was alone with Alice on Christmas Eve and Christmas night." Elliot stopped to catch his breath again.

"Don't listen to me or Mr. Tuttle." Elliot gestured to the defense table. "Listen to the evidence. Listen to the victim. Use your common sense. If you do that, I am certain that you will return a guilty verdict. Thank you."

Greg Elliot returned to the prosecution table, a female associate by his side.

Before the district attorney was seated, Norman Tuttle was on his feet and approaching the jury, looking slick in his black tailored suit, a major contrast to his beefy adversary. Norman rested a hand on the top of the wooden partition, separating him from the jury box. "Good morning."

The jurors sat stone-faced.

"Mr. Elliot's right. This case is heartbreaking, and this crime is particularly heinous. I'm not here to defend the brutal actions of a child rapist. I'm here to make sure we don't imprison the wrong man."

Norman showed his palms to the jury. "I know what you're thinking." He used a higher tone to mimic a random juror. "People aren't arrested and sent to prison for crimes they don't commit." He returned to his normal voice. "Unfortunately, it happens far more often than people realize. Based on Mr. Elliot's statements, it sounds like an open-and-shut case, but the devil is in the details."

Norman gestured to Jason. "My client, Jason Lewis, has never been arrested. He grew up poor and worked his rear end off to make something of his life. He didn't seek out the victim. Alice begged him to play with her. You'll hear testimony confirming that fact. If he was abusing Alice, why wasn't she afraid of him? Why did she appear to enjoy his company? In fact, you'll see Alice's deposition where she herself says that she likes Jason and is *not* afraid of him."

Norman rubbed his chin, as if he were thinking, his gaze on the jury. "If Jason didn't abuse Alice, then how did his DNA end up on her underwear? This is a great question. On Christmas night, Alice slept with Frank and Ruth Murphy, Jason's in-laws. You'll hear testimony from Jason's wife, Michelle, that he and his wife had sex on Christmas night. Jason was wearing a condom."

Michelle blushed at the mention of their Christmas night tryst.

Norman continued. "Jason deposited that condom in the bathroom trash can shortly before Alice peed the bed, and woke the house with the subsequent commotion. While Frank and Michelle cleaned up the bed, Ruth took Alice into the bathroom to get cleaned up, the very same bathroom where Jason had deposited his condom only hours earlier."

Norman nodded, making eye contact with several jurors. "The DNA evidence certainly sounds credible, but only a very small sample of my client's DNA was found on the underwear. It is my contention that the underwear was contaminated in the bathroom. In addition to being bloodstained and soaked in urine, the underwear was worn and threadbare. Maybe Ruth set the soiled underwear in the trash, with my client's condom.

"It is also my contention that Alice isn't afraid of Jason because Jason didn't hurt her. Someone else did. And that someone else coached her very well to tell police and psychologists that my client molested her. When you watch her deposition, watch the robot-like responses when she's asked who hurt her. She responds without emotion that my client was the one." Norman held up one finger. "But, when she's recounting the abuse that she suffered, you can see the pain on her face and hear the pain in her voice.

"There's a very important concept that Mr. Elliot failed to mention. If you are to convict my client, to send him to prison, you must find him guilty *beyond a reasonable doubt.*" Norman clasped his hands together, then kept them clasped, as if he were praying. "*Reasonable doubt.* That's a very important concept. If there are reasonable doubts to my client's guilt, you must find him innocent. I've already given you several reasonable doubts. Please don't compound this terrible tragedy by convicting an innocent man and allowing the real perpetrator to roam free."

Chapter 34: The Prosecution's Case

On Tuesday, they were not permitted in the courtroom until 9:30. The first hour was closed to the public as the jury watched Becky aka Alice's videotaped deposition. Michelle hadn't seen the deposition, but DA Elliot told Susie that Becky had done a great job. Despite her age and the obvious trauma she'd endured, she was a credible witness.

They'd spent the next hour listening to Ashley Watson from the Pennsylvania State Police Crime Lab explain the DNA science used to determine with nearly infinite probability that the semen stain on Alice's underwear did in fact match Jason's DNA.

"May I approach the witness?" Norman asked.

"You may," Judge Ames replied.

Norman Tuttle approached the chubby woman for his cross-examination. "Hello, Ms. Watson. I'm Norman Tuttle."

Ashley Watson gave him a tight smile and said, "Hello."

"I only have three questions." Norman reached into the inside pocket of his jacket and removed a small pair of girl's underwear, still in the package. He opened the package, shoving the plastic into his pocket. Then he unfolded the white cotton underwear and held them up to the DNA technician. "Is this underwear roughly the same size as Alice's underwear? The ones you examined?"

Ashley inspected the underwear. "I don't know if they're the exact same size, but they look pretty close."

"Great. Close will be fine for this exercise." Norman handed Ashley the underwear. "Please take these."

Norman reached into his inside jacket pocket and removed a black Sharpie marker. "Now, Ms. Watson, would you please use this marker to mark the spot on the underwear where you found my client's DNA, and also please color in the spot so we can see roughly how big the stain was." Tuttle handed Ashley the Sharpie.

Ashley spread the underwear out on the bar in front of her.

Many jurors leaned toward the nearby witness stand for a better view.

On the right-hand side, along the waistband, Ashley made a dot the size of a grape seed.

Norman inspected her handiwork. He cocked his head in confusion, facing the jury for maximum impact. "I can barely see that."

Ashley Watson frowned at the defense attorney.

Norman picked up the underwear from the bar and walked it closer to the jury box, holding it up for the jurors to see the location and the size of the mark. The jurors craned their necks to see the dot. An older woman put on her reading glasses.

Norman said, "I know. I had trouble seeing it too." Then Norman stepped back to the witness stand and spread out the underwear on the bar in front of Ashley. "Ms. Watson, is it possible that a stain of that size could come from touching a used condom in the trash?"

"If it were leaking," Ashley replied.

"Yes or no, Ms. Watson. Is it possible?"

Ashley pressed her lips together. "Yes."

"What if someone wrapped the condom in toilet paper? Is it possible for semen to leak through the toilet paper and cause a spot of that size?"

"Objection. Calls for speculation," Greg Elliot said, sitting behind the prosecution table.

"Ms. Watson is a DNA expert," Norman said to the judge.

Judge Ames addressed the witness. "Please answer the question."

"I've never seen something like that before," Ashley said.

"I didn't ask you if you've seen it before. Is it possible?" Norman asked.

"Yes."

Norman made eye contact with the jury, giving them a *this is important* look.

***

After lunch, they heard testimony from Ruth. She wore a long blue dress with a white cardigan. Her blond hair was tucked behind her ears, exposing the apple-shaped earrings she'd been given by a student.

District Attorney Greg Elliot stood behind the podium. "In your own words, please tell us what happened, when you woke up late on Christmas night."

From the witness stand, Ruth replied, "Alice peed the bed. My husband, Frank, woke us all up. He got some urine on his pajamas. Then my daughter, Michelle, woke up too. Frank and Michelle cleaned up the bed, while I took Alice to the bathroom to clean up. I helped her out of her nightgown and her underwear. That's when I noticed her underwear was stained with blood. I asked her what the blood was from. She said, 'A man hurt my pee-pee part.'" Ruth took a deep breath. "I realized then that the underwear in my hand might be evidence, so I took it to Frank. He put it in a plastic bag for the police."

"What happened after that?" Elliot asked.

"Frank called the police. I asked Alice who hurt her, but she wouldn't tell me."

"Do you know of anyone who was alone with Alice on Christmas night?"

"Jason Lewis was alone with her in the basement for around forty-five minutes, right before we went to bed," Ruth said.

Elliot made eye contact with the jury, letting that statement sink in. Then he addressed Ruth again. "Could you please point out Jason Lewis for the jury?"

Ruth pointed at Jason, sitting behind the defense table.

"Let the record show that Ruth Murphy identified the defendant." Elliot hitched up his pants and returned to his seat at the defense table. "No further questions."

"Mr. Tuttle," Judge Ames said from her desk on high.

Norman went to the podium, buttoning his jacket on the way. He stared at Ruth for a long moment. Then he said, "On the night of December 25th, did you take Alice to your bathroom after she peed your bed?"

"Yes," Ruth replied.

"Did you remove her nightgown?"

"Yes."

"Did you remove her underwear?"

Ruth hesitated for a beat. "Yes."

"When did you notice the blood on the underwear?"

"As soon as I took them off. It was very noticeable."

Norman nodded. "Was the underwear wet from Alice's urine?"

Ruth hesitated again. "Yes."

"Besides the stains, what was the condition of the underwear? Was it new or old?"

"I didn't really notice."

"If I were to show you the underwear, would you recognize it?"

"Yes."

Norman addressed Judge Ames. "May I approach the witness? I have questions that pertain to physical evidence."

"You may," Judge Ames replied.

Norman walked to the evidence table to the left of Judge Ames. He picked up the clear plastic evidence bag holding Becky's underwear.

Norman held it up and said, "Commonwealth's exhibit number four." As he passed Elliot and the prosecution table, Norman showed him the exhibit he was holding.

Elliot nodded in response.

Norman handed the exhibit to Ruth. "Is this the underwear you removed from your granddaughter on December 25th, 1999?"

Ruth inspected the underwear through the clear evidence bag. "Yes, it is."

Norman raised his eyebrows. "Does this underwear look old or new?"

Ruth cleared her throat. "Old."

Norman turned to the judge. "Permission to show the evidence to the jury?"

"You may," Judge Ames replied.

Norman took the evidence bag from Ruth to the jury. He handed it to the jury foreman and said, "Please pass it around, once you've noted the condition of the undergarment."

The old man nodded and passed the evidence to the juror next to him.

Norman waited for a few minutes for the jury to inspect the underwear. Then he returned to Ruth. "Where were you standing in your bathroom, when you took off Alice's underwear?"

"Next to the bathtub," Ruth replied. "I was planning to give her a bath, but, after she said that someone touched her, I knew it was important not to wash her."

Norman inched a little closer to Ruth. "How close were you to the bathroom trash can?"

Ruth shrugged. "I don't know exactly."

"Estimate."

"Objection. Calls for speculation," Elliot said.

Norman frowned at the judge. "She's talking about her own bathroom."

"Please answer, Mrs. Murphy," Judge Ames said.

"Not very far. Maybe five or six feet," Ruth said.

Norman tilted his head. "Did you throw away the underwear?"

"No."

Norman turned from Ruth to the jury. He rubbed his chin for a few seconds. Then he turned back to Ruth. "You're holding a threadbare, bloody, and pee-soaked pair of underwear, within five or six feet of a trash can. Why not throw it away?"

Ruth pressed her lips together. "I don't know."

Chapter 35: The Defense's Case

On Wednesday morning they listened to a child psychologist called by the defense. She talked about the unreliability of children as witnesses and the ease at which they can be suggestible, fitting the defense's narrative that Becky had been coached to accuse Jason of the molestation.

After the child psychologist was cross-examined by the prosecution, Norman Tuttle called Michelle to the witness stand. Michelle was led to the witness stand by a bailiff and sworn in by the court clerk. By the time she sat at the witness stand, her underarms were wet with sweat, and her face was flushed. She stared straight forward, resisting the urge to look at Jason sitting at the defense table.

Norman Tuttle stood behind the podium. "Good morning, Mrs. Lewis."

Michelle cringed at the association. Without making eye contact, she replied, "Good morning."

"Could you please state your full name and relation to the defendant?"

"Michelle Lewis. I'm the defendant's wife." She glared at Tuttle. "Soon to be ex-wife."

A few muted chuckles came from the audience.

Judge Ames stared down at Michelle. "Just answer the question, Mrs. Lewis. We don't need any additional commentary."

Michelle nodded to the judge.

Tuttle gave Michelle a small smile and asked, "How long have you been married to Jason Lewis?"

"Three years."

"How long did you date before you were married?"

"Two years."

"In your five years with Jason, has he ever done anything to make you think he might be capable of molesting children?"

"He preferred to play with Alice instead of visiting with the adults in my family."

Norman turned to the jury, rubbing his chin, as if he were thinking. Then he turned back to Michelle and asked, "Any other warning signs that he was a child molester?"

Michelle pursed her lips and said, "No."

"Where did Jason typically play with Alice?"

"Usually at my parents' house, in the basement. She has toys down there."

"Did this playing occur when you and Jason went to your parents to visit?"

"Yes."

"How often did you and Jason visit your parents?"

"Maybe once every month or two."

Norman glanced at the jury, then asked, "Is it safe to say that you visited your parents with Jason at least six times per year?"

"Yes."

"During these visits, how many times do you think Jason played with Alice alone?"

"I don't know. Maybe once."

"Who initiated the playing? Was it Jason who asked to play with Alice, or did Alice ask to play with Jason?"

Michelle hesitated. "Alice initiated."

"How many years has this playing between Jason and Alice been going on?"

"Three years maybe."

Norman looked up and rubbed his chin again. "If my math is correct, that means over a three-year span, Jason has played with Alice alone at least eighteen times. Would you agree with that estimate?"

"Sounds about right."

"Prior to the incidents on December 24th and 25th of 1999, has there ever been any indication that Jason was molesting Alice?"

Michelle pressed her lips together. "No."

"Was there ever any indication that he had abused her in any way physically or emotionally?"

Michelle hesitated again. "Not that I know of."

Norman glanced at the jury with arched eyebrows. Then he addressed Michelle again. "Prior to December 24th, 1999, did you ever suspect that Jason was a child molester?"

Michelle glanced at Jason, sitting at the defense table. He stared at Michelle, stone-faced, but his eyes were glassy. She looked back at Norman and said, "No."

"*Nothing?* Did he have secret computers that you couldn't get into?"

"He had computers at work that I didn't have access to."

"Did he ever take trips without you?"

"No."

"Did he ever lie to you about his whereabouts."

Michelle exhaled. "No."

Norman thrummed his fingers on the podium. "When Jason was arrested on January 11th of this year, did you think he was innocent or guilty?"

Michelle swallowed the lump in her throat. "Innocent."

"Did your parents or your sister try to influence you to believe that he's guilty?"

"I wasn't thinking clearly before."

"Please answer the question, Mrs. Lewis. Did your parents or your sister try to influence you to believe he's guilty?"

Michelle dipped her head and replied, "Yes, but they were right."

Norman nodded to himself and said, "Ah. I see. And your parents are always right."

"Objection. Argumentative," Elliot said from the prosecution table.

"Sustained," Judge Ames said.

Norman eyed Michelle for an instant before asking, "Who do you think knows Jason better? Your parents and your sister or *you*?"

"I don't know." Michelle wiped the corners of her eyes with the side of her index finger.

Norman glanced at the jury, giving them a *this is interesting* look. Then he asked Michelle, "Did you have sex with Jason Lewis on December 24th, 1999?"

Michelle blushed and replied, "Yes."

"Did you also have sex with Jason Lewis on December 25th, 1999?"

"Yes."

"Did Jason appear to be attracted to you, an adult woman, during these encounters?"

Michelle clenched her jaw and replied, "Yes."

"On the night of December 25th, 1999, did Jason use a condom during sexual intercourse?"

"Yes."

"Did he throw that condom in the bathroom trash can?"

"I didn't see him do it."

"After sex on December 25th, did Jason go to the bathroom?"

"Yes."

"Do you think he left the condom on his penis filled with semen, or do you think he threw it in the trash?"

Michelle cringed.

"Objection. Calls for speculation," Elliot said from the prosecution table.

"Sustained," Judge Ames replied.

Norman paused for a moment. "How many hours after you had sex with Jason on December 25th, did your parents wake you because Alice had peed their bed?"

"An hour or two."

"How long after you were awakened did you see your mother take Alice into the bathroom to be cleaned up?"

"A few minutes."

Norman eyed Michelle for a few seconds, building suspense for his final question. "Do you think it's possible that your husband is innocent?"

Michelle flushed.

Greg Elliot stood from his seat. "Objection. Calls for speculation."

"Sustained," Judge Ames said.

Norman waved it off. "Withdrawn. I have no further questions for this witness."

Chapter 36: Closing Arguments

On Thursday, Michelle and Danny were back in the courtroom audience. District Attorney Greg Elliot stood in front of the jury.

Elliot said, "This case is about the evidence. Pure and simple. Don't lose sight of the facts because Jason Lewis has a fancy fast-talking lawyer. According to several witnesses, Jason was alone with Alice on December 24th and December 25th in the basement of Frank and Ruth Murphy's home. This fact is *not* disputed by the defense. Jason Lewis's semen was found on Alice's underwear late on December 25th, after Alice was alone with the defendant. That is *irrefutable*. Even the defense acknowledges that fact."

Elliot paused, catching his breath. "The defense would have you believe that a condom wrapped in toilet paper magically jumped from the trash can to Alice's underwear. This isn't wonderland. Ruth Murphy testified that she took the underwear from Alice and gave it to her husband, Frank Murphy, who is a retired police officer. A police wife of thirty years knows what to do with evidence. Frank Murphy testified that he placed the underwear in a plastic bag and gave it to Detective Wells."

Elliot surveyed the jury, catching his breath again. "Finally, we have the deposition of the victim, detailing the sexual abuse, and naming Jason Lewis as the perpetrator." Elliot held up one finger. "Jason Lewis was alone with Alice." Elliot held up two fingers. "Jason Lewis's DNA was found on Alice's underwear." Elliot held up three fingers. "Alice identified Jason Lewis as the perpetrator. Three strikes, the defendant's out."

Elliot gestured to Norman and Jason at the defense table. "The defense's theory is just that, a theory with no evidence to support it." He turned back to the jury. "Follow the evidence. It will lead you to the truth. If you follow the conjecture and the theories from the defense, it'll lead you to doubt, which is exactly what they want. They know they can't convince you that the defendant is innocent, so they try to make you doubt. Don't fall for it. Jason Lewis is guilty on all charges. It is your duty to follow the evidence. It is your duty to convict. I am confident that the good people on this jury will do the right thing. Thank you." Elliot hitched up his pants and walked back to the prosecution table.

Norman Tuttle sat unmoving for several seconds. Jason sat next to him, staring at a yellow notepad before him. Norman stood and placed his hand on Jason's shoulder. Jason looked up, and his attorney nodded. Michelle wondered if this was theatrics or did Norman Tuttle believe Jason was innocent. Norman strolled across the courtroom to the jury.

"Good afternoon," Norman said.

A few jurors nodded.

"The prosecution wants you to believe that this case is simple. They have all the evidence, and the world is black-and-white. This case isn't near as simple as they would have you believe, and this world is full of gray." Norman's gaze swept across the jurors. "Yes, Jason was alone with Alice, but only because Alice wanted to play with Jason, not the other way around. According to the testimony of Michelle Lewis, Jason had played with Alice alone at least eighteen times, and there'd never been a problem."

Norman took a few steps along the jury box, stopped, and faced the jury. "Why now? I believe someone else molested Alice and coached her to identify Jason as the perpetrator. You saw Alice's deposition with your own eyes. When she detailed the abuse she suffered, you saw the pain on her face and in her voice. However, when I asked her questions about Jason, she was happy to tell me that she liked Jason and was *not* afraid of him. She said, 'He's my friend.'"

Norman nodded, scanning the jurors. "You heard expert testimony from child psychologist, Dr. Deborah Turner. She detailed the unreliability of testimonies from children and the ease with which an adult could influence their testimony."

Norman turned and took another few steps along the jury box. He stopped and faced the jury again. "The DNA evidence is suspect. You saw the commonwealth's DNA expert, Ashley Watson, draw that tiny speck on the waistband of the underwear, indicating the size and location of the DNA sample she had collected. It was a barely visible speck.

"I believe Ruth Murphy took off Alice's stained and tattered underwear and did what most people would do. She threw it in the nearby trash can. Then she grabbed it after Alice told her someone had hurt her. While the underwear was in the trash can, it touched the condom wrapped in toilet paper that Jason Lewis had deposited into the trash less than two hours earlier." Norman showed his palms. "I know Ruth Murphy testified to the contrary but put yourself in her shoes. Her granddaughter had just told her that a man molested her. If I heard something like that from my granddaughter, I might forget a few details too."

Norman took a deep breath. "This case is about reasonable doubt. The prosecution must prove that my client is guilty *beyond a reasonable doubt*. The evidence offered by the prosecution is filled with doubts that they failed to address." Norman paused. "Please don't compound this terrible tragedy by sending an innocent man to prison. If you have even *one* reasonable doubt, you must render a verdict of *not* guilty on all charges."

Chapter 37: The Verdict

The evening after the closing arguments, Michelle went to the grocery store to pick up a few things. She wore a knit cap and kept her head down to avoid being recognized. On the way back from the grocery store, she stopped by her parents' house. She parked her BMW behind her father's F-150. It was dark, but lights came from the garage, along with the sound of an electric saw. Michelle exited her car and glanced in the garage window. Ruth's Ford Taurus was parked on the right-hand side. The left-hand side housed Frank's fishing boat. Behind his fishing boat, Frank had his work benches, tools, and carpentry area. He was cutting wood on a table saw.

Michelle entered the garage through the side door. She walked along Frank's fishing boat toward her father. A propane heater warmed the space.

He looked up from the table saw, turned off the machine, and took off his safety glasses. "What are you doing here?"

Michelle forced a smile, standing before her father. "I wanted to talk to you."

"I'm assuming this is about the trial."

Michelle nodded. "I'm worried. Norman Tuttle's a good attorney."

Frank stacked a few two by fours. "Yep. I told you he was the best."

"You don't seem too worried. Am I not seeing this right?"

Frank met his daughter's gaze and said, "It'll work out. Don't worry."

Michelle tilted her head. "How do you know it'll work out? If I didn't know what I know about him molesting his sister, I might be swayed. The jury doesn't know about that. It was inadmissible."

"Maybe they do."

Michelle drew her eyebrows together. "What are you talking about? Did you do something?"

"Quite a few people saw the preliminary hearing. They saw his sister. She didn't get to say it, but everyone in that courtroom knew he molested his sister. You know how this town is with gossip. I'm pretty sure the jury heard about that."

"Did you have something to do with that?"

Frank flashed his palms, a smirk on his face. "That's jury tampering. I would *never* be involved with something like that."

***

After lunch on Friday, the jury filed into the courtroom. Michelle sat in her customary spot in the audience, on the side of the prosecution, a few rows back. Danny sat next to her on her right. Frank, Ruth, Susie, and Cody sat to her left.

The jury foreman, a white-haired man with a paunch, handed a folder to the bailiff, who handed the folder to the judge. Judge Ames opened the folder and read the form for a minute, then handed it back to the bailiff. The bailiff handed the form back to the foreman, and gave him a few muted instructions.

"Jason Lewis, please stand for the reading of the verdict," Judge Ames said.

Norman Tuttle stood, then Jason.

Michelle held Danny's hand tight, not thinking about other people noticing.

"You may read the verdict," Ames said to the jury foreman.

The old man stood in front of his seat on the jury, holding the folder open. He read from the form without emotion. "For the charge of involuntary deviate sexual intercourse with a child, count one, we find the defendant ... guilty."

Michelle let out a sigh of relief. Danny squeezed Michelle's hand. Cody put his arm around Susie, pulling her close, both of them with big smiles on their faces. Hushed murmurs came from the audience.

The foreman continued, unmoved by the audience. "For the charge of involuntary deviate sexual intercourse with a child, count two, we find the defendant ... guilty. For the charge of aggravated indecent assault of a child, count one, we find the defendant ... guilty. For the charge of aggravated indecent assault of a child, count two, we find the defendant ... *guilty.*"

The audience erupted into a cacophony of excited voices, cheers, and applause. Jason hung his head. His shoulders trembled. Michelle wondered if he was crying. Amid the jubilation, Norman patted Jason on the back, leaned over, and said something to him. Jason straightened up and stared straight ahead.

Danny hugged Michelle, lifting her from her feet.

PART II: Jason

No one can tell what goes on in between the person you were and the person you become. No one can chart that blue and lonely section of hell. There are no maps of the change. You just come out the other side. Or you don't.
—Stephen King, *The Stand*

Chapter 38: Chomo

Jason peered out the window of the prison bus. He wore a belly chain, which connected to his handcuffs and leg shackles. The mostly leafless trees along I-80 West passed by in an amalgamation of brown and gray, with the occasional splash of yellow or white from the forsythia and cherry blossoms. Each inmate had their own seat and were forbidden from standing or talking.

The man in front of Jason said, "I gotta piss."

Jason turned from the window. The guards were separated from the inmates by a locked metal cage.

A guard glared through the cage. "Shut the fuck up."

"I gotta go, man," the inmate said.

"If you piss on my bus, you'll lick it up."

The inmate mumbled to himself.

Jason went back to the window, watching the world go by. He thought about Michelle. *Did she ever really give a shit about me? I thought she did. And now? I don't know. I don't know anything anymore. I don't have anybody. Nobody will ever love me. Everyone knows who I am and what I did. It'll follow me for the rest of my life.*

An hour later, the bus drove toward the prison complex. They approached from a hilltop, giving Jason a bird's-eye view. The thirty-five-acre complex was surrounded by a ten-foot-tall chain-link fence, topped with barbed wire. Twelve two-story rectangular buildings were connected with corridors, in a circular pattern, reminding Jason of a virus. Three additional concrete buildings stood at the edges of the complex, along with a gravel track. The bus stopped in front of the chain-link gate. The sign read, The State Correctional Institution at Mill Creek.

The gate opened, and corrections officers waved the bus inside. The bus parked in front of a building marked Receiving and Discharge. Jason and the rest of the inmates were lined up single file and herded into the building, everyone shuffling with the leg shackles.

Once inside, the corrections officers marched them along a black line, stopping them before a square room with two doors. The inmate in front of Jason fidgeted, doing the pee dance. The COs all wore uniforms: gray button-down shirts and dark blue pants and black boots. A patch on their shoulders read Pennsylvania Department of Corrections. They all had keys, handcuffs, billy clubs, and pepper spray on their belts, but no firearms for the inmates to steal.

Four inmates were let into the room at a time, the rest waiting in line in the hallway, always being watched by several COs. Jason went inside with the first group. A corrections officer chaperoned each of the four inmates. Jason's chaperone was average height but muscular and wide, like an NFL fullback. He appeared to be in his late-twenties, with a curly blond crew cut. He reminded Jason of an angry Barney Rubble. His name tag read McCloud.

On the nearby table was a clipboard with paperwork and a small jailhouse picture of Jason on the upper-right corner. A rubber trash can stood next to the table, lined with a mesh laundry bag.

CO McCloud unlocked Jason's belly chain and removed his handcuffs and leg shackles. Jason rubbed his naked wrists. His wrists and ankles were marred with red marks.

"Take off your clothes," McCloud said, glowering at Jason. "Put 'em in the laundry bag."

Jason took off the light blue jumpsuit he'd been issued at the jail four days ago and tossed it in the laundry bag.

"Hurry up," McCloud said.

Jason removed his T-shirt, socks, and finally his boxers. He stood stark naked, his head bowed. Three other men did the same at their own stations.

"Run your fingers through your hair," McCloud said.

Jason complied.

"Open your mouth and lift your tongue."

Jason opened his mouth and lifted his tongue.

"Raise your arms."

Jason complied.

McCloud smirked. "Lift your sack."

Jason complied.

"Turn around, bend over, and spread your ass cheeks."

Jason complied without emotion.

CO McCloud handed Jason a stack of clothes. "Get dressed."

Jason dressed in white boxers, white socks, a maroon smock that read DOC on the back, maroon pants, and white slip-on shoes.

McCloud glanced at Jason's paperwork, a scowl on his face. "You have any medical or mental problems?"

"No," Jason replied.

McCloud flipped through the pages, then stepped into Jason's personal space. The CO's breath was hot and pungent. He said, "I grew up in Loganville. My father's a retired police officer. He's good friends with Frank Murphy."

Jason stared ahead, poker-faced, while his stomach turned, and his heart pounded.

McCloud leaned in real close and whispered, "I'd hate to be you. Wait until they find out you're a fuckin' chomo."

As Jason was escorted to another room for further processing, he thought about the word, *chomo*, wondering what it meant. He winced and thought, *child molester*.

Chapter 39: Cellmates

After the intake process, Jason and approximately fifty other inmates were divided into eight groups, based on which cell block they'd be assigned to. This was decided by the prison administration at intake. Members of the same gangs were kept in the same block or building, keeping the gang violence to a minimum. During intake, he'd heard one of the guards mention that Cell Block C was the Aryan Brotherhood.

Jason walked in single file with five other freshly incarcerated men, following the black line on the hallway floor to Cell Block C. They were escorted by several COs. Jason and the men were silent, their eyes darting about. An ID badge with Jason's picture was clipped to the breast pocket of his smock. He carried his bedroll, a laundry bag, and his intake paperwork. The bedroll contained fresh sheets, a pillow case, and a blanket. His laundry bag contained extra prison uniforms, underwear, socks, and toiletries.

They were buzzed into Cell Block C, which was a two-story rectangular building capable of housing 160 inmates. The door shut behind them, along with their escorts. The center of the building resembled an indoor courtyard, with stainless-steel tables and chairs bolted to the floors. A handful of guards patrolled the perimeter.

A cacophony of voices came from the inmates, loitering at and around the tables. The inmates self-segregated. The majority of the men were white, many of them with shaved heads, and face and neck tattoos. Jason had never seen someone with a swastika tattoo, but he'd seen several in his first few seconds on Cell Block C. Approximately one-third of the men were black, and a handful were Latino. Some of the segregated groups played cards. Some joked and laughed. But most leered and pointed at the incoming inmates. A few catcalled and threatened them.

"Fresh fish comin'," someone announced.

A few inmates blew kisses at the newbies.

"Look at these motherfuckers," another inmate said.

"Check out that white boy. He's too fuckin' pretty to be in here."

Jason followed the other newbies, his underarms sweating, trying not to make eye contact with anyone.

Prison guards watched the scene through the thick windows of the control room, which was a half-moon–shaped observation area situated along the west wall, with a wide view of Cell Block C. Along the perimeter of the cell block were two stories of open cells, and two metal staircases to access the cells on the upper floor.

Two of the new inmates went directly to the Aryans and greeted their brothers. Jason and the other fresh fish went to find their cell assignments. Jason gripped his bedroll to stop his hands from shaking. A few men deliberately stepped in front of Jason, forcing him to walk around or to cause a collision.

A muscular inmate, about the same height as Jason, but probably outweighing him by seventy-five pounds of extra muscle, sneered at Jason and said, "Punk-ass bitch." Up close, Jason saw a tear drop tattoo under his right eye and a neck tatt, both barely visible with his dark skin.

Jason pretended not to hear him and slipped by in the chaos. Jason climbed the stairs on rubbery legs to the second-floor landing. He found cell number 210. The sliding cell door was wide open. Jason stood in the doorway and stuck his head inside, bracing himself for the worst. A young man with red acne sat on the bottom bunk. He made eye contact with Jason.

"I'm supposed to be in here," Jason said, his voice wavering. "Is it okay if I come in?"

The young man nodded and stood from the bed. "Y-y-y-yeah." He was short and very thin, without a single follicle of facial hair. His brown hair was parted to the side, with a cowlick in back.

Jason stepped into the nine-by-twelve space, relieved that his roommate wasn't intimidating. It was only three steps from the door to the stainless-steel toilet and sink in the far corner. Bunkbeds were built into the concrete wall. There were two lockers, each with built-in combination locks. Jason tossed his stuff on the top bunk.

He held out his hand to the young man and said, "I'm Jason."

"I'm R-R-Ronnie." They shook hands. Ronnie's grip was weak, and his hand was sweaty. His mouth worked hard to overcome his stutter. "You c-can have the bottom b-b-b-bunk, if you want."

Jason shook his head. "You were here first. I'm fine with the top bunk." Jason went to the empty locker. "I should try this combination and make sure it works, before I put my stuff in it."

"You have to k-k-keep your stuff l-l-locked up." Ronnie sat on the bottom bunk again.

Jason consulted his orientation paperwork for the combination, committing it to memory. Jason mastered the combination, tried it twice, then locked his valuables inside. Jason turned from the locker and asked, "How long have you been here?"

"Two days," Ronnie replied.

Jason stepped closer to his roommate. Ronnie flinched, and Jason showed his palms. "I'm not gonna be a problem. You don't have to worry about me."

Ronnie nodded again. "Sorry. It's hard t-t-to know who to trust in here."

"I can see that. How old are you?"

"I'll be t-t-t-twenty in October."

Jason winced. "*Jesus*. How the hell did you end up in here?"

Ronnie dipped his head.

"You don't have to answer that."

Ronnie raised his gaze and said, "When I w-w-w-was eighteen, I had a g-g-g-girlfriend. My f-f-first. She was sixteen. I d-d-d-didn't know it was b-b-b-bad. Her parents c-c-came home early and saw us ..." Ronnie blushed. "You know."

Jason nodded.

"They c-c-c-called the p-p-police. Corruption of a m-m-minor. My p-p-p-parents are religious." Ronnie bowed his head again. His voice caught. "They d-d-d-disowned me."

Jason frowned. "That sucks. I'm sorry, Ronnie."

Ronnie shrugged and swallowed hard, his Adam's apple bobbing up and down.

"How long is your sentence?"

Ronnie raised his gaze again, his eyes glassy. "T-t-t-two years."

"It'll be over before you know it."

"What about you? Why are y-y-you here?"

Jason cleared his throat. "Insider trading."

Chapter 40: The Resource Center

The day after intake, Jason left Cell Block C, buzzed out by a CO in the control room, and escorted by CO McCloud to Jason's work assignment at the resource center, which was prison terminology for the library.

Jason walked along the black line, McCloud's heavy steps behind him.

"I went to school with Michelle and Susie," McCloud said to the back of Jason's head.

Jason didn't respond.

When Jason reached the open door to the resource center, McCloud said, "Stop."

Jason stopped in his tracks.

McCloud walked around to face Jason, his billy club in hand. He stared at Jason for a long moment. "Your wife was a nice girl in school." He smirked. "Susie was a wild child, but Shelly was a good girl. I always had a thing for Shelly. Everyone did. I was too much of a pussy to make a move."

Jason stared straight ahead, poker-faced.

"I'm sure she'll divorce your ass, assumin' she hasn't already." He poked Jason in the stomach with his billy club. "Has she divorced you yet?"

"No."

"Let me know when she does. Maybe I'll take a crack at her."

Jason clenched his jaw.

"What? You got somethin' to say?"

"No."

McCloud inspected Jason's face. "You don't say much. That's prob'ly good for you. You gotta big secret to hide. They'll find out sooner or later what you did, and they'll make you pay." McCloud cackled.

Jason swallowed hard.

McCloud stepped aside. "Get your ass to work."

Jason walked through the open doorway.

The resource center had five round tables and chairs, six computer stations, jam-packed bookcases, magazine racks, and a view of the gravel track and forest beyond.

Jason approached the counter. The library was empty except for the dark-skinned man behind the counter, who was reading *The Pilgrim's Progress* by John Bunyan. Jason said, "Excuse me."

The gray-haired man looked up from his book.

"I'm supposed to work here." Jason handed the man his paperwork.

The man took the documents. "Let's see what we got here." He skimmed the information, then held out his hand. "Welcome to the resource center, Jason."

"Thank you." They shook hands.

"I'm Terrance."

"Nice to meet you, Terrance."

"Are you a college boy, Jason? You look like a college boy."

"I went to Penn."

Terrance let out a low whistle. "Must be a rich boy too."

"I was on scholarship."

Terrance grinned. "Then you're a smart boy."

Jason grimaced. "I was. Until now."

"I suppose that's true for all of us. I guess you're gonna be my replacement."

"You're leaving?" Jason asked.

He smiled wide. "God willing, I'm outta here next week, and I'm never coming back."

Jason nodded.

"What about you? How long are you here?"

"Five years." That was a lie.

"That's not too bad." Terrance narrowed his eyes. "You look too respectable to be in here. What the heck did you do?"

Jason broke eye contact for a split second. "Insider trading."

"For the love of money is the root of all kinds of evil. By craving it, some have wandered away from the faith and pierced themselves with many sorrows. Timothy 6:10."

"It's hard to love money at thirty cents an hour."

Terrance chuckled. "Modern-day slavery. You make one phone call, and it costs a week's wage in here." Terrance gestured to the bookshelves. "Let me give you a tour and show you the ropes."

Terrance showed Jason the books, which were arranged on the shelves according to subject.

"Do you use the Dewey decimal system?" Jason asked. "The bindings have the numbers, but they're out of order."

"Don't bother. Most of 'em just read the magazines. The ones who read books just go to the subject and browse."

Terrance led Jason to the magazine racks, surrounded by old couches. Well-worn magazines were shoved into the racks: *Sports Illustrated*, *Time*, *National Geographic*, *Popular Mechanics*, *Road & Track*, *Motor Trend*, and others.

Terrance said, "Every weekday, one cell block has resource center privileges. This rotates each day. You usually only have five to ten guys who come in. Most of 'em will come here and read the magazines or go on the computers. We don't let 'em check out magazines. If we did that, we wouldn't have any magazines for the guys to read. They can check out books but no more than three at a time."

"Got it," Jason replied.

Terrance took Jason to the computers, with big fat monitors and dirty keyboards. "As you can see, we only have six computers. Sometimes more than six guys wanna use the computers at the same time. I make 'em draw names out of a hat. Don't let anyone intimidate you. You're the boss here."

Jason nodded again.

Terrance took Jason to the front desk and demonstrated the checkout procedure. Four large boxes of books were under the front desk.

Jason pointed to the boxes and said, "What about these books?"

"That's my busy work. When the guards come in, I start working on shelving the new books. Otherwise, they bitch at me and tell me to get to work. But there isn't much to do but read. This job is the best-kept secret here. I've read at least a thousand books in this library. Kept me sane for twenty-five years. Maybe it'll do the same for you."

Chapter 41: Unwritten Rules

The men from Cell Block B left the resource center, escorted by several COs.

"That's about it for today," Terrance said, shutting the novel he was reading.

Jason looked up from the book he was cataloging.

"Don't work too fast. You'll run out of stuff to do."

Jason set the book in the box, with the rest of the ones he'd labeled that day. "I'll keep that in mind. Thanks for showing me the ropes."

"No problem, young buck," Terrance said, with a smile. "You're Cell Block C, right?"

"Yes. What about you?"

"E."

Jason shoved the box under the counter. "I'll see you tomorrow."

"Before you go." Terrance hesitated for a beat, checking the CO, who was in the hallway, out of earshot. "Be careful. Guys like to test the new guy to see if he's a punk. Walk away if you can but don't be a coward. Keep a low profile. If you have to fight, put up a good fight. You don't have to win, but you have to try." Terrance raised one eyebrow. "You understand?"

Jason nodded.

"Don't get into debt or accept favors from anyone you don't trust. Debt is the thing that gets guys in trouble more than anything. If you owe someone, they'll get their pound of flesh, one way or another."

"Thanks for the advice."

Terrance held up one finger. "One more thing. No matter what happens, never snitch. It always makes it worse."

Jason walked back to Cell Block C, escorted by a lanky CO. Jason was buzzed into the cell block. He glanced at the analog clock on the wall—*4:32 p.m.* He still had a little time before dinner in the cafeteria. The common area of Cell Block C was bustling with activity. Inmates returned from their jobs and loitered, waiting for dinner. Jason avoided contact with any of the inmates, climbing the stairs, headed for his cell. Hushed voices came from his cell. Jason slowed as he approached, not sure what he was walking into.

"You wanna know what it's like to get fucked like a little girl?" The voice sounded familiar, but Jason couldn't quite place it.

"She w-w-w-wasn't a little girl," Ronnie said. "She was s-s-sixteen. I w-w-w-was only eighteen."

"That's what all you fuckin' chomos say. Tell the truth, motherfucker. You like little girls, don't you?"

"No. I s-s-s-swear to God." Ronnie's voice was whiny.

The familiar voice mimicked Ronnie's whine and stutter. "I s-s-s-swear to God."

Jason peered around the corner to see the muscular man who'd called Jason a "punk-ass bitch" the day before. He had Ronnie pushed against the far wall. Jason stepped into the doorway and spoke in a friendly tone. "What's going on in here?"

The muscular man turned around, his jaw set tight. "Get the fuck outta here."

Ronnie appeared terrified, with bulging eyes and a taut expression, like he'd been given a bad face lift.

"I need to get into my locker," Jason said.

"Do I look like I give a fuck?" the muscular man snapped.

"No, you do not. But, ... *um*, ... I still need my shit. We only have a few minutes until dinner." This was a lie, as they had close to thirty minutes. If everyone wasn't lined up for chow at 5:00 p.m. sharp, the COs would come looking.

This was enough to disrupt the man's plan. The muscular man turned back to Ronnie. "Sooner or later you're gonna give up that ass, or I'm gonna take it." He turned and marched toward the door.

Jason moved from the doorway.

On the landing, the man glared at Jason, his lips curled into a sneer. "Watch your back, bitch."

Then he was gone. Jason watched him greet another inmate at the stairs. The inmate referred to the muscular man as Duane. Jason went into his cell. Ronnie sat on the concrete floor, sniffling, his head hanging. Jason squatted in front of him.

"You okay, Ronnie?"

Ronnie shook his head. His voice quivered. Tears ran down his face. "He's gonna ... r-r-r-rape me."

"He's trying to scare you." Jason thought about the advice he'd gotten from Terrance. "They do that to the new guys. As long as you don't except any favors, you'll be fine. I'll watch your back, and you'll watch mine."

Ronnie sucked back mucus and wiped his face with his smock. Jason stood and held out his hand. Ronnie took it, and Jason helped him to his feet.

"He knew about m-m-my charges," Ronnie said. "How d-d-d-did he know?"

"I don't know." Jason wondered when Duane would find out about *his* charges.

Chapter 42: Safety in Gangs

After his second day working at the resource center, Jason was buzzed into Cell Block C. As usual, it was bustling with inmates loitering in the common area before dinner. As Jason headed for the stairs and ultimately his cell, Duane shoulder-checked him, causing Jason to bounce off the man like a pinball. Jason stumbled and regained his balance.

Duane said, "Watch your step, kiddie fucker."

A few nearby inmates glowered at Jason.

Jason hurried to the stairs, his heart pounding. Four Aryans blocked the staircase. They all had shaved heads and tattoos.

Jason said, "Excuse me."

The Aryans didn't move a muscle. The apparent leader stepped forward. He was stocky, with a barrel chest, and ink-covered pythons for arms. A chain tattoo ran around his neck, with a red swastika for a charm.

The man smiled, showing the gap between his front teeth. He held out his hand. "I'm Erik."

Jason hesitated, then shook his hand. "Jason."

Erik gestured with his chin in Duane's direction. "He givin' you trouble?"

"No."

The man arched his eyebrows. "He will if you don't do somethin'."

"I don't want any trouble."

Erik shook his head. "In this place, trouble finds you. Guys are talkin' about you bein' a chomo."

Jason swallowed. "I'm not."

"That may be, but Duane's already got his eyes on your ass, if you know what I mean. You and your faggot-ass cellmate. I can intervene. Make sure Duane doesn't turn you into a bitch."

Jason thought about what Terrance had said about accepting favors from people you don't trust. "I appreciate it, but it's not necessary. I'll handle it."

Erik chuckled. "I don't think that's gonna work out." Erik's grin evaporated, replaced by a hard stare. He pointed at Jason with a thick finger. "You gotta make a choice. Be with us or take your chances with Duane."

"I'll handle it."

Chapter 43: The Alchemist

"It looks like today's my last day," Terrance said, with a smile, standing next to Jason at the counter.

Jason turned from the book he was cataloging. "I thought you were leaving next week."

"I'm outta here on Monday morning, so …"

It was Friday, and Jason's third day working at the resource center.

"That's great." Jason forced a smile that didn't reach his eyes.

Terrance tilted his head. "You all right?"

Jason broke eye contact. "I'm fine."

"You don't seem fine. I know I don't know you very well, but you've been quiet all morning."

Jason exhaled. "I might have some trouble brewing."

"What kind of trouble?"

Jason glanced at the CO standing near the open door, just out of earshot. "A guy in Cell Block C thinks I'm a child molester—"

"Are you?"

"No."

Terrance nodded.

"This guy wants to … make me pay. The Aryans offered to help, but I declined. I remembered what you told me about accepting favors."

Terrance rubbed the stubble on his chin, thinking for a moment.

"Sooner or later you'll have to fight this guy. You think you can do that?"

"I can try. He probably outweighs me by seventy-five pounds."

"Is he a fat guy?"

Jason shook his head. "He's built like the Incredible Hulk."

"What's his name?"

"Duane."

Terrance winced. "*Shit*. This isn't good."

"I know."

"He's well-known for raping guys. A few years ago, he had one white boy acting like his wife. The boy started wearing makeup. Grew his hair out. Shaved his legs. Duane had him doing his chores, performing sexual acts that I'd rather not think about, but that wasn't even the worst part."

Jason leaned on the counter, his stomach in knots. "I'm not sure I want to know."

"You *need* to know. Duane started selling this white boy to other inmates to use."

Jason cringed. "What about the guards?"

"They don't give a shit. They need a complaint before they step in. Of course, you can't snitch in here. That white boy wasn't gonna snitch anyway."

"Why not?"

"Because that boy was broken. He ended up killing himself. Took apart a safety razor and sliced his own throat."

"*Jesus*."

"That didn't have anything to do with Jesus. That's for certain."

Jason rubbed his temples. "I don't know what to do."

"I wish I had an easy answer for you, but there isn't one. For most guys, you fight, and it's over. Nobody dies, and nobody's defiled. Duane's different. He wants to dominate, humiliate, and possess a man."

"I'm completely screwed."

Terrance took a deep breath. "I had a situation similar to you when I first came here."

"What did you do?"

Terrance lowered his voice. "I did what I had to do, but I paid for it. *Dearly*. I wouldn't recommend it, unless you're out of options."

Jason drew his eyebrows together and leaned toward Terrance, also lowering his voice. "What is it?"

Terrance glanced toward the open door, checking on the CO. He was talking to another guard in the hallway. "My name has to stay out of this."

"Of course."

"You didn't hear this from me. If you say so, I'll deny it."

"I won't say anything. I promise."

Terrance leaned toward Jason and whispered, "I'm gonna say this once, and I'm never gonna say it again. Understand?"

Jason nodded.

"I read a book called *The Alchemist* by Paulo Coelho. Don't read it, unless it's an absolute last resort."

"I don't understand. Does it tell you how to poison someone?"

Terrance put up his hand, like a stop sign. "I'm done."

Chapter 44: The Visitor

Jason had spent the weekend with Ronnie, doing their best to stay within view of a CO at all times. Duane and his crew had been watching them, waiting for an opportunity. Jason thought prison was a lot like high school, without girls. The inmates had their cliques. They jockeyed for popularity. They bullied. They were managed on a strict time schedule. Those in control rarely stopped horrible things from happening. At one point, Jason and Duane had locked eyes, and Duane had mouthed a kiss.

By Monday, Jason was exhausted from being on high alert for days. He'd had to leave the resource center in the late morning to meet a visitor. It was the first visitor he'd had since he was incarcerated. The CO assigned to the resource center kept watch while Jason was away, but he wouldn't be recommending any books or taking returns.

Jason was escorted to a visiting room by a CO. The visiting room was filled with perfectly spaced stainless-steel tables with attached stainless-steel disks that functioned as the most uncomfortable seats ever created. A few vending machines lined the walls with overpriced snacks and soda. Corrections officers patrolled the room, making sure nobody acted inappropriate or aggressive.

A short balding man with round glasses stood next to a table and said, "Jason Lewis?"

Jason nodded.

"I'm Les Goldman."

They shook hands. Jason already knew his name and the reason for his visit from Jason's visitation list.

"As you know, I'm your wife's divorce attorney," Les said.

Jason nodded again, looking down on the man with bloodshot eyes.

Les gestured to the table. "Mind if we sit?"

"Sure."

They sat across from each other at the table. Les placed his briefcase on the table and opened it. Other inmates sat at nearby tables, snacking, talking, laughing, and whispering with their friends and families. Les removed a stack of documents and a pen, and shut his briefcase.

"I have papers for an uncontested divorce. My client is being very generous." Les pushed his glasses up his nose. "Against my advice, I might add. She's highly motivated to settle this divorce quickly and amicably." He slid the papers across the table to Jason. "Michelle's only asking for $50,000, her car, and her personal items. If I were you, I'd sign it before she changes her mind."

Jason shook his head. "I'm not signing anything unless she comes to see me herself."

The papers sat in the middle of the table between the two men.

Les pressed his lips together. "She's made it clear to me that she will *not* come here under any circumstances."

"Not my problem."

"Don't you think you've put her through enough?"

Jason glared at the attorney. "I'm not signing *anything* until I talk to Michelle."

"What if she called you?"

Jason paused, thinking for an instant. "That'll work—on one condition."

"What's the condition?"

"She has to hear me out. She can't hang up on me, until I've said my piece."

Chapter 45: Commissary Day

The inmates of Cell Block C were given the opportunity to go to the commissary to spend their hard-earned money once a week. Ten inmates were escorted at a time throughout the day at scheduled intervals. Eligible inmates were expected to sign up ahead of time, so the prison could allocate the appropriate number of guards. Jason and Ronnie had signed up for the latest time slot, after dinner.

The commissary was divided by a concrete wall, with an open window for transactions. On the wall was a daily printed list of prices and items in stock. A long counter beneath the price list held order forms, with pens chained to the counter. Jason, Ronnie, and the rest of the inmates grabbed order forms and scanned the price list. The price list was alphabetized and divided into categories: food stuffs, pharmacy, toiletries, entertainment, electronics, and stationary. Jason was shocked at the prices. Everything was two to three times more expensive than normal. Sodas were $2. So were candy bars. Ramen noodles were $3. A single roll of toilet paper was $1.

"This is ridiculous," Jason said, holding his empty laundry bag.

"I know," Ronnie replied. "I can't b-b-b-buy much. I only have t-t-ten dollars in m-m-m-my account." The only money Ronnie had was from his janitorial job that paid twenty-five cents an hour.

"If you need something, I can help you out."

"Thanks. I'll p-p-pay you back."

Jason shook his head. "You don't owe me anything." Prior to incarceration, Norman Tuttle had advised Jason to give him a few thousand dollars to deposit into Jason's prison account if necessary. It felt like a bad omen at the time, but Jason was relieved that he didn't have to go without any necessities now.

Jason and Ronnie filled out their cards and turned them into one of the inmates working behind the counter. The inmate collected their order and set it in front of the corrections officer who ran the computer and register. The CO deducted the items and funds from their prison accounts.

Jason packed his purchases in his empty laundry bag. He had purchased a roll of toilet paper, soap, floss, underwear, socks, a pencil, some paper, plus some candy and potato chips for Ronnie.

Jason, Ronnie, and the eight other inmates were escorted back to Cell Block C. As soon as they entered the cell block, everyone was accosted, and Cell Block C turned into a market. Inmates haggled, begged, and cajoled for their desired goods.

"What did you get?"

"Lemme have some."

"I'll trade you for that candy."

"I'll pay you back next week."

Jason walked toward the stairs, intent on locking up his goods in his cell. Ronnie was right behind him. He and Ronnie had already discussed the importance of immediately locking up their commissary items. Jason held his laundry bag tight to his body. The Aryans blocked the stairs. The hair on the back of Jason's neck stood on end, and his heart thumped in his chest.

Erik lifted his chin to Jason. "What'd you get?"

"Some necessities." Jason pointed up the stairs. "Mind if we get through?"

"Gimme that," a voice said behind Jason.

Jason turned to the familiar voice to see Duane snatch Ronnie's laundry bag.

"Come on," Ronnie said, his voice whiny. "Give it b-b-b-back."

Duane grabbed a Snickers candy bar from the bag. He opened the wrapper and took a big bite. "I love me some Snickers," Duane said, with his mouth full.

Ronnie walked away, his head down. Duane turned back to his friends, savoring his candy bar. Jason approached from behind and snatched the laundry bag from Duane's grasp. Jason ran toward the stairs, right into the Aryans. Instead of letting Jason through, they blocked his path. Jason turned to face Duane, just as Duane's big fist connected with Jason's jaw.

Jason's body went limp, and he crashed to the concrete floor. When he came to, his head and jaw ached, and both laundry bags were gone.

Chapter 46: Last-Ditch Effort

A row of phones was attached to the wall in Cell Block C. Inmates could make outgoing calls between 8:00 a.m. and 10:00 p.m. All calls were collect, unless the inmate had a calling card from the commissary. The day before, Jason had made arrangements with Michelle's divorce attorney to call her collect at 8:00 p.m. at her parents' house.

Jason moved his jaw from side to side. It clicked and was still sore from Duane's knockout punch. He had a headache and a knot on the back of his head from the fall. When the COs had cleared the chaotic scene, they'd asked Jason what had happened. Jason had replied, "I slipped."

Jason took a deep breath and picked up the phone receiver, placing it to his ear. He dialed zero, then the phone number. The recording asked for his name, and he said, "Jason."

Ten seconds later he was on the line with Michelle. Her voice was clipped and cold. "What do you want?"

"How are you?" Jason asked.

"What do you want?"

Jason glanced around, making sure nobody was eavesdropping. "I need you to know that I'm innocent. Whoever's abusing Becky might still be doing it."

"Nobody's abusing Becky anymore because *you're* in prison."

"How do you know?"

"Because I see her almost every day. She's getting better."

"That's good to hear." He paused for a second. "I think you were right about your mom putting Becky's underwear in the trash can. That has to be how my semen got on her underwear."

"I was wrong, and the jury disagreed with that theory."

"You could ask your mom. Maybe she'll tell you the truth."

"Your attorney already asked her. I'm not going to make her relive the nightmare *you* caused."

Jason winced. "Please, Michelle. If you ever loved me, you have to believe me."

"*Stop.*"

"You could talk to Becky. Maybe she'll tell you the truth now. Somebody told her to say it was me. I need your help. *Please.*"

"Are you done?" Her voice was still as cold as ice.

Jason swallowed the lump in his throat. "Deep down you know I would never do this. I'm begging you. Please help me."

She hesitated for a moment. "If you have a single shred of decency left in your sick mind, you'll sign those divorce papers and forget I ever existed."

His shoulders slumped. *I've lost her. It's over.* "I'll sign the papers. I won't contact you again."

"Good." Michelle disconnected the call.

Jason slammed down the receiver.

A passing CO glowered at him. "Watch it, inmate."

Jason walked back to his cell, his head bowed, replaying the conversation, reliving the coldness in her voice.

Along the way, several inmates stared at Jason. One of them said, "Fuckin' chomo."

Jason entered his open cell.

Ronnie rose from the bottom bunk, his face and acne red with anger.

"What's wrong?" Jason asked.

"I heard you're a ch-ch-child m-m-m-molester."

"That's bullshit. Who told you that?"

Ronnie glared at Jason. "You think I'm s-s-stupid, don't you?"

Jason drew back. "No. Why would you think that?"

"I saw a n-n-n-newspaper article about your t-t-trial. Everybody saw it."

Jason let out a heavy breath. "God damn it. It's not what you think. I didn't do it. I was framed. I know it sounds crazy, but it's true."

Ronnie twisted his face in disgust. "You're a *fucking* l-l-l-liar. I'm gonna g-g-get a n-n-new cellmate."

Jason showed his palms and inched closer to Ronnie. "You don't have to do that."

Ronnie stepped back, shaking his head. "They s-s-s-said, if I stay w-w-w-with you, everyone w-w-w-will think I'm a chomo too."

"That's bullshit. Duane already thinks that."

"N-n-n-no. He doesn't."

"Please, Ronnie. I'm telling the truth."

"N-n-n-no. You're not. G-g-g-get away from me!"

Jason backed off.

Ronnie pushed past Jason and left the cell.

Chapter 47: The Most Hated Man in Cell Block C

The next morning Jason dined alone in the cafeteria. He ate powdered eggs, a single sausage link, and a piece of white bread with no butter. Several inmates mean-mugged Jason, and a few hurled insults under their breath, but nobody touched him. Jason finished his breakfast and returned his tray to the appropriate counter. On the way he saw Ronnie sitting with a few inmates, who worked on the janitorial crew. Ronnie saw Jason and said something to his buddies. They cackled like jackals.

One of them coughed into his hand and said, "*Chomo.*"

Jason had the urge to punch Ronnie in the face. Instead, he walked into the hall and lined up along the wall to be escorted back to Cell Block C. While Jason waited for the rest of Cell Block C, he wondered who would be his next cellmate, if and when Ronnie transferred.

***

In the afternoon, after work, Jason was escorted from the resource center back to Cell Block C. CO McCloud walked behind him, his heavy boots stomping on the linoleum.

"You're gettin' divorced, huh?"

Jason clenched his jaw.

"We see everything you put in the mail before it goes out. I told you she was gonna divorce your ass. She's a teacher, isn't she?" McCloud paused, waiting for a response that never came. "She can't be married to a fuckin' chomo." McCloud chuckled. "This is your life now. Stuck in this fuckin' hellhole, where you belong."

Jason stopped at the security door for Cell Block C.

McCloud faced Jason, close enough to smell the coffee on his breath. "I heard everyone on Cell Block C knows about you now. Tough break. You're gonna need to grow eyes in the back of your head. Did I ever tell you that my dad still lives in Loganville?"

Jason stared straight ahead, poker-faced, but his stomach lurched, and his underarms were sweaty.

"I think I did tell you that. He's a retired township cop. Gets the Loganville Times. Reads it every day. He never throws anything away, so he has piles of fuckin' newspapers. He sent me a good article about your trial. I bet you thought you were gonna get off with your money and that slick-ass lawyer." McCloud went to the door, signaled to the control room, and the thick metal door buzzed open.

They entered the vestibule, the door locking behind them. McCloud whispered in Jason's ear. "I bet you don't make it outta here alive."

Jason clenched his fists to stops his hands from trembling.

The door to the Cell Block C buzzed open, and Jason walked inside. He avoided eye contact with the other inmates. Laughing to his right caught his attention. He glanced that way. Jason was slack-jawed at the sight of Ronnie sitting and laughing with Duane and his buddies.

Chapter 48: My Struggle

Over the next two days, Ronnie hadn't moved cells, but he still ignored Jason, spending his time with his coworkers in janitorial or even with Duane and his crew. On Friday afternoon, several COs escorted inmates from Cell Block C to the resource center. Five of the six inmates who entered the resource center went to the magazine racks or the computers. Erik the Aryan approached the counter with a crooked grin. His head had been freshly shaved that morning. Twice a week, the guards issued safety razors to be used by the inmates in their cells and returned within fifteen minutes. All razors were checked out, returned, and inspected. If a single razor was missing, the entire cell block was locked down, and cells were ransacked until they found the razor.

"What's up, Jason?" Erik said.

Jason glanced at the tattooed swastika at the base of Erik's neck. "Not much. Need help finding a book?" Jason imagined him reading *Mein Kampf.*

"Your boy moved to a new cell. What's that all about?"

"He moved?"

"Yeah. A couple hours ago. What'd you do? Try to fuck him?" Erik cackled.

Jason dipped his head, not sure how to reply.

"Guess where he went?"

Jason shrugged. "I don't know. I know he's friendly with some of the guys in janitorial."

"He's with that big nigger, Duane."

Jason knitted his brow. "How did that happen?"

"I heard he asked for it."

Jason shook his head. "Why the hell would Ronnie do that?" Jason asked himself this question more than Erik.

"That nigger finessed him. Said he would protect him. Said he reminded him of his little brother." Erik cackled again and slapped the countertop. "He's fucked now."

"Is there something that can be done to help him? He's just a kid."

Erik scowled. "Like what? He made his bed. I wouldn't worry about him, if I was you. You need to worry about yourself. Plenty of guys want a piece of you. You need some friends. *Fast*."

"No thanks. I'm good."

"Are you?"

Chapter 49: Regret

That night, after lockdown and lights out, Jason lay on his back in the top bunk, his eyes closed. The bottom bunk was empty. Ronnie's locker had been cleaned out, along with all of his things. Jason thought about telling a guard about Ronnie's situation. *Snitching could get me killed or raped or both. It could happen even if I don't snitch.* Jason tried to think of something else. He wondered how long it would be until he had a new cellmate. *Hopefully the guy won't be a psychopath.*

He fidgeted in bed, trying to get comfortable on the thin mattress. He thought about the trial. *I still can't believe this happened. I thought for sure ... What the hell do I know?* Jason inhaled, the air stale. *I can't do this. Not for twenty years.* He did the math in his head. *Three hundred and sixty-five days for twenty years. Seven thousand three hundred of these nights. Seven thousand two-hundred and eighty-six left, if you count today and the four days at the jail after the trial.*

Muted shouts and screams came from nearby cells. Jason covered his face and ears with his pillow. *I'm hanging by a thread. I can't avoid the predators in this place for twenty years. I may not make it through tomorrow. McCloud's right. I'm not leaving this place alive. There has to be a way out. The only way out is through twenty years of hell.* He choked up, on the verge of tears. He felt sick to his stomach. *It's psychosomatic. Think about something else. Anything else.*

Jason thought about Michelle, trying to remember the good times, and trying to avoid another sleepless night. He pictured her face, like he had every night since he'd been incarcerated, but the image wasn't perfect. He concentrated, trying to remember her face in perfect detail, like a good photograph, but he couldn't. She was already fading from his memory. He blinked, and tears slipped from his eyes. He rolled over and buried his face in his pillow to muffle his sobs.

Chapter 50: Running with the Devil

The next morning, after breakfast, Jason and the inmates of Cell Block C queued up along the wall, waiting to be escorted outside. They were given two hours of outdoor rec time, three days a week. His fellow inmates were loud and obnoxious, like children who needed to go outside and play. Laughing, catcalling, and heckling came from behind him.

Jason turned to the commotion. Ronnie was the focus of their ire. Ronnie's maroon smock was tied in the front, exposing his thin stomach. His pants were rolled up to his knees, exposing shaved calves. He even wore dark eyeshadow. His head was bowed. Duane was beaming with his arm around the thin teen, like he was with his girlfriend.

A beefy inmate lifted his chin to Ronnie and asked Duane, "How much?"

"I'm still breakin' her in," Duane replied.

Jason cringed and turned away from the scene. He thought about snitching. *The guards already know. They can see what's happening, and they don't care.*

The door to the vestibule buzzed open. Several COs allowed the first ten men to go inside, Jason among them. The door to Cell Block C shut behind them. Then the door to the hallway opened. The COs escorted ten men at a time to the outdoor rec area, making multiple trips back and forth from the yard.

Jason walked along the wall, part of a single file line, chaperoned by multiple COs. Up ahead, the CO opened the door. Sunlight streamed into the hallway, the natural light mixing with the fluorescent. Jason stepped outside and surveyed the yard. Two blacktop basketball courts were to his right. Straight ahead was a gravel track, with a grass field inside the oval and short bleachers along one side. Beyond the track were two chain-link fences topped with barbed wire. A guard tower loomed over the yard, complete with a sniper.

The other nine inmates went to play basketball, immediately claiming a court. Jason walked out to the track, enjoying the sun on his face. A breeze kissed his neck. He stepped onto the gravel track and walked. After half a lap, he started jogging. His slip-on shoes weren't exactly running shoes, but they weren't terrible. As he jogged, he remembered finishing second in the eight-hundred meters his senior year in high school. He was less than a second from being the state champion. His coach used to say, "You're the maddest runner I've ever seen."

Jason always ran angry, often pushing himself to the point of nausea. At the time, winning was the only thing that made him feel good about himself. He had several track scholarships to go with his academic offers. He had vowed that he'd take his scholarship, make the most of it, and he'd never return to his family.

He had taken the academic scholarship, not wanting to be forced to run to stay in school. Jason had joined the track team at Penn, but he quit after the winter season. It had been too much, along with working and his studies. He had kept his vow too. When his classmates went on holiday breaks, he had stayed on campus, worked, and studied. He hadn't seen or talked to his mother and sister again.

The preliminary hearing was the first time he'd seen them in eighteen years.

Jason picked up the pace, stretching his long legs with each stride. The yard was filling up now. More inmates crowded around the basketball court. A few walked on the track. Some sat on the bleachers, playing cards, or simply enjoying the spring day. One wild-eyed inmate, who resembled a large Charles Manson, ran the wrong way around the track. He didn't run with any pace. Sometimes he sprinted. Sometimes he jogged slower than a walk. Each time Jason passed the man, Charlie stared with eyes that appeared almost black. A small effeminate inmate jogged along the outer edge of the track.

Jason pushed himself harder, running faster than he had in a decade or more. His breathing was labored, but his feet were still light, barely touching the gravel. Sweat beaded at his hairline and under his arms.

An inmate from the bleachers said, "God damn. That white boy's fast."

Jason continued around the circle, pushing harder, imagining the bell ringing, signaling the final lap. His legs and lungs burned, but he didn't stop. He pushed through the pain like he always had. Part of him hoped his heart would burst, and he'd die on that track.

On the final turn, Jason imagined the finish line up ahead. He imagined the effeminate jogger ten yards ahead of him was in the race. He dug deep to grab those reserves that he had buried deep inside, easily passing and lapping the jogger again. As Jason sprinted past the bleachers, more than a few inmates cheered. When he passed the imaginary finish line, he veered into the grass, fell to his knees, and vomited foamy scrambled eggs. It reminded him of track practice.

The peanut gallery commented from the bleachers.

"He's throwin' up."

"That's nasty."

"That's why I don't run."

"You don't run because you're a fat fuck."

Jason spat and looked up. The wild-eyed man was running toward him. A piece of sharpened metal glistened in the sunlight. Jason was too exhausted to defend himself. He cowered and braced for impact.

But the man ran right past Jason, attacking the effeminate jogger behind him. Jason turned to see the Charles Manson lookalike stab the jogger in the neck.

When Charlie removed the blade, arterial blood squirted through the air. The jogger grabbed his neck with both hands and dropped to his knees. Jason gaped at the bloody scene.

A siren came from the PA system. The inmates in the yard all lay on their bellies, their arms and legs spread out like an X. Jason did the same, knowing the rule. But Charlie was a man possessed, still stabbing the jogger repeatedly in his face, neck, and chest area.

A shot echoed through the yard. Charlie dropped to his side, his legs splayed awkwardly. Jason locked eyes with Charlie. They were vacant. Blood leaked from the red hole in his forehead. Jason imagined his own lifeless body on the gravel.

The peanut gallery lay on the ground nearby.

One of them said, "That motherfuckin' snitch had it comin'."

"Snitches get stitches."

"Shit. Snitches get *kilt*."

Corrections officers, dressed in riot gear, carried electrified shields and stormed onto the scene. The men of CERT—Corrections Emergency Response Team—found nobody to subdue and nobody to save. They were already dead.

Chapter 51: Settlement

The inmates of Cell Block C spent the weekend on lockdown, after the murder at the track. The COs ransacked every cell for contraband, specifically searching for homemade knives, known in prison as shanks. Several inmates were busted with drugs and homemade wine, made from fermenting fruit juice and crumbled white bread, but no shanks were found.

On Monday, Jason met with his attorney in a private room. Jason sat across the table from Norman Tuttle. A guard waited in the hall, his block head visible through the door window.

"Susan Murphy's suing you for sexual assault and intentional causing of emotional distress," Norman said.

Jason nodded. "I figured this was coming."

"So, did I. With your conviction, she has a very strong case. I spoke to her attorney on Friday. They're willing to settle for five million dollars."

Jason rubbed the back of his neck. "I don't have near that amount of money."

"How much do you have?"

"Around 2.2 million."

"What do you think about countering at one million?"

Jason shook his head. "If I settle, I'm admitting guilt."

"This is a civil case—"

"I understand that." Jason thought about Susie telling Michelle that the settlement was an admission of guilt. "I don't want to settle."

"We could offer 500,000."

"I'm not settling."

Norman frowned. "She might take everything you have."

Jason frowned right back. "That already happened."

Chapter 52: Gold Tooth and Face Tatt

After work, Jason was led back to Cell Block C. He walked back to his cell, thinking about his meeting with Norman and the possibility of starting over. *If I got parole in fifteen years, I'd only be fifty-one. With money, I could start over. I wouldn't have to worry about getting a job with multiple felonies on my record. But, if Norman's right, and Susie takes everything, I'll be destitute.*

Jason climbed the metal steps to access the second-floor cells. Two of Duane's buddies loitered on the landing, peering out over the railing, seemingly oblivious to Jason's presence. They were both young and muscular. One of them had gold front teeth. The other had a face tattoo that covered his right cheek. Jason walked toward them, treading lightly, eager to pass by unmolested and to return to his cell.

As soon as he reached the two, they turned from the railing and tried to push Jason into an open cell. Jason braced himself, dipping and jamming a shoulder into Face Tatt, holding his ground on the landing. Gold Tooth grabbed Jason by the collar. Jason rammed his knee upward, catching Gold Tooth on his scrotum. Gold Tooth went down, shrieking, and holding his crotch.

Face Tatt hit Jason with a straight right, smashing his nose, blood spurting from Jason's nostrils. Face Tatt tried to push Jason into the cell again, but Jason pushed back, and he was winning the tug of war. Then Face Tatt turned, his hands still gripping Jason's smock. Face

Tatt used Jason's momentum to throw Jason over the edge.

Jason pushed against an immovable object, then, in a flash, he wasn't. He flew through the air like Superman. Just before impact, Jason turned his body, taking the brunt of the landing with his shoulder, but the side of his head hit the concrete just after his shoulder, knocking him unconscious.

Chapter 53: Down but Not Out

Jason's eyes fluttered. The room was blurry. His mind was hazy, like he was in a dream or a nightmare. *Where am I?*

"He's waking up," someone said.

Something was in his throat. He thrashed and choked. His right shoulder burned with pain when he moved. His head pounded. Strong hands held him steady as the endotracheal tube was removed from his sore throat.

His eyes fluttered again. Dark forms hovered over him. The dark forms turned white and light blue. A doctor in a white coat and several nurses in blue scrubs stood alongside him. He closed his eyes, retreating to the darkness.

***

The lighting was dim. Jason lay on his back in the hospital bed in a drug-induced haze. Despite the drugs, his head still hurt. He wiggled his nose. That hurt too. He reached up with his left hand and touched his head. It was wrapped and bandaged. He touched his nose with the slightest of pressure. It was bandaged too. His right arm was hooked to an IV. Cool oxygen flowed into his nose from the nasal cannula. He moved his right arm, and pain radiated from his shoulder.

A young doctor entered the room, holding a file folder. He flipped through the file, then approached the bed. "Hello, Mr. Lewis. I'm Dr.

Gaynor. How are you feeling?"

Jason's voice was raspy. "I feel a little dizzy. My head's killing me."

"You had quite a fall."

"Where am I?"

"You're at Mill Creek Memorial Hospital. Do you remember what happened to you?"

Jason thought for an instant, recalling the fight, then flying over the railing, but not remembering the impact. "I was in a fight, and the guy threw me over the railing. That's all I remember."

"Thankfully your shoulder hit the concrete first, followed by your head, and not the other way around. You were in a coma for two days. You have a severe concussion. That's why you feel dizzy and your head hurts."

Jason nodded. "Did I break my shoulder?"

"It's badly bruised but not broken. You did separate your AC joint."

"What does that mean?"

"An AC joint separation is a dislocation of the clavicle from the acromion. This is the acromion." The doctor touched the outer edge of his clavicle to show the location of the acromion. "It's not a serious injury. Most people don't bother with surgery and do just fine. It'll heal in a few weeks." The doctor gave a reassuring smile. "You also have a broken nose, which may cause you some discomfort at the moment. We reset your nose. You might have a little wiggle, but it'll heal fine."

Jason squinted into the dim light. "How long do you think I'll be here?"

"Depends on your concussion. That's my biggest concern. We'll keep you here for observation until we're certain you're out of the woods. You have sixteen stitches on the side of your head. You're lucky to be alive."

Jason glanced to his right, toward the open door. From his perspective, he saw the sheriff's deputy, sitting in the hallway outside his room. He wondered two things. *How long can I stay here? Could I escape?*

Chapter 54: To Snitch or Not to Snitch

Jason had been in the hospital for nine days. His AC joint separation didn't hurt anymore, but when he moved his shoulder a certain way, his clavicle looked like it might poke out of his skin. He had two fading black eyes and a slightly crooked nose. The bruises on his shoulder had mostly healed. Even his headaches were gone, but that wasn't what he'd been telling the medical staff.

Warden Douglas Bates stood by Jason's bedside. "How are you feeling?"

"Not great," Jason replied, squinting into the dim light, giving his best rendition of a concussion sufferer.

Warden Bates clenched his jaw, staring at Jason for a long time. He was a big man with a second-trimester gut. His complexion was ruddy and pockmarked, and his flesh-colored lips were nonexistent. "Do you know Duane Griffith?"

"Not well," Jason replied.

"Do you two have a beef?"

"Not that I know of."

Warden Bates exhaled. "He won't stop unless someone talks. I hear his young cellmate's dressing like a woman. Your old cellmate. You know anything about that?"

Jason thought about the snitch who was stabbed in the neck at the track. "No."

Bates shook his head. "Inmate Griffith was in that cell waiting for you. Of course, he claims to have no idea why those inmates tried to push you into his cell. What do you think would've happened to you if they would've succeeded?" Bates waited a few seconds for a reply that never came. "The two inmates who jumped you are in seg."

Seg was short for segregation, meaning that the two were in isolated cells away from the general population.

Jason nodded.

"I'd like to put Griffith in seg too, but I need a reason. I need your help."

Jason hesitated. "I don't know anything."

Bates scowled. "There's no need to continue this charade. I spoke with your doctor. He thinks you're faking symptoms to extend your stay here."

Jason didn't respond.

"You're going back tomorrow." Warden Bates walked away, flipping on the bright lights before he left the hospital room.

Chapter 55: Back to the Jungle

The ride from Mill Creek Memorial Hospital back to The State Correctional Institution at Mill Creek was uneventful. Jason had had fantasies of stealing a gun from a deputy and escaping, but he was cuffed and shackled for the trip. Even if he hadn't been, Jason knew he didn't have the stones for that.

Jason went to Cell Block C, expecting the worst. As he walked through the common area, inmates lifted their chins to Jason. A few even verbally greeted him.

"Welcome back."

"What's up."

Nobody called him kiddie fucker or chomo.

Ronnie fluttered from inmate to inmate, flirting and shaking his ass. His smock was tied in the front. The collar was off one shoulder, exposing a bra strap. Jason diverted his gaze.

Jason climbed the metal stairs to the landing that accessed the second-floor cells. He glanced at the indoor courtyard below. He had a flashback. Flying through the air like Superman, then dropping like a stone, his head cracking on the concrete. His stomach churned, and a bead of sweat slipped down his spine.

Jason turned from the railing and continued to his cell. He stopped in the open doorway. An inmate lounged on the bottom bunk, leafing through a well-worn nudie magazine.

The inmate rose from the bunk and glared at Jason. "What the fuck do you want?"

Jason clenched his jaw. "This is my cell."

He lifted his chin. "You were in the hospital."

Jason held out his hand. "I'm Jason."

They shook hands. "Russ."

Russ was short, burly, and hairy, with wiry black hair coming from his V-collared smock. Most guys wore a T-shirt underneath the smock, but not Russ.

Jason caught of whiff of Russ's BO and turned away in disgust.

Russ stepped to Jason. "What the fuck's your problem?"

Jason took a step back. "Look, Russ. I'd like to have an amicable relationship with you, but you have to do something about your body odor. I'd be happy to buy you some deodorant from the commissary, but you have to make all the shower times."

Russ tilted his head and blinked his beady eyes rapidly, mimicking a girl. He spoke in a mocking high voice. "Hi, I'm Jason. I want everything to smell like roses, just like my pussy." His voice went back to normal. "Get the fuck outta my face."

Jason frowned and walked away.

"Yeah," Russ called out to Jason's back. "Walk away, bitch."

Chapter 56: The Prison Psychologist

After a sporadic sleep, inhaling Russ's BO and flatulence, Jason met with prison psychologist, Dr. Wendell Harrington.

Sunlight streamed through the open blinds. Jason sat on the ratty couch in the sitting area. Dr. Harrington sat kitty-cornered on the swivel chair that he'd moved from behind his desk. He was a small delicate man, with bronze skin and white hair parted to the side.

"Why am I here?" Jason asked, his arms crossed over his chest.

"I like to meet with inmates after they've suffered a trauma to see how they're doing and to see if I can be of any assistance," Dr. Harrington replied, with a notepad and a pen in hand.

"I'm fine."

Dr. Harrington adjusted his invisible frame glasses. "Any adverse effects from the fall?"

"I'm mostly healed."

"Mostly?"

Jason uncrossed his arms and exhaled. "I have an AC joint separation, and my nose is crooked but no pain. I still have stitches in my head, but medical will take them out in a few days."

Harrington made a few notes in his notepad. "Any headaches or dizziness?"

"No."

"Were you able to contact your family while you were in the hospital to let them know about your fall?"

Jason shook his head.

"You've only had two visitors since you've been in prison and no mail."

"Chomos aren't exactly popular, doc."

Dr. Harrington tilted his head. "Is that how you see yourself?"

Jason wrung his hands in his lap. "That's how everybody sees me."

"How do you see yourself?"

"I don't know." Jason glanced at the closed door, suddenly feeling claustrophobic.

"When was the last time you had any contact with your parents?"

Jason fidgeted on the couch. "I'd rather not talk about that."

Dr. Harrington made a note. "Okay. How are you getting along with your new cellmate?"

Jason frowned. "Just peachy. Apart from the fact that he smells like shit."

Harrington smiled.

"Aren't you going to ask me how I feel about that?"

"How *do* you feel about that?"

"I'd rather live with a goat. I'm applying for a transfer."

A moment of silence passed between the two men.

"What happened between you and Ronnie Cunningham?" Harrington asked.

Jason looked down, thinking about the teen being bought and sold like a prostitute. "You should already know. He applied for a transfer."

"How do you feel about the transfer?"

Jason turned his gaze back to the doctor. "It was a mistake."

Dr. Harrington slid his glasses down his nose and peered over the top of his lenses. "How was it a mistake?"

Jason let out a ragged breath. "Is this confidential?"

"It is. Unless you indicate that you're a danger to yourself or someone else."

Jason pressed his lips together, thinking about the potential ramifications of what he was about to do. "Ronnie was manipulated into rooming with Duane Griffith, so Duane could rape him and turn him out."

"Would you be willing to go to the warden and make a formal complaint?"

Jason hesitated. "I would need some assurances that nobody would find out that I snitched."

"Only certain prison staff would be privy to those records."

Chapter 57: One Month Later ...

A month went by, and Jason fell into the prison routine. He worked at the resource center, ran at the track, and read many books. He'd reorganized the resource center, updating the card catalogue, and shelving all the books according to the Dewey decimal system.

Jason had withdrawn his transfer request a few days after he'd submitted it. Russ paid more attention to his hygiene after other inmates had roasted him mercilessly, calling him dick breath, pigpen, Russ Stanky, and telling him to check his drawers because he smelled like shit. Jason had figured it was better to stick with Russ, given that he could physically overpower Russ. Transferring could put Jason in close quarters with a powerful predator. Russ was a con man and a thief, but he wasn't violent, as far as Jason knew.

Jason did file a formal complaint against Duane, with anonymity assurances from Dr. Harrington. Duane was immediately put into seg, and Jason hadn't seen him since. There had been rumors that Jason had snitched, but his name had been circulated along with Duane's numerous enemies. Nobody had proof, and, with Duane out of sight, along with two of his buddies, everyone had moved on.

Ronnie had been transferred to Cell Block E. Rumors were that Ronnie was being passed from inmate to inmate, still playing the part of the prostitute. Once an inmate was "broken in," unless he was placed in seg, he would be raped regardless of where he was transferred.

On the last Thursday in May, Jason met with his attorney in a private room. Jason sat across the table from Norman Tuttle. A guard waited in the hall, ready to escort Jason back to the resource center after his meeting.

"The trial is set for July 24th," Norman said. "I plan to push for a change of venue. I don't think you'll receive a fair trial in Loganville."

Jason nodded. "Do you think they'll change the venue?"

"I don't know. The plaintiff will argue that they can easily find twelve people in Loganville, who don't know who you are, and they'll be right. People forget pretty quickly, and some never paid attention in the first place."

Jason looked down. "My case doesn't look good, does it?"

Norman shook his head. "No, it doesn't. I'd like to put my PI to work. New evidence is the only way we'll win. Sometimes witnesses change their stories. Sometimes they remember things. Is there anyone you think we should talk to?"

"Becky. I know that's probably not possible, but she might tell the truth this time."

"I've already tried. The Murphys aren't letting anyone near her. I do have an interesting lead though. Not sure if it'll turn into anything."

Jason perked up. "What's the lead?"

"I heard through the grapevine that Cody Price and Susan Murphy called off their engagement. I contacted Cody, and I'm meeting with him next week. In my experience, exes can be a treasure trove of dirt."

Chapter 58: Worthless

"I'm surprised to see you," Dr. Harrington said, standing from his desk.

It had been over a month since their first and last session.

Jason and Dr. Harrington shook hands. "Thank you for meeting with me," Jason replied.

"Of course. Anytime." Dr. Harrington gestured to the sitting area. "Have a seat." He moved his swivel chair next to the couch.

Jason sat on the couch.

Dr. Harrington sat on his chair, flipped open his notepad, and removed the pen clipped to the pad. "What brings you here today?"

Jason took a deep breath. "I guess I needed to talk to someone who doesn't charge me $300 an hour."

"Are you referring to your attorney?"

Jason nodded.

"I'm all ears."

Nobody spoke for several seconds.

"I'm not really sure where to start," Jason said.

"Start anywhere you like," Dr. Harrington replied.

"I, *um*, … I was getting used to this place. I settled into the prison routine. I have my job at the resource center, which I actually like. I'm no fan of my cellmate, but it could be worse. I'm getting by. I started to think I could do this. I could do my fifteen years, get my early parole, and get out of here. I'll only be fifty-one. I have money. I could start over. Now … that's no longer an option."

Dr. Harrington knitted his brow. "How so?"

"I'm being sued. The lawsuit stems from my criminal charges. My attorney interviewed a witness yesterday, hoping to find new evidence, but he came up empty-handed. I spoke to him on the phone earlier today. He didn't sound confident. I had convinced myself that he would find something. It's hard to have any hope in here." Jason hung his head and rubbed his temples.

"What do you think you'll do when you're released?"

Jason raised his gaze. "I don't know. It'll be difficult to get a job as a felon. I'm not sure my skills will be relevant in fifteen years."

Dr. Harrington jotted down a note. "You were a financial advisor, right?"

"Yes."

"Are you not able to be a financial advisor with a felony record?"

"Technically, yes, but who the hell wants to entrust their money to a convicted felon? I was hoping to invest my own money when I got out, but there's a good chance I'll lose everything in this lawsuit. It's a lot easier to make money if you have money."

Dr. Harrington cocked his head. "And this feels unfair to you?"

"What if I didn't do it? What if I'm innocent?"

"Are you?"

Jason frowned. "How many guys come in here and tell you that they're innocent?"

"I'm not here to judge either way."

"If I'm innocent, how am I supposed to feel? How much more do I have to take?"

"Don't worry about how you're supposed to feel. How do you feel right now?"

Jason swallowed hard. "Hopeless. Worthless. My life has no meaning."

"Everyone's life has meaning."

Jason shook his head. "You're wrong. If I died tomorrow, not one person on this Earth would give a shit. In fact, I can think of quite a few people who would be happier that I was gone."

Chapter 59: Imminent Danger

Jason stood at the front desk in the resource center, stamping returns with today's date, 5-31-2000. He didn't bother to penalize the overdue books. It wasn't worth the possible beef it could cause.

Seven men from Cell Block C were led into the resource center by several COs. Most of the inmates went to the magazines and computers.

Erik the Aryan approached the front desk, with a shit-eating grin. "What's up, Jason?"

"Not much. Need any help?" Jason replied.

"I was gonna ask you the same thing."

Jason tilted his head.

"I heard Duane's gettin' out of seg next week, and he's comin' back to C Block."

Jason stood stunned and slack-jawed.

Erik chuckled. "I also heard that CO McCloud told Duane that you snitched on him."

Jason winced. "*Shit.*"

"Now might be a good time to make some friends. We're always lookin' for new brothers."

Chapter 60: Real Friends Are Rare

"I'd like to make a family tree for you," Dr. Harrington said, sitting on his swivel chair.

"Why?" Jason replied, sitting kitty-cornered from Harrington on the couch.

"Families have a huge impact on our feelings and behaviors. If I know about your family, I have a much better chance of helping you."

"Who says I need help?"

"By coming back to therapy, you did."

Jason nodded. "That's a fair point. What do you want to know?"

Dr. Harrington held his notepad open, his pen in hand. "What's your relationship like with your father?"

Jason shrugged. "I've never met him."

Harrington wrote in his notepad. "Do you know who he is?"

"No. My mother claims not to know."

"Do you think she's lying?"

"I don't know, and I don't care."

Harrington made another note. "What about your mother? What's your relationship like with her?"

Jason let out a heavy breath. "We haven't spoken in eighteen years. Not since I left for college."

Dr. Harrington widened his eyes. "Why don't you speak to your mother?"

"She's a mess. She's always been a mess. My childhood was chaotic and dysfunctional. She had substance abuse issues. She hung out with losers and druggies. I knew I needed to get away from her if I wanted to make something of my life." Jason grimaced. "Ironically, she's doing better than me."

"How do you know that?"

"Well, ... she's not in prison."

"She could be. You said you haven't talked to her in eighteen years."

"I saw her in court at my preliminary hearing, but I didn't talk to her."

Dr. Harrington rubbed his chin. "Why do you think she was there?"

Jason broke eye contact. "I don't know." This was a lie.

"Do you have any siblings?"

Jason stared at the coffee table in front of him. "A half sister. She's three years younger than me."

"Do you have any contact with her?"

Jason made eye contact again. "No."

Dr. Harrington made another note. "Why not?"

Jason fidgeted in his seat. "We were never close."

"What about extended family? Do you have any close relatives?"

"No."

"What about friends?"

"I had a few friends in high school and college, but I've never had any close friends, ... not until Michelle, ... my ex-wife."

"Why do you think that is?"

Jason rubbed the back of his neck, thinking for a moment. "I guess I've always been kind of a loner. In high school, I was either studying, working, or running. College was more of the same. After I graduated, I worked nonstop to build a business. Some of my clients were acquaintances, borderline friends, but I didn't have a real friend, until I met Michelle."

"What made her a real friend?"

"She cared about me for me." Jason dipped his head. "Or at least I thought she did."

A moment of silence passed between them.

"What do you think now?" Dr. Harrington asked.

Jason raised his gaze. "About Michelle?"

"Yes."

Jason swallowed the lump in his throat. "I disgust her. The last thing she said to me was, 'If you have a single shred of decency left in your sick mind, you'll sign those divorce papers and forget I ever existed.'" Tears filled his eyes. "I signed the divorce papers, but I can't seem to forget about her. I should've ..." Jason wiped the corners of his eyes with his index finger.

Several seconds of silence passed between them again.

"You said, I should've, but you didn't finish the sentence," Dr. Harrington said, leaning forward in his seat.

"She wanted to have children, but I ... I didn't want children. I kept trying to delay it."

Dr. Harrington made a note. "Why didn't you want children?"

Jason frowned. "I didn't exactly have a charmed childhood. Maybe I didn't want to inflict that on a child."

"But you were financially secure and married. Why wouldn't you have happy, well-adjusted children?"

"You're right, doc. I could've. I *should've*." His voice wavered. "It was the biggest mistake of my life."

Chapter 61: Reckoning

A bank of ten showers were accessible through two locked doors along the north wall of Cell Block C. Every Monday, Wednesday, and Friday morning, inmates were given the option to shower. On Wednesday morning, Jason and his fellow inmates lined up along the wall to the showers, their towels over their shoulders.

CO McCloud opened the door to the locker room and four COs went inside. Then McCloud said, "First ten. Let's go."

Jason was fourth in line behind Russ, which was odd because Russ wasn't an early riser. He was usually one of the last to shower. Jason glanced back at the line, making sure he wouldn't be in the shower with Duane.

Duane had been released from seg two days ago, but Jason hadn't had any contact with him. Jason had heard that Gold Tooth and Face Tatt had been released a week ago, but they'd been moved to Cell Block D.

CO McCloud let the first ten inmates into the locker room, locking out the others waiting in line. As soon as they were let into the room, Jason and the rest of the inmates rushed to a cubby and undressed. They all knew they only had five minutes, so they focused on the task at hand. Jason placed his clothes in the cubby marked #8. He put his towel around his waist and turned around. Jason thought he saw Duane walk into the shower room. *That can't be right. He wasn't among the first ten. Did he cut the line right before we came in? I'm being paranoid.*

Inmates walked into the shower room, wearing nothing but towels around their waists and shower shoes on their feet. A few didn't bother with shower shoes, and others didn't bother with any modesty whatsoever, placing their towels over their shoulders instead. Jason walked toward the shower room with his towel wrapped around his waist and shower shoes to protect his feet from the various fungi and viruses being transmitted throughout the prison.

Russ sat on one of the benches, his shirt off. He groaned and held his hairy gut. "I'm not feelin' good."

Jason stood by the door to the showers, watching Russ.

CO McCloud shoved Jason into the shower room. "Hurry up."

The shower room consisted of ten showerheads, each separated by a chest high wall. Blots of mold crept up the walls and covered the tile grout. Three COs watched the shower stalls, including McCloud. Jason went to the first open shower stall he came across, scanning for Duane. Steam came from the showers, obscuring Jason's view. Inmates who were first in line for shower day were rewarded with scorching hot water. Inmates toward the end of the line had only cold water.

Jason hung his towel on the wall separating his shower from the next, and grabbed his soap from his plastic container. In his plastic container, he had a small squirt of shampoo for his hair. He didn't like bringing the bottle to shower day because every inmate would ask for a squirt. Jason turned on the shower head, checking the water with his palm. He stepped into the hot water and grabbed the soap. Jason washed quickly, knowing he only had two or three minutes left.

A commotion came from the locker room. Two of the three guards ran from the shower room. One of the guards in the locker room shouted, "He's having a seizure."

Jason glanced toward the door to the locker room. CO McCloud guarded the door, glaring at Jason. The hair on the back of Jason's neck stood on end. A thick black arm wrapped around Jason's neck from behind and hooked into place with the assailant's other arm. The man's left hand was behind Jason's head, pushing forward, tilting Jason's neck toward his chest. Jason pushed and struggled against the immoveable force behind him, the thick arms squeezing like pythons. Hot water from the showerhead peppered Jason's chest and face. He could breathe, but Jason felt weak, his vision hazy. Jason rammed his elbow backward, but it had no effect.

"You're mine now, bitch."

It's Duane. Jason eyed McCloud for help. The CO locked eyes with Jason, then turned his back. The steam seemed to thicken and darken. His legs felt rubbery. Then, everything went black.

Seconds later, Jason woke, disoriented, like he was in a dream or a nightmare. Duane's heavy body pinned him to the tile floor. Jason's penis, knees, and the left side of his face ground into the hard tile. Shooting pain came from his rectum as Duane grunted in his ear. Hot water came from above, splashing the wet tile. Steam covered them like a blanket.

Jason bucked, desperately trying to get the man off him. Duane grabbed a fistful of Jason's hair and slammed his face into the tile over and over, until it all went black again.

Chapter 62: Déjà Vu

Jason lay on his back in the hospital bed in a drug-induced haze. Despite the drugs, his face and head still hurt. He raised his head and dropped it immediately. The movement sent shooting pain to his abdomen and anal region. He wiggled his nose. That hurt too. He reached up with his left hand and touched his skull. It was wrapped and bandaged. He touched his nose with the slightest of pressure. It was bandaged too. His right arm was hooked to an IV. Cool oxygen flowed into his nose from the nasal cannula. He felt a powerful sense of déjà vu.

Jason tried to remember how he'd gotten there, but everything was hazy. *I fell off the second story landing and hit my head. Right?* He searched his fuzzy memory. *No, that already happened.*

A doctor entered the room and approached Jason's bedside. She was small and thin with jet-black hair. "Hello, Mr. Lewis. I'm Dr. Chung. Remember me?"

Jason glanced at the doctor and nodded almost imperceptibly. He remembered that she was his surgeon.

"I'm happy to report that your surgery went well. Usually, my patients are much older, and *they* recover well. I expect you to make a full recovery in four to six weeks. Your stomach may be a little sore for a week or so. I made an incision in your stomach to pull your rectum back up and into its proper position."

My rectum? Then it came back to him in a wave. The sleeper hold. Waking with Duane on top of him. *He was so heavy. I couldn't move him. I tried. He smashed my face into the tile. Broke my nose again. Split my forehead open.* Jason closed his eyes and turned away from Dr. Chung.

He wished Duane had killed him.

Chapter 63: On Your Own

Three days later, Warden Douglas Bates stood at Jason's bedside. Jason lay with the bed slightly propped. His head and nose were still bandaged, but the pain had subsided. His stomach still hurt from the surgery, but it wasn't unbearable.

"You gonna tell me what happened?" Warden Bates asked.

Jason stared straight ahead.

"I'm trying to help you."

No reply.

"Your cellmate faked a seizure in what I believe was an attempt to create a diversion so you could be assaulted. He won't admit to it, and I have no concrete evidence, other than that he was medically fine shortly after the supposed seizure, and he has no history of seizures."

Jason still stared straight ahead, his jaw set tight.

Warden Bates glared at Jason. "I also have no witnesses to the assault—or at least no one willing to talk. If you don't talk, I can't do anything. That means, when you return, your attacker will still be there, waiting for you." He paused for a moment. "You have to help me, so I can help you. Who was it? Duane Griffith?"

Jason turned his gaze to meet Bates. "I don't trust you. I told you about what was happening to Ronnie Cunningham. Now he's being passed around on E Block. Your prison is a living hell that does nothing to rehabilitate. It only dehumanizes and degrades. You can't control the evil inside. You can't even control the evil within your own guards."

Warden Bates was slack-jawed for an instant. Then his mouth curled into a sneer. "Don't you dare lecture me, *inmate*. You're a child molester. Nobody cares that some sick pervert was raped. What do you think's gonna happen to you when you get back? Once an inmate is branded by rape, they become a target for every single sodomite in the prison."

Jason applauded with a slow rhythmic clap. "That was the first honest thing you've said today. With all due respect, Warden, go fuck yourself."

Warden Bates pointed at Jason, his ruddy complexion bright red. "You're on your own. Don't come crying to me for help next time." He marched from the hospital room.

Chapter 64: Can I Babysit?

Jason watched the television that hung in the upper corner of his hospital room. The newscast showed a crowd of people, chanting in front of the Loganville Township Police Station.

"Who do we want?" a man chanted through the bullhorn.

"Luisa!" the crowd chanted back.

"When do we want her?"

"Now!"

The newscaster spoke over the images. "Luisa Sandoval's family and over one hundred Loganville residents protested the lack of police progress on the recent disappearance of six-year-old Luisa Sandoval, who went missing one week ago."

The program showed graffiti of a devil within view of a playground. Then they cut to a Latino man with a weathered face. A caption identified the man as Hector Cruz, Community Organizer. "This is the second child who has disappeared from our community in the past six months, and the police have done *nothing*. People say the kidnapper is the devil, but he's just a man. If the police won't find him, *we will*."

Dr. Harrington walked into the hospital room.

The news cut to a Latina with dark curly hair and glasses. The caption under her likeness read Carmen Sandoval, Luisa's Mother. Her eyes were glassy. "We just want Luisa to come home. I'm begging whoever has her to just let her go."

"Hello, Jason," Dr. Harrington said, as he approached the bedside.

Jason muted the television with the remote on his overbed table. "Dr. Harrington." His bed was propped in the sitting position.

"Mind if I sit?"

"It's up to you."

Dr. Harrington grabbed a nearby chair, moved it next to Jason's bedside, and sat down. "How are you doing?"

"Fine."

"The warden told me that you won't identify your attacker."

Jason clenched his jaw. "Snitching only makes it worse. The warden doesn't give a shit about what happens to me."

"We could have your attacker put into administrative segregation. Was it Duane Griffith?"

Jason shook his head. "How did that work out for Ronnie? I'm not snitching again. I'm done talking about it."

Dr. Harrington adjusted his glasses. "Even if you won't identify your attacker, I'll have Duane Griffith transferred out of C block."

Jason nodded.

"Then I'm going to recommend that you be put into segregation, at least until you've fully healed from your surgery."

"Do what you have to do."

"I'm sorry that this happened to you."

Jason shrugged, watching the Ford truck commercial on the muted television.

Nobody spoke for a minute.

Dr. Harrington broke the silence. "On the drive over here, I was thinking about our last conversation."

Jason turned his gaze from the TV to Harrington.

"I was wondering if you had any male role models growing up?"

Jason hesitated for a few seconds. "I guess my high school track coach. I had a few teachers who were good male role models."

Dr. Harrington nodded. "What about inside your home? Did your mother have any boyfriends who were role models?"

Jason frowned. "Most of them weren't interested in me."

"Were there any who were?"

"A few." Jason stared at his overbed table, thinking about his mother's carousel of loser boyfriends. The ones who smacked him around. The stringy-haired piece of shit who used to come to his room, while his mother was passed out. *Lenny*. Jason had preferred the beatings to Lenny's touch. Afterward, Lenny had always asked, "You liked it, didn't you?"

"What were they like?" Dr. Harrington asked.

"What do you think they were like?" Jason replied.

The doctor spoke in a calm voice. "I don't know. I wasn't there."

Jason chewed on the inside of his cheek, still not making eye contact. He spoke barely above a whisper. "They were abusive. Physically. Emotionally."

"Sexually?"

Jason shook his head.

"What happened with these men?"

Jason glared at Harrington. "I'm done talking."

Dr. Harrington paused for an instant. "I think this is important. It might provide some insights into your behavior—"

"Fuck you. You think I molested children because some scumbag molested *me*?"

Dr. Harrington slid his glasses down his nose and peered over the top of his lenses. "What do you think?"

"You don't fucking get it, do you? It doesn't matter what I think or say or what I do. People will always see me as a child molester. If I told you that I was innocent, would you let me babysit your kids?"

Dr. Harrington opened his mouth, but nothing came out.

"I didn't think so. The fact that I was abused doesn't give me a fucking excuse to abuse a child. What happened is in the past. My choices are my own."

"It's not uncommon for victims of abuse—"

"Get the fuck out." Jason pointed to the door. "I said I was done."

Dr. Harrington pressed his lips together. "We're making progress."

Jason spoke through gritted teeth. "We're not. Please leave."

Dr. Harrington stood from the chair. "I hope we can resume our sessions once you're out of the hospital."

"I'm not talking to you anymore." Jason glowered at Harrington for a long beat. "You understand me?"

Chapter 65: Seg

Jason lay in his bunk, reading *The Rainmaker* by John Grisham. It was first published five years ago, but it was one of the newer novels in the resource center. When he finished the chapter, he used his bookmark to hold his spot and stood from his bunk. His cell in seg was six by nine, with a single metal bunk and a toilet with an attached sink. Light came from the fluorescent tube overhead, and a small sliver of a frosted window that offered no view whatsoever.

He was in his cell twenty-three hours per day. All his meals were delivered through the food pass on his door. Most days he was given rec time in a segregated outdoor cage. Three days a week he was taken to the showers. Since he'd returned from the hospital six days ago, he'd seen the medical staff twice. Once to remove his stitches, and once to check that he was healing okay from his surgery.

He paced in his cell, which amounted to walking three steps, turning around, walking three steps, and turning around again. He wanted to do push-ups, but Dr. Chung had instructed him not to exert himself for at least four weeks, and even then he was supposed to ease back into activities.

As he paced, he thought about his dilemma. Warden Bates was right. Once an inmate was "broken in," it was open season. He'd be sent back to general population in a month. *What then? I have to send a message to the first guy who tries. How? I'll still be weak from the surgery. I can't exercise yet. I'll need the element of surprise somehow.*

The food pass opened, and a covered plastic container appeared. Jason went to the door. CO McCloud's grinning face was in the door window. Jason hadn't seen him since the attack in the shower. Jason grabbed his lunch and turned around.

McCloud rapped on the window with his billy club. "Don't fuckin' turn your back on me."

Jason faced him, his jaw set tight.

"How did it feel to get fucked?"

Jason stared blank-faced.

"Now you know what Becky felt like."

Jason still stared blank-faced.

"I can make your life a livin' hell."

"I'd like to eat my lunch."

"Go right ahead. I put some special sauce on it for you." He cackled and walked away.

Jason went to his bunk and opened the plastic cover to find a peanut butter sandwich on white bread with canned green beans. The bread was compressed in spots with what appeared to be someone's fingertips. He pulled the bread apart, wondering if McCloud spit in his food, or worse. Jason took his lunch to the food pass, sliding it back without taking a single bite.

Chapter 66: Back to Gen Pop

Jason was escorted back to Cell Block C on July 20, carrying his belongings in his laundry bag. He entered the vestibule with the CO. The door to the hallway shut behind them. The next door opened. A cacophony of shouts, laughing, and talking came from Cell Block C. It was jarring after thirty-six days in the relative quiet of seg.

"Move it, inmate," the CO said.

Jason stepped into Cell Block C. The door to the vestibule shut behind him. It was just before dinner, and the inside courtyard was bustling with activity. A few inmates noticed Jason, and they alerted their friends. As Jason walked toward the stairs, most of Cell Block C watched his every move.

Someone shouted, "Faggot."

The crowd laughed.

A few inmates blew kisses.

Someone else said, "Bitch gonna be my prison wife."

Another inmate said, "Hey, white boy."

Jason ignored the comments.

"Hey, white boy. You're gonna give up that ass."

Jason climbed the metal steps toward his original cell. Russ had been given another cellmate while Jason was in seg, but it hadn't lasted. The day before Jason's release from seg, McCloud had taunted Jason with the fact that he was back with Russ. McCloud had said, "He's gonna make you his bitch."

Jason entered his old cell. The smell of feces was in the air.

Russ was on the toilet. He grinned at Jason. "Look who's back."

Jason tossed his laundry bag on the top bunk. He eyed his old locker, eager to lock his possessions inside, but it was only a few feet from the toilet.

Russ leaned forward on the toilet and wiped his ass. He glanced back at the shit stain before dropping it in the toilet. He stood from the toilet, flushed, and pulled up his pants. He didn't bother washing his hands.

Russ sauntered to Jason. "This is *my* cell. You can live here, but you're gonna do what I say."

Jason dipped his head and nodded.

Russ grinned again. His teeth had a yellow film. "That's what I thought." Russ moved into Jason's personal space. His breath smelled worse than his shit. Russ grabbed Jason's hand and placed it firmly on his crotch. "We're gonna have some fun tonight." Russ left the cell, headed to dinner.

***

That night, after lockdown and lights out, Jason lay on his top bunk, waiting for the inevitable. Dim light came from the door window. Rustling came from the bottom bunk. Russ rolled out of bed and stood. Jason closed his eyes, feigning sleep.

Russ grabbed Jason and shook him. "Get up."

Jason opened his eyes and turned his head to Russ.

Russ shook him again. "Get up. Come down here."

Jason climbed down from his bunk, moving slowly and deliberately. Jason faced his cellmate, his head bowed in deference.

Russ's hairy gut hung over the waistband of his white boxers. He wore nothing else. He pulled his boxers down to mid-thigh, releasing his penis. He masturbated with a smirk on his face. "Suck my dick. And watch your teeth."

Jason cringed and said, "I'll do it, but I need you to do one thing."

"What?"

"Close your eyes and pretend I'm a beautiful woman."

Russ narrowed his eyes. "What the fuck are you talkin' about?"

"Otherwise, we're both faggots."

Russ grunted his understanding. He closed his eyes, still stroking his penis.

Jason reared back and threw a right cross, connecting perfectly with Russ's jaw. Russ fell back, his body seemingly useless. He hit the back of his head on his locker and slumped to the floor, now sitting, his head hanging to his chin. Jason grabbed a fistful of his hair, lifted his face, and gave him another right cross, opening his lip, blood staining his teeth. Jason pounded his face again and again. He wanted Cell Block C to know. Russ moaned, his face covered in blood.

Then, Jason wrapped his large hands around Russ's neck and squeezed. Russ tried to hit Jason's arms, but he was too weak. Jason held firm, staring into Russ's wide-open eyes. Jason imagined he was choking Duane. He imagined he was choking Lenny, his mother's old boyfriend. Lenny's face was beet red and terrified. He turned from red to blue. Then, Lenny's face was gone, replaced by Russ. Jason let go and stepped back.

Russ wheezed and gasped for air.

Jason watched the man struggle for air, without an ounce of sympathy. When Russ's breathing normalized, Jason stepped closer, leaned in, and said, "Next time, I'll fucking kill you. You understand me?"

Russ hung his head and wept.

Jason grabbed a fistful of his hair and raised Russ's gaze. His other arm was cocked for another straight right. "You understand me?"

"Yes. Yes. I understand," Russ said, his face covered in blood and tears.

Chapter 67: No Escape

The next day Jason expected to be put back into seg for rearranging Russ's face, but that's not what happened. Russ had two black eyes, a split lip, bruises on his left cheek, a cut under his eye, and fingerprint bruising around his neck, but Russ didn't snitch. The rest of Cell Block C got the message though. Once word got around that Jason had pummeled Russ, the catcalling and disrespect stopped.

In the afternoon, Jason browsed the bookshelves in the resource center, removing out-of-place books, and placing them on his cart to be reshelved. The inmate who had taken Jason's place at the resource center hadn't organized the books properly.

Seven inmates from Cell Block D were escorted into the resource center. Jason set a book on his cart and glanced at the front desk to see if anyone needed help. The inmates walked toward the computers and magazines, but one inmate spotted Jason between the bookcases and sauntered his way.

For a split-second, Jason couldn't place the man. Then the man grinned, showing his gold teeth. Jason turned to exit the situation, but another man sauntered toward him, blocking his escape. Jason recognized the muscular inmate and his face tatt. They moved closer, trapping Jason between the bookcases and the two inmates.

"Remember us?" Gold Tooth asked.

"You need something?" Jason replied.

Duane appeared behind Gold Tooth and joined the party.

Jason trembled and bowed his head in deference.

"He's shakin' like a punk-ass bitch," Gold Tooth said.

Face Tatt cackled.

Duane smiled wide, his mustache spreading across his lip. "You didn't think we were gonna forget about you, did you?"

Jason showed his palms. "I don't want any more trouble."

Duane chuckled. "Too late for that, white boy." Duane's face turned serious. "How did it feel to get fucked like a bitch? I heard I tore up your little pussy."

Jason peered over Duane's shoulder, hoping to spot a CO, but seeing nobody.

Duane glanced back. "Ain't nobody comin' to save you." Duane poked Jason's chest with his thick finger. "I got this place wired. I can get you anywhere, anytime I want. The COs don't give a shit about a fuckin' chomo snitch, like you. I own your ass." Duane lifted his chin to Face Tatt.

Face Tatt grabbed Jason from behind, pinning his arms. Gold Tooth tried to grab Jason's legs, but Jason bucked frantically, kicking the bookshelf with both legs, causing the shelf to fall into the next shelf like dominoes, before crashing into the wall. Many of the books slid off the shelves to the floor.

The racket caused a CO to appear at the end of the row. "What the hell's going on?"

Face Tatt let go of Jason.

Another CO appeared, inspecting the leaning bookshelves and the books all over the floor. "Fuckin' idiots. What the fuck are y'all doin'?"

Jason still trembled, adrenaline coursing through his veins.

Duane and his boys walked toward the COs, showing their palms. Duane said, "White boy knocked over the bookshelf."

"Clean this shit up," one of the COs barked to Jason.

Duane and his boys were sent back to Cell Block D.

Jason sat on the floor and hung his head. *I can't keep doing this.* After a few minutes, he steeled himself and rose from the floor. He righted the bookshelves and began organizing the books on the floor to be reshelved. As he was organizing the books, he came across *The Alchemist* by Paulo Coelho. This was the book that Terrance the old librarian had told him to read if he was desperate—but only as a last resort.

I have nothing to lose. Jason looked around, making sure nobody was watching. He opened the book slowly, as if it might hold a bomb. He let out a ragged exhalation, staring at the open book. *Could be a lifeline or a death sentence. Probably both.*

Chapter 68: The Civil Trial

Jason spent the next week in court. It felt like a repeat of the criminal trial, complete with many of the same witnesses. Norman Tuttle had wanted to include Michelle on his witness list again, but Jason had asked him not to. Jason didn't want to see Michelle's look of disgust, and he knew she didn't want to be put on the stand again. Instead, Norman had used her prior testimony at the criminal trial as evidence for the defense.

The civil trial had gone much like the criminal trial, with the witnesses testifying more or less the same as they had in the criminal trial. Norman had made a big show of the tiny semen sample found on the waistband of Becky's underwear. The plaintiff's attorney had included heartbreaking evidence of the suffering that Becky had endured after the sexual assault, as well as expert testimony from a child psychologist who detailed the trauma she'd likely endure for the rest of her life.

On Friday afternoon, after the morning of jury deliberations, the jurors filed back into the packed courtroom.

Judge Ken Hamilton sat behind his desk on high. He was a portly man with a long gray mustache that covered his lips. He leaned into his microphone and said, "Please be seated."

The audience settled into their pews. Jason sat at the defense table with his attorney, Norman Tuttle. Susie Murphy sat at the plaintiff's table with her attorney. Frank and Ruth were in the audience, right behind the plaintiff's table.

The jury forewoman, a white-haired lady with glasses, handed a folder to the bailiff, who handed the folder to the judge. Judge Hamilton, opened the folder, read the form, then handed it back to the bailiff. The bailiff handed the form back to the forewoman and gave her a few muted instructions.

The judge addressed the jury. "This will be the last time I see you, so I'd like to take this opportunity to thank you for your service. You've all been very attentive and very conscientious. Thank you very much." He cleared his throat. "You've given a verdict in this case, and, just so you know, after the jury forewoman reads the verdict, the attorneys may ask that you be polled to make sure that each of you say it's your verdict." He turned to the defense table. "Jason Lewis, please rise for the reading of the verdict."

Norman Tuttle stood, followed by his client. Jason had been more confident last time. His criminal conviction had come as a shock. He wasn't confident this time. He was hoping that the amount would be something less than what he had. He was hoping not to be destitute when he was released from prison in fifteen to twenty years.

"You may read the verdict," Judge Hamilton said to the jury forewoman.

Jason's heart thumped in his chest.

The old woman stood in front of her seat on the jury, holding the folder open. She read from the form without emotion. "Question number one. Was the defendant negligent? Unanimously, yes."

Jason winced.

Hushed murmurs came from the audience.

The jury forewoman continued. "Question number two. If yes, was the defendant's negligence the proximate cause of the plaintiff's injuries? Unanimously, yes."

More murmurs came from the audience.

"Question number three. If yes, did the plaintiff's conduct contribute to her injuries?" The jury forewoman clenched her jaw and glanced across the courtroom to Jason. "Unanimously, *no.*" She took a deep breath. "Question four. How much should the plaintiff receive?"

Susie leaned forward, on the edge of her seat, her hands clasped, as if she were praying.

"We the jury award the plaintiff the sum of 2.5 million dollars."

Excited chatter came from the audience. Susie shook her fist, beaming.

Jason stared straight ahead, showing no emotion. He thought, *I'm bankrupt.*

Chapter 69: Smack

The Monday after the verdict, Jason walked on the black line to the resource center, his shoulders slumped. CO McCloud walked behind him.

"You got fucked in the ass in court." McCloud cackled. "Two point five million bucks. God damn. There is justice in this world."

Jason stopped at the resource center door.

CO McCloud unlocked the door but didn't open it right away. "I have a three-year-old daughter. What do you think about that?"

Jason didn't respond.

McCloud removed his billy club from his belt. "Answer me, inmate."

Jason still didn't respond.

McCloud moved closer, poking his billy club in Jason's stomach. "When you get out in twenty years, are you gonna go back to rapin' little girls?"

"Your daughter will be twenty-three when I get out and looking for a way to get back at her asshole father."

McCloud punched Jason in the stomach, causing him to double over and cough repeatedly. "Say somethin' else smart. I'd love to beat your fuckin' ass."

Jason stood upright.

McCloud opened the door and shoved Jason inside. "Get to work, faggot."

Jason went to his cart, which was filled with books that needed shelving. He pushed the cart along the bookshelves, shelving the books according to subject and their numerical place in the Dewey decimal system. He stopped midway down a bookshelf. He ran his fingers across the spines of famous novels, stopping at *The Alchemist* by Paulo Coelho. He removed the novel next to it—*The Pilgrimage* by the same author. He looked around, making sure nobody was watching. Then he reached into the waistband of his boxers and removed a small plastic baggy, partially filled with a white powder. He flattened the baggy, placed it in the middle of the novel, and reshelved the book.

Chapter 70: The Inevitable

The inmates from Cell Block D had resource center privileges on Friday afternoons. Jason thought about faking an illness to hide from Duane and his boys, but Jason knew Duane could get to him anywhere through proxies and even the guards. Ultimately, if it were going to happen, it was better that it happened on familiar ground.

Jason spent that first Friday in August on pins and needles, his stomach sick, and his body flinching at the slightest sound. After lunch, Jason purposely spent his time between the bookshelves, shelving books, waiting for the men of Cell Block D.

In the afternoon, CO McCloud led the inmates from Cell Block D into the resource center. Jason immediately moved to the next bookshelf over, midway down, in the company of the great novelist, Paulo Coelho.

Between the bookcases, Jason watched five inmates walk to the magazines and computers. Duane, Gold Tooth, and Face Tatt searched the front desk, then the bookshelves. CO McCloud stood by the entrance, like a sentry. Jason knew he wasn't protecting him.

Face Tatt saw Jason first. "He's right here." Face Tatt strutted between the bookshelves, coming toward Jason, with Gold Tooth in tow.

Jason stood still, his eyes locked on Face Tatt, and his hands trembling. Jason heard footsteps behind him. He turned to see Duane coming from behind, a smirk on his face. Duane threw a right hook that connected with Jason's jaw. Jason's head rotated, his brain jostled, and he fell awkwardly, his body limp.

Jason lay on the carpet, his world spinning, the three inmates standing over him laughing. Jason reached for the bookcase, trying to pull himself upright, but he lost his grip, falling to the floor again. Duane and his crew laughed again. Jason lay on the carpet, trying to get his bearings. Duane bent down and slipped his massive hands around Jason's neck and squeezed like a python.

Jason gasped, peering into Duane's dark eyes.

"Ain't nobody gonna save you this time," Duane said, still squeezing. "You're gonna do what we want, or I'm gonna fuckin' kill you." Duane let go.

Jason choked and wheezed, sucking in air.

"On your knees, bitch," Duane said, rubbing his crotch.

Face Tatt and Gold Tooth grabbed Jason under his arms and pulled him up so he was on his knees.

Duane pulled his pants down, exposing his erection. "You better suck it good, bitch."

Jason showed his palms in surrender, still on his knees. His voice was shaky. "Please. I'll do everything you want, but I need to take something first. I have cocaine. It's good shit. You can have some too."

"Where?" Duane asked, his eyes narrowed, one hand on his erection.

"Right here." Jason grabbed *The Pilgrimage* from the bookshelf. He opened the book exposing the flattened plastic baggie with white powder inside.

Face Tatt snatched the plastic baggie. "Aw, shit. It's a party now."

Duane pulled up his pants and snatched the baggie from Face Tatt. They huddled around the book cart, turning it so it blocked the row, and using it as a table. Duane was nearest to Jason, while the other two were on the opposite side of the cart. While still on his knees, Jason grabbed *The Alchemist* from the bookshelf, his body turned from the men, shielding the book from their view. Gold Tooth ripped a page out of *The Pilgrimage*, expertly rolling the paper to create a snorting straw. Duane dumped the white powder on a hardback book. Jason opened *The Alchemist* to reveal a narrow cutout in the middle of the pages. The cutout held a metal blade with a grip made from electrical tape. Jason removed the shank from the novel. Jason pivoted, now on one knee, his right hand behind his back, gripping the shank.

Duane turned and pointed at Jason. "Don't fuckin' move. We ain't done with you."

Duane used a bookmark to cut the powder and arranged it in neat lines. As Duane snorted his first line of confectioner's sugar, Jason sprang to his feet, and plunged the blade into the back of Duane's neck. Jason was possessed, stabbing over and over again. Blood spurted in pulses from Duane's neck.

Face Tatt and Gold Tooth were stunned for a moment. Face Tatt pulled one side of the cart toward him to make a space to squeeze through. When he pulled the cart, Duane dropped to his knees, then toppled to the side, the bookshelf partially propping the big man, and his body creating another obstacle in the row. Face Tatt slipped between the bookcase and the cart, but Jason didn't run. Instead, Jason rushed to meet him, jumping over Duane, and stabbing Face Tatt in the chest. Face Tatt shrieked and turned, causing Jason to lose his grip on the shank. Gold Tooth ran away from Jason, hollering for help. Face Tatt followed his boy, the shank still stuck in his chest.

Jason stared at Duane, lying against the bookcase, his eyes still. Blood pooled on the book case and the gray carpet beneath him. Jason spat in the dead man's face. Then he sat next to his handiwork, his back against the bookshelf, and smiled to himself.

Heavy boots entered the resource center. The men from CERT with their electrified shields and riot gear. Jason didn't resist as the first man smashed into him with his shield, jolting him with eighty thousand volts of electricity.

Chapter 71: Sentencing

Six months later, Jason sat at the defense table again, this time with a public defender at his side. Norman Tuttle didn't work for free. The judge sat behind his desk on high, the state flag of Pennsylvania and the American flag hanging limp behind him. Only a few people came to watch the sentencing.

Judge Sutherland appeared to be in his late-forties, with brown hair parted to the side. His black robe had a V-collar, showing his red tie. His face was full, giving a clue to his heavy-set frame concealed beneath his robe. He said, "Yesterday, the defendant was convicted of voluntary manslaughter, a first-degree felony, which carries a maximum sentence of up to twenty years. However, the defendant has three or more violent offense convictions. For these repeat offenders, Pennsylvania law requires a minimum sentence of twenty-five years in prison, with the option of increasing the sentence to life imprisonment without parole, if necessary for public safety."

The judge addressed the prosecution. "Mr. Harrison, in the matter of the sentencing, is there anyone who would like to speak on behalf of the victim in this case?"

Mr. Harrison spoke from behind the prosecution table. "Yes, Your Honor. Eunice Griffith, the victim's mother, would like to make a statement." Harrison gestured to the middle-aged woman, sitting in the first row of the audience, behind the prosecution table.

Judge Sutherland said, "Mrs. Griffith, you're welcome to stand where you are and address the court, or you may use the podium."

Eunice Griffith stood from her seat and made her way to the podium placed between the defense and prosecution tables, and facing the judge. She was a large heavyset woman, with dark skin. She wore a black dress fit for a funeral. She unfolded a piece of paper and spread it out on the podium. She read from the paper without looking up. "My name is Eunice Griffith. My son was Duane Griffith. He made his mistakes, but he never killed nobody. He was a good son, and he was gonna turn his life around. He only had four years left in prison." Eunice grabbed a tissue from the box on the podium and dabbed the corners of her eyes.

She sniffled and continued. "He wasn't always there for his children, but, when he was, he was the best father. Now Aisha and Jordan will never have the chance to know their father. I believe only God should take the life of a human being." Eunice turned and glared at Jason. "That man is pure evil. He deserves life in prison." She turned and walked back to the audience.

Jason stared forward, blank-faced.

"Thank you, Mrs. Griffith." The judge addressed the defense. "Mr. Goodman?"

The public defender spoke from his seat. "We don't have anyone to speak on behalf of the defense."

"Mr. Lewis, you have the last word. Is there anything you'd like to say before I impose the sentence?"

Jason stood from his seat, wearing a jail jumpsuit, hand and leg cuffs, and a belly chain around his midsection. "For punishment to mean something, I would have to believe that I've done something wrong. You could sentence me to a thousand years in prison, and I will never regret killing that rapist piece of shit."

Gasps came from the audience.

Eunice sprang from her seat and shouted, "Give him life!"

Judge Sutherland banged his gavel. "Order in the court."

The audience quieted. A bailiff approached Eunice with a scowl. She sat down.

The judge glowered at Jason. "I was tempted by your story of self-defense, but I believe you had ill-intentions, which you so clearly demonstrated just now. You could've asked for protection from the prison staff, but you chose to take a life instead, with the most brutal stabbing I've seen in my fifteen years on the bench. However, the law states that increasing the sentence to life imprisonment without parole can be done if necessary for public safety. Fortunately, for you and the public, you'll be a very old man when you're released from prison, so I believe your risk to the public at that time will be very low. I hereby impose the sentence of twenty-five years in prison." The judge smacked his gavel.

Jason knew that meant if he served both his sentences in their entirety, he'd be eighty-one years old when released.

PART III: April

Things come apart so easily, when they have been held together with lies.
—Dorothy Allison, Bastard Out of Carolina

Knowing can be a curse on a person's life. I'd traded in a pack of lies for a pack of truth, and I didn't know which one was heavier. Which one took the most strength to carry around? It was a ridiculous question, though, because, once you know the truth, you can't ever go back and pick up your suitcase of lies. Heavier or not, the truth is yours now.
—Sue Monk Kidd, The Secret Life of Bees

Chapter 72: He's Back

"I need to have some fun," Travis said, sitting in the front passenger seat. "I'm so fucking bored. Connor's parties are epic. Everyone's gonna be there."

April Gibbs drove her Honda Civic through a neighborhood of brick ramblers and colonials built in the fifties and sixties. Many lawns featured Trump 2020 signs. She glanced at her boyfriend. "It's too dangerous."

Travis groaned. "I call bullshit. Nobody our age gets sick."

April pulled into the driveway of a redbrick rambler, with a manicured lawn and several Trump 2020 signs. She parked behind her grandpap's trailered fishing boat and next to her mother's minivan. April pulled the emergency brake and turned to her boyfriend. "Even if young people don't usually get sick, I could still give it to my parents or, even worse, my grandparents."

Travis rolled his eyes. His six-foot-tall frame was slumped in his seat. "Whatever. You think you know everything. You're not a doctor yet."

April frowned. "No shit, but I listen to doctors." April was a rising sophomore at Penn and a biology major with aspirations of going to medical school and becoming a pediatrician. Travis was taking a few classes at the local community college.

"Fine. I'll go by myself. I'm not gonna live my life in fear," Travis said.

April glanced at her surgical mask and hand sanitizer sitting in the center cupholder. "I'm not living in fear. I'm trying to make smart decisions."

Travis tilted the rearview mirror toward himself, checking his blond hair and face that resembled a young Ryan Gosling. "You're such a goodie-goodie. Don't you ever wanna do something dangerous? Don't you ever wanna break the rules?"

April adjusted the rearview mirror, making sure she could see out the back window. "I'm not a goodie-goodie. I'm just not a dumbass."

"I'm going with or without you."

April turned to Travis. "If you go, you can't see me until you quarantine for two weeks."

Travis shook his head. "Don't you miss parties?"

"We're at a party right now." She glanced at the clock—*1:03.* "Come on. We're late."

Travis cackled. "Only a goodie-goodie would think three minutes is late."

April stepped out of her car and shut the door. The bright sun warmed her skin. She walked toward her grandpap's boat, then stopped, waiting for her boyfriend. Travis exited her car. He rolled his neck, then strolled toward April. He wore a T-shirt with an American flag for the occasion. The tight sleeves and fitted shirt highlighted his muscular upper body. April wore a red T-shirt and short but not obscene khaki shorts.

April led Travis past the garage to the backyard and the ground-level deck, where the festivities were already underway. The picnic table was covered in a red, white, and blue tablecloth. Pappy Frank stood by the grill, tongs in hand. April's younger twin brothers were tossing a Nerf football in the grass. Her mother, Michelle, sat at the picnic table with Grammy Ruth. April's father, Danny, was working, taking advantage of the holiday double-time.

Ruth was the first to notice April and Travis. "April! Hi, honey. Hi, Travis."

April and Travis climbed the two steps to the deck area.

Grammy Ruth stood from the table and approached the couple. Ruth held out her flabby arms and said, "Give your grammy a hug."

April hugged her grandmother. Travis stood off to the side, trying to avoid the hug, but Ruth gave him a hug too.

"Look at you two," Ruth said, inspecting them. "Such a gorgeous couple."

April blushed, not from the compliment but from the lie. Travis was gorgeous. She was average in the looks department. Her straight brown hair hung to her shoulders, with no body and no highlights. The epitome of average and boring. She had brown eyes, a round face, and a medium build. Her face was cute, but her nose was a little crooked, and her smile was a little too toothy.

She'd met Travis in high school, when she'd been assigned to him as a peer tutor. She'd single-handedly kept him on the football, basketball, and baseball teams. Without her help, he might not have graduated.

"Thanks, Grammy," April replied.

"Hi, Mrs. Gibbs," Travis said, waving.

Michelle smiled at Travis from the picnic table. "Hi, Travis. Happy Fourth of July."

"Thanks, you too." Travis glanced at the boys playing catch. "Watch this interception." Travis ran off the deck into the lawn and stepped in front of Dylan, snatching the Nerf football from the air.

April said hello to her mother and walked over to her grandpap, at the far end of the deck, following the smell of grilling burgers.

"Hey, young lady," Grandpap Frank said, smiling.

Frank was a big man, with a shock of white hair and a white beard to match.

"Hi, Grandpap," April replied. She hugged her grandfather. When they separated, she asked, "Is Aunt Susie coming?"

Frank opened the grill lid. "She'll be here eventually." He turned the burgers with his tongs. "You know your Aunt Susie. She's on her own time."

"What about Becky?"

Frank frowned. "Your grandmother invited her, but I doubt she'll show."

"I love Becky, but maybe it's better she doesn't come. You know she was in Las Vegas last week for her birthday. She posted a bunch of pictures on Instagram. Nobody was wearing masks either." April thought about grabbing her mask from the car in case Becky showed. However, that was futile because the rest of her family wouldn't be wearing masks, so, if Becky were infected, they would all get it eventually.

Frank grabbed the spatula hanging from the shiny grill. "I don't think the masks make one bit of difference."

"Then why do doctors and nurses wear them?"

Frank pressed on the burgers with his spatula. "Explain to me why Fauci told us not to wear masks in the beginning, and now he's telling us to wear masks."

April put her hands on her hips. "He admitted to lying because they were worried about not having enough masks for health care workers."

"Maybe that was part of it. The bigger picture is the liberals are trying to make things as bad as possible, so Trump isn't reelected. Look at all the riots. These leftist governors and mayors are letting these thugs destroy their cities."

"People are really mad about all the racism and the police brutality. I know you and my dad aren't like that, but a lot of police officers are."

Frank glared at April. "You don't really believe that bullshit, do you?"

April dipped her head. "I've seen lots of videos."

"Don't believe everything you see on the internet."

April raised her gaze. "Those videos aren't fake."

"That's not what I'm saying. The media highlights these videos and blows them out of proportion. Now the public hates the police and thinks we're all shooting unarmed black men. Did you know that, if you control for crime rates, whites are more likely to be shot and killed than blacks?"

April tilted her head. "Really?"

Frank nodded. "Yep."

"The other side says that the police target people of color. That's why the crime stats show that black people commit more crime than white people."

Frank shook his head. "Police officers are usually called to situations. They don't have any control over that. I'm sure there are racist individuals, just like in any profession, but police officers generally aren't racist, and they're certainly not killers." Frank removed a burger from the grill, placing it on the nearby plate. "I'm glad I'm retired. I wouldn't wanna deal with this bullshit." He removed another burger from the grill. "I'm sure it's rough on your dad."

"He hasn't said much. My mom's worried that he'll get COVID. Thankfully, we don't have any riots around here."

Frank smirked. "Because everyone has a gun."

The rumble of a flat-six Porsche engine followed the screech of tires in the driveway.

April turned around, facing the back of the garage, but still standing next to Frank. "I think that's Aunt Susie."

Frank checked his watch and chuckled. "Your grandmother told her that we were eating at noon."

Susie marched between the garage and the house to the backyard, carrying an envelope. She made a beeline for Michelle.

"Hi, honey," Ruth said, standing from the picnic table to greet her daughter.

But Susie ignored Ruth, glowering at Michelle. "I need to talk to you. *Now.*"

"About what?" Michelle asked, standing from the picnic table.

"Inside."

Michelle and Susie entered the house through the back door.

April turned to Frank. "What do you think that's about?"

"I don't know. Let them work it out." Frank removed another burger from the grill. "We're about ready to eat. Why don't you go get Travis and your brothers?"

"Okay." April walked back toward the picnic table at the opposite end of the deck.

Ruth was setting the picnic table with American flag–themed paper plates and cups. April stepped off the deck and walked into the lush lawn. Travis played quarterback, and Dylan ran pass patterns against his twin brother, Lance. Travis launched a bomb over Lance's head, dropping the football into Dylan's hands for the touchdown.

Dylan spiked the Nerf football. "You got burnt."

"Shut up," Lance replied, with slumped shoulders. "I burned you last time."

Her twin brothers were fourteen and big for their age—nearly six-feet tall.

"Burgers are ready," April called out to Travis and her brothers.

"We're coming," Travis said, holding up his hand.

April turned around to walk back to the deck. A Nerf football sailed through the air and bounced off the side of her head, nearly knocking her off her feet. She steadied herself and turned to her brothers, with a look that could kill.

"Sorry," Dylan called out, raising his hand. "It got away from me."

Lance laughed into his fist.

"You all right?" Travis called out, suppressing a grin.

April touched the side of her head. No damage. "I'm fine." She went back to Ruth and the picnic table. Muffled voices came from the house. April gestured to the house. "What's going on with my mom and Aunt Susie?"

Ruth removed cling wrap from the bowl of macaroni salad and looked up. "I don't know."

April pivoted to go inside.

"Don't bother them, sweetheart."

April turned to Ruth. "I have to use the bathroom."

Ruth nodded.

April went inside. Voices came from one of the bedrooms. She walked past the dining room to the hallway that led to the bedrooms and the bathroom. She crept down the hallway, the voices increasing in volume with each step. They were in Michelle's childhood bedroom, with the door shut. April tiptoed near the bedroom and cupped her ear to the door.

"I thought he was in for forty-five years," Michelle said. "I don't understand."

"Neither do I," Susie replied. "I got this letter that says he was released yesterday."

"Is there anything that we can do?"

"I doubt it. It's done. Now Becky and I have to go through it all over again. I can't believe this is happening. This is *your* fault. *You* let him into our lives."

Michelle's voice was whiny. "It's his fault. Not mine. I had no idea. You know that."

"Do I?"

"I'm not a liar. When have I ever lied?"

"You have a child who looks like Jason."

What the hell does that mean? April thought about the fact that she didn't look like her father.

Chapter 73: Too Many Questions

"Susie was on the rag," Travis said, slouched in the front passenger seat.

April glanced from the road to Travis, frowning. "Don't say that. It's misogynistic."

"Whatever. She was being a total bitch. You seem mad too." He paused. "I mean, you're not a bitch or anything, but you seem a little mad too."

April turned onto Valley View Boulevard. "I heard Susie and my mom arguing." They drove by the Dairy Queen and the Weis Market.

Travis sat up straighter in his seat. "Really? What did they say?"

"I didn't hear the whole argument, but it sounded like some man was released from prison, and Susie's super pissed about it."

"What did he do?"

April glanced from the road to Travis and back again. "I don't know. It must've been something bad though. He was supposed to be in prison for forty-five years, but he got out early for some reason."

"Maybe he's one of Susie's sketchy ex-boyfriends."

"I thought that too, but Susie said it was my mother's fault that this guy was around them. She said something about her and Becky having to go through something again. I got the impression that this guy did something to Becky and Susie. Maybe he was my mother's ex-boyfriend?"

"Why don't you ask your mom?"

April gripped the steering wheel, stopped at a traffic light. "My mother said she wasn't a liar, but then Susie said, 'You have a child who looks like Jason.'"

Travis drew his eyebrows together. "What does that mean?"

"Do you think I look like my dad?"

A horn came from behind them.

April looked up at the green light and pressed on the accelerator. They drove past a Subway and a Burger King.

Travis said, "You look like your mom. I don't get it. Are you saying this Jason person could be your father?"

April swallowed hard. "I don't know. Maybe."

"That can't be right. That would mean your parents have been lying to you, like … your whole life."

"I know."

Travis shook his head. "Damn."

They drove past the cemetery and neared Travis's neighborhood.

"I have to talk to my mom."

Travis pointed to his street. "Can you drop me off at home?"

April switched lanes and slowed the car. "You don't want to come over?"

"You should talk to your mom alone."

April pursed her lips and turned onto Sycamore Street. "I guess I'll call you later then."

"Yeah, cool."

April drove into a small neighborhood of vinyl-sided split levels. She parked in Travis's driveway. "You're not going to that party, are you?"

"Nah. I don't think so." He smirked. "I don't wanna quarantine for two weeks." Travis leaned over and kissed April, slipping his tongue into her mouth. When they separated, he said, "Good luck talking to your mom. I'm sure there's a reason."

"I hope so."

Travis exited the Honda, waving to April, as he walked toward his parents' front door.

April drove home, which was only two miles from Travis's house. She parked along the curb in front of a white colonial with black shutters and a basketball hoop in the driveway. She used to park in the driveway, until Dylan and Lance dented her hood with their basketball.

April exited her car, walked up the driveway and walkway, and entered the front door. Dylan and Lance were playing video football in the living room.

"You suck," Lance said.

Dylan threw his controller. "Whatever. You were lucky."

April stopped at the edge of the living room. "Where's Mom?"

"Don't know," Lance replied.

April went upstairs to the master bedroom. She knocked on the door.

No answer.

April knocked harder.

"Who is it?" Michelle called out.

"It's me," April replied. "I need to talk to you."

There was a long pause. "Come in."

April entered her parents' bedroom. The room was dominated by a king-size bed and framed by dressers and bedside tables. Her mother sat up in bed, her back against the headboard, the covers over her legs.

April approached the bedside. "Are you okay?"

Michelle's eyes were puffy. "I'm fine. What do you need?" April's mother was nearly fifty, but she could pass for thirty-five. She had deep laugh lines and crow's feet, but she also had high cheekbones and a toned body.

"Did something happen with you and Aunt Susie?"

"We're fine. Don't worry."

April sat on the edge of the bed, her head turned to her mother. "I heard you two arguing."

Michelle knitted her brow. "You were eavesdropping?"

"Who's Jason?"

Michelle's face reddened. "He's nobody."

April cocked her head. "I don't think that's true. What did he do to Susie and Becky?"

"What did you hear?"

April narrowed her eyes. "Does it matter? What's this about?"

Michelle shook her head. "This isn't any of your concern. This is between your aunt Susie and me. I really don't want to talk about this anymore."

April took a deep breath. "Is dad really my biological father?"

Michelle's body went rigid. Her eyes bulged. "What? Why would you say something so awful?"

"Is he?"

"Of course he's your biological father. Don't ever let your father hear you talk like that. You'll break his heart."

April chewed on her lower lip.

Michelle reached out and took her daughter's hand. "You must've heard something out of context, which is why you shouldn't be eavesdropping."

April hung her head. "Susie accused you of lying and said, 'You have a child who looks like Jason.' She was talking about me, wasn't she? I don't look like Dad."

Michelle let out a heavy exhalation. "What I'm about to tell you has to stay between us. Okay?"

April raised her gaze and nodded. "Okay."

Michelle hesitated for a moment. "I was married before your father."

April arched her eyebrows, her eyes wide open. "What? Nobody ever told me that."

"It's not a chapter of my life that I'm particularly proud of."

"Why?"

"Well ..." Michelle swallowed hard. "He was convicted of molesting Becky, when she was six."

April was slack-jawed. "Oh my God. That's awful."

Michelle nodded. "Now he's out of prison, and Susie's mad at me because, on some level, she blames me for bringing him around our family." Michelle dipped her head. "If it wasn't for me, that never would've happened to Becky."

"Oh, Mom. That's not your fault."

Michelle raised her head. "Well, I still feel terrible about the whole thing, and there's nothing I can do to fix it. I tried to help Becky, but I didn't do a very good job, I guess."

"You're not a psychologist."

Michelle shook her head again. "I don't think they helped much either."

April's mouth turned down. "Why did Aunt Susie say that I look like him?"

"When all this happened, I separated from Jason, and I got together with your father very quickly. We were high school and college sweethearts. I got pregnant right away. You weren't planned, but we were thrilled to have you. You were this blessing, and I needed a blessing after everything that had happened. When your aunt Susie gets mad at me, she likes to throw that in my face, just to be mean, but it's not true." Michelle leaned toward her daughter, holding her gaze, and still holding her hand. "I'm 100 percent certain that your father is your biological father. Jason has absolutely nothing to do with you, and he never will."

Chapter 74: The Party

April climbed into bed with her phone. She thought about calling Travis, but they'd spoken earlier on the phone, after April had talked to her mother. She sent a text instead.

April: Thank you for listening to me earlier. I love you. Good night.

April set her phone on her bedside table and turned off the lamp. She tossed and turned, replaying the conversation she'd had with her mother. It had ended amicably, with her mother answering all her questions, but something still nagged April. *I think she's hiding something.*

Her phone buzzed with a text. April grabbed her phone from the bedside table, expecting a reply from Travis. She glanced at the time on her phone—12:07 a.m.—then checked the text.

Becky: Hey PP. Your bf all over some skank

PP was an abbreviation for April's nickname that Becky had bestowed on her many years ago. A picture was attached to the text, showing Travis with his arm around Kyra, his hand gripping her hip, and his other hand gripping a red Solo cup. Kyra was seventeen, a recent high school graduate, and known as the school slut. April's entire body tensed. She sent a text to Travis.

April: CALL ME NOW!!!

April stared at her phone, her stomach turning, waiting for Travis to call back. After exactly five minutes, she called Travis. Her call went straight to voice mail. She slammed her phone on the bedside table. It might've broken, if it wasn't in a protective case.

She turned on her lamp and climbed out of bed. She threw on a pair of jeans, a bra, and a T-shirt. April grabbed her keys and her purse, slipped on her sneakers, and left her room. The hallway was dark, the house dead quiet. She tiptoed downstairs, out the front door, and across the lawn to her car. Her sneakers got wet from the dew on the grass.

April drove across town to Sylvan Heights, otherwise known as Sylvan Snobs. Travis's best friend, Connor, lived in Sylvan Heights, with the rest of the rich kids and the Loganville elite.

April drove into the neighborhood, driving faster than normal. McMansions sat on half-acre lots with four-car garages and hilly lawns. April followed the winding road past the sleepy houses. A deer bounded into the street, illuminated by her headlights. April slammed on the brakes, skidding to a halt, narrowly missing the animal. The doe bolted across the road. followed by three of her buddies. April sat in her car, catching her breath for a minute.

She resumed her trip, following the curvy road to the back of the neighborhood. Connor's parents' house was the last house on the dead-end street. The Tudor-styled home backed up to state game lands. Connor's mother was a professor, and his father was a novelist. They often traveled, leaving their nineteen-year-old to his own devices.

Two dozen cars were parked in the driveway and along the curb in front of the house, including Becky's yellow Corvette. Music came from the house but not loud enough to disturb the neighbors. April parked her car along the curb. She put on her surgical mask and slipped her little bottle of hand sanitizer in her pocket.

Then she walked up to the house. A couple, who she recognized but didn't know, argued in the driveway. April walked by them, taking a wide berth. She eyed the front doorknob, thinking about all the hands that had touched it. She took a deep breath, turned the doorknob, and stepped inside, without knocking.

A techno beat came from the basement. The pitched foyer had exposed beams and wood floors in a herringbone pattern. April squirted hand sanitizer in her hands and rubbed them together. She walked beyond the foyer, into the dimly lit living room, scanning the area for Travis. Couples made out on the couches, but she didn't see Travis. She was the only person wearing a mask. She did see a few people she knew, but she didn't want to interrupt.

April turned and followed the techno beat to the basement. The *thump* of bass and the hooting and cheering of boys increased, as she descended the steps. The basement was decorated like a ski lodge, with dark wood, dark leather furniture, and exposed beams overhead. A wet bar, displaying a wide array of alcohol, sat at the far end of the basement. The boys stood in front of the sectional couch in a circle, cheering and whistling. April approached the crowd. She stood on the leather couch to see over the crowd.

Becky gyrated to the techno beat, standing on impossibly high heels, and not wearing a stitch of clothing. She was thin and blond, with fake breasts. The boys threw money at her. April wondered if that was what boys wanted. Becky bent over and the crowd went wild. April gawked, unable to look away, like it was a bad accident. Becky slowly stood, biting her lower lip, and giving a good show. As she stood upright, she locked eyes with April.

April dipped her head, not wanting to see anymore. She turned, climbed over the back of the couch, and ran up the stairs, back to the living room. April walked into the kitchen, catching her breath. A group of boys huddled around a keg, chugging beer from red Solo cups. A group of girls sat at the counter, chatting and nursing their drinks.

She recognized three of the girls from high school.

April approached them. "Hey. Have you seen Travis Redner?"

A raven-haired girl with clusters of bracelets and a low-cut shirt smirked at April. "What?"

April pulled down her mask, hoping she was a safe-enough distance away from them. "Have you seen Travis Redner?"

"I think he's upstairs."

"Thanks." April pulled up her mask. When April turned to go upstairs, the group of girls burst into laughter.

She climbed the stairs to the second-floor hallway and bedrooms. She crept down the hallway. Doors on either side of her were shut. Giggles came from one room. Moans and a squeaky mattress came from another. A bathroom door was open and unoccupied. At the end of the hall, the door to the master bedroom was shut. She raised her hand to knock.

A door opened behind her.

April turned to see Kyra, exiting one of the guest bedrooms. Kyra turned her head back to the room and said, "I'll be right back."

Kyra was short and voluptuous, with auburn hair to her shoulders. She wore short shorts, a T-shirt without a bra, and no shoes. Kyra turned and walked down the hall toward the bathroom and April. Kyra squinted at April but didn't recognize her with the mask. Kyra went into the bathroom, shutting the door behind her.

April went to the open guest bedroom. The bedside lamp provided dim light. Travis lay on the bed, the comforter covering his lower half, his upper body bare, and his hands behind his head. Travis recognized April, his eyes bulging in shock. He inhaled sharply and sat up.

April pointed at her boyfriend, her finger jabbing with each syllable, and her vision blurry from her tears. "You're a piece of shit. I never want to see you again." April ran from the bedroom.

Travis called to her back. "April, wait."

April ran down the stairs, with heavy steps behind her. She ran through the living room to the foyer and out the front door.

"April, wait," Travis called out.

April stopped and turned, standing on the front walkway. Travis walked toward her, wearing jeans and nothing else.

April held out her hand like a stop sign, glaring at her boyfriend. "Don't come near me. You might have COVID or fucking herpes."

Travis stopped about six feet away, showing his palms. "It's not what you think. I drank too much, and I went upstairs to take a nap. Kyra came in my room by accident."

April sniffled and wiped her eyes with her T-shirt. "I don't believe you."

"I swear to God. Nothing happened." He stepped closer, but April backed up.

"Don't come near me."

"Please. I swear I didn't do anything."

"I know what I saw. She wasn't wearing a bra."

Travis ran his hand over his face. "Let me explain."

The front door opened, and Kyra appeared behind Travis.

Travis continued to plead his case, unaware of his audience. "Kyra was hitting on me all night. She got in bed with me, but I told her no. She's not even that pretty."

"Asshole!" Kyra said, her arms crossed over her chest.

Travis turned around. "Wait, Kyra. That's not what I meant."

Kyra stomped inside, and Travis chased after her, leaving April on the front walkway alone. Becky appeared, wearing a short dress and high heels, the glitter on her face catching the light from the house. She sauntered toward April, vaping marijuana concentrate.

April backpedaled on the walkway, keeping her distance from the marijuana vapor. She showed her palms. "We shouldn't get too close."

Becky stopped and laughed. "Damn, Princess Perfect. You really are freaked about the 'rona, huh?"

"I don't want to give it to my parents or our grandparents."

Becky nodded and put her vape pen to her mouth, inhaling. Then she turned her head, exhaling a cloud of marijuana-laced vaper away from April. "What happened with Travis?"

April shook her head, tears filling her eyes again.

Becky put her empty hand on her hip. "He's a little douche. You're too good for him anyway. Don't cry over him. He's not worth it."

April wiped her eyes. "You're right." April forced a smile under her mask. "Thanks, Becky."

Becky winked. "Anytime, Princess Perfect. I should get back to work."

"Can I ask you something?"

"Yeah."

April hesitated for a beat. "Did you know that my mom was married before?"

Becky tilted her head. "What did you say?"

April took a step back and pulled down her mask. "Did you know that my mom was married before?"

Becky narrowed her eyes. "I guess you heard Jason's getting out of prison."

April nodded. "Your mom is really mad at my mom."

"Susie lost her shit when she found out." Becky took another hit from her vape pen.

"What about you? Are you okay?"

Becky shrugged; her mouth turned down. "It doesn't matter."

April chewed on her bottom lip. "Your mom said I look like him, and she insinuated that he's my father. My mom said that's not true, but ..."

"But what?"

April frowned. "I think there's a lot I don't know."

Becky took another hit from her vape pen. With vapor still spilling from her mouth, she said, "You might be right."

"Is he my father?"

Becky stared at April, as if deciding whether or not April was ready. "I don't know."

"Do you know what he did?"

Becky nodded, her gaze downcast.

"Did he do something to you?"

Becky raised her gaze. "Yeah. He did. Sometimes I think he's still doing it."

Chapter 75: The Morning After

Sunlight slipped between the blinds, warming April's face. A knock came at her door. Her eyes fluttered and opened. She grasped for her phone, knocking it off her bedside table.

Another knock came. "April? Are you okay?" Michelle called out through the door.

"I'm fine," April replied, her voice raspy.

"Can I come in?"

"Yes." April reached over the edge of her bed, grabbing her phone.

Michelle opened the door and walked to the bedside. April checked her texts, hoping to see an apology from Travis. Nothing. She slapped her phone on the bedside table and lay on her back.

Michelle squinted, searching April's face. "It's almost noon. Are you sick?"

April sat up, her comforter still covering her lower half. "I couldn't sleep last night."

Michelle sat on the edge of her daughter's bed. "How come?"

April swallowed hard. "Travis and I broke up." She grimaced. "Actually, he didn't even have the common courtesy to break up with me. He went running after his *new* girlfriend."

Michelle took April's hand in hers. "I'm so sorry, sweetie. Is there something I can do?"

April shook her head. Tears welled in her eyes.

Michelle leaned forward and hugged her daughter. April sobbed, her face buried in her mother's shoulder. Michelle rocked her daughter, rubbing her back.

After a long moment, they separated. April sniffled. Michelle grabbed the box of tissues from the bedside table and handed it to her daughter. April took three tissues and wiped her face.

April eyed her mother and asked, "Have you ever been cheated on?"

"Yes."

April's eyes widened. "Dad?"

Michelle broke eye contact for a split second. "No."

"Jason?"

"It doesn't matter. I know how you feel. It'll pass. You'll meet someone wonderful, who treats you the way you deserve to be treated."

April pulled her knees to her chest. "You think so?"

"I know so."

April forced a small smile.

"You must be hungry. Would you like some lunch? I could make breakfast for lunch. Blueberry pancakes? We have fresh blueberries."

"I love you, Mom."

Michelle beamed. "I love you too, sweetie." She stood from the bed. "I'll call you when brunch is ready."

"Can I ask you something about Jason?" April asked.

Michelle's body stiffened. Her smile evaporated. "I'd rather not talk about him."

"I know. It's just ..." April pursed her lips. "What did he do before he was arrested? What was his job?"

Michelle exhaled and replied, "He was in finance."

"Is that where Susie and Becky got all their money?"

Michelle nodded. "There was a civil trial and a settlement, after he was convicted and sent to prison."

"How much money did they get?"

Michelle scowled. "Not enough for what he did. Please let this go. It was a terrible time for everyone. I'd rather not revisit it." Michelle left April's bedroom.

April sat on her bed, thinking about her mother's reluctance to talk about Jason. This only fueled her curiosity. April grabbed her phone and sent a text to her aunt Susie.

April: I need to talk to you. Can I come over?

Chapter 76: Creep

After brunch, April drove to Sylvan Heights, the same fancy neighborhood where she had found Travis the night before. Aunt Susie's brick McMansion was built into the hillside. April drove up her driveway—which wrapped around the back of the house—parking in front of her three-car garage. April grabbed her hand sanitizer, put on her mask, and exited her car. The oaks provided a dappled shade, muting the summer sun.

April went to the back door and knocked. A minute later, Susie's face appeared in the sidelight window.

Susie opened the back door, wearing yoga pants and a tank top. "Come on in."

April stepped inside, the back door opening to the kitchen. A pile of unread mail sat on the kitchen counter. Unwashed dishes packed the sink. The smell of cigarettes hung in the air. Talk-show television blared from the living room.

Susie stared at April for a beat. "You don't need to wear that thing. I was around you yesterday."

April pulled down her mask. "I know. I'm just trying to be careful."

Susie went to the fridge, inspecting the contents. "You want something to drink? I have some orange juice and milk." She picked up the milk carton, inspecting the date. "I think the milk's bad." She put it back in the fridge and turned to April. "I have beer and wine too."

April showed her palms. "I'm not thirsty."

Susie shut the fridge and walked toward April. Susie used to be prettier than April's mother, but smoking had given Susie wrinkles, especially around her mouth. Drinking had made her puffy and her skin splotchy. Susie gestured to the kitchen table. "Have a seat."

April sat at the round table.

Susie sat across from her. She picked up the open pack of cigarettes, retrieving a single cigarette. "What's this about?"

April took a deep breath. "I heard about Jason."

Susie grabbed the lighter from the table, flicking it several times, her hand unsteady, before finally lighting her cigarette. She inhaled deeply, turned her head, and blew the smoke away from April. "What about him?"

April hesitated. "Is he … my biological father?"

Susie arched her eyebrows. "What makes you think that?" Susie took another drag from her cigarette.

"I heard you say that I look like him."

Susie glared at April. "You were listening to my conversation with your mother?"

April dipped her head. "I'm sorry."

Susie tapped ash from her cigarette into the ashtray. "Did you ask your mother?"

April raised her gaze. "She said he's not my biological father."

Susie took a drag from her cigarette, exhaling the smoke away from April again. "She's right. He isn't."

"Then why did you say I look like him?"

Susie shrugged. "I don't know. I guess I was mad at your mom." Susie tapped more ash into the ashtray. "Sometimes your mother acts like she's perfect, and I'm the fuckup in the family. There was a little overlap between Jason and your father. I was just reminding her that she's not always perfect."

April furrowed her brow. "What do you mean by overlap? Was my mom still married to Jason when she got together with my father?"

"You'll have to ask your mother about that but don't bring my name into it."

April nodded. "Did you know Jason?"

"Yes." Susie took another drag from her cigarette.

"What was he like?"

Susie crushed her cigarette in the ashtray, smoke spewing from her mouth. "He's a fucking creep. That's all you need to know."

Chapter 77: More to the Story

After visiting with Aunt Susie, April returned to her bedroom and sat at her desk. She opened her laptop and waited for her computer to load. While she waited, she glanced at the picture of her and Travis, smiling, their arms around each other. She opened the frame, removed the picture, balled it up, and tossed it in the trash can. The icons appeared on her computer. She double-clicked the Google icon and typed Loganville Pennsylvania child molester Jason 2000 into the search bar. She was guessing on the date, based on what her mother had said about the timing of her relationship with Jason and her father, using her likely conception date as an estimate.

A slew of articles appeared, featuring child molester cases from Pennsylvania. The most prevalent articles featured a story from 2016 when the Pennsylvania attorney general announced that a statewide grand jury had determined that at least fifty "predator priests" had been involved in sexual abuses of hundreds of children.

April scanned ten pages of molestation articles, but none of them featured a Jason in Loganville from 1999 or 2000, and the farther down in the search she ventured, the less relevant the articles became.

April went back to Google and typed *how to find old newspaper articles*. One of the suggestions she found was to go to the local library. So, she grabbed her keys and her purse, left her house, and drove to the Loganville Public Library.

The library was a two-story square building with a flat roof. If not for the windows and stone on the first floor, the metal building resembled a warehouse. April parked in the mostly empty lot, put on her mask, and slipped her hand sanitizer in her pocket. She walked across the hot macadam to the front door. She entered the library, immediately sanitizing her hands after touching the door. Despite the industrial exterior, the interior was inviting, with neatly arranged bookshelves, cushy couches, and local art decorating the walls.

April approached the front desk.

A female librarian, wearing a mask, asked, "Can I help you?"

"I'm looking for information about a child molestation case in Loganville from late 1999 or early 2000," April said.

"Do you know the name of the defendant?"

"Only his first name. Jason."

"That'll be tough. The internet was still pretty young then. Unless it was a case that had nationwide coverage, it's probably not something you can simply search on Google or Bing or even the Library of Congress's searchable database."

April frowned. "What about going to the courthouse?"

"You could try that, but I'm nearly certain you'll need more information than you have to obtain the court records. We do keep a paper archive of the *Loganville Times* from that time frame. It might be time-consuming, but you could search through the papers."

April nodded. "I'll try that. Could you show me where they are?"

The librarian led April upstairs to the newspaper section. Physical newspapers were stacked and arranged on shelves by publication and date. The librarian showed April the *Loganville Times* from 1999 through 2000.

Based on what her mother and her aunt had said, April believed that Jason and her mother broke up because Jason had molested Becky. Shortly after or even before they broke up, her mother had gotten together with her father. April was born on September 18, 2000. April had used a conception date calculator to figure out she was likely conceived around Christmastime 1999, which made sense because the family would've been together, and Jason would've had access to Becky during that time. If the crime happened then, April figured the trial had to be at least a few months after that. So, she started her search in February of 2000.

April searched for several hours, scouring the daily paper for articles relating to sexual assault or child abuse or molestation or rape. If she saw any headlines that resembled what she was searching for, she read the first sentence or two to rule it out. When she hit April Fool's Day of 2000, she gaped at the headline on the front page.

Child Rapist Found Guilty
By: Harold Swanson
Saturday, April 1, 2000

After a brief deliberation by jurors, Jason Lewis of Villanova, PA, has been found guilty of two counts of involuntary deviate sexual intercourse with a child and two counts of aggravated indecent assault of a child. According to the Loganville County District Attorney's Office he will serve up to 120 years in a state correctional institution.

District Attorney Greg Elliot said, "The only way to keep our children safe from Jason Lewis is to put him in prison for life. The jury did their part today. Now it's up to Judge Ames to finish the job."

Defense Attorney Norman Tuttle said, "I'm disappointed by the verdict. The physical evidence was likely contaminated, and Mr. Lewis has no prior arrests. It's a grave miscarriage of justice. I hope that Judge Ames will consider the facts of the case at sentencing."

Sentencing is scheduled for Monday morning, April 3rd.

The article was accompanied by a mugshot of Jason Lewis, scowling for the camera. April stared at the image, searching his dark eyes for clues. She did look a little like him, but it certainly wasn't definitive. They shared the same hair color, and the shape of their noses were similar, except his was pointier. April actually looked more like her mother than Jason Lewis.

April removed her phone from her purse. She went to Google and typed *Jason Lewis Child Rapist Villanova PA*. She tapped on the top article in the search. It was from three days ago.

Villanova Man Freed Amid Prison Scandal
By: Rod Melville
July 2, 2020

A Villanova man who had been convicted in 2001 for voluntary manslaughter had his conviction overturned by a judge.

Jason Lewis, 56, had been incarcerated at The State Correctional Institution at Mill Creek in 2000 for involuntary deviate sexual intercourse with a child and aggravated indecent assault of a child. In 2001, during an altercation with three inmates, Lewis stabbed two of the inmates. Duane Griffith died from the stabbing. Mr. Lewis was subsequently convicted of voluntary manslaughter and twenty-five years were added to his existing twenty-year sentence.

Seventeen years after the stabbing case, former prison guard Charles Wolfe, 50, met with Jason Lewis at Mill Creek. Mr. Wolfe admitted that he witnessed fellow guard, Damon McCloud, 48, facilitate and allow the attack against Mr. Lewis, which led to the death of Duane Griffith. Mr. Wolfe offered to testify on Jason Lewis's behalf. With new evidence, Mr. Lewis enlisted help from the Innocence Project.

Despite the new evidence, the appeal was denied. The dedicated lawyers and law students at the Innocence Project continued to work on Jason Lewis's behalf.

Almost two years later, they had an unlikely break in the case. Braylon Samuels, the inmate who had also been stabbed by Mr. Lewis but survived, recanted his original story, which painted Jason Lewis as the aggressor. Mr. Samuels admitted that he and his two fellow inmates had initiated the altercation with Jason Lewis. He admitted that Mr. Lewis likely feared for his life and acted in self-defense. Mr. Samuels also corroborated the accusations made by former prison guard Charles Wolfe.

After Mr. Samuels came forward, over one hundred inmates made formal complaints of abuse and impropriety suffered at the hands of Damon McCloud.

With the additional evidence, Judge Cummins overturned Jason Lewis's involuntary manslaughter conviction. Mr.

Lewis had recently completed his original twenty-year sentence. Consequently, he is due to be released from The State Correctional Institution at Mill Creek tomorrow, July 3, 2020.

Damon McCloud's employment at The State Correctional Institution at Mill Creek has been terminated. He is currently under investigation.

Chapter 78: Faded Memories

The next morning April sat at her desk, thinking about her mother's reaction, when April had asked if her father had cheated on her. *She said no, but she looked away. Then, when I asked if it was Jason who had cheated on her, she said that it didn't matter. If it was Jason, why wouldn't she say so? She hates him. If it was some other boyfriend, why not say that?* April grabbed her phone and typed a text to Becky with her thumbs.

April: Did my father ever cheat on my mother?

A knock came at her bedroom door.

April swiveled in her desk chair to face the door. "Come in."

Her father entered the room, wearing his Loganville Township Police uniform. His short sleeves barely contained his muscular biceps. He was clean-shaven, with a crew cut. His brown hair was mixed with gray. "Hey."

"Hi, Dad. What's up?"

He walked toward April, stopping a few feet away. "I heard about Travis, and I wanted to see how you're doing."

April shrugged. "I'm okay."

He wrung his hands. "You're better off, if you ask me. Once a cheater, always a cheater."

April narrowed her eyes at his hands. "I know."

"Well, I should get to work." He leaned over and kissed his daughter on the crown of her head.

April forced a smile. "Have a good day, Dad. Be safe."

He smiled back. "Thanks. Love you."

"I love you too."

Danny left her bedroom, shutting the door behind him. Her phone buzzed with a text. April grabbed her phone, thinking it was from Becky.

Travis: I'm sorry about what happened. It was nothing. I swear.

I don't love Kyra. I love you. Text me back. PLS

April thought about her father's comment. *Once a cheater always a cheater. Was he speaking from experience?* April blocked Travis from her phone. Then she tried calling Becky, but her call went straight to voice mail.

April grabbed her keys and her purse and left her house. Outside on the driveway, her brothers played one-on-one. Neither boy wore a shirt. They both had mild sunburns on their shoulders.

As April walked past, Dylan stopped dribbling and said, "Hey, April."

April turned to her brother.

Dylan mimed passing the basketball to April, causing her to flinch.

Dylan and Lance laughed.

"I owe you two for flinching," Lance said.

"Shut up," April replied, with a scowl.

April drove a few miles down the road to Becky's neighborhood. Pleasant Hills was an upper-middle-class neighborhood of colonials, ramblers, and Cape Cods on quarter-acre lots. Many houses had Trump 2020 yard signs. Biden signs were less common. A teen boy pushed a lawn mower in front of a redbrick rambler, but nobody else was outside. She parked along the curb in front of Becky's Cape Cod. The house had gray siding, dormer windows, and white columns holding up the front porch. April remembered when Becky bought the house. She was only eighteen years old, but Aunt Susie and Becky couldn't live together anymore. They fought like cats and dogs.

Becky's lawn was overgrown, and her flower beds were filled with weeds, which wasn't uncommon. Three cars were in the driveway, which also wasn't uncommon. April put on her mask, grabbed her hand sanitizer, and walked to the front door. She pressed the doorbell.

A minute later, a shirtless man opened the door. His hair and beard were disheveled. He leered at April and pumped his eyebrows. "Are you a dancer?"

"Becky's my cousin. Is she here?"

He grinned, blocking the doorway. "Yeah, she's here. You gotta pay the cover to get in."

April frowned. "Would you move please?"

He tapped his lips. "One kiss. You can keep the mask on, if you let me grab your ass."

April put her hands on her hips. "If you won't let me see my cousin, I'll have to assume that you did something to her." She removed her phone from her back pocket.

He narrowed his eyes. "What are you doing?"

"Calling my dad. He's a police officer."

The man stepped aside. "I was just kidding. *Damn.* You don't have to be such a bitch."

April replaced her phone in the back pocket of her shorts. She stalked past the man without a word.

"She's in her bedroom," the man called out to April's back.

The house smelled like marijuana. The television was audible from the living room down the hall. The kitchen was a mess, not unlike Susie's house. Mail was strewn about the counter. A few of the envelopes were adorned with red lettering that read PAST DUE.

She walked past the kitchen and dining area to the stairs. April climbed the carpeted staircase to the second floor. Snoring came from one of the guest bedrooms. The door was open. April peeked inside. Three bodies were in the bed. Two women were under the covers. One man lay facedown atop the comforter, his hairy butt on full display. The smell of cigarette smoke, sweat, and sex wafted into the hallway. April continued to the end of the hallway, stopping at the double doors to the master bedroom.

April knocked.

"Come in," Becky called out.

April opened one of the double doors and stepped into the master bedroom. The large room was dominated by the king-size bed. Becky sat up in her bed, tapping her phone, still wearing her pajamas.

Becky looked up from her phone and said, "Princess Perfect. You don't give up."

April approached her bedside. "I'm assuming you got my text."

Becky frowned. "Leave it alone."

April held out her hands, like a beggar. "Please, Becky. I feel like everyone's lying to me. I know you—"

"Don't give a fuck?"

"You'll tell me the truth, even if it hurts."

Becky pursed her lips. "You can take off that mask."

"I'm trying to be safe."

Becky rolled her eyes. "You sure you wanna know the truth?"

April nodded. "I'm sure."

Becky sighed. "You know that your parents were together in high school and college, right?"

"Yes."

"They were engaged right after college, then your dad ... cheated on your mom with her best friend."

April winced. "Ouch."

Becky arched her eyebrows. "Told you."

April sat on the edge of the bed, feeling woozy from the bombshell. April turned her head to Becky. "What happened after that?"

"Your mom broke it off and moved to Villanova to work at some school."

"Is that where she met Jason?"

Becky stared through April.

April looked down. "I'm sorry I brought him up."

Becky shook her head. "I've been thinking a lot about him lately. Maybe it's because he's out."

April made eye contact with her cousin again. "Are you afraid of him?"

"No. It's funny. I don't even remember what happened anymore. The only thing I remember about Jason is that I liked him. I remember him playing Ice Cream Shop with me. I had these plastic ice creams and bowls and fake money. You probably played with them too. They're in Grammy's basement."

April nodded.

"I remember giving him the ice cream and him acting like I did something so great. He got my trust and took advantage, but I only remember the good stuff about him." She let out a heavy breath. "How fucked up is that?"

April leaned toward her cousin. "You don't remember when he …"

"Molested me?"

April nodded again.

"I remember pieces of it, but it's not clear. My shrink says it's my mind's way of protecting myself. I used to have this nightmare, where Jason came into my bedroom at night while I was sleeping, put his hands around my throat, and choked me. I would wake up actually choking. It was terrifying."

"You don't have that nightmare anymore?"

"No. That was years ago." Becky hesitated for a moment. "My mom's so freaked about him getting out, but I feel nothing. I know I should feel something, but I feel *nothing*. Sometimes I wish he would come here and choke me to death." Becky chuckled, her eyes still.

April wasn't sure if that was a joke or not.

Chapter 79: The Dirty Secret of the Legal System

April drove home from Becky's, gripping the steering wheel with white knuckles. She thought about her mother lying about her father cheating. *Is she lying about who my father is too?*

April went to her bedroom and opened her laptop. After the icons loaded, she went to Google and typed *how to get court transcripts*. After reading several articles, she realized that the court likely has an audio recording but no transcripts, unless someone had already paid to have the trial transcribed. Either way, it would likely take at least thirty days to obtain the recording or a transcript.

She typed *Norman Tuttle Attorney Loganville* into the search bar. His website appeared as the first search result. Tuttle and Associates. She clicked on the site. On the home page was a smiling group of lawyers, paralegals, and administrative assistants. April checked the address. It was located in downtown Loganville on Sixth Avenue. Then she found the phone number, grabbed her cell, and dialed the number.

A woman answered. "Tuttle and Associates, how may I direct your call?"

"May I speak with Norman Tuttle please?" April asked.

"He's not in at the moment. Would you like his voice mail?"

"Could I set up an appointment to meet with him?"

"Are you a potential client?"

April hesitated for a beat. "Yes."

"I'm sorry. Mr. Tuttle isn't taking any new clients these days, but we have five very good attorneys in this office. If you tell me what this is regarding, I can schedule you a Zoom appointment with the appropriate attorney."

"I'm actually a former client of his—or at least this matter is related to his former client."

"What's your name?"

April hesitated again. "April Gibbs. My mother used to be married to Jason Lewis."

"Could you hold please?"

"Of course." April sat at her desk, her knee bouncing, waiting for the receptionist to return.

Several minutes later, the receptionist said, "He's in tomorrow from ten until three. He's available at 10:30, if you'd like to meet with him via Zoom."

"How much, um, does it cost?"

"Consultations are free. If Mr. Tuttle retains you as a client, he will inform you of his fees."

***

The next day at precisely 10:30 a.m., April sat in front of her laptop and clicked the link for the Zoom appointment with Norman Tuttle. The old attorney had a full head of white hair parted to the side and beady eyes. His face was pulled tight as a drum, multiple face lifts eliminating his wrinkles but making him appear unreal, almost plastic.

"Hello, Ms. Gibbs," he said. "I'm Norman Tuttle. What can I do for you?"

April smiled nervously. "Hello, Mr. Tuttle. I'm April Gibbs." She frowned. "You know that already. Sorry. I'm looking for transcripts or a recording of the trial for Jason Lewis. My mother used to be married to him."

"Your mother ..." Norman placed his fingertip to his temple. "Don't tell me. Let me see if I can remember. Everyone says I forget things, but my mind's like a steel trap. Her name was ... Mandy."

"Michelle."

Norman snapped his fingers. "Close but no cigar."

"Do you have the transcripts from the trial?"

"I'm sure they're in storage. If my memory serves me correct, there was a civil trial after the criminal trial, and we made transcripts for our defense."

Michelle leaned closer to the screen. "Would I be able to borrow them?"

"The courthouse has copies too. You'd have to fill out a form, and it might take a few weeks."

"I looked into getting them from the court, but it might take thirty days."

Norman paused for a second.

April thought Zoom froze.

Then he said, "Why do you want to see the transcripts?"

April tried to think of a lie, but the truth was better. She took a deep breath, then said, "Jason might be my father. I've heard what he did, but I'd like to see for myself."

Norman was slack-jawed for an instant. "Well, I suppose I could let you look at our copies, but I don't think I should let you take them."

"When can I come by?"

"Anytime. I'm here until three."

April smiled again. "Great. I can be there in forty minutes or so."

"I'll have someone bring the files up from storage."

***

April drove into downtown Loganville, past gothic churches, bars, offices, and apartment buildings. She parked in the small lot in front of a five-story office building. April put on her mask, grabbed her hand sanitizer, and walked across the parking lot to the building. Thankfully, it was overcast and cooler than the day before. She wore slacks and a blouse for the occasion, figuring she should dress up for a lawyer's office. She took the elevator to the top floor.

The elevator doors opened. April stepped out and walked to the reception desk. A woman was on the phone, her mask pulled down. April waited a polite distance away.

The receptionist hung up the phone, raised her mask, and asked, "May I help you?"

"I'm April Gibbs. I'm here to see Norman Tuttle."

She nodded. "One moment." She picked up the phone, dialed, and said, "April Gibbs is here to see you." She paused. "Okay. I'll bring her back." The receptionist hung up and stood from her chair. "I'll take you back." The receptionist led April down a hallway with offices on either side. Norman's office was at the end of the hall. The door was open. She gestured to the open door.

April stepped inside Norman's corner office. The furniture was dark wood and black leather. It smelled faintly of old books and cologne. Thick legal texts adorned the floor-to-ceiling bookshelf. He stood from his desk with a grin and no mask. His posture was slightly stooped. He held out his hand to shake. April didn't budge.

Norman glanced at April's mask and retracted his hand. "Sorry. I forgot." He waved and said, "It's nice to meet you in person."

"You too," April replied, smiling under her mask. "Thank you for helping me."

Norman gestured to the round table beyond his desk. A box sat on the table. "Those are the transcripts. They're in order by date. You'll start with the arraignment and then the preliminary hearing."

"What's a preliminary hearing?"

"It's a hearing to determine whether there's enough evidence to require a trial."

April nodded. "Thank you, Mr. Tuttle."

"If you need any help, let me know."

April went to the box and opened the lid. It was filled with file folders and documents, all dated and labeled. She sat at the table, opened the file, and began to read about the arraignment. This file was small. The charges were announced by the judge, and the attorneys argued over bail, but that was about it.

While April read, Norman worked on his laptop.

The preliminary hearing was much more interesting. The file was also ten times as thick. She read about the DNA evidence. Jason's semen was found on the victim's underwear. They never used Becky's name during the hearing. She read her grandmother's testimony. Ruth had found the bloody underwear and asked Becky what had happened. Becky had replied, "A man hurt my pee-pee part."

Norman snored. April looked up from the file. Norman slumped in his chair, sleeping.

April went back to the preliminary hearing. She was shocked by the testimony from Jason's half-sister, Lori Grasso.

District Attorney Greg Elliot had asked her, "How long did you live in the same house with the defendant?"

"Until I was fifteen and he went away to college. So, I guess fifteen years," Lori had replied.

"How much older than you is the defendant?"

"Three years and a few months."

"Did he ever molest you as a child?"

April thought, *Holy shit. He did it before.*

"Objection, Your Honor," Norman Tuttle had said. "This is extremely prejudicial. What Mr. Lewis allegedly did as a minor has no relevancy in this case. This is pure character assassination."

Elliot had said, "It's very relevant, Your Honor. It's the exact same crime. It establishes a prior pattern of deviant behavior."

Judge Ames didn't let Lori Grasso testify further.

Detective Wells had the most heart-wrenching testimony.

Elliot had asked Detective Wells, "Did the victim identify the defendant as the perpetrator?"

"Yes, she did," Wells had replied.

"What exactly did she say? If you can't remember, I'm sure Judge Ames will let you borrow the transcript."

"I remember. I asked her who hurt her private part. She said, 'Jason,' without hesitation."

"Did you ask her what he did specifically?"

"Yes, I did."

"What was her response?"

"At the time we were using dolls to identify where she was hurt. She said, 'He poked me with his finger.' When she said that, she pointed to the doll's crotch area. She also said, 'He made me put my mouth on it.' The victim demonstrated oral sex by placing the crotch of the boy doll on the girl doll's face."

April hung her head. Tears slipped down her cheeks. She sniffled and wiped her eyes with the sleeve of her blouse. Her ears hurt from wearing her mask.

Norman's phone chimed. He awoke from his slumber and turned off the alarm. He rubbed his eyes and gazed at April from his desk. "Are you all right, dear?"

"I'm fine," April replied.

Norman stood with a groan, stretching out his arms. "It's about time for me to go home. You can come back tomorrow at ten, if you like."

"Thank you." April stood from her seat and glanced at the clock on the wall. She'd been there for almost three hours. She placed the file back in the box. It was tight, so she tried to push the files back to make room, but something at the other end was blocking the files. She turned the box around to get a better view. A stack of ten CDs banded together was on the bottom of the box. She removed the stack and showed them to Norman. "What are these?"

"That's the audio."

"Could I borrow them?"

Norman stretched out his arms. "I suppose so. I forgot they were in there."

April shouldered her purse and grabbed the stack of CDs. "Do you think Jason was guilty?"

Norman stared at April, his thin lips pressed together for an instant. "No."

"Then why was he convicted?"

Norman shook his head. "It's the dirty secret of our legal system. Sometimes innocent people go to prison." He rubbed his eyes, then blinked rapidly, his tired eyes settling on April again. "I've been practicing law for fifty-five years, and I'm usually right about juries, but I was wrong on that one. I always wondered if there was jury tampering."

April tilted her head. "What's jury tampering?"

"It's when someone tries to influence the jury outside of the court proceeding."

"And you think someone did that?"

"I don't know. I never found any proof of that, but ..." Norman exhaled. "In the preliminary hearing Jason's half-sister claimed that he molested her. She didn't say those words exactly, but she said enough."

April nodded. "I read that in the file."

"Then you know I was able to eliminate her as a witness on the grounds that her testimony was prejudicial, but I always wondered if she contacted a juror, or maybe somebody who was in the audience that day contacted a juror. It is a small town."

Chapter 80: Everyone's Hiding Something

April had spent Tuesday night and Wednesday morning listening to Jason's criminal trial and taking notes, breaking only for a five-hour sleep. She'd had to use an old laptop with a CD player to listen to the audio of the trial. She'd spent almost twelve hours listening at 2x speed, slowing it down in places, and skipping forward at other places.

She sat up in her bed, listening to the guilty verdict, and the cheering from the court audience. April stopped the CD and removed her headphones. She imagined that she was on the jury. Objectively, she thought Norman Tuttle proved reasonable doubt. *But, if I factor in Jason's molestation of his half sister, I would probably convict too.* April tapped her lips, thinking. *The most important piece of evidence was the semen found on Becky's underwear. Norman thought it was contaminated by Jason's condom in the trash.*

April sucked in a breath, realizing that, in her focus on the case and her tired mind, she'd overlooked something very important. *My mother was having sex with Jason at Christmas, the same time I was conceived. They did use a condom, but condoms aren't 100 percent. Was she sleeping with Jason and my father at the same time?* April rubbed her temples, her head hurting from lack of sleep.

April stood from her bed and changed from her pajamas to a pair of shorts and a T-shirt. She put her hair into a ponytail, grabbed her keys and purse, and walked downstairs. Her mother was in the kitchen, chopping vegetables.

Michelle looked up from the cutting board. "Where are you going?"

April hesitated. "Grammy's."

Michelle was a teacher and off for the summer. Ruth was a retired teacher and off forever.

Michelle arched her eyebrows and set down her knife. "Any special reason for the visit?"

"I just wanted to see how she's doing."

Michelle smiled. "Well, that's sweet of you. I'm sure she'll be thrilled to see you. Lunch should be ready soon, if you'd like to eat before you go. We're having grilled chicken salads."

"I'll eat when I get back."

"Okay, sweetie."

April left the house, slipping past her video-game-playing brothers. She started her car and powered down the window, letting out the heat. She lowered her sun visor and drove the short distance to her grandmother's house. April parked in the driveway, next to Grandpap's trailered fishing boat. Grandpap's pickup truck was gone. Ruth was in the front yard, kneeling on a pad in the front flower beds, planting red begonias. April exited her car and approached Ruth.

Ruth turned from her work and smiled. She stuck her garden trowel into the loose soil, stood from the pad, and wiped her bare knees. "This is a pleasant surprise."

"Hi, Grammy." April hugged her grandmother.

When they separated, Ruth asked, "What brings you over here?"

"I, *um*, ... I wanted to ask you about the Jason Lewis trial."

Ruth scowled. "I, I don't want to talk about that."

"But Grammy—"

"Absolutely not!"

April flinched.

Ruth trembled with rage. "You don't know what that man did to this family. I won't waste another second of my life on him. If that's all you came here for, then you can leave."

"Fine." April turned and stalked away. She entered her Civic, backed out of the driveway, and drove away. As she left the scene, she saw Ruth back on her knees, stabbing the soil with her garden trowel. April drove home, thinking, *They're all hiding something.*

April parked in front of her house and went back inside. She walked past her brothers in the living room. Machine gun fire and explosions came from the first-person shooter game.

Dylan turned from the video game to April. "Who peed in your corn flakes?"

Lance continued to play, unfazed.

April glared at her brother but said nothing. She walked into the kitchen, following the smell of grilling chicken.

Michelle turned from the stovetop, a spatula in hand, chicken strips sizzling in the frying pan. "That was quick. Lunch is almost ready."

"Can you put my salad in the fridge? I'm not hungry."

Michelle narrowed her eyes. "Are you okay? Did something happen at Grammy's?"

"No. She's busy gardening, and it's hot, so I came home."

"Okay, sweetie. I'll put your lunch in the fridge."

April went to her bedroom and shut the door behind her. She set her purse and keys on her dresser and sat at her desk. She opened her laptop, waiting for the icons to load. When they did, she clicked on Google and typed *background check* into the search bar. Then she clicked on PublicRecords.com. *If I want the truth, maybe I need to go to the source.*

The headline on the home page read Background Checks. Underneath were three information cells. They were labeled First Name, Last Name, and Where to Search. April typed *Jason Lewis.* Where to Search was a drop-down menu of states, so she selected Pennsylvania and clicked the big orange button that read Search Now.

Another window opened, and headshots appeared in a little box, flashing so quickly that you couldn't see the pictures clearly. A green bar was at the top of the screen, growing in size, with a percentage attached to it. As it grew, the percentage grew, marking the search progress. A question appeared on the screen, asking for Jason's age. You could check unsure, but April knew his age from the article she'd read. She typed *56*. Then she was asked if she knew where he lived. April typed in *Villanova*, thinking that the search might connect his old residence.

When the search concluded, dozens of Jason Lewises were listed, but the most relevant one had lived in Villanova, was fifty-six years old, and had a criminal record. April paid ten bucks with her credit card and received access to the report. She also checked the box to allow email updates, whenever changes occurred to the background check. April's bank account was low, given that she couldn't waitress that summer because of COVID, but she still had some savings.

The report showed several addresses where he'd lived. It showed Michelle Murphy as his ex-wife. His criminal charges were listed. He'd never been arrested prior to the molestation charges. April was disappointed that the report didn't show a current address.

Jason's mother was listed. So was his half sister Lori. Their names were hyperlinks. April clicked on Jason's mother, Barbara Lewis. She purchased the background check. Barbara Lewis was seventy-two years old and lived in Portage, Pennsylvania. She had a long rap sheet of drug offenses, larceny, grand larceny, burglary, and fraud. Lori Grasso was listed as her daughter. April clicked on Lori and purchased her background check too.

April scanned Lori's information. She was divorced from a Tony Grasso and apparently hadn't bothered to change her name back to her maiden name. She had two adult children. Lori also lived in Portage. In fact, she lived on the same street as her mother. Lori's rap sheet was almost as long as her mother's: drugs, fraud, and shoplifting.

April thought about what Norman had said about Lori's testimony possibly being used as jury tampering. April also wondered if it was true. *She doesn't appear to be an honest person. But, why would someone lie about something like that? Jason had money. Maybe they wanted to sue.*

Chapter 81: Family

April drove through the Portage trailer park, slowing for the speed bump. Single-wide and double-wide trailers of various colors dotted both sides of the macadam road. Two boys on bikes pedaled past, going the opposite way. The Allegheny Mountains loomed large and green in the distance, with a cloudless sky overhead. April found trailer number 162. The single-wide trailer had beige siding with maroon shutters and skirting to cover the bottom of the trailer.

April parked along the road, not wanting to block the tiny empty driveway. She checked her phone—*4:12 p.m.* April knew from the background check she'd purchased the day before that Lori Grasso worked for Larry's Landscaping. So, April figured she'd try to catch her after work.

While she waited, she thumb-typed a text to her grandpap.

> **April**: It's been a while since we went fishing. What do you think about going to the lake?

A knock came at April's window, startling her. A short chubby woman with gray hair and a saggy face stood with her hands on her hips. April put on her mask and powered down her window.

"You can't park here," the woman said.

"I was just waiting for Lori Grasso, and I didn't want to park in her driveway," April replied.

The old woman narrowed her blue eyes. "Who the hell are you?"

April drew her eyebrows together. "Who are you?"

"I'm Barb. Lori's mother." She moved her head side to side, as she announced her position of authority in Lori's life. "Now, who are *you*?"

April pursed her lips. "I'm April. I might be Jason Lewis's daughter."

Barb was wide-eyed and slack-jawed. "How the hell do you know that?"

"I don't know for sure."

She inspected April, bending at the waist, so her face was in the open window. "Lemme see your face."

April pulled down her mask.

Barb squinted at April, her hot breath wafting into April's mouth and nose. "You do look a little like him."

April raised her mask.

"That would make you my granddaughter." Barb smirked. "What do ya think a that?"

"Well, I don't know if he's my father yet."

Barb stood upright. "What do you want with Lori?"

April felt trapped in her car, with Barb blocking her door and standing over her. "Do you mind if I get out?"

Barb stepped back.

April exited her car, shutting the door behind her. "I wanted to ask Lori some questions about Jason."

Barb crossed her arms over her chest. "What kinda questions?"

"I wanted to ask her about the trial. She was going to testify, but they ruled her testimony was inadmissible. I just wanted to hear what she was planning to say."

Barb raised one side of her mouth in disgust. "I can tell you everything you wanna know."

"What was Jason like?"

"He's a lyin' piece of shit. I raised him right. Gave him everything he needed. Hell, I was a single mom, before it was cool. But, there's somethin' wrong with him. Always has been. When I found out he was touchin' his sister, I stopped it, but the damage was already done."

"How old was he when that happened?"

"Thirteen."

A silver Hyundai puttered toward them. They both glanced back at the car.

"There she is, if you still wanna talk to her," Barb said.

Lori parked her Hyundai in her small driveway. She exited the vehicle, staring at Barb and April. Barb waved her over. Lori walked toward them, her purse over her shoulder. Lori was thin, with a platinum-blonde dye job.

Lori lifted her chin to April. "Who's this?"

Up close, Lori had wrinkles around her lips, likely from smoking, sunken cheeks, and hooded eyes.

"This is April. She might be Jason's daughter. Could be your niece." Barb addressed April. "How old are you?"

"Nineteen," April replied.

"Your mom must've got pregnant right before he went to prison," Barb said.

April nodded. "If he's my father, yes."

Barb addressed Lori again. "She wants to ask you a few questions about Jason."

Lori put her hands on her hips, not unlike the posture Barb had taken, when they first met. "What do you wanna know?"

"Would it be okay if we talked alone?" April asked Lori.

"That's bullshit," Barb said, glowering.

"Anything you say to me, you can say in front of my mother," Lori said.

April wrung her hands. "Okay. *Um*, … You weren't allowed to testify at Jason's trial. What were you planning to say?"

"I was gonna tell the truth. He molested me when we was kids."

"Do you remember how old you were?"

"You were ten when I found out about it," Barb interjected. "He was thirteen."

Lori looked to Barb, then back to April. "I don't remember the exact age, but, if my mom says I was ten, I was ten."

"This might be too sensitive. If you don't want to answer, I understand—"

"Spit it out," Lori said.

April took a deep breath. "Do you remember exactly what happened with the molestation? What did he do?"

Lori's jaw tensed. She pointed at April. "Who the fuck do you think you are? You don't fuckin' know me. All up in my business."

April drew back and showed her palms. "I'm sorry. I was just trying to find out about Jason."

"He was a fuckin' piece of shit," Barb said. "Still is."

Lori lifted her chin to the road behind April. "I think it's best you get up outta here."

"I'm sorry to have bothered you." April turned, opened her car door, and drove to the end of the street, turning around at the cul-de-sac. As she drove back, she passed Lori and Barb, both of them giving her the evil eye. April thought, *I don't believe them.* Her phone buzzed with a text. Once she was out of their sight, she parked her car along the road and checked her text.

Grandpap: Anytime. I'm always up for fishing.

April: How about tomorrow?

Chapter 82: Fishing for Information

Grandpap Frank killed the outboard motor on his fourteen-foot fishing boat as they coasted near a cove. It was one of Frank's favorite fishing spots. April and Frank knew a ledge was beneath them, where the depth cratered. Fish congregated near these ledges because they offered food, cover, and a variety of water depths. As they slowed to a stop, April tossed the anchor into the lake.

The morning sun reflected off the blue water of Raystown Lake, like tiny starbursts. They were surrounded by the Tussey Mountains and the bright green leaves of the oak forest.

"It's gonna be a beautiful day," Frank said, opening his tackle box. His fishing pole stood upright and secure in a holder on the side of the boat. He grabbed a lure and baited his hook.

April walked wide-legged toward her grandpap, eyeing the lures. "Can I have a worm?"

"Help yourself."

April selected a soft plastic worm and shut the box. She walked back to the opposite side of the boat and baited her hook.

At each end of the aluminum boat, they cast their lines into the depths. They fished in silence for several minutes, casting and reeling, casting and reeling.

April glanced at her grandpap. "Did you ever take Becky fishing?"

Frank cast his line into the lake. "Yep. A few times when she was young."

"Did she like it?" April reeled in her line.

"I think so. It was a long time ago."

"Why did she stop coming?"

Frank gave April a look. "What's with all the questions? You're scaring the fish."

April set her fishing pole in a holder on the side of the boat. "I wanted to ask you about Jason."

Frank frowned. "I should've known. Ruth mentioned you were asking about him. Here I thought we were fishing for bass. Turns out you're fishing for information."

April sat on the bench, facing Frank. "Come on, Grandpap. I feel like everyone's hiding stuff from me. Whatever the truth is, I can handle it. I'm almost twenty."

Frank reeled in his line and set his pole in a holder. He sat on the bench facing April, eight feet away. "These are old but very deep wounds. We have to tread lightly. You understand?"

"Yes."

He paused for a second. "What do you wanna know?"

"What was he like?"

Frank exhaled, his shoulders slumped. "Strange. Quiet. Didn't interact much with adults. He liked to spend time with Becky more than the adults." Frank clenched his jaw. "I should've known back then."

"I listened to most of the trial."

Frank knitted his brow. "You what?"

"I got a copy of the trial, and I've been listening to it."

Frank scowled. "What you're doing is gonna hurt this family."

April held out her hands. "Why?"

"Because this was a terrible time in our lives. None of us wanna relive it."

"I need to know the truth. The whole truth."

"You already know the truth. Everything's in the trial."

"That's the problem. The trial wasn't definitive."

Frank shrugged. "The jury disagreed with you on that. They were very definitive. They were unanimous."

April pressed her lips together. "What if mistakes were made?"

"What mistakes?"

"Why didn't Grammy put the underwear in the trash? They were worn out and stained. The trash can was right there. Maybe she forgot that she put the underwear in the trash."

Frank shook his head. "That's not what happened."

"How do you know? You weren't in the bathroom with Grammy."

His face reddened. "*Jesus*, April. You sound like his defense attorney. Becky IDed him. A doctor confirmed the abuse. His DNA was on her underwear. He was alone with her. I've seen many men sent to prison for a lot less."

"But my mom testified that Jason played with Becky a bunch of times and nothing happened. Why would it happen all of the sudden?"

"I don't know. Maybe he was grooming her. Maybe he was waiting for her to reach a certain age. These child predators have specific ages they target."

"But—"

"That's *enough*." Frank glared across the boat at April. "This may seem like a Nancy Drew game to you, but Becky's never been right since and neither has your Aunt Susie. This nearly destroyed our family. Now that you know, I need you to let it go."

April dipped her head, chastened. "I'm sorry. I'm not trying to upset anyone."

Frank's expression softened. "I know you're not. You've always asked so many questions. I remember taking you out here when you were little and you'd talk my ear off. Asking me how fish breathe. What do they eat? How do they have babies? How many types of fish are there? How big do they get? On and on." Frank chuckled.

April smiled. "I remember."

"That's why you're so smart."

"One more question? I promise this is the last one."

Frank sighed. "I can't stop you from asking."

"Is that why Susie never got married?"

"I know it ruined one potential marriage." Frank stood from his seat and grabbed his fishing pole. He cast his line into the lake, no longer making eye contact with his granddaughter.

April stood from her seat and grabbed her fishing pole. "Susie was engaged?"

"Yep. They broke up because Becky needed so much attention. I guess it was too hard to build a marriage, when Becky consumed every last ounce of Susie's energy."

April cast her line into the lake. "Did you like Susie's fiancé?"

"I did. He was a hard worker. He's a successful real estate developer now." Frank's line tugged and the pole bent toward the water. He tugged back, setting the hook and reeling in his catch. "Got one!"

Chapter 83: So It Begins

Over the past two weeks, April had listened to the trial over and over again, becoming an expert on the arguments. She hadn't asked her family about Jason since her fishing excursion with Grandpap Frank. She had thought very seriously about going back to Portage with a DNA test to determine for certain if she was Jason's daughter. She still hadn't decided whether or not to do it.

April sat at her desk, scrolling through pictures of Travis on her phone. She swallowed the lump in her throat. Tears welled in her eyes. Three weeks ago, she had Travis, and she didn't even know Jason Lewis existed. A big part of her wished she'd never found out about Travis cheating *or* Jason's existence.

An email notification appeared on her phone. She tapped the notification, taking her directly to the email.

From: updates@publicrecords.com
To: aprilgibbs2234@gmail.com
Date: July 24, 2020, 10:03 AM
Subject: Update Jason Lewis

You're receiving this email because you elected Public Records to notify you if there were any updates to the following background check:

<u>Jason Lewis</u>

The following update(s) have been made.

<u>Address</u>
Second Chance House
340 Eighth Avenue
Loganville, PA 16666

April sucked in a sharp breath and said to herself, "He's here."

Chapter 84: Second Chances

April drove into downtown Loganville, passing brick and stone row homes used as offices and storefronts. She slowed her Civic as she neared the police station. A crowd of Latinos shouted and held various signs that read Find Rosa, Justice for Rosa, No Justice No Peace, Save our Children, and Racist Police.

As April drove past, she cracked her window, listening to their chant.

"El Diablo está aquí! El Diablo está aquí! El Diablo está aquí!"

April had taken Spanish in high school, and she knew that meant the devil is here.

A few blocks from the police station, April parked along the street, in front of a line of brick row homes. She put on her mask and slipped her hand sanitizer in the front pocket of her jeans. She walked to the brick house at the end of the block. A sign next to the front door read Second Chance House.

She entered. The wood floors creaked under her feet. A wooden staircase and a hallway lay before her. An open room was to her left, down the hall a few steps. A man's voice came from the room. April stepped forward and peered into the room.

A man sat behind a metal desk, talking on his cell phone. He glanced up at April and said, "I'm gonna have to call you back." He paused. "Yeah. Okay. I'll call you back." He disconnected the call and eyed April. "What can I do for you?"

April stepped into the office, stopping a few feet from the man's desk. Metal filing cabinets lined one wall. Motivational posters hung from the walls. They all featured one word, followed by a sentence or two of wisdom. *Success. Renew. Commitment. Excellence. Attitude.* Beautiful images accompanied the words of wisdom: beams of sunlight on a putting green, a raging river, a rocket ship blasting off, a soaring eagle, and a cresting wave.

April said, "I'm here to see Jason Lewis."

He narrowed his eyes. "He's not here at the moment."

"Do you know where he is?"

"I can't give out that information. What is your relationship with Mr. Lewis?"

April hesitated. "I'm a friend. Can I leave him a message?"

He stared at April for a few seconds. "Sure."

April scrawled a short message with her phone number on her notepad, asking Jason to text or call her. She signed her name as Teresa.

Chapter 85: COVID Karen and Broken Becky

April had checked her phone obsessively on Friday, after she'd left a message for Jason, but he never called. She'd thought about whether or not she should tell her family that Jason was living in town. She'd come to the conclusion that they probably already knew, given that her father was a police officer, and, if she did tell, they would be irate that she had located Jason.

On Saturday night, she went to the one person in her family who she could tell without judgment, the person who should know above anyone else. April parked her Civic along the street in front of Becky's Cape Cod. Light came from the windows and the porch lamps, brightening the night. Several cars were parked in the driveway. The *thump* of bass came from the house. April put on her mask and grabbed her hand sanitizer. She walked up the driveway and walkway to the front door.

She entered Becky's house, without knocking. Rap music blasted from the speakers. A large man was in the kitchen, his head in the empty refrigerator. He slammed the door shut. He turned to grab his half-empty beer from the counter, noticing April walking past him.

He lifted his chin, his eyes crawling over April. "What's up?"

April didn't respond. She walked down the hall to the living room, where a dozen or so partiers snorted lines of cocaine off the glass coffee table, or made out in various stages of undress, or gawked at the half-naked women.

Becky snorted a line of cocaine through a short metal straw. She giggled and handed the straw to the young woman sitting on the floor next to her. "Your turn."

April walked around the couch and tapped Becky on the shoulder.

Becky turned, looked up at April, and beamed. "Hey, everyone. This is my cousin, April. She's a bit of a COVID Karen, but I *love* her."

One of the guys said, "What up, April."

Another guy said, "Why don't you take off that mask, so we can see your pretty face?"

April ignored the guys. "I need to talk to you."

Becky gestured to the cocaine. "You wanna party first?"

"Please. I have to tell you something important."

Becky struggled to her feet on high heels. "Big surprise. Princess Perfect doesn't wanna party."

A few boos came from the party crowd.

April frowned and took Becky by the elbow. April led her wobbly, giggling cousin to the office. Becky's "office" was a room with five rolling racks of clothes spanning the length of the room, with enough space between for Becky to browse. April shut the door behind them. Becky used a rack to steady herself. She wore a tight white dress, her nipples showing without a bra.

"Jason's living in Loganville," April said.

Becky laughed. "So what?"

"I thought you'd want to know."

"I don't give a *fuck*." She sang the last word in her statement.

Clearly, April thought. "Why do you think he came back here?"

Becky shrugged. "Don't know. Don't care."

April furrowed her brow. "How can you say that after what he did?"

Becky groaned, her head lolled to the side. "I don't even remember."

"What do you mean, you don't remember? You IDed him. You gave testimony."

Becky shrugged again. "We thought he did it, so he did it."

April drew back. "What does that mean? Who's *we*?"

Becky scowled. "This is bullshit. He did it. It's over. I got bigger shit to deal with now." Becky brushed past April, opening the "office" door.

April turned to face her cousin. "What are you dealing with? Maybe I can help."

Becky turned from the door, one side of her mouth raised in contempt. "You wouldn't understand. You never have. You're so fucking perfect, and I'm so fucking … *broken*." She whispered the last word.

"Try me. I'll try to understand."

Becky swallowed hard. Her eyes were glassy. "I'm gonna lose this house. With COVID, I can't even work. Dancing at private parties isn't enough. I'm gonna lose everything. My car. My house. Everything."

"What about your mom? I'm sure she'd help."

Becky cackled. "My mother doesn't give a shit about me. She got millions from the civil suit. Gave me a fraction of that money, just so I'd leave her house. All of that money should've been mine." Becky shook her head. "My *mother* hasn't worked a fucking day since then. Always blamed it on me. Saying she needed to be home with me, but that was bullshit. She didn't help me. Now, I hear she's broke too."

"I'm sorry, Becky. I didn't know."

"Save it. I don't want your pity. All I have is right now. I plan to enjoy it while I can." She turned and wobbled back to the party.

Chapter 86: Men at Work

On Monday morning, April parked two houses down from the Second Chance House on Eighth Avenue. She watched the brick row house, with a clear view of the front door. The sun barely peeked over the horizon. She perked up each time the door opened, and some man exited.

The third man to leave that day resembled the online pictures she'd seen of Jason Lewis. He was tall and thin and carried a backpack over his shoulder. A little gray mixed with his brown hair. He wore canvas pants, work boots, and a T-shirt. He walked with his head bowed to the bus stop across the street. April tilted her rearview mirror to keep him in sight. At the bus stop, Jason kept his distance from the other people waiting on the bus. He reached into his backpack and retrieved a surgical mask and a book. As he waited, he put on the surgical mask, and he read the book.

Shortly thereafter, a bus rumbled down the street. April started her engine, still watching the bus stop through her rearview mirror. The bus stopped and picked up a handful of people, including Jason. April reversed her Honda from the parking spot and followed the bus across town.

Five minutes later, Jason exited the bus at the edge of the Loganville city limits. The bus turned right and drove away, black smoke billowing behind. April illegally parked at the bus stop, watching Jason. He crossed the highway and walked over a bridge on the sidewalk. April drove over the bridge, passing Jason on the way. She pulled into a Sheetz convenience store, situated just beyond the bridge. She parked, insuring a clear view of the bridge.

April waited for Jason to make it across the bridge. When he did, he kept walking up a steep hill into a residential neighborhood of old single-family homes on small lots, mostly craftsmen, bungalows, and Victorian architecture. April waited until she could barely see him, then she started her car and followed him up the hill. She parked behind him, waiting for him to walk nearly out of view again.

April did this several times until Jason walked into a newer neighborhood of vinyl-sided colonials and ramblers. He had hiked at least three miles. In the back of the community, several houses were under construction. April parked in front of a fully built, but unsold home across the street from the construction site.

Jason entered the construction office trailer. He exited shortly thereafter, without his backpack, wearing leather gloves and a hard hat.

April spent the morning watching Jason carry sheets of particle board to the carpenters. By ten o'clock his shirt was soaked with sweat. All morning, that's all he did, taking only one break to use the porta-potty. At lunch, he sat on a cinderblock by himself and ate sandwiches from his backpack. Fifteen minutes later, he was back to hauling particle board.

The men on the construction site often took breaks to smoke, to drink water, to eat, or to shoot the shit. From what April had seen, Jason hadn't touched a tool and rarely took a break. April had lunch and had used the bathroom at the Sheetz down the road.

In the afternoon April received a text.

Mom: Where are you?

April: I'm fine. I'll be home soon

Mom: Where are you exactly?

April didn't answer her mother's last text, not wanting to lie, knowing that her mother would be upset if she told her the truth.

Two hours later, at four o'clock on the dot, the construction stopped, and the men packed up their tools and left the job in their pickup trucks. Jason grabbed his backpack from the trailer, returned his hard hat, and walked back the way he came. April stared out her windshield, as he walked toward her. He walked slower than he had that morning. His shirt had salt stains from sweating all day.

A ringing bell made April turn away from Jason. A little girl rode her bike up the street, ringing the bell on her handlebars. She appeared to be seven or eight. Her mother jogged behind her wearing spandex shorts and a tank top. April watched Jason's face as the little girl rode her bike past him, followed by the attractive woman. April expected Jason to leer at the little girl or at least glance at her. But he didn't look at either of them. He didn't look at April either, as he walked past her car.

On an impulse, April exited her car and called out to his back, "You need a ride?"

Jason stopped in his tracks and turned around. He forced a smile at April and replied, "No thank you." Then, he turned and kept walking.

April walked after him. "Hey, I was hoping to talk to you."

He stopped and turned around again, his forehead creased. "Do I know you?"

April stopped ten feet away, not wearing her mask. "I'm Teresa. I'm the one who left you a message."

He narrowed his dark eyes. "What's this regarding?"

April had already rehearsed the lie. "I'm a reporter from *The Daily Pennsylvanian*. It's the student-run newspaper at the University of Pennsylvania."

Jason nodded. "I know. I used to go there."

April smiled. "Really? That's great. I'm a sophomore, or I will be if we go back in the fall. Anyway, I wanted to talk to you about your trial back in 2000."

Jason frowned. "I don't have anything to say about that."

"I've listened to the audio recording of your trial several times. I think there are some loose ends."

"No. There aren't."

"Please—"

"No." His body was tense. "You go ahead and write your story. Tell the world what I did. I don't care. But I won't participate. Please leave me alone."

"Why did you come back to Loganville?"

He opened his mouth, but nothing came out.

A siren blared in the distance. Jason turned around, gazing at the oncoming police car, the lights whirling. The car skidded to a halt several feet in front of Jason. He immediately raised his hands over his head.

April's eyes bulged at the sight of her father, as he exited his squad car, wearing a mask, his eyes laser-focused.

Danny removed the billy club from his belt and addressed April. "Are you okay?"

April drew her eyebrows together. "I'm fine."

"Go home, April. *Now.*"

April walked back to her car, still watching over her shoulder.

Danny then pointed his billy club at Jason. "You remember me, you sick fuck?"

Jason stood still, his hands in the air.

April stood next to her car, watching the scene, still within earshot.

"I asked you a *fucking* question," Danny said.

Jason responded, barely above a whisper. "Yes. I remember you."

"Take off that backpack, put your hands on the hood, and spread your legs."

Jason took off his backpack and dropped it on the macadam. He placed his hands on the hood of the police car.

Danny holstered his billy club and kicked Jason's feet apart. Then, Danny patted him down. "Don't move," Danny said. He picked up Jason's backpack, opened it, and dumped the contents on the ground. An empty water bottle, two empty Ziploc bags, gloves, and a paperback book fell to the macadam. The water bottle rolled to the curb. He checked the small pocket, pulling out a surgical mask. Then, Danny threw the empty backpack on the ground and turned to Jason, with one side of his mouth raised in disgust. "If you ever come near my family again, I'll make sure you go back to prison for the rest of your sorry life. You got me?"

Jason nodded.

"I didn't hear you."

"I understand." Jason's voice was unemotional and monotone.

"Now pick up your shit and get the fuck outta here."

Jason bent down and collected his things, placing them back in his backpack.

April had an urge to help Jason collect his things, but she didn't move.

Jason shouldered his backpack and walked away from the scene.

Danny stalked to April. "What the hell were you thinking?"

April scowled at her father. "Why did you do that? He didn't do anything."

Danny's lower jaw jutted forward. His neck vein pulsed. "He didn't? He's a murderer and a child rapist!"

April dipped her head, chastened.

"I know you must be curious about what happened, but you can't talk to him. He's dangerous, and he has nothing but bad intentions coming back here."

April raised her gaze. "How do you know?"

"I know men like him. Trust me."

April didn't respond.

"Text your mother back and tell her that you're coming home now. She's worried sick."

April nodded.

Danny gave April a stern look. "I expect you to go straight home."

Chapter 87: Facing the Music

April drove straight home from the construction site, as her father had demanded. She walked through the front door, bracing herself for her mother's wrath. Dylan and Lance turned from their video game to stare at the dead woman walking.

"Where were you?" Dylan asked.

"Mom's pissed," Lance added. "What did you do?"

"Nothing," April replied, annoyance in her voice. She walked past the living room and into the kitchen. Her mother stood at the center island, texting on her phone.

Michelle looked up from her phone, her face like stone. "We need to have a talk."

April swallowed. "Fine."

"Upstairs."

April trudged upstairs, her mother hot on her heels. April walked into her bedroom, dropping her purse on her dresser. Michelle shut the bedroom door behind them. April slumped into her swivel chair, facing her mother.

Michelle spoke with a hushed fury. "Why are you doing this?"

April chewed on her bottom lip and lifted one shoulder.

Michelle put her hands on her hips. "No. That's not good enough. I told you to let it go, and you deliberately defied me."

"How did Dad know where I was?"

"What difference does it make?"

April glared up at her mother. "Do you have a tracker on my phone or something?"

Michelle let out a heavy breath. "Of course not. We're not the Gestapo. We're your parents. Your dad found out that Jason's in town. I tried texting you, but you were very vague in your response, so we figured you might've gone to see him."

"I'm nineteen. You can't tell me who I can and can't see."

Michelle's face reddened. She turned and paced away from April; then she paced back to her daughter. "I don't understand why you can't get this through your head. He's *dangerous*. He's a murderer and a child rapist."

April narrowed her eyes. "That's not true. He was acquitted of murder. He acted in self-defense. The prison guard set him up."

"*Jesus*, April. Will you listen to yourself? This isn't a game."

"You and Dad and everyone else are treating this like a game. I'm the only one who cares about the truth."

Michelle glowered at her daughter. "You think I don't care about the truth? I stood by Jason until the preliminary hearing. Until I heard the evidence. I almost lost my whole family."

"What if it's all a lie? I listened to the trial."

Michelle put up her hand like a stop sign. "Wait. What? How did you listen to the trial?"

April winced. "I got a copy from Norman Tuttle."

Michelle hung her head and rubbed her temples. When she raised her gaze, her eyes were glassy. "I don't understand why you're intent on digging this up. It caused so much pain."

"I'm sorry, Mom. I don't want to hurt anyone. It's just that Norman Tuttle made a good case that he could be innocent. What if someone else hurt Becky?"

"You think I didn't consider that? Jason was my husband. Believe it or not, I loved him. I wanted it to be someone else more than anyone."

"It could've been a teacher or a coach. Becky played basketball. She must've had male teachers."

"First of all, your grandpap was her basketball coach. Second of all, there was never any evidence of anyone else hurting Becky."

"What about Susie's fiancé? The real estate guy."

"Cody? No way. I've known him since we were kids. So has your father. Cody's DNA wasn't found on Becky's underwear. Becky didn't ID Cody. She IDed Jason." Michelle sat on the edge of April's bed and slumped her shoulders.

April swiveled her chair to the right, facing her mother. "But the DNA could've come from the condom in the trash, and little kids aren't reliable witnesses."

"I might've thought that too, but he molested his sister."

"Did you know that Jason's sister has been arrested multiple times? Maybe she's lying."

Michelle shook her head. "He admitted it to me."

April was slack-jawed for a moment. "I … I didn't know that."

"It's not for you to know."

"I'm sorry, Mom."

Michelle wiped the corners of her eyes, sniffed, and stood from April's bed. She peered into her daughter's eyes and said, "Please stay away from him." Then she left the room, shutting the door behind her.

April sat on her swivel chair, thinking about the revelation. She had judged Lori, believing she was a white-trash liar. A wave of sadness broke over April. She held her head in her hands and cried. After a few minutes, she walked to her bedside table, grabbed a few tissues from the box and wiped her face.

I don't even know why I'm crying. What difference does it make if he's guilty? He's not my father. She knew she was lying to herself. *I don't know that yet for sure. My mother had sex with Jason around the same time I was conceived. I look more like him than Danny. Would they lie about something so big? If he's a pedophile, maybe they would. I have to talk to Jason again.*

April went back to her swivel chair, turning in her seat to her desk. She opened her laptop. While the icons loaded, she thought about Becky saying that Susie took her money. *Would Susie manipulate this whole thing to get Jason's money? She had nothing to do with Lori being molested by Jason. I doubt Susie would tell the truth if she did something like that. What about Cody? He might talk. Exes love to talk trash.*

April googled *Real Estate Loganville PA Cody.* The top website was PricePropertyDevelopment.com. April clicked on the website. The front page showed a model townhome, with a little patch of green grass and pink petunias in the flower beds. Underneath the picture was the message: From the 150s. Townhomes at Mountain Manor. Schedule your tour today!

She clicked on Our Team. A list of employees appeared, each with a headshot and a bio. The top picture featured, CEO Cody Price. He had a manicured beard and bright green eyes. His light-brown hair was mixed with white and parted to the side. Based on Aunt Susie's age, April guessed he was in his late-forties.

His bio said he'd been the CEO for fifteen years, taking over from his late father. He'd grown the company four-fold since that time. He was an avid triathlete, winning the Loganville Triathlon twelve times in various age groups.

April clicked around the website, learning a little about Price Property Development. They built and sold custom homes, townhomes, and multifamily units. They also maintained and leased apartments.

April minimized the website and navigated to PublicRecords.com. She signed in to her account. Then, she went to the Search page. She typed *Cody Price Pennsylvania.* As the page scrolled through profile pictures, it asked for a city of residence. April entered Loganville. Then, she entered an age range of forty-five to fifty-five, as well as his place of employment.

She purchased Cody Price's background check and opened it. He was fifty years old. No criminal record. He had an address in Duncansville, which was about fifteen minutes from Loganville. No marriages. No children. *A good-looking rich guy with no kids and no wife. Could be gay. Or a player. Or a workaholic.*

April remembered a YouTube video she'd seen about asexuality. *Asexual people are usually female. He could be a pedophile. Don't pedophiles usually have jobs that give them access to kids? Like a teacher or a priest? He's in real estate. That doesn't fit the profile, but he* was *with Susie when it happened. Besides Susie, he must've had the most access to Becky back then.*

April navigated back to PricePropertyDevelopment.com. She clicked the hyperlink beneath the model town house that read, Schedule your tour today! April was taken to the Contact page. She filled out the contact form. In the comment section she explained that she was interested in purchasing a new town house at Mountain Manor and asked to meet with Cody Price.

She hovered the cursor over the Send button, then realized her mistake. She should've used a fake name. Also, her contact email was AprilGibbs2234@gmail.com. If Cody knew her parents, which he likely did, he would make the connection. Her parents would blow a gasket if Cody told them what she was doing. So, she minimized the window and went to Google.

April created a new email address. TeresaJohnson34511@gmail.com. Then she went back to the contact page and replaced her name and email address with the new one.

Chapter 88: Who's Your Daddy

The next afternoon, April sat at her desk, checking her new email address. "Teresa" had two new emails, a welcome email from Google and another from Brooke. April clicked the email from Brooke.

From: brooke@pricepropertydevelopment.com
To: teresajohnson34511@gmail.com
Date: July 28, 2020, 1:08 PM
Subject: Tour of the Townhomes at Mountain Manor

Hi Teresa,

I received your request for a tour of the Townhomes at Mountain Manor. The model home is open Monday through Friday from 10:00 a.m. until 6:00 p.m. You are welcome to walk in and talk to an agent during those times. If the agent is with a customer, you may have a short wait.

Alternatively, you can make an appointment for a specific date and time, if you'd rather not run the risk of waiting. If you'd like to set an appointment, please let me know. If you choose to walk in, please wear a mask.

The address of the model home is:
100 Manor Drive
Loganville, PA 16666

Best,
Brooke Bollinger
Senior Agent
Price Property Development

April clicked Reply.

From: teresajohnson34511@gmail.com
To: brooke@pricepropertydevelopment.com
Date: July 28, 2020, 3:48 PM
Subject: Re: Tour of the Townhomes at Mountain Manor

Brooke,

Thank you for returning my message. I would like to set up an appointment with Cody Price to look at the model home. I work from home, so my schedule is flexible. Whatever date and time works for him.

Let me know.

Thanks!
Teresa

The alarm on her phone chimed. April silenced it. *Time to go.* She grabbed her keys and her purse and tiptoed down the stairs. She peered into the kitchen. It was empty. Music and the clanging of weights came from the basement. Her brothers were lifting weights in preparation for the upcoming football season. With the pandemic, it was still undecided whether or not there would be one. April crept through the living room, out the front door.

Her mother bent over on the front walkway, touching her toes, her butt facing April. Michelle stood and turned toward her daughter, glaring, and wearing spandex running shorts and a sweaty T-shirt. "Where do you think you're going?"

"Travis called me. He wants to talk in person," April replied.

Michelle's face softened. "You don't have to talk to him, if you don't want to."

"I know. I feel like I need closure."

Michelle nodded. "Don't be too late."

April forced a smile. "Okay, Mom."

April walked across the lawn to her car. She glanced at the clock on her car radio—*3:53. I need to hurry.* She lowered the sun visor and drove across town to the construction site, parking a few houses away, like she'd done the day before. She checked the time—*4:01.* Workers were already driving away from the site in their pickup trucks. Jason exited the construction office, his backpack over his shoulder, and his clothes covered in dirt and sweat.

April stepped out of her car, waiting for Jason, not wearing her mask. She hoped to social distance, but she didn't want the mask to obscure what she needed to ask. He walked in her direction. He recognized April and her car and moved to the opposite side of the street. April walked across the street, intercepting him.

"I need to talk to you," April said.

He didn't break stride. "You can't be serious."

April followed, walking alongside Jason, but keeping a safe distance. "I'm sorry about yesterday."

"It's fine, but we shouldn't be talking."

They walked downhill, past newly built single-family homes. A man mowed his grass on a lawn tractor, wearing ear muffs.

"I'm April Gibbs. You used to be married to my mom." She spoke loud enough to be heard over the mower.

Jason continued to walk, unfazed by the revelation. "I'd rather not go back to prison."

He already knows who I am. "I just need to talk to you for a few minutes."

"Please leave me alone." He picked up the pace, his long strides leaving April and the mower behind.

"I think you might be my father," April called out to his back.

Jason stopped in his tracks and stood still for several seconds. Then, he turned around, his forehead creased. "What?"

April walked closer, staying six-feet away. "I think you might be my father."

He stared at her, slack-jawed, studying her face. "When's your birthday?"

"September 18th, 2000. Conception was likely around Christmas Day 1999, give or take a week. I already checked a conception calculator online."

He bent over, his hands on his knees. Then he sat on the curb, his legs wobbly, and his face red.

April stood over him. "Are you okay?"

He didn't respond for a long time. "I think I'm just a little dehydrated."

"I can drive you to Sheetz for some water."

Jason shook his head. "I'll be fine in a minute."

"Do you think you could be my father?"

Jason took a deep breath. "Did you ask your mother?"

April wrung her hands. "She says that you're not."

"I must not be then. Michelle and I didn't part on good terms, but she was never a liar."

April arched her eyebrows. "But there's a big problem with the date."

Jason swallowed hard and looked down between his legs. "I know."

"If my conception was around Christmas of 1999, then my mother was either cheating on you, or you're my father. Did you ever suspect her of cheating?"

Jason shrugged, his eyes on the macadam. "I'm sure you know that your parents were together in high school and college."

"Yes."

Jason raised his gaze to April. "I used to worry that Michelle still had feelings for Danny, but I never thought she'd cheat. I guess I was wrong."

April held out her hands. "What if you're not wrong?"

"If your mother says I'm not your father, I believe her. She wouldn't lie about something like this." Jason stood from the curb with a groan.

"I'd really like to drive you to Sheetz. You don't look so good."

Jason glanced down the road, heat reverberating off the macadam. "All right. Thank you."

April led Jason to her car. She thought about being in tight quarters with Jason. *What about COVID?* When they reached the car, it was as if he read her mind.

Jason said, "If you're worried about COVID, I can wear my mask."

"Thanks," April replied, opening her driver's side door. She climbed into her car, put on her mask, and started the car. She put the air-conditioning on full blast.

Jason opened his backpack, grabbed his mask, and put it on. He climbed into the passenger seat, and powered down his window, his backpack in his lap.

April gestured to the air conditioner. "I have the air on."

"If I have COVID, you probably don't want to be sealed in here with me."

April powered down her window and turned off the air conditioning. "Good point." She turned the car around and drove down the hill toward the Sheetz convenience store. April glanced at Jason. "Did you know who I was yesterday?"

Jason nodded.

"And you let me lie? Why?"

"Why did you give me a fake name?"

April lifted one shoulder, her eyes on the road. "I don't know. I really don't know you. You could be …"

"Dangerous?"

"I'm sorry. I should've told you the truth."

"It's fine. I don't know you, and you don't know me."

April's eyes flicked to Jason, then back to the road. "How did you find out about me?"

"It's easy to look up exes on social media."

"You looked up my mom?"

"I guess I was wondering about her life." He exhaled. "I know it's pathetic."

"I wasn't judging." April turned into the Sheetz gas station, parking near the convenience store. She turned in her seat toward Jason. "Did you ever think I could be your daughter?"

Jason shook his head. "It hadn't occurred to me. I didn't know your birthdate." He glanced at the convenience store. "I should go." He opened the passenger door. "Thanks for the ride."

"Do you need a ride home?"

"No, thanks." He exited the car and shut the door.

April leaned toward the open passenger window and called out, "Jason." He bent down, his masked face in the open window.

"Why are you here? You're not from Loganville."

"Thanks for the ride, April." He turned and walked into the convenience store.

April's phone buzzed with an email.

From: brooke@pricepropertydevelopment.com
To: teresajohnson34511@gmail.com
Date: July 28, 2020, 4:26 PM
Subject: Re: Re: Tour of the Townhomes at Mountain Manor

Hi Teresa,

You're in luck! Cody has an opening tomorrow, Wednesday, July 29, at 3:00 p.m. If that's too soon, his next available appointment is August 6 in the afternoon. We have other agents available, if those dates and times don't work for you.

It's not a requirement for the tour, but it might be smart to bring your preapproval letter from your lender. If you don't have one yet, we can help with that. It's good to be ready. Despite the pandemic, we're selling these homes like hotcakes.

Please let me know to confirm, and I will put you on the schedule.

Best,
Brooke Bollinger
Senior Agent
Price Property Development

Chapter 89: The Townhomes at Mountain Manor

The next day, April drove into an upscale community with a few hundred town houses—half of them complete. The community center featured a playground, a pool, and a gym. Many lawns were brown, the shallow-rooted sod not able to survive the summer heat. April parked in a visitor's spot across from the model home. She glanced at the clock on her car radio—*2:59. Right on time.* A banner hung across the model home that read The Townhomes at Mountain Manor, From the 150s.

She put on her mask, grabbed her hand sanitizer and purse, and exited her car. She wore a dressy skirt and a blouse for the occasion, thinking it made her appear older. The three-story end-unit townhome resembled the picture she'd seen on their website. Someone had obviously been watering the grass and the pink petunias.

April climbed the stairs on the side to the second-floor entrance. She stepped inside, without knocking. The open-concept floor plan was staged with dark wooden furniture. Cody and a woman stood in the dining room to April's left. Cody waved at April and raised his mask over his face. He wore slacks and a polo shirt embroidered with Price Property Development over his left pectoral. Cody approached April at the front door. He was tall, maybe six two.

He stopped a polite distance away. "You must be Teresa."

April waved. "Hi. You must be Cody."

He grinned under his mask, his green eyes squinting. "Guilty as charged. Would you like me to show you around?"

"That would be great."

"Let's start in the basement and work our way up."

"Sounds good."

Cody led April downstairs to the basement. It didn't feel like a basement though. Large windows in front and back let in the sunlight. April scanned the spacious living area. It wasn't furnished like the second level. The ceiling felt higher than a normal basement.

"As you can see, the walkout basement is completely finished," Cody said. "Wall-to-wall carpet. A large bedroom, bathroom, laundry room."

April peered into the open bathroom door, as if she cared.

"A full bath with a shower stall."

"It's nice," April said.

Cody showed April the bedroom and then the laundry room. He gestured to the front-loading washer and dryer. "We have a special for deals signed in July for a free washer and dryer. I'm not trying to pressure you of course. We have more buyers than we know what to do with."

April nodded, noncommittal.

Cody showed her the one-car garage. "This is the garage. Could also be a nice workshop. Are you married or single?"

"Single," April replied.

"I doubt you'll be on the market too much longer." Cody winked.

April blushed.

Cody led her back through the living area and out the back door. They stood on a stone patio, overlooking a little green patch of grass, surrounded by a wooden privacy fence. A wooden deck overhead shaded the patio. "This is a perfect place to play for small kids, when you find that special someone, or for a dog or even for a vegetable garden." He stared at April. "Has anyone ever told you that you look awfully young?"

"I'm older than I look."

Cody showed his palms. "It's a good thing, as far as I'm concerned. What is it that you do, if you don't mind me asking?"

"I'm a nurse."

"Really? I used to be an EMT at Loganville General."

"I work for a pediatrician. It's a small family practice."

Cody tilted his head. "Brooke said you requested me specifically. Do I know you from somewhere?"

This is my opening. "Susie Murphy said I should talk to you." April eyed Cody, watching for a reaction.

His face turned to stone for a split second, then softened. "Susie Murphy? How do you know her?"

April had already prepared for this question. "The doctor I work for is a mutual friend. We met at his birthday party a few years ago, and we hit it off. She's hilarious." April smiled under her mask. "She said you were the best real estate agent in town."

Cody took a step back, examining April. "What is this? Who are you?"

"You know who I am." April touched her chest. "I'm Teresa Johnson."

"Can I see some ID?"

April glared at Cody. "I'm not showing you my license."

"You don't have to show me your license." He gestured to her purse. "Show me anything with your name on it. I don't care if it's a library card."

April pressed her lips together, unsure how to respond.

"If you wanna buy a house, you'll need to provide identification. If you can't do that now, this showing is over. I'm a busy man, *Teresa*, if that's your real name. I'll show you out." He gestured to the open door back to the basement.

"I'm April Gibbs."

Cody drew back. "Danny and Michelle's daughter?"

April nodded.

"I don't understand. What's with the ruse? Why are you wasting my time?"

"I'm sorry. My parents would kill me if they knew I was here. I need to ask you some questions about Jason Lewis."

He shook his head. "I won't tell your parents that you were here, but you should go home."

April flashed her palms. "Please. I think Jason Lewis might be my father."

His eyes bulged. "Whoa. Look. I feel for you, but this is none of my business."

"I just have a couple of questions. *Please.*"

Cody blew out a heavy breath. "Go ahead."

"Did you think Jason was guilty?"

"The jury sure thought he was guilty, and I certainly agreed."

"Why did you and Susie break up?" April peered into his eyes, searching for signs of deception.

He broke eye contact for a beat. "It was too hard. To be honest, I wasn't mature enough to handle Becky after that mess. It was awful. I'm sure you know that we were engaged."

"I do."

He swallowed hard, his Adam's apple bobbing up and down. "I wish I would've handled it differently. I'm sure Susie still hates me."

"I've never heard her say anything about you."

"Well, I'd hate me if I was her. I should've been there for her, but I wasn't." He glanced back to the open door to the basement. "I should get back to work. I can take you out through the garage."

"Okay."

Cody led April back through the basement and into the garage. He pressed the button on the wall and the garage door opener rumbled to life, letting in the sunlight. They walked outside to the driveway.

April turned to Cody. She was a few steps down the sloped driveway, so Cody towered over her. "Do you ever see my parents?"

"I haven't seen them in years," Cody replied, squinting into the sun. "We're Facebook friends, but … you know how it goes. We all have our own lives."

April nodded again. "I'm sorry again for bothering you."

"I hope you find what you're looking for."

April forced a smile and said, "Thanks." She turned and walked to her car in the visitor's parking spot. She sat behind the wheel and glanced back at the house. Cody was gone, and the garage door motored down. She thought about his reaction when she had first mentioned Aunt Susie. *It was brief, and he covered it up, but it was there. He reacted with something. Anger? Fear? He's hiding something too. It's like they all agreed on a big lie.*

Chapter 90: Cody's House

The next morning, April sat at her desk, browsing Cody's background check on her laptop. *Something's off about him. Too perfect?*

A knock came at April's door. April closed her laptop and said, "Come in."

Michelle stepped into April's bedroom. "I'm going to the grocery store. Do you need anything?"

"No, thank you."

Michelle offered a small smile. Maybe as a way to let her daughter know that she wasn't mad at her anymore. Michelle left April's room, shutting the door behind her.

April opened her laptop, grabbed Cody's address from the background check, and programmed the location into the GPS on her phone. She stood from her desk, slipped on her sneakers, and grabbed her keys and her purse. She went to the window and parted the blinds. Her mother's minivan backed out of the garage.

April left her bedroom and crept down the hallway, not wanting to wake her brothers. They had been staying up too late, playing video games. Each day it seemed like they slept in a little later. April left her house and walked to her Honda.

Inside her car, she set her phone in the cradle and tapped on the GPS. It was already set to go to Duncansville. She drove out of Loganville via 17th Street. Then she drove south on I-99 through the

Allegheny Mountains. The traffic was light. Windmills rotated on the distant mountaintops. The valley below was bright green and dotted with farms.

Five miles later, she took a left exit toward Duncan Boulevard. She drove for a few minutes on Duncan Boulevard until the GPS said, "Turn right on Blair Hill Road." April turned her car onto the narrow two-lane road. She drove past farmland and forest. The GPS said, "You have arrived at your destination on the right."

April slowed her car, trying to read the numbers on the upcoming mailbox. She recognized that the numbers did, in fact, match Cody's address, but the house was obscured by the forest and not visible from Blair Hill Road. The shoulder was crowded with brambles. She drove two hundred yards past Cody's driveway, finally finding enough shoulder to park on the side of the road. Brambles scratched her car as she parked. She stepped out of the car and peered back at the lonely road. Cody's mailbox wasn't visible from her perspective, as she'd parked just beyond a hairpin turn.

"This is crazy," she said to herself. She had been hoping to just drive by his house and check it out, thinking that his house might tell her something important about him that wasn't on his background check. She had envisioned a neighborhood like Sylvan Heights. *I should've looked it up on Google Earth. I'm so stupid.* April blew out a breath. *Even if it was a regular neighborhood, what did I think I'd find? A freaking NAMBLA flag? I'm already here. I'd like to see his house. I could walk through the woods. He's probably at work anyway.*

She grabbed her cell phone and her keys and exited her car. She hiked along the shoulder back toward Cody's mailbox. As soon as she cleared the hairpin turn, she saw Cody's mailbox in the distance. As she neared the mailbox, she slipped into the woods, the brambles tugging on her jeans. Once she was under the canopy of the great oaks and hickories, the forest floor was relatively clear, except for leaves and saplings struggling for sun. She walked through the woods parallel to the driveway, her steps crunching the dried leaves underfoot. A squirrel darted away from April and up a tree.

She stopped at the edge of the woods, partially concealed by brambles, but with a view of the front of Cody's house. April scanned the house for several minutes, wondering if it looked like the house of a decent man. It was a two-story stone house with a three-car garage. A wooden privacy fence surrounded the backyard. She stood still, listening to the squirrels scurrying across the leaves and the birds chirping overhead. *Why would he need a privacy fence? Nobody's out here. I could walk through the woods to the back fence and look over the top. See what's in back.*

A rumble diverted April's gaze to the garage. The left-hand garage door opened. She expected to see a car drive out, but instead Cody zipped from the garage on a racing bicycle. He wore spandex shorts, a yellow jersey, and an aerodynamic helmet. He coasted down the driveway to the road. Then he turned left, and he was gone.

The left-hand garage door was still open. A BMW sedan and a white van with a ladder rack were parked inside. The van was only partially visible from her vantage point, obscured by the closed garage doors. She considered inspecting the open garage. *Isn't that breaking and entering? Or is it just entering? Either way, it's probably against the law. I should just check out the backyard.*

April walked around the house, staying concealed by the woods. She crept to the six-foot-tall privacy fence. She tried to peek between the boards, but the wood was tight together and in good condition. She reached and grabbed the top of the fence, and hoisted herself upward, using her feet against the boards for assistance. April was never good at pullups, but she was able to hold her head over the fence for a few seconds before her arms tired.

A green lawn was in the backyard, along with a rectangular pool, the blue water rippling with the breeze. *Perfect for laps.* April sighed. *I should go. This was a big waste of time.* April hiked through the woods, leaving the same way she'd come. As she walked, she thought about what she'd seen. *He has a nice house, which looks normal. He likes to bike, which makes sense, considering he's a triathlete. Makes sense that he'd have a lap pool too. Maybe he has the privacy fence to keep animals out. He has a nice car and a van. Windowless vans are creepy, but his company builds and maintains houses and apartments. It's probably a work truck. Although, I doubt he's doing any construction himself. He is the boss. Maybe he's into DIY stuff. It is weird that he's home on a Thursday morning. Maybe he works late. Don't real estate agents work late so they can see clients after the workday? My appointment with him was in the afternoon. Or maybe he works whenever he feels like it.*

A twig snapped causing April to stop in her tracks and scan to her left, listening for the culprit. It was eerily quiet. She looked around, suddenly aware that she was alone, and nobody knew she was here. *How far away is the nearest neighbor?* A chill ran up her spine, and the hair on the back of her neck stood on end. Another twig snapped, this one directly behind her, causing her to bolt, like a frightened deer. She sprinted through the woods, avoiding trees, adrenaline coursing through her veins.

The road and her car appeared in the distance. She glanced back but didn't see anyone chasing her. When she looked forward again, she nearly collided with an oak tree. She sidestepped the tree and ran to her car.

April got into her car, still breathing hard from her run. She started the vehicle and drove away from the scene, like she'd robbed a bank. She didn't turn around because she didn't want to drive back by Cody's house. She let the GPS take her home. It wanted her to turn around for a few miles, but it eventually found an alternate route. April giggled to herself, relieved. *I'm being paranoid.*

Chapter 91: Self-Destruction

Later that evening, April sat at her desk, thinking about Cody breaking the engagement because of Becky. *I wonder how Susie felt about that. What about Becky? Does she remember him?* She called Becky's cell. Her call went straight to voice mail.

The message said, "This mailbox is full. Goodbye."

April glanced at the time on her phone—*10:47*. Becky was a night owl, used to partying or working late and sleeping all day. She sent Becky a text.

April: I really need to talk to you. I'm coming over.

April changed from her pajamas to jeans and a fleece. She grabbed her keys, her purse, and her sneakers. She crept down the hall in stocking feet. Her brothers were awake, a sliver of light coming from the bottom of their bedroom doors. Thankfully, her parents were asleep. She left the house without incident, slipping on her sneakers on the front stoop. April walked across the lawn to her car.

She drove the short distance to Becky's house. At least thirty cars were crammed into her driveway, lawn, and along the curb. Music boomed from the house. People were visible through the windows, many with drinks in hand. It was a Thursday night. *The neighbors must be pissed. This is over-the-top, even for Becky.* In response to the pandemic, there was a ban on indoor gatherings over twenty-five people in Pennsylvania. *This has to be more than twenty-five people.* She put on her mask, grabbed her hand sanitizer, and exited her car. She walked to the front door, the party volume increasing with each step.

April opened the door and stepped inside. In the dining room, two couples played Beer Pong. One side cheered as the Ping-Pong ball landed in a cup of beer. A group of guys crowded around a keg in the kitchen. April walked down the hall to the living room. A disco ball projected and rotated red, green, and purple dots around the room. Several women were in various stages of undress, gyrating to the rap beat, giving the men lap dances. Cash littered the floor in front of them. More bills were tucked into their G-strings. One woman was between a man's legs, her head bobbing in his lap, her long hair shielding the deed. April didn't see Becky, so she went upstairs.

Giggling, moans, and bed squeaks came from the guest bedrooms. April walked to the end of the hall to the master bedroom. Shouting came from Becky's bedroom.

"Get the fuck out of my room!" Becky shouted.

"You're a fuckin' bitch!" a man shouted back.

"I said, get out. Limp-dick douchebag."

April heard a smack of skin on skin, followed by a yelp, and a crash to the floor. April opened one of the double doors. Becky sat on the carpet, her hand to her cheek, a large shirtless man standing over her. His body was covered in tattoos, an amalgamation of faded purple ink.

April ran to Becky, standing between her cousin and the sneering man. "Leave her alone."

"What the fuck are you gonna do about it?" the man said.

"My dad's a police officer."

He stepped into April's personal space, towering over her. "I don't give a fuck." He spat on the carpet near Becky. "She ain't worth it." Then, he pivoted and walked away, snatching his shirt from the floor on the way.

April kneeled next to Becky. "Are you okay?"

Becky wiped the corners of her eyes. "I'm fine." She stood from the floor, wearing a tight black dress. One side of her face was still scarlet from the slap.

April stood with Becky. "You sure?"

Becky smirked. "Don't worry, Princess Perfect. I'm not your problem." She walked to her bedside table. Becky opened the top drawer and removed a glass vial, filled with white powder.

April walked closer, stopping six feet away, and eyeing the cocaine vial. "Why did that guy hit you?"

Becky unscrewed the lid and used her long red pinkie nail to scoop some of the powder. She snorted the cocaine off her fingernail, then placed the vial on the bedside table. Becky turned to April. "He wanted me to do some shit that I didn't wanna do. These fucking assholes think because I'm a stripper they can do whatever they want to me."

April stared at her cousin, unblinking. "I'm sorry, Becky."

She lifted one shoulder. "It is what it is."

"I was thinking about your money problems."

"Yeah? You gonna fix that for me?"

"I was thinking you could fix it yourself. I'm sure Grammy would let you live in her basement. You could go to school. Figure out what you want to do. I'm sure everyone would pitch in to help you." April wrung her hands. "But ... I think you'd have to stop taking drugs."

Becky cackled. "I'm just gonna go to school and become a doctor or a lawyer or some shit?"

"If that's what you want."

"You're living in a fantasy world."

April held out her hands. "You'll lose everything. You have to do something."

"Don't worry about me. I've got a plan."

April cocked her head. "What plan?"

"It's none of your business." Becky sighed. "What the hell are you doing here anyway?"

"Do you remember Cody Price?"

Becky frowned. "Vaguely. He was engaged to my mother, until I supposedly ruined it."

"He said he was too immature to handle everything that happened to you."

Becky narrowed her eyes. "You *talked* to him?"

"Earlier today. I think he might be hiding something. I just wanted to know if you remember anything about him."

Becky sat on the edge of her bed. "How do you know he's hiding something?"

April shrugged. "I don't know. Just a feeling, I guess."

"Everyone's hiding something."

Shrieks and shouts came from downstairs, followed by heavy boots and the sound of people running and being tackled to the ground. The music was cut.

A male voice boomed from downstairs. "Loganville Police! Everyone on the fucking ground. On your stomachs. Arms and hands out, like a starfish."

Becky's eyes went wide. She sprang from the bed, grabbing her vile of cocaine from the bedside table.

April stood in shock.

Becky glared at April. "Get out of here."

April blinked, waking from her stupor. "Where do I go?"

Becky gestured to the windows that overlooked the backyard. "The window."

April rushed to the windows, while Becky ran to her dresser, fishing through the top drawer, then removing a plastic bag full of pills. April opened a window and gaped at the grass below. Heavy footsteps climbed the steps. Becky ran to the master bathroom. April climbed out the window, her hands shaking. She hung from the window sill, an eight-foot drop below her.

A police officer shouted, "Loganville Police! Stop right there."

April dropped reflexively. She hit the ground with bent knees and rolled on the grass.

The same police officer stuck his head out the window. "Don't move! Stop right there!"

April wanted to run, but his commanding voice pinned her in place.

"We ran your plates. We already know who you are. Don't make this worse."

April rolled to her back and gazed at the stars. Her eyes welled with tears and slipped down the side of her face. *I'm going to prison. My life is over.*

Chapter 92: Princess-Not-So-Perfect

Thirteen female partygoers were crammed into the holding cell, with a single stainless-steel toilet in the corner. April sat on a concrete bench next to Becky, wondering what would happen to her, and thinking about how much she had to pee. The other partygoers lounged on the benches too, some already asleep and coming down from their highs.

A deputy approached the cell. "April Gibbs?"

April sprang from her seat. "Yes?"

He beckoned her with his index finger. "Let's go."

Becky scowled. "I saw this coming. Princess Perfect with her *get out of jail free* card."

A few of the other girls grumbled.

April gestured back to Becky. "What about my cousin, Becky Murphy?"

The deputy glowered at April. "If I wanted her, I would've asked for her. Let's go." The deputy opened the cell, and April stepped into the hall. He didn't bother handcuffing April. As the deputy escorted April away from the cell, she glanced back at her fellow jailbirds. Smudged makeup, too short dresses, and red eyes in the harsh fluorescent lights made them appear battered and used, more like victims than criminals.

The deputy led April beyond the holding cells to a waiting room. April's parents rushed toward her.

"Thank you, Lucas," Danny said to the deputy.

The deputy nodded to Danny and left the waiting room.

Michelle grabbed April by the shoulders. "*What* is going on with you?" April burst into tears. Michelle held her, as she sobbed. When the tears subsided, Michelle said, "Let's go home."

Danny opened the door for them, his face like stone. Michelle had her arm around April, as they walked through the parking lot. Danny walked a few paces ahead, his fists clenched. Michelle opened the back door to the minivan. April crawled into the second-row seat and curled into a ball. Danny got into the driver's side, slamming the door unnecessarily hard. Michelle sat in the passenger's seat.

Danny started the minivan but didn't drive. Instead, he turned and glowered at April, his neck vein pulsing. "You're lucky you're not going to prison."

April didn't acknowledge her father.

"Sit up!"

April flinched. She sat up. "What do you want from me?"

"I want you to recognize that you made a stupid decision, and you're lucky you have a father with connections. Forget about the COVID restriction violation. Your cousin's going to prison for dealing drugs. Did you know that she had thousands of dollars' worth of Vicodin?"

"I didn't know." April's voice was whiny.

Michelle touched Danny's forearm. "Let's go home. We'll figure it out in the morning."

"No." Danny turned his glare on Michelle. "Do you know how embarrassing this is for me?" Danny turned back to his daughter. "You humiliated me. Do you understand that?"

April crossed her arms over her chest. "You humiliated *me. Both* of you did."

Danny pointed at his daughter. "You won't talk to me or your mother that way. You're already on thin ice. We're taking your car away until further notice."

Michelle touched Danny's forearm again. "We should talk about this first."

"No. We've been too lenient with her. That's the problem." Danny turned back to April. "If you ever do something like this again, I won't help you."

April clenched her jaw. "You're such a hypocrite. You can't tell me anything anymore. You're not even my *father!*"

Her parents were slack-jawed.

Michelle recovered first. "*April.* That is *not* true."

April addressed her mother, her voice trembling. "You were *married* when I was conceived. Are you a cheater or a liar?"

"That's *enough*," Danny said, red-faced. "You are the most self-centered child on this fucking planet. You have no *fucking* idea what your mother and I went through for you."

"Danny, stop," Michelle said.

Danny kept talking, ignoring his wife. "You're right. Your mother was still married to that sick pedophile, when we got together. You don't know the hell that your mother endured, and I, for one, don't wanna hear another word out of your mouth about it. You have no idea what it was like. By the way, we had a paternity test, when you were born. You're mine, whether you like it or not."

April peered out the window, deliberately shunning her father. She thought, *I'll find out for myself.*

Chapter 93: Sometimes Lies Are Easier to Live With

A knock came at April's bedroom door. April lay in her bed under the covers, unresponsive. Another knock came, and then Michelle entered her bedroom.

"I'm going to visit with Grammy. Would you like to come?" Michelle asked.

April shook her head, not making eye contact with her mother.

"I'll be back in an hour or so to make dinner."

April didn't reply.

Michelle stood in the doorway for a few seconds, then she left.

April rolled out of bed, wearing jeans and a T-shirt. She grabbed her phone and tapped her Uber app. She requested the nearest available driver, which was seven minutes away. A faint rumble came from the garage door opener. April went to her window and split the blinds. She watched her mother's minivan back out on the road and drive away.

April's Honda Civic was parked along the curb. Her parents had picked it up that morning from Becky's house, but they had confiscated the keys. A notification came from Uber. The driver accepted the fare and was on his way.

April slipped on her sneakers, grabbed her purse, and left her room. Her brothers were in the basement, lifting weights. Her father was at work. She left the house and sat on the front stoop. Dark clouds gathered from the east. A cool breeze cut through the heat. April checked the weather on her phone. There was a 60 percent chance of thunderstorms but not until late that night.

Four minutes later, a Ford Escape SUV pulled into the driveway, a young man behind the wheel. He pulled up his mask and waved.

April put on her mask, climbed into the back seat, and said, "Hi, I'm April."

He turned in his seat and replied, "Hi, I'm Gino. You ready?"

April nodded.

Gino appeared to be college age and Italian, with tan skin and dark wavy hair. He drove April a few miles down the road to Rite Aid.

"I'll be right back," April said.

Gino smiled under his mask. "I'll be here."

April walked into the Rite Aid. Shortly thereafter, she came out carrying a plastic bag with a small box inside.

Gino drove April toward her second destination. April glanced at the time on her phone—*4:09. Shit. I'm late.* She shoved her bag from Rite Aid into her purse. They drove through downtown Loganville, passing churches and storefronts and bars and restaurants. They left the city limits, driving over a bridge. Jason walked on the bridge sidewalk, going the opposite direction.

"Can you turn around?" April asked. "I need to talk to that man we just passed."

Gino peered into his rearview mirror, spotting Jason. "I can't turn around on the middle of a bridge. As soon as I cross, I'll turn around. We'll catch him."

"Thanks."

Gino turned around at the Sheetz convenience store, just after the bridge. He drove back over the bridge, his foot heavy on the accelerator. As they cleared the bridge, April spotted Jason at the bus stop.

"Can you drop me up here on the sidewalk?" April asked.

"No problem."

Gino parked along the curb with his hazard lights blinking.

"I'll just be a minute. Could you wait?"

Gino saluted and said, "You're the boss."

April hopped out of the car, her purse over her shoulder, still wearing her surgical mask. She looked both ways and ran across the street to the bus stop. Jason sat on the bus stop bench alone, reading a book. As April neared, he looked up from his book, his eyes wide.

April scowled at Jason, standing six feet away.

Jason slapped his book shut. "This can't be good."

"Your victim's in jail," April said.

Jason arched his eyebrows.

"Becky was arrested last night." Her voice quivered. "It's your fault she turned out this way."

"I'm sorry about your cousin."

April glared at Jason. "Are you sorry about molesting her?"

He dropped his gaze and said, "No, but I am sorry that it happened to her."

April put her hands on her hips. "Tell the truth. You did it, didn't you?"

He raised his gaze to meet hers. "Maybe it's better if you leave it alone."

"That's what everyone's been saying. But I think everyone's *lying*."

Jason exhaled. "Sometimes lies are easier to live with."

April reached into her purse and removed the DNA Paternity Test. "I'd like to know the truth."

Chapter 94: The Test

April sat on her bed cross-legged, stalking Travis's Instagram page. She scowled at a picture of Travis with his arm around Kyra, the happy couple smiling for the camera. She thought about Becky and the time she texted her when she saw Travis with Kyra. *For all her faults, Becky's always had my back.*

Becky's arraignment had been heartbreaking. Frank and Ruth had paid for the attorney, but they wouldn't pay for bail, believing that Becky would likely violate her bail by doing drugs. They had reasoned that going to jail might get her clean. An email notification appeared on April's screen. She sucked in a sharp breath and tapped the notification, taking her to the email.

From: info@paternitydna.com
To: aprilgibbs2234@gmail.com
Date: August 6, 2020, 11:48 AM
Subject: Paternity DNA Test

DNA TEST REPORT
For Personal Knowledge Only

Case Number: 234969

Name: April Gibbs
Relation: Daughter
Test Number: 234969-1
Date Collected: 7-31-2020

Name: Jason Lewis
Relation: Alleged Father
Test Number: 234969-2
Date Collected: 7-31-2020

April skimmed over the DNA data to the results at the bottom of the email.

The alleged father is not excluded as the biological father of the tested child. Based on testing results obtained from analyses of the DNA loci listed, the probability of paternity is **99.9993%**.

April stared at the screen slack-jawed, her eyes like saucers. A lump formed in her throat. Tears welled in her eyes. *They lied to me.* April slipped on her sneakers and took her phone downstairs, following the smell of French fries and grilled cheese sandwiches. Michelle was at the stovetop. She flipped a grilled cheese sandwich on the frying pan. French fries were in the oven below.

April stopped at the center island. She swallowed the lump in her throat and said, "I need to talk to you."

Michelle flipped another sandwich, replying without looking back. "Lunch is almost ready. Can you get your brothers? They're out back."

April glanced out the sliding glass door. They were playing catch. She clenched her fists and spoke through gritted teeth. "You *lied* to me."

Michelle removed the frying pan from the burner, turning it off at the same time. She pivoted to April. "What did you say?"

Tears slipped down April's face.

Michelle knitted her brow, searching her daughter's contorted face. "Sweetie, what's wrong?" Michelle walked around the center island.

April showed her palms. "Don't *touch* me. You *lied* to me!"

Michelle flinched and stopped a few feet away from April.

"I know Jason's my father."

"We've been through this, sweetie. We had a paternity test done when you were born—"

"Stop lying!" April sneered at her mother. "How *stupid* do you think I am? I had a DNA test done."

Michelle opened her mouth to speak, but nothing came out.

"You and *Danny* have been lying to me my whole life."

Michelle shook her head, her eyes glassy. "It's not like that."

April crossed her arms over her chest. "What's it like then?"

"I was pregnant before I knew about the evidence against Jason. I never thought he could do such a thing, but ..." Michelle wiped the corners of her eyes. "I left Jason, and I reconnected with Danny. Your father was like a shelter in the storm. I fell in love with him all over again. I found out I was pregnant shortly afterward. Your dad was so excited."

April tilted her head. "Does he know the truth?"

"Yes. I told him right then. He was disappointed that you were Jason's, but he wanted you from the beginning. He wanted us to be a family. We didn't want you to know what your biological father had done. We didn't want you to be forced to visit him in prison—"

"So you lied?"

Michelle sniffled and said, "We did what we thought was best."

"This is so *fucked up*."

Michelle approached April, with her arms out for a hug.

April walked away.

Michelle followed her daughter through the living room. "Where are you going?"

April spoke over her shoulder. "I need some air."

"Please. I love you. I didn't mean to—"

"Leave me alone."

Michelle stopped in her tracks.

April left the house, slamming the door in her wake.

Chapter 95: Home

Billowy clouds partially covered the sun. April marched around the corner, just out of view of her house. She sat on the curb between two of her neighbors. She tapped on her phone, opening her Uber app. She entered her destination. Gino was nearby, so she requested a ride from him. He responded almost immediately, accepting the fare.

As she waited for Gino, she hugged her knees, her head resting on her arms, and sobbed. A few minutes later, Gino's Ford Escape stopped alongside her. April wiped her face with her T-shirt and rose from the curb.

Gino stepped out of his car. He pulled up his mask. "Are you okay?"

April nodded. "I'm fine."

He narrowed his dark eyes. "You don't look fine."

"I'm *fine*." She opened the rear passenger door.

"Do you want a mask?" Gino asked.

April frowned. "Shit. I forgot."

"I keep extras." Gino reached over the front seat to the center console. He handed April a new surgical mask in sealed plastic.

"Thank you." April opened the plastic and put on the mask.

Gino drove them through downtown Loganville. April sat in back, staring out the window in silence. They drove across the bridge, leaving the Loganville city limits. Gino finally parked the SUV across the street from the construction site. Workers and machines labored in and around the wooden skeletons that would soon be someone's home.

"I can wait if you need me to," Gino said.

"That would be great," April replied, opening the door.

"You sure you're okay?" Gino, asked, turning around in his seat.

"I will be."

April stepped out of the car and approached the construction site. She scanned the men, searching for Jason. Two men sat on a truck tailgate, eating their lunch. Several others walked to their trucks parked along the street. They drove away, intent on eating out. Jason sat on a cinderblock, alone, eating a sandwich. She spotted him first. As if he sensed her gaze, he turned to her. Jason placed his sandwich in a Ziploc bag and shoved it in his backpack. He stood from the cinderblock, left his backpack, and walked to April. He stopped on the street, a polite distance away.

April pulled down her mask, not wanting any misunderstanding. "I got the DNA test."

"You look upset," Jason replied, his eyebrows drawn together.

April removed her phone from her back pocket and walked closer to Jason. "You can see for yourself." She tapped to the email in question and handed her phone to Jason. "Here's the results."

Jason tilted the screen so he could see better in the sun. Then he scrolled, his face twisting in anguish as he read. "I'm sorry, April. I know this isn't the result you wanted." He returned her phone.

April snatched her phone from his hand, stashing it in her back pocket. "No *shit*. My parents have been lying to me my whole life."

Jason looked down for a beat. "It's just DNA. Danny's been your father your whole life. This doesn't have to change anything."

April threw up her hands in frustration. "This changes *everything*! I'm in an impossible situation. If you're guilty, I can walk away knowing that my parents did the right thing, shielding me from you, but, if you're innocent, my whole life's a lie. My parents aren't the people who I thought they were."

"What do you want from me?"

April put her hands on her hips. "The truth. Did you molest your sister?"

He cocked his head. "How did you …"

"I listened to her audio from the preliminary hearing, and I talked to her. She and your mother both said you molested her. Did you do it?"

His eyes were glassy. "Yes."

"What about Becky?"

He blinked, and a tear snaked along his nose. "Yes."

"I wish I never knew you existed." April ran back to Gino's SUV. She climbed into the back, put her face in her hands, and cried.

"Are you okay?" Gino asked.

April looked up, her face red and tear-streaked. "Just go."

Gino turned around, driving back the way they came. "Where to?"

"Home. Take me home."

Chapter 96: Nine Months Later

Azaleas bloomed pink along the edge of the ground-level deck. The sun played peek-a-boo with the clouds. Everyone wore light jackets or sweatshirts. Frank and Ruth Murphy and the Gibbs family crowded around the Murphys' patio table and sang happy birthday to Dylan and Lance.

The twin teens blew out their candles.

Everyone cheered, including April. It had been nine months since she'd found out the truth about her father. She hadn't had any contact with Jason since. It had taken several months of professional therapy to repair her relationship with her parents. Given Jason's confession of guilt, April eventually forgave her parents for hiding the existence of her biological father, now understanding the difficult choice they had to make.

At the height of the pandemic, she had completed her first semester of her sophomore year online, but, as new cases slowed, she'd gone back to the University of Pennsylvania for the spring term. It had been good for her to spend time with her friends from college, who vastly outnumbered those from high school. After acing her exams, she was back home for the summer.

Ruth cut the cake, and Michelle used the spade knife to set squares of cake on the birthday-themed paper plates.

The newly minted fifteen-year-olds scarfed down their cake and went to the lawn to throw the football. April ate her cake at a leisurely pace, listening to the adult conversation.

"Any word from Susie?" Michelle asked Ruth.

Michelle had extended a party invitation to Susie through Ruth because Susie had blocked Michelle's calls. Michelle had said, "Maybe if it's at mom's she'll feel more comfortable."

Susie and Michelle's relationship had fractured, after Susie lost her house to foreclosure. Susie had blamed her misfortune on Michelle for exposing her and Becky to Jason and his dirty money. April had wondered if Aunt Susie was simply searching for someone to blame for her poor choices.

Ruth frowned at Michelle. "I'm sorry, honey. She said she has to work."

Susie had updated her license and had gone back to work as a nurse.

"Anything new on Maria?" Grandpap Frank asked Danny.

Danny swallowed his cake and shook his head, a scowl on his face. "She disappeared into thin air, just like the rest of them." Danny let out a breath. "I'd like to be optimistic, but she's been gone for almost three weeks. The chances of recovery now, ... well, you know."

Frank nodded and clenched his jaw. "I keep thinking I should've done something. I should've seen something."

"Stop beating yourself up," Ruth said, placing her hand atop Frank's. "Basketball season had been over for months when she disappeared. How could you've known?"

Maria was the latest child to be taken from Loganville, and she had been on Frank's basketball team.

Frank shook his head. "I don't know. Her mom never came to pick her up on time. I used to stay after practice, waiting with her, because I didn't wanna leave her alone. Her mom was always in a rush. She always appeared tired. Maria wasn't really interested in basketball. I think her mother signed her up for free after-school care. I never even thought about what might happen after basketball season." Frank stared at his half-eaten cake. "Now she's gone."

"Do you think it's a serial killer?" April asked.

Everyone turned their attention to April.

"There's no evidence of that." Danny huffed. "There's no evidence period."

"I saw that community organizer guy, Hector Cruz, on the news. He said, there's been nine missing girls from Loganville, all Latinas between five and seven years old. He said the first one was Nina Diaz in 1999."

"The first one might've been Heather Sample in '97," Frank said. "She disappeared without a trace, just like Maria."

***

Later that afternoon, April sat at her desk, her laptop open in front of her. She signed on to her CorrLinks account, which was an email messaging service to communicate with incarcerated persons. All incoming and outgoing messages were monitored by prison staff before delivering. She had a new message from her cousin. Becky had been sentenced to two years in prison for trafficking Vicodin, which was a Schedule II substance. With her time served, she had another fifteen months to go.

> **Becky**: Hey, PP. What up! Miss you girl. I hope you are home from school.
>
> I was wondering if you would come see me next Saturday? We have visiting hours from 10-4. It would mean a lot to me. It's part of my recovery. Please come alone. We need to have some real talk without the parental units. Also I'm finished with your CDs, if you want them back. I love you.
>
> **April**: Hi, Becky. It's great to hear from you. I miss you too.

I hope you're doing well with your recovery. Grammy Ruth tells me that you're doing really great. I'm sorry I haven't been to visit in a while. I've been really busy with school and everything. I know that's not a good excuse. I will be there on Saturday. I look forward to seeing you. I'll be there around noon, if that's okay with you. The CDs are Norman Tuttle's. I'm pretty sure he forgot about them, but I'll take them back to him, if you're finished. I love you too!

An email notification appeared on the bottom corner of her laptop screen. April clicked on the notification.

From: updates@publicrecords.com
To: aprilgibbs2234@gmail.com
Date: May 8, 2021, 4:20 PM
Subject: Update Jason Lewis

You're receiving this email because you elected Public Records to notify you if there were any updates to the following background check:

Jason Lewis

The following update(s) have been made.

Address
200 Valley View Drive
Apartment 3F
Loganville, PA 16666

April clicked the link at the bottom that read *Click here if you no longer wish to receive notifications regarding this record.*

Chapter 97: Clean

April wanted to hug her cousin but waved and smiled under her mask instead. Becky smiled back, the evidence coming from her eyes, her mouth also covered by a surgical mask. Inmates weren't required to wear masks, unless they were sick or visiting with the public.

Becky appeared a little heavier in a good way. "Thanks for coming, PP."

"Of course," April replied.

Becky grabbed a stack of bound CDs from the nearby stainless-steel table and handed them to April. "Thank you for letting me borrow these."

"You're welcome," April replied, taking the CDs. "I forgot you had them." At Becky's request, April had lent the recording of Jason's trial to Becky, shortly after she was incarcerated.

Becky gestured to the table. "You wanna sit?"

April sat across from Becky at the table. She set the stack of CDs on the seat next to her. A folded note sat in front of Becky on the table. Like her fellow inmates, Becky wore a maroon smock and matching maroon pants. DOC was etched across her back in big white letters. The tables around the meeting room were filled with female inmates, talking and laughing with their families, everyone muffled by a mask and social distancing.

Several inmates gazed at their children playing or coloring, desperate to touch them. Some met with older people, who appeared to be their parents. Several guards watched over the scene, also wearing masks. One inmate wiped tears from her eyes, the man in front of her delivering distressing news.

Becky rested her elbows on the table, her hands folded. "So, what are you planning to do this summer?"

April shrugged. "I'm not sure yet. I need to get a job. I may go back to waitressing, but I wanted to take a few weeks to decompress after the school year."

"Are you still seeing that cute Italian boy?"

"Gino?"

Becky giggled. "Is there another cute Italian boy in your life?"

April frowned. "No. We broke up."

Becky mimicked April's frown, the evidence in her eyes and on her creased forehead. "Why? What happened?"

"Before the spring semester, we got in this big fight about long-distance relationships. We were both going back to school in the spring, and we wouldn't be able to see each other much, so I suggested we take a break. He freaked. Thought I didn't care about him."

"I'm sorry."

April lifted one shoulder. "It's okay. I'm thinking about calling him and apologizing. I've been stalking him on Instagram. It doesn't look like he's dating anyone."

"Go for it. If I was you, that's what I'd do."

April nodded.

Becky cleared her throat. "So, the reason I asked you to come see me is because of my recovery and my therapy."

April leaned forward, her elbows on the table, and her hands folded like Becky's.

"As part of my recovery, I'm supposed to make amends." Becky stared into April's eyes, unblinking. "I'm so sorry for subjecting you to drugs and alcohol and all the scumbags at my house. You always said

346

no, but I was wrong to offer you drugs and alcohol. It was like I wanted to ruin your perfect life. I was wrong, and I'm so sorry."

April nodded again. "That's really nice of you to say. I forgive you."

"Thanks, April."

This made April smile. Becky rarely called her April. "You're welcome. Is that what you wanted to tell me?"

"There's more. As you know I've been in therapy. The therapist here is really nice. She's really helped me."

"I'm so happy for you."

"We've talked a lot about my mother and her addictions. I've learned a lot about myself and why I do the things I do. I'm trying to break my bad habits for good."

"That's great," April said.

"I've been clean, and my mind's been so much clearer. Anyway, I uh, started to remember things from the past. I think listening to the trial and my deposition helped too." Becky took a deep breath. "One of the things that I remembered was from when I was a little girl. It was a man telling me that Jason touched my pee-pee part. That's the word I remember him using. Pee-pee part. He told me this over and over again, like he was trying to hypnotize me or brainwash me. And then I used that same word in my deposition."

April's eyes widened. "Who was it?"

Becky shrugged. "I don't know. The face is a blur. I'm pretty sure it was a man though."

"I don't understand." April glanced around, making sure nobody was listening. Then she spoke in a hushed whisper. "Does this mean you don't think Jason molested you?"

"I don't know for certain, but I doubt it was him."

"But ..." April pursed her lips. "He admitted it to me."

Becky knitted her brow. "He did?"

"Yes. When I found out he was my father, I confronted him. I told him that …" April put her hand to her mouth. "Oh, my God."

"What?"

"I told him that, if he's guilty, I can walk away, knowing that my parents did the right thing, but, if he's innocent, my whole life's a lie."

"You think he lied for you?"

April shook her head. "I don't know. You really think he didn't do it?"

"No. I don't."

"Somebody did." April whispered again, "You had trauma."

Becky exhaled. "I know."

"Then who?"

Becky shrugged again. "I really don't know. Maybe it'll come to me in time. Maybe it won't."

"What about Jason? He went to prison for twenty years."

Becky stared at the table for a few seconds. "I know. I've tried to contact him to apologize, but I've been unsuccessful. I'd be willing to testify in court, if he wanted to clear his name. I was hoping you could get in touch with him for me."

April hung her head and rubbed her temples.

"Are you okay?"

April raised her gaze. "This is so crazy. Everyone said he did it. Now you say he didn't. I don't understand. There was DNA." April whispered, "He molested his sister."

"I don't know about his sister, but, if you wanna know the truth about the DNA, I know a way to find out. If you don't, it's okay."

April hesitated for a long moment. "I do."

Becky picked up the folded note in front of her and handed it across the table to April. "Give this to Grammy."

Chapter 98: No More Secrets

April drove from the women's prison directly to her grandparents' house. She parked in the driveway next to Frank's Ford F-150. Ruth stood along the front flower beds, watering her pink petunias. April cut her engine and walked over to her grammy. It was sunny but cool—in the sixties.

Ruth set down the hose, the trigger nozzle stopping the flow of water, and turned to greet her granddaughter. "Hi, sweetheart."

April hugged Ruth.

When they separated, Ruth asked, "What are you doing here?"

"I went to see Becky today."

Ruth drew her eyebrows together. "Is she all right?"

April put her hands on her hips. "She's fine. Better than ever actually."

Ruth beamed. "I hate to say it, but her being arrested might've been the best thing for her."

"She likes her therapist, and she's clean. No drugs. No alcohol."

"I'm so proud of her."

April nodded. "I have a question to ask you, and I need you to be honest."

Ruth tilted her head.

"Did you put Becky's underwear in the trash that day?"

Ruth broke eye contact, her face reddening. "I thought we were finally over this nonsense."

April stared at Ruth. "Becky told me that Jason didn't do it."

Ruth's eyes widened. "That can't be true. She's too young to remember."

April reached into the back pocket of her jeans and handed Becky's note to Ruth. "She asked me to give you this."

Ruth took the note, opened it, and read it silently.

April already knew what it said. Becky had asked April to read it, so she'd be ready for Ruth's possible objections. It read:

Grammy,

I don't think Jason molested me. Someone coached me to say it was Jason. I don't know who. I also think you lied. I know you did it to protect me, but it's time to tell the truth. You don't need to protect me anymore.

Please tell April the truth. She deserves to know.

I love you,
Becky

Ruth looked up from the note, her eyes glassy. "I wanted to tell the truth, but it was too late."

The front door opened, and Grandpap Frank appeared. Ruth and April gaped at Frank.

He narrowed his eyes, walking toward them, trying to access the situation. "What's going on?"

A tear slipped down Ruth's cheek. She handed the note to her husband. Her voice quivered. "Becky wrote this to me."

Frank read the note, his jaw clenching. "This is bullshit. No way she's a reliable witness, especially after twenty-one years."

Ruth shook her head. "I never should've listened to you."

Frank addressed April. "Your grandmother's tired."

"No, she's not," April replied, her hands on her hips.

"I should take her inside." Frank put his arm around Ruth and tried to guide her to the house."

"Let me go!" Ruth shouted.

Frank startled and removed his arm from his wife.

Ruth pointed at her husband, her face blotchy and tear-streaked. "You told me to lie. You told me that it wouldn't matter. You told me that we were just making sure he didn't get off."

"He's still guilty," Frank said. "You did the right thing. If you would've said the underwear was in the trash, he would've gotten off. He was alone with her. He molested his sister for Christ's sake. It had to be him."

"I have to tell the truth."

Frank glared at his wife and grabbed her by the upper arms. "Absolutely *not*. You could go to prison for perjury. *Prison*, Ruth. Do you understand me?"

"Like Jason?" April asked, interjecting.

Frank let go of Ruth and turned his glare on April. "This has to be kept secret. Do you understand me?"

"No more secrets." April pivoted and walked to her car.

"April! Where are you going? April. Wait!" Frank shouted.

April climbed into her Civic, slammed the door, and started her car. She reversed wildly out of the driveway, put it in Drive, and sped away.

Chapter 99: Dirty Money

April drove a few miles down the road to an apartment complex. She parked in a visitor spot in front of building 124, a three-story brick apartment building, with four apartments on each floor. She walked to the apartment building and pressed the buzzer next to apartment 2B. There was no response. Susie's red Chevy Cavalier was in the lot, so she knew she was home.

A resident exited the apartment building. April grabbed the door before it was locked shut. She entered the building. April took the stairs to the second floor and knocked on 2B. The TV blared from the apartment. April knocked again—this time hard enough to pass for a cop, serving an arrest warrant.

"I'm … comin'," Susie said, her voice raspy, and her words slurred. She opened the door with a scowl, her eyes and face droopy. "What are you … doin' here?" The smell of alcohol came from her breath.

"I need to talk to you," April replied.

Susie shrugged. "Whatever." Susie staggered back into her apartment, leaving the door open.

April stepped inside the apartment, shutting the door behind her. Just beyond the front door was the living room and the kitchen. Susie slumped on the couch, staring at the TV, like a zombie. Two bottles of vodka were on the coffee table—one empty, the other nearly empty. Her face was red and puffy. Her midsection was puffy too. April remembered how glamourous her aunt had been when April was young. Rich and beautiful, always wearing fashionable clothes and driving the coolest cars.

April walked over to the coffee table, grabbed the remote, and turned off the television.

Susie glowered at April. "Hey?"

"We need to talk." April stood in front of the coffee table, facing her aunt on the couch.

"Talk then."

"Becky told me that Jason didn't molest her."

Susie gaped back, blank-faced.

April leaned toward Susie. "Did you hear me?"

Susie was still blank-faced. "Yeah, ... so?"

April knitted her brow. "So? That's all you have to say?"

"You don't know ... shit. Becky's a ... liar." She grabbed the mostly empty bottle of vodka and took a swig.

April stared at her aunt, and then it hit her. "You knew! Didn't you? And you let him rot in prison."

Susie broke eye contact for a split second. "I don't know what you're ... talkin' about."

"Why?" April paused for a response that never came. "It's because of the money, isn't it? If Jason's innocent, you don't get to take his money in civil court."

Susie pointed vaguely in the direction of her door. "Get out."

April raised one side of her mouth in disgust. "Becky told me that a man coached her to say it was Jason. Who was it?"

Susie sneered. "She's ... a liar."

"Was it Cody Price?"

Susie stood from the couch, her legs wobbly. She pointed at the door again. "Get the fuck out."

"Not until you tell me the truth."

Susie staggered around the table. She raised her flabby arm and swung at April, but she sidestepped her aunt, and Susie fell face-first on the carpet. Susie groaned and rolled to her back, blubbering now, her eyes filled with tears. "I don't know ... who did it."

April looked down on her aunt. "You knew it wasn't Jason, but you wanted his money."

"I wish ... it never happened." Susie curled into the fetal position and sobbed.

April knelt next to her aunt. "Tell me the truth. Was it Cody?"

Susie continued to sob.

April shook Susie. "Tell me the truth. Was it Cody?"

"I don't know."

"Did you suspect it was him? Is that why he broke off the engagement?"

In between sobs Susie said, "He was ... in Becky's room ... late at night."

"Did he touch her?" April shook her aunt again. "Did you see Cody touch her?"

"No. He was ... watching her. I know ... that look."

April stood, glaring at her aunt. "You let an innocent man go to prison."

"It was ... already done."

Chapter 100: Redemption

April sat in her car in the apartment complex parking lot, tapping on her phone. She searched her deleted emails to find the recent one from updates@publicrecords.com. She tapped the email, finding Jason's new address. Then she set her GPS to 200 Valley View Drive.

April drove through downtown Loganville on Valley View Drive. The sun was still high in the sky. She turned into the parking lot, beside the six-story apartment building. April parked in a visitor spot. She grabbed her surgical mask but changed her mind, leaving it in the car. April had been vaccinated, and she didn't want her voice to be muffled. She walked to the front door of the apartment building and pressed the buzzer for 3F.

A few seconds later Jason's voice came back, "Who is it?"

"It's April. I need to talk to you."

Jason hesitated for an instant. "Okay. Come on up."

The front door buzzed open, and April walked into the apartment building. She took the stairs to the third floor. The stairwell smelled faintly of urine. She found apartment 3F. A spray-painted message was on the door. El Diablo está aquí. April knocked.

Jason answered the door. He had two black eyes, bruising on his cheeks, and a scab on his lip.

"Oh my God," April said.

"I know I look rough." Jason stepped aside. "Come in."

April walked into his apartment. It was mostly empty. The living room was furniture free, the gray carpet stained. A card table was setup near the tiny kitchen, with two plastic chairs. A small stack of paperbacks sat on the table.

Jason shut the door and turned the dead bolt. He walked toward April and said, "You want something to drink?"

"No, thank you."

He gestured to the table. "You want to sit down?"

April sat at the card table, staring at Jason's battered face. "What happened to you?"

Jason exhaled. "I'm a registered sex offender. With these girls going missing, my neighbors are especially sensitive."

April's eyes widened. "That's not right. They can't do that. Did you call the police?"

"I'd rather not involve the police. I imagine they'd think I got what I deserved."

"I could talk to my dad—"

"Please, don't do that." Jason grabbed the empty chair from under the card table and moved it several feet away. Then, he sat in the plastic chair.

April eyed him, with a furrowed brow.

"You forgot your mask," Jason said. "You probably want me to keep my distance."

"It's okay. I'm vaccinated. What about you?"

"Not yet. I'm still on the fence about it."

April nodded.

Jason didn't move closer. "I'm surprised you're here."

"Me too. I didn't think I'd ever contact you again."

"What changed?"

"I have a question for you." April paused for a beat. "It's about your sister, Lori."

Jason frowned. "I already told you. What more do you want from me?"

April peered into his dark eyes. "I want you to tell me exactly what happened."

"I'd rather not talk about it."

"Please. I'm trying to piece things together, but I can't explain this. It doesn't make sense. How old were you? Your mom said you were thirteen when it happened."

Jason grunted. "That's bullshit. My mother's lying to conceal her own guilt."

"How old were you then?"

"Seven." He cleared his throat. "It was when my mother's boyfriend molested me." Jason dropped his gaze, no longer making eye contact with April. "He told me that the things he was doing to me was how you showed someone love, ... so I did the same thing to my sister." He shook his head. "I touched her but I didn't know what I was doing. I didn't know any better. I was just a child." Jason stared at the tabletop for a long time, his eyes distant.

"Jason?" April finally said.

He wiped his eyes and raised his gaze.

"It's not your fault."

He swallowed hard and shrugged.

April took a deep breath. "I think you're innocent. I think you lied to me nine months ago because you didn't want me to hate my parents."

"You can't know that."

"Becky told me that she thinks you didn't do it."

Jason's eyes welled with tears again.

"My grandmother admitted that she put Becky's underwear in the trash. My aunt Susie just told me in so many words that she thinks it was Cody Price."

Jason hung his head and cried softly.

April leaned forward in her chair. "I'm sorry. Did I say something wrong?"

He covered his face with his hands, still crying.

She stood from the table and walked to her father. Jason put up his hand to keep her away from him, but she ignored his dissent and bent down and hugged him. She wrapped her arms around his back. His body convulsed as he wept. After a long moment, April let go, now standing over him.

Jason wiped his face with his T-shirt and swallowed the lump in his throat. "I'm sorry."

April blinked, her own eyes glassy in empathy. "It's okay. Did I say something wrong?"

He shook his head again. His voice wavered. "After all these years … you're the first person to believe me."

"I'll tell my dad everything. The police will reopen the case. Becky already said she'd testify, if you want to clear your name. You might get a settlement for all the prison time you served—"

"No. That's not how the system works. The justice system doesn't fix mistakes. It covers them up. They won't reopen the case unless there's physical evidence against Cody, and even then they might not. What's the evidence against Cody?"

April slumped her shoulders. "My aunt saw him staring at Becky late at night in her room. I know that's technically nothing but …"

"That's not evidence, April."

"I'm sorry."

"Don't be. I'm grateful that you believe me. That's what matters."

Chapter 101: The Cover-Up

April walked into her house, her purse over her shoulder. Her brothers were in the living room, playing video games on the big screen. She stepped through the living room to the kitchen. Michelle stood at the center island, slicing tomatoes with a serrated knife.

Her mother looked up from the tomatoes and smiled. "You're back. How was Becky?"

April sidled up to the center island, resting her hands on the edge. "She's doing great. You and Dad should go for a visit."

Michelle nodded. "It's been too long. I'm glad she's doing well."

"Me too."

Michelle glanced out the sliding glass door to the patio. "You're just in time. Your dad's making burgers for dinner."

April forced a smile. "Great. Are we eating outside?"

"Yes. It's still so nice."

April went to the sliding glass door and opened it. She shut the door and descended two steps to the patio.

Danny turned from the open grill, a spatula in hand, the breeze carrying the smoke away from them. "Hey. Burgers are almost ready. How was Becky?"

"She's really good." April pursed her lips. "She told me that Jason never molested her."

Danny's face twisted in confusion. "What are you talking about?"

"She's in therapy at the prison. Says she remembers a man coaching her to say it was Jason."

"She was only six. That can't possibly be a reliable memory. That's great that she's doing better, but she's still a drug addict with severe mental problems."

April stepped closer to Danny. "There's more. Grammy admitted that she put Becky's underwear in the trash."

"You talked to Ruth about this?"

"Yes."

Danny glared at April. "I thought we agreed that this was over. Your grandmother doesn't need this stress."

April glared right back. "Becky sought me out, not the other way around."

Danny pointed his spatula at April. "But you interrogated your grandmother."

"Aunt Susie knows it wasn't Jason either. She thinks it was Cody Price."

Danny cocked his head, his face reddening. "Susie doesn't think that."

April crossed her arms over her chest. "She just told me."

"Was she sober?"

April opened her mouth, then shut it.

"That's what I thought."

"Cody had access to Becky. He could've coached Becky to say it was Jason."

Danny put up his hand. "That's *enough*."

April spoke faster, trying to finish her argument. "He's like fifty, and he's never been married. Never had any kids. Did you know that he has a creepy white van?"

"That's not evidence. Do you have any physical evidence to support your theory?"

"Not exactly, but—"

"*Jesus*, April. You can't keep turning this family upside down."

"You don't want Jason to be innocent because you took Mom from him."

Danny clenched his jaw. He spoke through gritted teeth. "You will *not* talk to me that way."

April narrowed her eyes at Danny. "You lied about my father for twenty years. Did you plant evidence too? Did you frame my real father so you could have Mom?"

He spiked his spatula on the patio and stalked toward April, grabbing her by her upper arms. "I raised you as my own, and *this* is the thanks I get?" He shook her as he made his point, his hands gripping like pythons.

April wriggled in vain, her eyes bulging. "You're hurting me."

The sliding glass door opened.

"*Danny*! What are you doing? Let her go," Michelle said from the doorway.

His grip loosened. Danny let go and stepped back. He dipped his head. A wave of shame passed over his face. "I'm sorry, April."

"Fuck you!" April ran from the backyard.

"April," Michelle called out.

"Let her go," Danny said.

April ran to her car, started the vehicle, and drove away.

Chapter 102: Dangerous Evidence

April drove south on I-99 through the Allegheny Mountains, gripping the steering wheel with white knuckles, still seething. The sun was bright and high in the sky. She glanced at the time on her radio—*5:26*. Sunset wasn't until 8:30. She took a left exit toward Duncan Boulevard. She drove for a few minutes on Duncan Boulevard, until the GPS said, "Turn right on Blair Hill Road." April turned her car onto the narrow two-lane road, past farmland and forest.

A cyclist approached, pedaling toward her in the opposite lane. April rubbernecked as she drove past the man on the bike. "That's Cody," she said to herself. He didn't appear to notice April or her car. She thought about turning around and following him. *No. Stick to the plan. You'll just have to wait until he gets back.*

The plan was to call Danny when she made it to Cody's house, to let him know what she was doing, then to hang up when he inevitably ordered her to come home. She'd have to wait until Cody returned to make that call, otherwise her parents would be at Cody's doorstep before she even had a chance to confront him.

She'd planned to confront Cody with what Becky and Susie had said, with her phone recording the conversation in her open purse. She'd planned to lie and say that Becky remembered Cody coaching her to blame Jason for the molestation. She would make sure Cody knew that Danny knew where she was to ensure her safety. Hopefully, she'd record him saying something incriminating. At the very least she'd give him a piece of her mind.

April drove past Cody's house and parked her car alongside the road, after the hairpin turn. She wanted to maintain the element of surprise, so she didn't want Cody to see her car before the confrontation. She remembered the last time she'd been to Cody's house. He'd been out for a bike ride then too. *His garage might be open again. Maybe I could look around while he's gone. What if he comes back? He's a triathlete. He'll be out for a long time. Even if he does come back early, I'll hear the garage door. I can slip out the back. … This is crazy. No, this is an opportunity. Danny wants evidence. I'll find some evidence.*

April grabbed her keys and her phone and exited her car. She jogged along the road, then up Cody's driveway toward the two-story stone house. The left-hand garage door was open. She stopped in front of the open door, catching her breath. She turned around, half-expecting to see Cody on his bicycle. As her breath regulated, she realized how quiet it was, like she was the only person for miles.

April scanned the area one more time, listening to the squirrels scurrying on dry leaves and the birds chirping overhead. Then she stepped into the garage, her heart pounding. Cody's BMW and van were parked inside. April walked through the garage, stopping at the door to the house. Part of her hoped it was locked.

It wasn't. April stepped inside and shut the door behind her. She walked past the laundry room to the open-plan kitchen, with its massive commercial appliances and an indoor grill built into the center island. She whirled around, searching for anything incriminating. She went to the counter and flipped through his mail. *Bills and junk mail, like everyone else.*

A 2D replica wooden house hung from the wall, with two hooks at the bottom, holding two key rings. April walked beyond the kitchen, passing a formal dining room to her left, and entered the living room.

The floors were shiny hardwood with Oriental area rugs. Much of the furniture was white with glass tables. Everything was sparkling clean and impeccably decorated, like one of his model homes.

To the left of the living room was a family room, with black sectional couches and a sixty-inch television on the wall. The living room and family room were separated by a staircase that led upstairs.

April walked beyond the living room and family room to Cody's office. A massive mahogany desk dominated the room. A laptop sat open on the desk. It was in Sleep mode. April sat in the cushy leather chair and pressed the space bar, waking the computer. It prompted April for a password. *Shit.* She had no clue what Cody might use as a password. She riffled through his desk drawers, thinking he might've written it down. His drawers were organized to perfection, with every office supply in its place, but no passwords. She stood from the desk and went to the floor-to-ceiling bookshelf. It was filled with hardback books. Not a single paperback. April checked the bindings. A chill ran down her spine. *They're alphabetized. Someone this organized wouldn't leave incriminating evidence lying around. I need to get out of here.*

She left the office, going back the way she came. On the way, a door on the staircase separating the living room and family room caught her eye. *Is that a dead bolt?* She approached the single door. It resembled a heavy-duty exterior door, and it did in fact have a dead bolt. April tried to open the door, but it was locked. *He has to be hiding something behind this door.*

Her stomach fluttered. She ran to the kitchen, snatched the two key rings off the hooks, and ran back to the door. She matched the manufacturer listed on the dead bolt, Kwikset, with the same manufacturer on the key. She found three Kwikset keys on one of the key rings. The second one turned the lock.

April flipped on the light, illuminating the white-carpeted stairs going down. She crept downstairs, wondering how much time she had until Cody came back. The basement was an immaculate man cave and a tribute to Pittsburgh sports. Signed Steelers, Pirates, and Penguins jerseys hung from the walls. A black leather sectional wrapped around the room, facing a massive projector screen. Trophy cases lined one wall, filled with triathlon trophies and medals and framed photos of Cody standing at the top of various winner's podiums, sweaty and smiling. *Why would he lock this room from the outside?*

April surveyed the room. She saw something on the carpet under the couch. *Is that hair?* April walked closer to the mysterious hair. She knelt, reached under the couch, and pulled the hair, revealing a doll from under the couch. *Holy shit. He doesn't have kids.* She shoved the doll back under. *I need to get out of here.*

A clanging sound made April freeze, like a deer in headlights. *Where did that come from?* More clanging came from the wall behind the trophy cases. April crept to the trophy cases. She leaned toward the wall, listening for several seconds. It was dead quiet, until a *clang* made her flinch. April called out, "Hello?"

A tiny voice replied, "Hello?"

April's eyes bulged. "Where are you?"

"In here."

"In where?"

"My room."

"How do I get in there?"

"The door."

"What door?"

"The *door.*"

"Hold on." *There can't be another door. This is underground. It has to be here.* April checked along the edges of the trophy cases, frantically searching for a hidden door. Between the last two cases were hinges, barely visible, and painted black to match. April tugged on the last trophy case, groaning from the effort, but it didn't move. She glanced at the carpet. A curved line of compressed carpet came from the outer edge of the last trophy case on the row. She checked the back edge of the last case. Nothing. Then, she slipped her hand behind it and felt a handle. She pulled down the handle, and the trophy case moved an inch toward her. She grabbed the edge and pulled, the case opening on a hinge, like a door, the weight of the case being supported by wheels underneath.

She stared into the secret room, stunned, her mouth an O. The walls were bright white, with several posters of cartoon characters. A small bed sat dead center. A door was open in the back corner, exposing a small bathroom. A few scattered dolls were on the pink shag carpet. Chains hung from one wall, attached to thick steel rings. A little girl stood by the chains, clanging them together. April eyed her wrists, relieved that she wasn't bound.

The dark-haired girl turned to April and asked, "You wanna play?"

That's when it all clicked. "Are you Maria?" Before the girl could answer, an inhale of breath made April turn around. She saw a flash of his yellow jersey, followed by his fist. Then everything went black.

Chapter 103: In Over Her Head

Hot pain radiated from the back of April's head and her jaw. She lay on her side, on hard tile. Her eyes fluttered, opened, and focused. Two boots covered in blue booties stood before her. She tilted her head upward. Cody stood over her, wearing medical coveralls with latex gloves, and goggles around his neck. He smelled like sweat. April groaned and sat upright, her back against the wall. Her right hand was cuffed to one of the chains on the wall.

"There she is," Cody said, his hands on his hips.

April touched the back of her head with her left hand; it was slick. She pulled her hand back into view. Her fingertips were red with blood.

"You took quite a fall," Cody said.

April glanced around the room, searching for Maria, but she was gone, and the room no longer resembled a little girl's room. It was mostly empty now, except for the pink shag carpet that was rolled up and leaning against the wall. A drain was in the middle of the tile floor. The bathroom door was shut. "Where's Maria?"

Cody smirked. "I don't know what you're talking about. It's just you and me. We have a big night ahead of us." Cody turned and walked to the carpet leaning on the wall. He hefted it over his shoulder and walked out of the room.

As soon as he left, April quickly checked her jean pockets, keeping an eye on the open door for Cody's return. Her keys and her phone were gone. Her hands trembled, and her heart pounded in her chest. April rose to her feet and yanked on the chain with both hands, using all her weight to try to dislodge it from the wall. The metal ring that the chain was attached to didn't budge. *Damn it.* April tried pulling down on the chain with both hands and pushing off the wall with her legs. The metal ring still didn't budge. *Shit. I need to get out of here. Think.* She inspected the thick metal cuff around her wrist. It was fastened by a screw. She tried sticking her fingernail in the flathead screw and turning left, but it didn't move. It was too tight. *God damn it.*

April walked as far as the chain would allow, which was three steps from the wall. She scanned the area for anything she could use. *Think.* The room was barren. *Oh my God. I'm in big trouble.* She sat on the tile and cried, thinking about how stupid she'd been.

"There, there," Cody said, as he entered the room.

April looked up and sniffled.

Cody placed a bucket of water and a large jug of bleach in the corner of the room, far out of April's reach. Then he left the room again. He returned a minute later with a circular saw, a plastic case, and a sheathed knife. He set the items near the bleach.

April stared at the items, wide-eyed, her stomach in knots. *He'll kill me and cut me up.* She scooted back until she hit the wall again.

Then, he removed the child-safe covering over the electric outlet, plugged in his saw, and sauntered over to April, the saw in hand. When he got close, he revved the saw in April's face. She flinched, her head hitting the concrete wall, sending a fresh burst of pain through her already tender head wound.

Cody let off the trigger, the *whiz* of the blade stopping immediately. He laughed. "This is a bone saw. Fresh blade too. It'll cut through you like a hot knife through butter."

April trembled, her voice shaky, still sitting against the wall. "What do you want from me?"

"You're gonna answer some questions, and you're gonna tell the truth. For every lie, I'll cut off a finger." He pulled the trigger, buzzing the saw in April's face again.

April leaned away from the saw, her entire body taut.

Cody let off the trigger. "Who knows you're here?"

April hesitated for a beat. "My father."

He smirked. "Which one?"

"The *police officer*. He's on his way. If you let me go—"

Cody snatched the chain attached to April's hand, and pulled it toward the middle of the room, dragging April's arm and her body with him. He pulled the chain taut, as far as it would reach. April was flat on her stomach now, her right hand straight out on the tile. Cody stepped on her hand with his full weight, causing April to cry out in pain. The bone saw *buzzed*. "Here goes your first finger." He bent over, lowering the bone saw toward her hand.

April clenched her fist.

"I'll just take the whole hand," Cody said, the saw now millimeters from her wrist. "Unless you wanna retract that lie."

"Nobody knows I'm here!" The *buzzing* ceased, and Cody stepped off her hand. April recoiled to the wall, rubbing her hand, tears streaming down her cheeks. "Please don't do this. I won't tell anyone. I promise. Just let me go. *Please*."

Cody rolled his eyes. "It doesn't work that way. This is your fault. I was ready for a nice relaxing Saturday night. You ruined that for both of us. Don't worry. I'll put you to sleep first." He walked to the corner, near the bleach. He set down his saw and kneeled next to the plastic case. Cody opened the case, revealing a set of small glass bottles and syringes.

April eyed the syringes. Her voice quivered. "Is that what you do to the girls? Drug and kidnap them?"

He grinned, as he filled a syringe from one of the glass bottles. "It's a little more complex than that." He grabbed an elastic tourniquet and walked over to April, still holding the full syringe.

"Are you a racist? Do you hate Latinx people?"

"*Latinx.*" Cody chuckled, standing over her. "Aren't you the good little progressive. Not everything in this world is about race. They're just convenient. It's a good demographic for what I do. Many illegals work two jobs to make ends meet. They leave their kids alone as a consequence. They're all afraid to call the police because of deportation. To be honest, I don't think the police try quite as hard for them either. Your grandfather thinks *El Diablo* is some unpaid coyote. How fucking stupid can he be? Coyotes are paid up-front."

April glared at Cody, her tears dry. "Why did you molest Becky? She's not in your *demographic.*"

"I almost went to prison on that one. I lucked out. Your grandmother's lie put the spotlight on Jason. It's a good thing children are so easily suggestible. I learned my lesson. I never touch a child who I don't completely control anymore."

"So you keep them locked up in here?"

Cody grinned.

"Where are they? Do you kill them?"

"That's enough talking." He knelt in front of her. "Give me your arm."

April squirmed away from him. "No. Please."

Cody sighed. "We can do this the hard way or the easy way, but it's happening. You have a choice. You can be awake, while I hack off your limbs, or I can put you to sleep. Either way, this is it for you. You only get to choose whether or not you feel the pain."

April burst into tears again. She blubbered. "Please. Please don't do this. I won't tell. I promise. *Please.*"

His face turned to stone. "The needle or the saw? You choose." He set the syringe on the ground behind him and moved into her personal space. He grabbed her right arm by the wrist and pulled it toward him. He took the elastic tourniquet and tied it around her upper arm. Then he turned and grabbed the full syringe from the floor. April cowered against the wall, curled into a ball.

He knelt next to her again. "It'll all be over soon enough. No pain. I promise."

April's vision was blurred by her tears.

Cody grabbed her right arm.

The faint sound of glass breaking came from upstairs.

Cody cocked his head, his eyebrows drawn together. He stood and went to the case, setting the syringe back inside. He grabbed his sheathed knife, removing it from the protective case, exposing the shiny blade. Then he rushed from the room, leaving the hidden door open in his wake. His heavy boots climbed the stairs. A door opened. Grunting and another crash of glass came.

April screamed toward the open door, "Help! I'm down here! Help me!"

Maria moved into her line of sight.

April's eyes bulged. "Maria. Help me. I need a screwdriver. Do you know what a screwdriver is?"

Maria took two steps and stopped. Her little leg was bound by a cuff. The chain was stuck to the bottom of one of the couches.

April screamed again, "Help! Help me!"

The door to the basement opened again, followed by heavy steps. April prayed that someone other than Cody was coming down those stairs. Maria cowered as the heavy steps descended the stairs. Cody snatched her under her armpits and carried her away from the door back to the couch. The girl didn't resist or even make a sound.

"Be a good girl. Play with your doll," Cody said.

Then, he returned to the hidden room with his bloody knife in hand, and his medical coveralls also covered in blood. He went to the bathroom, his gloved hands staining the doorknob as he entered. He left the door open and washed his gloved hands at the sink, then his knife.

April screamed one more time. "Help! Help me!"

Cody returned from the bathroom. His eye was starting to swell, and his lip was bloody. "You're wasting your breath." He spit blood in the drain on the floor. "Your dad came by, but don't worry. I took care of him."

April shook her head. "No. You're lying."

"Care to guess which one?"

April hung her head.

"Your real father. I think he came here to kill me. Can you believe that? He almost did. Then you started screaming your head off. He was distracted by that. I think he recognized your voice."

April raised her gaze, sneering at Cody.

Cody thrust his knife at the air like a swordfighter. "But I got him good. It's poetic, don't you think? He died thinking of you. The daughter he never knew." Cody sighed. "It's been an eventful night. Where were we?" He paused, waiting for April to respond, but she didn't. "The pain meds." He went back to his case and retrieved the full syringe. Then he returned to April's side, kneeling in front of her. "I have to admit, I'm a bit stressed. I like things to be orderly. When I get stressed, I have to concentrate on one thing at a time. First, give me your arm."

April drew back, hugging herself, expecting a tug of war for her arm.

Cody punched her in the face with a straight right.

The back of April's head smacked the concrete again. She was dazed, blood streaming from her nose.

Cody snatched her arm, pulling it straight. He found a vein and injected the pain meds. "All done." He stood and leered at April for a long moment, as if waiting for a reaction.

April held her nose, groaning, blood slipping between her fingers. She felt fuzzy. The hand that covered her nose felt heavy. Her arm felt heavy too.

"I have a confession to make. I didn't exactly give you pain meds. I actually injected you with a paralytic. Your body will become paralyzed, but you'll be very awake. You will feel everything, but you won't be able to move a muscle."

April's eyes widened. Her arm dropped, and blood ran from her nose over her lips and down her chin. Her head lolled to the side. She toppled to her side, unable to hold herself upright.

"Based on the dose I gave you and your size, I'm guessing you have eight to ten minutes until you stop breathing, so I better get started. I like to start with the hands. Shit. I forgot my screwdriver." Cody hurried from the room. A few seconds later, he returned with a flathead screwdriver. He unscrewed April's cuff and dragged her to the middle of the room, leaving her on her back.

April watched in terror, unable to move, as he positioned her hands so they were flat on her chest.

"By putting your hands on your chest like this, if I cut too far, I won't ruin my blade on the tile. I used to use a block of wood, but then you have blood DNA in the wood to dispose of." Cody put on his goggles, grabbed his bone saw, and hovered over April's hands. He pressed the trigger, the saw *whizzing* in response.

April closed her eyes, not wanting to watch.

A crash came from Cody's man cave. Cody retracted the saw. April opened her eyes, her gaze on the open secret door.

"Fuck!" Cody said.

Groaning came from the stairs. Cody set down his saw and stalked to his man cave. He returned, dragging Jason by his underarms into the room, leaving a trail of blood.

Jason's breathing was raspy. He reached for the bone saw.

Cody pushed it out of reach with his foot. "Well, you've made a bloody mess of my house, but maybe this'll be better." Cody rolled April on her side, positioning her so she looked at Jason's face.

Jason lay on his back, barely breathing, his head turned to her. His lips moved, but no words came. His face was pale. April peered into his glassy eyes. He moved his hand a few inches, their pinkies touching.

Cody grabbed his bone saw and stood over April and Jason. "So, who wants to watch who die? Or is it whom? I don't think either of you can answer, so I'll have to make that decision." He pressed the trigger, the saw *buzzing* in response.

April concentrated on Jason's face, trying to block out the saw. *My father.*

Three gunshots echoed through the room. The saw fell to the concrete, inches from April's head. The *buzzing* ceased. Cody fell to his knees, then toppled forward on April. She didn't see the man wielding the gun. Then, the weight of Cody was pulled off of her, and Danny was at her side. He wasn't in uniform.

Danny checked April's body for injuries. "Can you talk? Why can't you move?" He searched the room, manic. He discovered the drugs. Then he was on his phone, speaking clearly but rapidly. "I need an ambulance at 1120 Blair Hill Road. Immediately. My daughter was given a paralytic drug. She needs a ventilator. Her breathing is shallow. Also, there's a man here who's been stabbed. I'm putting the phone down to stop the bleeding. *Hurry.*"

Chapter 104: Making Amends

Her mind was hazy. April squinted into the light. Dark forms hovered over her. Something was in her throat. She choked and thrashed. Strong hands held her steady as the endotracheal tube was removed from her sore throat. Her eyes adjusted to the light. The dark forms turned white and light blue. A doctor in a white coat and several nurses in blue scrubs stood at her bedside.

"April, how are you feeling?" the doctor asked.

April groaned. "Tired." She closed her eyes and fell back into the darkness.

***

The lighting was dim. April lay on her back in the hospital bed in a drug-induced haze. Despite the drugs, her face and head hurt. She moved her sore jaw from side to side. She reached up with her left hand and touched the bandage on her head. She touched her nose lightly. It was bandaged too. Her right arm was hooked to an IV. Cool oxygen flowed into her nose from the nasal cannula.

April turned her head to her right. A curtain. Probably another patient on the other side. She turned her head left and saw her parents asleep, each in their own chair. Michelle must've sensed her daughter's awakening. She opened her eyes, saw her daughter, and smiled. She stood from her seat, wearing sweats, and approached April's bedside.

"Mom," April said.

Michelle wiped the corners of her eyes. "I'm so sorry. For everything."

"It's okay."

Danny stirred in his seat and opened his eyes. He approached April's bedside with his head bowed. "How are you feeling?"

"Not too bad." April motioned with her chin to the IV. "Maybe it's the drugs."

"Look. *Um,* … what I did was … unforgiveable." He swallowed hard. "I never should've grabbed you like that. I'm sorry. And I'm sorry that I didn't listen to you. If I had, you wouldn't have felt the need to find the truth all by yourself. What you did was reckless but also incredibly brave. You saved that little girl. I'm so proud of you. I wasn't there for you when you needed me, and we almost lost you. I don't know what I would've done …"

"I love you, Dad," April said, holding her gaze on her father.

Danny smiled, his eyes misty. "I love you too."

Then April addressed Michelle. "I love you too, Mom."

Michelle bent over the bed, hugging April. Danny hugged the both of them.

April giggled. "You guys are crushing me."

Her parents stood, all smiles.

"Where's Jason?" April asked. "Is he okay?"

"I think he's still in surgery," Michelle said. "The doctor said he'd let us know."

"How serious is it? Will he be okay?"

Michelle dropped her gaze.

Danny placed his hand atop April's. "Jason was stabbed multiple times. He lost a lot of blood and had internal injuries. The doctor wasn't confident that he'd survive the surgery."

Chapter 105: The Van

Lighting came from the lamp on her bedside. Her roommate watched television, separated by a curtain. April lay on her back in the hospital bed, her drug-induced haze subsiding. She had two black eyes, a bandage over her nose, and another bandage wrapped around her head.

"How did you know where I was?" April asked her parents, the hospital bed propping her upright.

Michelle sat on the edge of April's bed, near her feet.

Danny sat in a chair at April's bedside. "You told me that Cody had a van. I dismissed it initially, but it stuck in my craw. I kept thinking about it, and I remembered something that your grandpap said to me a long time ago. He said that when he was working on the Heather Sample case, one of the witnesses talked about a suspicious van."

"That's what made you go to Cody's?" April asked.

"Not exactly. Just because Cody has a van now doesn't mean he was the owner of the suspicious van from twenty-four years ago. It bothered me though, so I called your grandpap and asked him about it, and he corroborated my memory, telling me there was a suspicious van with a ladder rack near the location where Heather Sample disappeared. Then I talked to your mom about everything." Danny glanced at Michelle, then addressed April again. "I told her what you'd told me, and I asked her if she thought it was possible that Jason was innocent."

April's gaze flicked to her mom. "What did you say?"

"The truth. That I thought it was possible," Michelle replied.

"Then your mom tried to call you, but it went straight to voice mail," Danny said, his hands folded in his lap. "We both started to worry. I didn't know where you went, but I figured you either went to see Jason or Cody. I was more worried about you confronting Cody, than telling Jason you thought he was innocent, for obvious reasons. So, I went to Cody's. Your grandpap checked Jason's apartment for me."

A doctor walked into the hospital room and approached April's bedside. "Excuse me, Mr. and Mrs. Gibbs?"

Everyone turned to the surgeon in her scrubs.

"May I talk to you in private for a moment?" the doctor asked.

"Is Jason okay?" April asked.

The doctor didn't answer.

Danny stood from his chair.

Michelle stood from the bed. "We'll be right back, sweetie."

April's parents and the doctor left the hospital room.

Why didn't she just say he was okay? April's stomach turned. *He's gone. I know it.* Her throat tightened. Tears welled in her eyes.

Michelle came back to her bedside, her eyes glassy. She took April's hand, her arm still attached to the IV. Michelle smiled and said, "He's alive."

PART IV: JASON

Everything which is done in the present affects the future by consequence and the past by redemption.
—Paulo Coelho

The day misspent, the love misplaced, has inside it the seed of redemption. Nothing is exempt from resurrection.
—Kay Ryan, *Say Uncle*

Chapter 106: Intent

Jason had been stabbed six times by Cody, but the blade had miraculously missed his vital organs. Jason would've died if not for the emergency medical attention given to him by Danny, prior to the arrival of the ambulance. Still, Jason had lost a lot of blood and was in a coma for two days afterward.

On his fourth day in the hospital, the doctors finally allowed a detective from the Duncansville Township Police to interview Jason. With the late-morning sun streaming into the hospital room, Detective Harry Hollis stood at Jason's bedside, a notepad and pen in hand. He wore an ill-fitting gray suit, the trousers too short and the jacket too big for his shoulders but struggling to contain his gut.

"Why were you at Cody Price's house?" Detective Hollis asked.

Jason lay flat on his bed, his head propped on a pillow. An IV was attached to his right arm, and his midsection was bandaged. He eyed the beefy detective. "I want an attorney."

Detective Hollis frowned. "Were you there to kill him?"

Jason swallowed, his throat dry.

"It's quite a story." Detective Hollis flipped through his notepad, reading. "You're incarcerated for twenty years for a crime that Cody Price likely committed. You lost your wife. Your business. Your money. Then, you're barely into your sentence and you murder an inmate, adding another twenty-five years to your sentence for voluntary manslaughter."

He looked up from his notepad. "Do I have that about right so far?"

Jason nodded.

Detective Hollis went back to his notes. "Then a prison guard admits that you were setup and the murder was actually self-defense. *But* that didn't get you a new trial. It took one of the alleged victims to come forward and to admit that they were the aggressors to get the case overturned." Detective Hollis closed his notepad and locked eyes with Jason. "Then you decide to settle in Loganville. The scene of the crime. You're not from Loganville." The detective tilted his head. "This is strange, don't you think? Why come back here, unless you're looking for revenge? Is that what this was about? Revenge?"

Jason stared back poker-faced. "I want an attorney."

Detective Hollis smirked and put his notepad into his inside jacket pocket, exposing his concealed handgun as he did so. "I'm the type of guy who has to know everything. That's the way I am. Always been that way. What I don't understand is your relationship with the Gibbs family. I know that Michelle Gibbs is your ex-wife, but what's your connection to their daughter, April?" Hollis waited a few seconds for a response that never came. "I'm pretty good at math too. Based on April's birthdate, she was conceived while you and your ex-wife were still married. Did you know that?"

Jason looked away.

"I'm guessing you knew. I'm also guessing she's your daughter."

Jason glared at the detective. "Leave her out of this."

Detective Hollis flashed his palms. "Don't worry. I'm not interested in April. I'm interested in what happened four days ago. You have abrasions on your fists and defensive wounds. A sidelight window was broken by the front door, telling me there was forced entry. You were fighting Cody Price inside his home. Had he killed you, he would've been justified. The important question is why." Hollis narrowed his eyes. "Why were you there?"

Jason kept his mouth shut.

"Officer Gibbs said he asked you to go there to check on April? Is that what happened?"

Jason furrowed his brow.

"That's how I'm gonna write it up. Officer Gibbs asked you to go to Mr. Price's home to see if April was there. You showed up, and you heard April scream, so you broke the sidelight window and entered the home. Cody Price tried to kill you in the living room. You defended yourself, but you were stabbed six times in the process. You were defending yourself, April, and Maria. I suggest you keep this story straight, if anyone else comes knocking." Detective Hollis smiled. "You're a good man, Mr. Lewis. I hope you have better luck in the future."

Chapter 107: Heroes

The hospital room was jam-packed with flower arrangements and cards, mostly from the Loganville Latino community. Jason had been in the hospital for a week, recovering from his stab wounds. He sat with his bed propped up, reading a paperback. April waltzed into his hospital room, with two faded black eyes and a smile. Jason set down his paperback on the overbed table—*The Pilgrimage* by Paulo Coelho—and smiled back.

"You look better today," April said, sitting in the chair next to his bedside. She had visited Jason every day since he woke from his coma.

"I feel a little better," Jason replied.

April glanced around the room. "These flowers are getting ridiculous. You're the most popular person in Loganville."

"It's really nice, but I feel undeserving." Jason frowned. "All I did was get stabbed and fall down the stairs. Your dad saved the day."

"You both did." April held his gaze to cement her point.

Jason smiled.

April took a deep breath. "My mom wanted me to ask you if you'd be open to a conversation with her."

Jason arched his eyebrows. "Really? About what?"

April shrugged. "She didn't say. She just said that she wanted to ask before just showing up to your hospital room. She thinks you hate her ..." April paused, hoping for Jason to contradict her statement, but he didn't. "Anyway, she wants to talk to you, but only if you want to. She told me to make sure you understand that it's okay to say no."

Jason hesitated. "Okay. That's fine."

"She's actually in the waiting room. I think she's hoping to talk to you, after we're done talking."

Jason's eyes widened. "She wants to talk right now?"

"After we talk. Is that okay?"

Jason hesitated again. "That's fine."

April removed her phone from her purse and tapped with her thumbs. "I'm sending her a text. I told her to give us an hour." April slipped her phone back in her purse. "Have you been watching the news?"

"I haven't even turned on the TV." Jason tapped his paperback. "I've been reading."

"You missed a lot. The police found keys to the apartments of the victims in Cody's house. They found a maintenance uniform and a large rolling tool box in his van, along with a ventilator and an intubation tube. They also found hidden cameras in his apartment buildings." April leaned forward, like she was sharing a juicy piece of gossip. "The police think he watched his tenants, then picked a girl who was left alone in his preferred age group. Then he would use a key to get in, and he'd inject the girl with a paralytic, stuff her in the tool box, and wheel her out through the service elevators. Then he would intubate her and put her on a ventilator in his van."

Jason raised one side of his mouth in contempt. "That's awful. I'm glad your dad shot that piece of shit."

April nodded, her mouth turned down. "I can't even imagine what those poor girls went through. My dad said they're going to search Cody's property. He thinks the bodies are buried there."

"How are you doing with all this?" Jason asked.

April lifted one shoulder and looked down. "I have a recurring nightmare where I can't move, and he cuts off my hands. We don't need Jung to analyze that dream."

"Are you talking to anyone?"

April raised her gaze. "My mom's making me see a trauma therapist. She's nice. I saw her yesterday."

"Good."

"What about you?"

"I'm fine." He broke eye contact for a beat.

"Are you sure?"

Jason fidgeted in the bed, adjusting his blanket. "I sometimes have flashbacks to my time in prison. I'll see something or feel something, and it takes me back. This has brought some of those memories to the forefront."

April nodded again. "That must be hard. I'm sorry."

Jason shook his head. "Don't be. I'm happier than I've been in a long time. That's all because of you."

April smiled. "I'm glad you feel that way. I want us to have a relationship. Do you think you'll stay in Loganville?"

"I'd like to." He chuckled to himself. "I used to hate visiting this place when I was married to your mom. Now … I could see myself living here. You're here. It's nice to be treated like a hero, even if it's misplaced."

She reached over and placed her hand on top of his. "If you hadn't been there, I'd be dead. You're a hero in my mind."

"That's nice of you to say, but you're the hero. You're the one who risked everything for me. You believed in me, when nobody did for twenty-one years." His voice wavered. "That meant more to me than you can imagine. Thank you."

"You're welcome, Dad."

Jason was stunned. She'd never called him dad. She rarely even used his name.

April retracted her hand. "I'm sorry. That was weird, wasn't it?"

Jason shook his head again, his eyes glassy. He turned his hand over. April placed her hand in his.

He squeezed his daughter's hand and said, "It's not weird at all. I'm honored."

Chapter 108: Twenty-One Years Too Late

Michelle knocked on the open door to his hospital room. She wore skinny jeans and a blousy top. Her brown hair was in an updo, wisps of hair framing her face.

"Come in," Jason called out, sitting up in his bed.

Michelle approached the bed tentatively, her head bowed. She forced a smile. "Hi."

Jason stared at her face. She had crow's feet and laugh lines, but she was still so beautiful. "This is so strange."

"I know. You must …"

Jason gestured to the chair next to his bed. "You can sit, if you want."

"Thanks." Michelle walked around his hospital bed and sat in the chair. "You're probably wondering what I'm doing here."

"I didn't have much time to think about it."

"Sorry, I wasn't sure you'd even talk to me, after what I did to you."

"Why are you here?"

Michelle wrung her hands in her lap. "I wanted to thank you for saving April's life."

"I think that was more Danny than me."

"That's not what he said. He said, if you hadn't been there, he would've been too late. So, thank you."

Jason nodded. "You're welcome."

Michelle took a deep breath. "I *um*, I also wanted to apologize to you, knowing that there's nothing I can ever say to … fix what I did to you." Tear welled in her eyes. "I can't imagine how much I must've hurt you." She wiped the corners of her eyes.

Jason didn't respond for a long moment. He swallowed hard and said, "Back then, this was all I wanted. You meeting with me face-to-face. I thought that, if we met in person, you would see that I was telling the truth."

Michelle sniffled. "I don't think it would've mattered. I was too influenced by the people around me to think for myself. You deserved better. I'm truly sorry."

Jason blinked, and a tear slipped down his face. He wiped his eyes discreetly with his index finger. "I regret not wanting to have children with you. If I had listened to you that Christmas night at your parents. If I hadn't worn that condom, none of this would've happened. You and I would be married, and maybe we'd have other kids too."

"I don't doubt it. I'm sure we would've been happy."

Jason exhaled. "But we can't go back."

She nodded. "You're right. We can't go back. We can only move forward." Michelle sat up straighter in her seat. "I know April's twenty and can make her own decisions, but Danny and I want you to be in her life. You're welcome in our home for family get-togethers. Christmas, Thanksgiving, birthdays. All of it. I know your family isn't welcoming to you."

Jason shook his head. "I can't imagine Danny's on board with that."

"He is. We've already discussed it. That's why I'm here."

"I don't think it's a good idea. I'm happy to show up to neutral places, like her college graduation or her wedding, if I'm invited, but I don't think I can be a part of your family like that. I don't think I can watch what could've been. There's too much …" He looked down.

"I understand. If you change your mind, you're always welcome."

He nodded again.

"What will you do now?"

He raised his gaze. "I don't know, but I feel like I have a second chance on life. I plan to take advantage of it."

If you enjoyed this novel, ...
you'll love *Cesspool*.

Would you become a criminal to do the right thing?

Disgraced teacher, James Fisher, moved to a backwoods town, content to live his life in solitude. He was awakened from his apathy by a small girl with a big problem. James suspected Brittany was being abused and exploited by his neighbor. He called the police but soon realized his mistake, as the neighbor was related to the chief of police.

Most would've looked the other way. Getting involved placed James squarely in the crosshairs of the local police. James lacked the brawn or the connections to save himself, much less Brittany. The police held all the power, and they knew it. But that was also their weakness. They underestimated what the mild-mannered teacher and the young runaway would do for justice.

Buy Cesspool today if you enjoy vigilante justice page-turners with a side of underdog.
Adult language and content.

<u>What Readers Are Saying</u>

"Wow. Just wow. This book was amazing. Every chapter, every page had me thinking about ideas, philosophies, current events, and history in a different way." - Elaine ★★★★★

"The writing is excellent, the pace quick, the characters and dialogue believable. An excellent read." - Dusty Sharp, Author of the Austin Conrad Series ★★★★★

"I have enjoyed this author before, but this is his best yet. If you want a story that will keep you reading, this is it. The story, the characters, and the cunning displayed by the hero is some of the best fiction I've had the pleasure to read. Do yourself a favor and pick up this book. You won't lay it down until the end." - Patrick R. ★★★★★

"Wow! This was one of the best books I've read in a while. Twists, turns, and unexpected events in every chapter. What a movie this would make." – Kindle Customer ★★★★★

"This book was incredible! I read it in three days—the entire story is a whirlwind of fantastic characters, a perfect constancy of ups and downs throughout." - Rae L. ★★★★★

For the Reader

Dear Reader,

I'm thrilled that you took precious time out of your life to read my novel. Thank you! I hope you found it entertaining, engaging, and thought-provoking. If so, please consider writing a positive review on Amazon and Goodreads. Five-star reviews have a huge impact on future sales. The review doesn't need to be long and detailed, if you're more of a reader than a writer. As an author and a small businessman, competing against the big publishers, I greatly appreciate every reader, every review, and every referral.

If you're interested in receiving my novel *Against the Grain* **for free and/or reading my other titles for free or discounted, go to the following link:** http://www.PhilWBooks.com. You're probably thinking, *What's the catch?* There is no catch.

If you want to contact me, don't be bashful. I can be found at Phil@PhilWBooks.com. I do my best to respond to all emails.

Sincerely,

Phil M. Williams

Gratitude

I'd like to thank my wife for being my first reader, sounding board, and cheerleader. Without her support and unwavering belief in my skill as an author, I'm not sure I would have embarked on this career. I love you, Denise.

I'd also like to thank my editors. My developmental editor, Caroline Smailes, did a fantastic job finding the holes in my plot and suggesting remedies. As always, my line editor, Denise Barker (not to be confused with my wife, Denise Williams), did a fantastic job making sure the manuscript was error-free. I love her comments and feedback.

Thank you to my good friend Barry for his invaluable legal knowledge. Any mistakes regarding the legal system were mine alone. Also, thank you to my big brother, Chris, for his help with prison life. For the record, he used to *work* in a prison. Again, any mistakes were mine alone. And lastly, thank you as always to my mother-in-law, Joy, one of the best nurses on this planet. She is always gracious with her time and extremely knowledgeable about all things medical.

Thank you to my beta readers, Sue, Ray, Saundra, and Matteo. They're my last defense against the dreaded typo. And thank you to you, the reader. Without you I wouldn't have a career. As long as you keep reading, I'll keep writing.

www.ingramcontent.com/pod-product-compliance
Lightning Source LLC
Chambersburg PA
CBHW021214260626
47172CB00002B/420